A LADY'S DREAM
COME TRUE

TRUE GENTLEMEN, BOOK NINE

GRACE BURROWES

A Lady's Dream Come True

Copyright © 2020 by Grace Burrowes

All rights reserved.

DEDICATION

A Lady's Dream Come True

To the artists and to the galleries who preserve and protect the artist's legacy

CHAPTER ONE

Throughout the length and breadth of England, fair summer days enjoyed a certain sameness. The blue of the sky rarely varied; the cheerful sun shone alike on cattle, sheep, country manor, or urban market with a predictably mellow, golden quality.

Before Oak Dorning had turned fifteen, sunny days had ceased to surprise his artist's eye.

Rainy days, by contrast, varied from location to location. In the north, the rain took on an icy gleam. Along a shoreline, a storm could turn rainclouds a brooding jade green. In the uplands, a driving wind made rain more of a grim blur than actual precipitation.

A mile and a half outside Little Bathboro, along a glorified, double-rutted sheep track, a rainy day was the embodiment of every misery a man who'd recently splurged on a pair of new boots could imagine. A penetrating chill had gripped Oak a mile out from the Bathboro crossroad. The wind kicked up a quarter mile beyond that, and after topping yet another rise, Oak saw that the weather would not relent for the foreseeable future.

The entire vista before him was shades of desolation and damp, with contrasting dashes of flooding and mud. A square, gray edifice squatted on a slight hill a half mile in the distance, and if that wasn't Merlin Hall, Oak would lay himself down in the nearest puddle.

He hefted his sodden valise and was preparing to negotiate slippery downhill footing, when he noticed a darker patch along the hedge-lined track below. A gig pulled by a sopping wet bay had become mired in the ruts, and though the horse hopped gamely forward in the traces, the wheels were stuck fast.

"Well, hell." Part of Oak's mind noticed the interplay of the melancholy clouds and the grass and gorse undulating in the gathering wind.

Another part continued cursing silently. "Seems you're a bit stuck," he said, approaching the vehicle. "Perhaps I can help."

The driver was veiled in widow's weeds, a heavy black wool blanket across her lap. "I can manage, thank you. Get up, Dante." She waved the whip at the horse's quarters without touching lash to hide. "Get up, boy. *Get up.*"

Oak set down his valise and ignored the icy trickle of rain dripping from the back of his hat brim directly onto his nape. The gig rocked, it jostled, it lurched forward only to sink back more deeply into the ruts. The beast was giving the job a good go, but the steep angle of the rut worked against him.

"You're in want of a boost," Oak said, when the driver allowed the horse a pause in his labors. "As it happens, I enjoyed a rural upbringing. I've unstuck a gig or two, ma'am, and I can have you on your way in a moment."

She had good posture, whoever she was. Her back was as straight as a marble column, and her hands on the reins gave with the horse's attempts to win free. A competent whip, as many rural ladies had to be.

"With another half hour or so of rocking your cart and hopping about," Oak went on, squishing his way closer to the gig, "your gelding might bounce you loose. Or he might bounce you the rest of the way into the ditch and snap an axle. Your decision."

The horse hung his head and sighed, his coat curling wetly along his shoulders and flanks.

"I hate this." The lady sounded dejected and tired.

Had Oak not been assessing the shine of the waning light on the jet buttons of the lady's cloak, and thus looking more or less *at* her, he'd not have associated those three plaintive, muttered words with her straight spine and graceful hands.

"Dante is not precisely thrilled with the day either," Oak said, "while my own sentiments regarding this weather aren't fit for a lady's ears. Your horse seems a sensible sort, and we can take comfort from that."

"He's an utter love, and if he pulls a shoe in this muck, my stable master will give notice."

What had sent this woman careering across the countryside on such a day? If she had a stable master, she likely had a closed carriage, but then, heavier vehicles became more easily stuck.

"He won't pull a shoe. Dante knows what the job entails." Oak offered a final, silent curse in the direction of gentlemanly obligations and stripped off his damp gloves. "When the gig comes free, you don't stop to congratulate the horse, you don't take a bow for your fine skill with the reins. Trot on. Don't canter, don't walk. Keep moving enough to not get stuck again, not so much that you career into another ditch."

"I really wish—"

Whatever she wished was cut off by a crack of thunder that had Dante's head coming up sharply.

"The idea is to rock the gig gently," Oak said as the rumbling faded. "At the opportune moment, I will lift the wheels, and you will be on your way. Agreed?"

She nodded, causing droplets to fall from the jet beads weighting the hem of her veil.

Oak slogged around to the rear of the cart, put his shoulder to the back of the seat, and found what purchase he could in the slick footing. He knew what was coming, he knew what honor required, and

he knew he truly should have remained in Dorset sketching butterflies and threatening to make a trip to Paris.

Except he couldn't afford a trip to Paris. "Ready?" he asked.

She took a firmer hold of the reins. "Get up, Dante."

The horse really was a saint. He seemed to grasp exactly what
the exercise was about, and when Oak hefted the back wheels
straight up at the apex of a particularly vigorous rocking arc, the
gelding gave a mighty heave forward.

The driver let out an unladylike whoop, and the cart jaunted off
down the lane.

Without the support of the vehicle, Oak pitched to his knees, as
he'd known he would. Unsticking carts was not a business for the
faint of heart or high of fashion.

"Thank you, kind sir!" came trilling back to him over the splash of
the wheels, the drip of the rain, and the moan of the wind.

He pushed to his feet and waved. "Godspeed!"

What a fool he'd look if the lady could see him. He'd ruined his
boots *and* his breeches, his hat had gone tumbling into the bracken,
and he still had another half a mile to slog. A shiver passed over him,
and another crack of thunder boomed as the gig bounced out of view
around a grassy swale.

What little daylight there was would soon be gone.

Oak wasted another ten minutes locating his hat, picked up his
valise, and trudged in the wake of the cart. If he'd pondered for the
rest of the summer, he could not have conjured a gloomier scene. The
sky was shifting from bleak to positively dire, and with every step,
Oak's boots squelched.

And yet, that whoop of joy, that merry, "Thank you, kind sir!" cut
through all the misery and chill, as a single shaft of sunlight
confirmed the existence of heaven even in the midst of the most deso-
late, sodden wasteland.

Oak traveled the rest of the way to the manor, mentally
composing a sketch of the stuck gig, the lowering sky, and the

brooding house in the background. All quite Gothic, quite dramatic, and awfully muddy.

A similarly doleful and Gothic butler let him into the entrance of Merlin Hall, after keeping him waiting on the front step for a frigid eternity. Oak's prospective employer was apparently a thrifty sort, for only a minimum of sconces had been lit, sending flickering shadows dancing along the stone walls.

"We did not expect you until later this week, Mr. Dorning," the butler said, casting a meaningful look at Oak's much-abused valise. "I'll have *that* taken up to your room, and perhaps you'd like a bath."

"A bath would be lovely, and a tray if it's not too much trouble. Bread and cheese, a pot of tea, nothing complicated."

The butler was white-haired, solid, of African descent, and about as disapproving as a butler could be without audibly sniffing in disgust. Oak's mother would have adored him.

"I will alert the kitchen to your arrival. The mistress won't expect to see you until breakfast tomorrow."

An entire lecture lay in that last sentence: By which time, you, Mr. Dorning, will be presentable, in dry clothing, free of mud, and no longer wearing the stench of Eau du Hampshire Hog Wallow.

Such a scold, added to cold, fatigue, and ruined boots, might have provoked Oak to sketching a most unflattering caricature of the butler, but Oak's habitual visual inventory of his surroundings at that moment fell upon a hat on a peg beside the front door.

And not just any hat. This hat was a mourning bonnet, all black, and the veil that would cover the lady's face to below her chin was weighted with jet beads. A slow, steady drip fell from the trailing end of the veil onto the stone floor. In the subdued illumination of the sconces, no light had ever flared more brightly in Oak's imagination than did those shiny jet beads, dripping rainwater all over the foyer of Merlin Hall.

~

THE TUB WAS a bit cramped for a man of Oak's proportions, but he made do, and the heat of the water was exquisite. He scrubbed off and lay back, happy to soak until the water had cooled a bit more.

Night had fallen, hastened by the miserable weather, and thus Oak's chamber was illuminated by only candles and the fire roaring in the hearth. Mrs. Channing apparently did not skimp on fuel, nor did she believe artists should be housed in drafty garrets.

Oak's bedroom came with a cozy sitting room, and both chambers sported lit fires. A dressing closet off the bedroom added further to the sense that Oak was a guest rather than an itinerant tradesman.

He took another nibble of a pale, blue-veined cheese and washed it down with a sip of excellent port. He'd begun the argument in his head—to doze off in the tub or climb out before the water grew cold—when a quiet snick sounded from the other side of the fire screens.

"I'll unpack the valise myself," he said, giving up on the nap. "You needn't bother. I'll see to it later." God willing, his clothes weren't entirely soaked. His trunks would probably not arrive for another few days, and damp shirts were a misery not to be borne.

He expected a footman's cheery greeting, or maybe a disapproving comment from the butler, Bracken. Instead, he heard a quiet rustling.

"Halloo," Oak said, sitting up, though the fire screens blocked his view of most of the room. "Who's there?" Had a maid stumbled into his room by mistake? Did somebody think to rifle what few belongings he'd brought with him?

He stood reluctantly, water sluicing off him into the tub and cold air chasing the drowsiness from his mind.

"Show yourself," he said, grabbing a towel and wrapping it around his middle. "I already have an extra bucket of coal in both rooms." More evidence that Oak was to be well treated at Merlin Hall.

Over the top of the fire screens, Oak saw the door to the corridor open. Soft footsteps pattered from the room, though in the gloom, all he could make out was a shadow slipping into the greater darkness beyond the doorway.

"Bloody hell." A thief stealing his sketch pad would not do. Oak extricated himself from the tub and bolted for the open door. "Get back here, whoever you are. Stealing from a guest is not the done thing." Though Oak wasn't quite a guest. He was an employee at Merlin Hall, an artisan rather than an artist.

The air in the corridor was even colder than the air in the sitting room had been, and Oak hadn't gone two yards from his doorway before it occurred to him that he was racing about a strange house wearing nothing but a towel.

He came to an abrupt halt just as footsteps faded around a carpeted corner. "Christ in swaddling clothes. What was I—?"

A throat cleared.

Oak turned slowly, clutching his towel about his waist with one hand.

"I see the swaddling clothes," the lady said. "I rather doubt the son of the Almighty stands before me."

She wore an aubergine dress so dark as to approach black in the corridor's shadows, and she held a carrying candle that flickered in the chilly breeze. The candle flame found brilliant highlights in her auburn hair and cast high cheekbones into dramatic relief.

"Oak Dorning, no relation to the Almighty. I would bow, but a man wearing only a towel has no wish to look yet more ridiculous."

The lady cast an appraising eye over him. "I assure you, Mr. Dorning, you do not appear ridiculous, though I can understand why you'd be a bit self-conscious. I am Verity Channing."

Oak considered himself too slender, at least when compared to his brother Hawthorne. Compared to Valerian, his toilette and manners were unpolished. He lacked Casriel's Town bronze. He hadn't Ash's head for business, Sycamore's cunning, or Willow's imperturbable calm.

But Verity Channing apparently saw something in Oak's nearly naked form that held her interest. Her gaze conveyed no prurient curiosity, but rather, the same assessment Oak made when he considered sketching a subject. How did the light treat this particular complexion? Was a slightly different angle more revealing? More honest?

Candlelight was said to be flattering, but Verity Channing needed no shadows to obscure her flaws, if any she had. Her eyes tilted ever so slightly, the perfect complement to a strong nose, full lips, and swooping brows. Her features had a rare symmetry and came together in ideal proportions. Brows, chin, jaw, cheeks... All the structures of a human face were presented in her physiognomy on the balancing edge between grace and strength, beauty and perfection.

She was, quite simply, stunning. So lovely to look at that, for a moment, Oak forgot he was wearing only a towel, forgot she was his employer, and forgot that he stood gaping at her in the middle of a chilly corridor.

He'd heard her laugh out on the cart track, heard her whoop with glee, though now she was utterly composed, inspecting rather than gawking.

"I owe you a favor, Mr. Dorning," she said, lowering the candle. "You extracted my gig from the muck and spared Dante and me a long, chilly walk home. For that reason, I will promise never to mention to another soul the circumstances of this meeting."

He could not tell if she was teasing him, but he believed she'd keep her word, and thank God for that, because his brothers would never stop laughing if they learned of this encounter.

"I don't suppose you might *forget* the circumstances of this meeting, ma'am? Wipe them from memory, perhaps?"

He'd have to pass her to return to his room. Her smile, so slight, so devilish, suggested she knew that.

She approached and handed him the candle. "When I am an old woman who hums under her breath to the distraction of all who must endure my company, I will still recall the sight of you clad in only a towel." She made a slow inspection of his chest, his arms, his shoulders, his face. "And the memory will make me smile. Good evening,

Mr. Dorning. I'll see you at breakfast, though lamentably for me, somewhat less of *you*, I trust. One wouldn't want such a fine specimen to come down with a lung fever."

She sauntered off into the darkness, and Oak remained in the corridor, sorting through his thoughts. He could not recall anybody—male or female—regarding him with such frank appreciation. The attention was unnerving, but also gratifying in an odd way.

And besides that lingering sense of gratification, he had the artist's aching need to render on paper something he'd experienced mostly through his visual senses—but not entirely. A hint of cinnamon hung in the air, a throb of awareness lingered such as a man felt toward a woman who had impressed him viscerally.

"That smile," he murmured, gathering up his toweling and returning to his sitting room. "That knowing, impish, female..."

When three footmen arrived to deal with the tub, Oak barely noticed. He sat swathed in towels and blankets on the sofa, trying to sketch Verity Channing's smile.

~

OAK DORNING MADE AN EVEN STRONGER impression fully clothed than he did wearing only a towel—which ought not to have been possible.

Perhaps the difficulty lay in the fact that Vera had seen him nearly naked and knew that the lean torso clad in a lawn shirt and blue paisley waistcoat was wrapped in muscle. Those long legs were similarly powerful, and those shoulders, which filled out a brown morning coat to perfection, could heft a gig from deep mud.

Worst of all, though, the man had been able to carry on a coherent conversation in a situation that ought to have left any mere mortal awash in mortification. What sort of upbringing produced such savoir faire?

And from what progenitor had he acquired eyes the hue of bluebells blooming in shade?

"Mrs. Channing, good morning." Mr. Dorning bowed over her hand as she sat at the head of the breakfast table. "You are looking well this morning."

While you are looking dressed. "Mr. Dorning, help yourself to the offerings on the sideboard and have a seat. I trust you slept well?"

"Quite. And yourself?"

He *looked* well rested and exceedingly self-possessed, but then, artists were generally nonchalant about nudity, a skill Vera had never acquired.

"Storms make me nervous," she said. "I once saw a tree struck by lightning. A young oak in all its wet leafy splendor one moment, then illuminated brighter than day the next."

He collected a plate from the table and went to the sideboard. "Did the tree survive?"

"No. At first, I thought my eyes must have deceived me, for there was no fire, but a few moments later, the highest branch was in flames despite the rain. The tree was consumed from within." An oddly disturbing sight, for there had been no helping that tree, no saving it as might have been done if the fire had been where the rain could put it out.

Mr. Dorning heaped a pile of scrambled eggs onto his plate. "How old were you?"

"Eight. I spent that summer with my grandmother in Sussex. I've disliked storms since."

A second large spoonful of eggs joined the first on his plate. "I enjoy a dramatic sky, but I know better than to be out in bad weather if I can help it. Would you care for more eggs?"

Did he intend to consume the entire tray? "No, thank you. Do you drink tea or coffee?"

"Tea will do," he replied, taking the seat at her left side, "or chocolate if you have it."

Vera set a rack of toast by his elbow, as well as a pot of chocolate, the butter plate, the honey pot, and a basket of cinnamon rolls.

"Tell me about your paintings," he said, draping his table linen across his lap. "My equipment and supplies will be a few days getting here, but I'd like to see the canvases this morning if you can spare the time."

Mr. Dorning's manners were almost delicate, and yet, he ate with the businesslike focus of a large, fit, hungry male. Vera had forgotten what that looked like and how gratifying the sight.

"I've found more old paintings since last we corresponded. My husband claimed they were worth a pretty penny, though Dirk's judgment was often colored by optimism. He said this house held more treasures than he had time to catalog, but I suspect he was mostly repeating family legends."

Mr. Dorning set down the chocolate pot without pouring himself a serving. "Dirk? Dirk Channing? You are his widow?"

She hadn't seen this reaction for several years and found Mr. Dorning's astonishment discomfiting.

"I have that honor. Were you acquainted with my late husband?"

"I met him once at a lecture. I would not say we were acquainted. I had just gone up to university, where my family was desperately hoping I'd outgrow my artistic fancies. They longed to see me safely pursuing a career in the Church, of all things."

He took up the butter knife and added a full pat to a half slice of toast. "Dirk Channing's paintings of the American rebellion and the Irish uprising convinced me that art is more than simply adornment for the idle rich. He was kind to a youth much in need of kindness, told me to be patient, dedicated, and determined. I have been dedicated and determined ever since."

Dirk had been so many things. A rascal, a romantic, a genius, and a fool. Then he'd been ill, and none of those other roles mattered. To be reminded that he had also been generous and encouraging was heartwarming.

"Have you been patient, Mr. Dorning, or did you flirt with the temptation to join the Church after all?"

He considered his toast, and Vera had the sense he was about to offer her platitudes rather than confront a sensitive topic.

"I am from a large family," he said. "Two sisters, six brothers. My oldest brother inherited the usual mixed blessings—land and standing —and he would and will provide for any sibling in need. Our lot as younger sons has been to aid him in any regard we can, whether that's laying a hedge, balancing a ledger, clearing a ditch, or standing up with the wallflowers when Dorning Hall hosts entertainments. My art is an indulgence in that context. I have been as patient as possible, but I haven't submitted to the exhibitions, haven't made the right connections. It's time I got on with my aspirations."

"You are ambitious." Vera ought not to fault him for that, but ye gods, ambition had driven Dirk nearly to Bedlam.

"I have dreams," he said, smiling at his toast. "I suspect you do too."

Vera had nightmares, though most mothers could likely say the same. "I have plans, Mr. Dorning. I plan to see those old paintings cleaned up and sold off. I will show them to you as soon as I've met with my housekeeper and made a call on the nursery. I hope to unearth all the treasure Dirk claimed he bequeathed to us—and to sell the lot of it. What good is treasure that remains buried?"

Vera looked up from stirring her tea to find Mr. Dorning studying her. His expression was abstracted, his gaze narrow. He wasn't frowning, so much as he was visually investigating her.

"May I?" he asked, his hand poised near her chin.

She knew that look, knew that particular intensity in a man's eyes, though she hadn't seen it for ages. She'd told herself that grief and the passing years had safeguarded her from this sort of attention, but she'd apparently been spinning a tale for her own amusement.

She nodded.

Mr. Dorning shifted the angle of her jaw, such that the morning sun pouring through the windows struck her profile. The heat of the summer morning was soothing, though a lady was supposed to avoid direct sunlight at all costs.

"You've a faint scar," he said, his thumb brushing over her cheek. "A childhood injury?"

His fingers were warm, his touch confident. He doubtless *handled* his models. Most artists did, most *male* artists.

"Fell from a tree, got scratched on the way down."

He withdrew his hand. "I beg your pardon for my forwardness, but your looks are striking, as you have probably been told more often than you care to recall. Might I sketch you if some free time arises?"

His casual question brushed over a *very bad idea*. Dirk had begun wooing her with the same request, and from there, matters had blossomed in unforeseen directions.

Vera stalled by taking a sip of tepid tea. "You needn't flatter me, Mr. Dorning. Dirk always said beauty is boring. Artists are supposed to know that. Quirks and unexpected flaws, asymmetries and imperfections are what make a subject worthy of notice."

"Perhaps to your husband you were merely beautiful," Mr. Dorning replied, buttering another half slice of toast. "To me, you are interesting."

He smiled and saluted with his toast, and Vera realized she had invited trouble into her home. Serious, handsome trouble. Oak Dorning was equally poised whether wearing a towel or London morning attire. He could compliment without flirting, and he wanted to sketch her.

Sketching meant artist and subject shared proximity, sometimes close proximity, and often conversed for the duration of the exercise. Sketching meant allowing an artist to inspect, touch, arrange, and question his subject.

Sketching, when Oak Dorning wielded the pencil, would be dangerous.

Vera was mentally rehearsing a demurral, some reference to summer being a busy time at a functioning estate and motherhood putting endless demands on her energy, when Jeremy Forester sauntered into the breakfast parlor.

Blond, scholarly, and slightly rumpled, he was in every way a welcome diversion from Mr. Dorning's darker and more intense presence, much less from thoughts of sketching.

"Good morning, all," Jeremy said, bowing in her direction. "I take it this fellow is the estimable Mr. Dorning, who braved the storm to join us at Merlin Hall. I'm Jeremy Forester, tutor to the terror. Don't suppose you'd like to teach him the rudiments of drawing? I say, Mrs. C, might I have that teapot?"

Mr. Dorning rose and bowed. "Good morning, Mr. Forester, pleased to make your acquaintance. Who or what is the terror?"

Jeremy launched into a doting, not entirely factual description of his responsibilities regarding Alexander, while Mr. Dorning sipped his tea and demolished cinnamon buns. Men looked at mothers differently, or some men did, regarding a woman with children as either out of bounds or devoid of feminine allure.

Mr. Dorning offered her the basket of cinnamon buns before passing it across the table to Jeremy.

"He's my favorite kind of little boy," Jeremy was saying. "Thoroughly rotten, lazy, and smart. I'll make a decent scholar of him despite his natural inclinations."

He smiled at Vera, and she obligingly smiled back, though Mr. Dorning wasn't smiling. She'd been married to an artist, so she knew what that distracted, half-puzzled expression meant.

In his head, Oak Dorning was already drawing her likeness, and that was not a good thing.

CHAPTER TWO

Oak had originally put Verity Channing's age at early to mid-twenties, but morning light suggested she was somewhat older. Not yet thirty, would be his guess, and her looks were unlikely to change substantially over the next fifteen or even twenty years.

She cared for her complexion, though she was also blessed with good, durable bone structure. High cheekbones, a strong jawline, a defined chin that stopped short of angularity. Good teeth too. He had become distracted by the sight of her biting into a cinnamon bun then licking her fingers.

What sort of girl had she been, and what had prompted her to marry the much older Dirk Channing?

"I can introduce you to my charge," Jeremy Forester said when Mrs. Channing had taken a quiet leave of the table. "He's a nosy little bugger, always fidgeting. Mostly, the lad's bored. Widows tend to coddle their sons, and next thing you know, we have a stage-play villain where a decent young man should be. I'm about to eat my third cinnamon bun, unless you care to arm-wrestle me for the basket."

"Perhaps another time. I've eaten my fill of sweets." Oak would be famished by noon, which prompted him to butter two more pieces of toast and make them into a sandwich.

"You needn't tuck away a snack," Jeremy said. "Mrs. Channing doesn't run that sort of household. Old Bracken plays the stern major-domo, because a widow must be careful, but we're free to impose on the kitchen for a tray if we're peckish. Late at night, I've been known to raid the larder, though you mustn't tell Alexander. He has a boy's exalted notions of fairness, which are most inconvenient when a tutor is a mere mortal fellow. More tea?"

"Please."

Forester poured for them both. "You're wondering if she'll pay you on time, but you don't want to make a bad impression by raising that question with a near stranger. I asked Miss Digg the same thing before we'd shared our first cup of tea."

"Who's Miss Digg?"

"Tamsin Diggory, the governess. She and I are distantly connected by marriage, or steps, or halves, or removes. I never can quite recall which."

Forester put three lumps of sugar in his tea before going on. "Miss Digg sometimes takes breakfast with Catherine on the upstairs terrace, though I suppose I ought to call her Miss Catherine. She's fourteen, and that is such a difficult age, particularly when you're enduring it in your step-mama's household. Alexander is a squirmy, saucy, naughty little boy, but that's the extent of the challenge he poses. He's educable, as we all were at six years of age. Catherine is a female who fancies herself the toast of London one minute and Mrs. Siddons's more talented understudy the next. Lord, I do love a good strong cup of tea."

Oak generally preferred a quiet start to his day, but Forester put him in mind of noisy, nosy brothers, a not-unpleasant association.

"Wages are paid timely in this household?" he asked.

"To the penny, absolutely. Mrs. Channing is a good employer. I haven't been here that long myself—only arrived in April—but she's fair, doesn't put on airs, listens when I have advice to offer regarding her son, and looks after her domestics. Take your time dusting off those old portraits, Mr. Dorning. Hampshire's as pleasant a place to spend your summer as anywhere."

Jeremy winked at him, then took a slurp of tea.

"If a fellow would rather be in London," Oak said, "Hampshire can be isolated."

"Do you have a particular reason for preferring London? I can't afford Town myself. I go up to visit an uncle at Yuletide, and I suppose the city air isn't so bad in spring and fall, but the coal smoke in winter and the stink in summer disagree with me."

"The Royal Academy is in London," Oak said, regretting the admission as soon as he'd made it. His brothers regarded his artistic aspirations with fond puzzlement now, but growing up, he'd been the butt of more fraternal humor than any one boy should have to endure.

He'd hidden in trees to escape his brothers' notice, and found the perspective offered by a higher vantage point worth sketching for its own sake.

"So you're a *serious* artist," Forester said, making a joke of the observation. "If you're looking to Mrs. Channing to become your patroness, you're bound for disappointment. The late, great, much-lamented Mr. Channing rather put her off artists. I gather he was the mercurial sort. I don't intend to let such tendencies take root in the boy."

"Mr. Channing apparently left his family awash in old paintings, which I hope to restore to salable quality. That is the extent of my engagement and of my ambitions here." That Forester would imply otherwise sat slightly ill with Oak. A widow of means generally needed those means—if Mrs. Channing was even as comfortably situated as she appeared to be.

Why sell art unless the coin was needed? But then, cinnamon buns, roaring fires, and a well-stocked breakfast buffet didn't argue for want of means. The lady's finances were none of Oak's business, provided he was adequately and timely compensated for his efforts.

"She's pretty," Forester said, considering his tea. "You get used to that. She's also a genuinely nice woman, which comes as something of a surprise."

A full stomach and a decent night's sleep made idling around the breakfast table much longer an impossibility. After a long day shut up in a coach, Oak needed to move.

He also, though, needed to get off on the right foot with Jeremy Forester. "Are nice women a rarity here in Hampshire? We have some in Dorset, and my brothers have a knack for marrying nice women."

Forester pulled a face. "I realized before completing my first year at university that to be a fortune hunter takes *some* means. One must have lodgings, decent attire, and belong to a club or two. My uncle paid for my education, he wasn't about to pay for me to idle around Town, dangling after women who could buy and sell my family forty times over. I saw the pretty ladies in their fine carriages every afternoon in Hyde Park, and they had no time for me. The local widowers and swains would dote on Mrs. Channing even were she a shrew, but she's not."

She also hadn't remarried, which struck Oak as curious. "Do you suppose she'd allow me to paint her portrait?"

"Ah, so that's your interest. Makes sense." Forester swirled his tea, nodding as sagaciously as if he were some sort of professional tea taster employed by Twinings to perfect their blends. "You'd have to ask her. Catch her in the right mood, and she might allow it. Be charming and winsome, though she's not much for outright flirtation. Miss Diggory warned me about that. Still, getting Verity Channing to sit for you would be quite a coup, and a man can but try, right?"

Oak left Forester sorting through the remaining cinnamon buns, looking for the largest of the lot no doubt.

A portrait of Verity Channing, done right, could launch Oak's career. She was stunning, complicated, somewhat familiar to the artistic community as Dirk Channing's widow, and as far as Oak knew, nobody had done her portrait yet. He could submit the finished painting for inclusion in the Academy's annual exhibition, and if chosen, paying commissions would be sure to follow.

He was halfway to the front door, hoping to locate Bracken, when it occurred to him that he hadn't asked Mrs. Channing about last evening's intruder in his rooms, nor had she mentioned the incident. Did she think Oak had gone larking up the corridor in nothing but a towel for the pleasure of taking the evening air?

Exactly how mercurial had Dirk Channing been, and why hadn't he ever painted his lovely wife's portrait?

~

"BUT WHAT DO we know of this widow?" Grey Dorning, Earl of Casriel, asked. "Who are her people, and why did Oak hare off to restore her paintings when he could have whiled away his summer here, amid the home vistas of Dorsetshire?"

Valerian Dorning poured his oldest brother two fingers of brandy, though afternoon had not yet yielded to evening. Clouds to the north promised rain, which meant Valerian needed to be on his way.

First, his lordly brother required sorting out. "Oak has painted every vista Dorning Hall has to offer," Valerian said, passing Casriel the half-full glass. "You told the lot of us to go forth and make our way in the world. Oak is an artist. He's making his way."

Casriel, mannerly to his bones, waited until Valerian had filled his own glass. "To the health of our ladies."

Valerian lifted his drink a few inches. "To the health of our ladies." Emily, his wife, was a blessing recently added to his life, and he looked forward to ending his day in her company. "Oak found this job on his own, and I suggest we leave him to it."

Casriel prowled over to the library desk, a massive expanse of carved mahogany that could have done service as an altar for pagan sacrifices.

"But why a job restoring paintings?" Casriel asked, taking the wing chair behind the desk. "Oak is an artist. Artists create, particularly if they want the notice of the Royal Academy and the lucrative commissions that follow therefrom. This is good brandy."

"Sycamore sent me a case as a wedding present," Valerian said, getting comfortable on a window seat. "I passed along two bottles to the Hall."

Casriel scowled and held his drink under the lordly beak. "Sycamore is a case in point. He wanted to be a man-about-town, so he acquired a club, and now his days are spent man-about-towning. If Oak is an artist, he ought to be artist-ing. Setting up his easel in Hyde Park, ingratiating himself with wealthy cits, advertising his skills. Not banishing himself to bedamned Hampshire so some crotchety old beldame can begrudge him his wages."

"We don't know if she's a crotchety old beldame or a young merry widow, Casriel. A concerned patriarch might put pen to paper and inquire of his younger sibling through the post. Just a thought."

Casriel took another sip of his brandy. "How did she learn of Oak's skills? He's never held himself out as one who restores cast-off attic portraits."

This concern would be touching if it weren't so belated. "I believe she wrote to a connection at the Academy, and he referred her to Oak."

"Why not send her an Academy member?"

Ye gods, when had Casriel become so dunderheaded? "Because those good fellows are absorbed with painting lucrative portraits, as you noted. Oak is willing to spend a few weeks restoring the lady's collection. He's out from underfoot here at the Hall, a consummation you devoutly wished for, and he's earning his keep, a goal he doubtless aspired to. What is this show of worry really about?"

Casriel set down his drink. "Beatitude is a widow."

Beatitude being the present Countess of Casriel and a thoroughly lovely woman. "Your point?"

"Society is inordinately invested in supervising the conduct of widows, particularly widows of means. We ought to have heard something of this Mrs. Channing. Beatitude knows nothing of her, and yet, Mrs. Channing owns a sizable estate and an *art collection*."

Laughing at Casriel's concern would be unkind and might result in an attempted thrashing for old times' sake.

"You say that as if only pirates and smugglers own *art collections*. Dorning Hall is full of portraits, landscapes, and still lifes, as are most country houses. The king himself sets great store by his art as well." Valerian's little estate, Abbotsford, had a few nice pieces, and Emily would doubtless acquire more over the years.

Emily, whom Valerian missed, though he'd parted from her not three hours previously. Married life was certainly a change. Valerian had never slept so well nor gone to bed so early or so happily.

"Oak wants to become a member of the Royal Academy some fine day," Valerian went on. "Therefore, if an Academy member recommended him for a job, he was all but duty-bound to accept the work. Very likely, he can charm a commission or two out of the old dear, and she will happily write him a glowing character. Not all battles are won with an artillery barrage and a cavalry charge, Casriel. Some of us must resort to strategy, diplomacy, and patience."

"Sycamore won his objective with boldness. Willow certainly didn't shilly-shally in the shires when he realized where his future lay. Hawthorne was similarly direct about pursuing his dreams, and you stole a march on the lot of us, marrying an heiress who appears to adore you."

A frowning perusal followed, with unspoken, well-intended, and unforgivably nosy questions hanging in the air.

"I adore her too," Valerian said, smiling at his brandy, "and married life is off to a splendid start."

"As it should be." Said quite fiercely.

"Would you presume to lecture Emily if I said we were having to make some adjustments?" They were. A lot of adjustments, but nothing that laughter, consideration, and mutual devotion couldn't surmount.

"Adjustments are part of the marital terrain, and just wait until fatherhood befalls you. There be dragons in that land, Valerian. Enormous, hungry dragons that cinder a man's peace." Casriel downed the rest of his drink. "Dear Oak has chosen the terrain of Hampshire, and we have no idea what adjustments he's having to make."

Valerian took a modest taste of his brandy. "When you hold Sycamore up as a good example, the realm is in peril. Think of it this way, Casriel: Hampshire is on the way to London. Oak wants to end up in London, a sought-after painter of portraits, and he's thus moved closer to his goal. Stop fretting and write our brother a letter. Have Beatitude send a cordial note to the widow. Show some faith in Oak's resourcefulness."

Casriel rose to return his glass to the sideboard. "Beatitude gives me the same sermon. Trust my brothers, she says. She hardly *knows* my brothers, but she admonishes me to trust the lot of you, wretches and scoundrels that you are. Oak likes to sit in trees sketching by the hour. He forgets to eat when a painting is going well and forgets his name when it's going poorly. He will wander into a bog because he's too taken with the colors of the sky to watch where his feet are going. He'll forget to collect his wages."

"No, he will not. Oak has more sense than most of us. He simply keeps his conclusions to himself, a habit foreign to your lordly nature."

Casriel approached, appropriated Valerian's glass, took a sip, and handed it back. "What if she's the bitter sort, a pinchpenny cheeseparer who will never write Oak a decent character? She'll instead malign his best efforts and set him back rather than advance his cause. We know nothing about her except that she haggled over terms and demanded he abandon all of his loved ones for a summer in blasted Hampshire."

"We know Oak," Valerian replied, passing Casriel the last of his drink. "We know he haggled right back, that he's merely on the other side of the New Forest rather than off to darkest Peru. We know that meddling in his affairs shows disrespect toward him. We also know that I am newly married and have *much* better things to do than pester our brother about the first artistic post he's ever landed."

"But you'll be nipping up to London from time to time, won't you?" Casriel asked, ever so casually. "I understand Emily's papa has business responsibilities in Town that yet require attention."

"You want me to *spy* on Oak?"

"Either you pay a passing call, or I've no doubt Sycamore will drop in on Oak when Cam next makes a raid on Dorning Hall. Ash could probably be persuaded to abandon Town in summer's heat, but one doesn't like to impose on Ash."

"One doesn't hesitate to impose on me, though? Emily and I are in our *honey month*, Casriel. Have you no shame?"

"Think about it," Casriel said, appearing quite pleased with his latest scheme. "Oak hasn't any allies in Hampshire, and I'm not suggesting you depart at first light."

No, but Monday would probably suit the earl's plans splendidly. Valerian rose from his window seat, escape having become imperative.

"Do you know something about Mrs. Channing, Casriel? Something you're not telling me?"

Casriel studied his drink—Valerian's drink. "Beatitude can't be sure, but she has former in-laws in Hampshire, and she recalls some mention from them about unpleasant doings at Merlin Hall. Nothing recent, nothing detailed, but a bad taste. Whispers and innuendo."

"I am not about to abandon my new wife for the sake of old whispers and innuendo, Casriel. Write to Oak and ask him how he's going on. Brothers do, you know. Write to each other."

Valerian bowed, intent on extricating himself from Casriel's plotting, but whispers and innuendo surrounding a rural widow were not good. Not good at all.

～

A SMART MAN, upon hearing heartbroken feminine sobbing,

would execute a silent about-face and go back up the path without intruding. Such a retreat would bear no shame, but rather, be an exercise in gentlemanly consideration—or so Oak's father had once declared.

The damsel venting her tears was not in distress, she was in high dudgeon. How Oak knew that likely had to do with his sisters, and with his late mother's penchant for dramatic displays. This female had also not quite attained damsel status. She was more a maiden of tender years.

Oak cleared his throat, which occasioned a pause in the lachrymosity.

"Go away, sir. You're on Merlin Hall land, and you are not welcome."

"You must be Miss Catherine." She was also blotchy-faced, and her nose was an unbecoming shade of pink. If looks could kill, Oak would be greeting Saint Peter at any moment.

Oak passed her his handkerchief and appropriated a place about two feet from her on the fallen log where she was staging her tragedy.

"You are not to menace me," she said, blowing her nose on his linen. "The stable boys will come running if I scream."

"I would not dream of menacing a lady so clearly having a bad moment. I'm Oak Dorning. I've come to Merlin Hall to restore some paintings for Mrs. Channing."

"I'm Catherine Channing." She peered at the flowers stitched onto the corner of the handkerchief. "This is very fine embroidery. Please don't show it to Miss Diggory, or I'll be walled into the nursery until I can duplicate the pattern."

"You may keep it," Oak said. "Duplicate the needlework in your spare time and impress Miss Diggory with your ingenuity when you've completed the project. Bracken suggested I might enjoy sketching along this path." He brandished his sketch pad and pencil and considered the setting.

The little copse lay about a quarter mile behind Merlin Hall, a former patch of hedgerow grown into a spinney. A stream meandered several yards away, the dark water suggesting drainage from a peat bog or fen. Ferns grew in abundance, giving the air a mossy scent.

Pretty, though well short of fascinating for a man who'd spent many a long hour sketching botanical specimens for his father. Today, Oak's objective had been some fresh air and perhaps a drawing of Merlin Hall itself to send back to his brothers in Dorset. On a sunny summer morning, the Channing abode showed to good advantage. A handsome country manor in a verdant bucolic setting.

"Stay on the path if you must go for a walk," Catherine said. "Do you know what a quaking bog is? It looks solid, but in a quaking bog you're not walking on earth. You're walking on a mat of plants and dirt, and if you jump up and down, you can make the ground ripple— or you can break through the mat and ruin your boots or even *die.*"

Hence the dark water and peaty scent. "A thick mat of moss, *Sphagnaceae*, according to Linnaeus."

"Who?"

"Linnaeus. A Swedish fellow who knew a lot about a lot of things. Ask Miss Diggory who he was. What had you so upset?"

Oak began to sketch Catherine out of habit—and because she was a perfect example of the human female with one foot in adulthood and one in childhood. Her shorter skirts still showed trim ankles and slender calves, but her figure had left behind the coltish angles of girlhood. Her honey-blond hair was pulled back and allowed to cascade over narrow shoulders, while her profile was a cameo-perfect landscape of young female pulchritude.

Her chin tended to a point, her nose tilted slightly. A piquant face, and Oak could see traces of Dirk Channing around the girl's blue eyes.

"I was crying because of *everything,*" she said, heaving a sigh that ought to have set the whole earth to quaking. "I'm suffering the regular inconvenience to which my gender is condemned. Do you know what that means?"

Oak tried to capture the blend of fierce indignation and dismay in her expression. "Is this an inconvenience a man with sisters ought to comprehend?"

"Yes, if he is not a complete lackwit. It's not fair. I had hoped the pain was simply a first-time thing, but here I am, a month later, and completely out of sorts and uncomfortable. I hate it."

Boggy ground, indeed. Six months from now, she'd be mortified to have had this conversation with him at all. Hell, *he* was mortified, but also a little touched. Was there nobody in whom this girl could confide her miseries? Nobody who could suggest she curl up with a hot water bottle, a drop of the poppy, and a lurid novel?

"What does Mrs. Channing suggest for your discomfort?"

"*Her.*"

Nobody conveyed disdain as effectively as an upset adolescent. "I take it your step-mother is among your many afflictions?"

Catherine pooched out her lips, which made her look about four years old. "I like Alexander well enough, though he's only a boy. He's had a hard time of it since Mr. Forester joined the household. I wish I could trade Alexander the use of Diggory for Mr. Forester's instruction, I truly do. Step-mama, though... She took advantage of Papa's grief. My mama, my *real* mama, was his muse. His work was never as good after Mama died. Everybody says."

Such hope colored that declaration, such sadness. "Everybody?"

"My aunt Winters, who is quite knowledgeable about art. What are you drawing?"

"I draw what I see. Is your step-mother a gorgon, forcing you to memorize entire books of the Bible or live on bread and water?"

"No, but she's always busy, and she's *beautiful*. Even Papa said she was beautiful. He was lonely, I know, but mightn't he have settled for a woman people don't gawk at?"

Oak had no answer for that query. He'd thought only to have a short ramble, then meet Mrs. Channing in the gallery. Still, he did not want to take an abrupt leave of Miss Catherine, as if her concerns were inconsequential.

"What does Miss Diggory say about your discomfort?"

"That pain is normal, the price all women must pay for Eve's betrayal. That I'm not to indulge in hysterics. That only *little girls* try to win pity by whining. You should see her when she has a megrim. We all tiptoe about, and heaven help the maid who closes a door firmly."

"I don't agree with Miss Diggory, if I can say that without sounding disrespectful. Turn your face a bit,"—he touched her chin —"like that, so you aren't in shade. Miss Diggory likely means well, and in her way she might be trying to jolly you away from thinking about the hurt, but there's no ignoring a bodily misery, in my experience."

"Exactly. It's misery. Worse than a silly old megrim, though Diggory treats a megrim as if she's been delivered a mortal blow."

Ah, there was the hint of humor, the hint of womanly self-posses-sion. "Then tell her you have a megrim. Some ladies find the two symptoms overlap, the megrim and the other. And as for your step-mama..."

Catherine scowled at him. "The megrim bit is a good idea, but Step-mama is a different matter entirely. Mr. Forester says she's exquisite."

When had Jeremy said that, and had his words been meant for Catherine's ears? Was the girl, in the tradition of youngsters the world over, given to spying on her elders? Sneaking into guest rooms, perhaps?

"Some people are physically attractive," Oak said. "They can't help it, any more than you can help having blond hair that puts me in mind of gold sovereigns or eyes the color of polished blue john."

"What's blue john?"

"A semiprecious stone mined only in one corner of Derbyshire. Don't judge your step-mother too harshly for her beauty." He tore loose his sketch and passed it to Catherine. "I ought to have asked your permission before I drew that, so I will offer the drawing to you by way of apology for my lapse. My subject is rather pretty, don't you think? I'd hate for anybody to hold that against her, as I suspect the condition is likely to grow more apparent as she matures."

He left Catherine gaping at the sketch, but stopped and turned before the path curved around a sizable yew.

"Did I meet you out here, Miss Catherine, or does discretion suggest I make no mention of this delightful encounter?"

She grinned, the mischief adding an adorable aspect to her features. "Alas, no delightful encounter for you today, Mr. Dorning. I'm in my room reading quietly. Thank you for the sketch."

He bowed and left the young lady to contemplate her likeness. She'd been smiling, an improvement over the tearful state in which he'd found her. That a sketch could bring good cheer to an unhappy heart pleased him, though it would take much more than good cheer to gain admittance to the Royal Academy.

~

VERA OCCASIONALLY CAUGHT Jeremy Forester studying her with a less than respectful gaze. She didn't blame him for that. He was a young man isolated in a rural household, while she was the closest thing to an *available* female, merry widows being a fixture in popular novels, if not in actual Society. He likely regarded Miss Diggory in a similar fashion from time to time and turned the same speculative consideration on the older housemaids.

He would be let go without a character if he trifled with the help. Vera had made sure he knew that. She did not feel the need to deliver the same warning to Oak Dorning, who hadn't so much as glanced at her since they'd entered the gallery.

"You're quiet," she said. "I realize you're only gathering first impressions, but have you an opinion you can share?"

Dirk had been more of a collector than a creator toward the end of his life, and his tastes had been eclectic. Some pieces Vera liked, others she would be only too happy to sell.

Mr. Dorning left off peering at the signature in the corner of a

French portrait of a wealthy young mother with her two smiling children.

"My preliminary opinion is that your situation is complicated, Mrs. Channing."

Not at all what she wanted to hear. "Cleaning paintings is complicated?"

"The challenge is not simply one of restoration. Take a look at this painting, for example. How old would you say it is?"

"Based on the fashions, perhaps... Fifty years? Seventy?" The lady wore an ensemble Vera associated with Louis XV, colorful and graceful with wide panniers that showed off exquisite fabrics. Her hair was powdered and sported a sort of crownpiece, not quite a cap, and she had a beauty patch near the corner of her mouth.

"I am certain," Mr. Dorning said, "if we were to turn this work over and examine the canvas, we'd find it nearly pristine, suggesting that what you have is a recent work intended to look venerable. Notice her headwear, called a *fontange*. They became fashionable in the 1680s, but Louis XIV took them into dislike when they grew ridiculously large and ornate. By 1700, they were no longer worn."

"Perhaps the lady wasn't a slave to fashion?"

"Perhaps she was an independent spirit, but consider her beauty patch. When the Duchesse du Maine brought beauty patches back into fashion, the custom became to wear several, as many as half a dozen at once, and they were of black silk. This lady's single patch is red."

"Because colored patches are a more recent trend," Vera murmured. "But this is a signed painting."

"Signatures are the easiest part of a painting to forge," Mr. Dorning said, bending close enough to sniff at the canvas. "Brushwork is much harder to duplicate, and many artists have peculiarities of palette that come from the specific dyes available to them in their locality and period. This painting doesn't smell fifty years old."

"I beg your pardon?"

"Take a sniff."

Sniffing paintings was decidedly eccentric. Mr. Dorning apparently sniffed paintings as a matter of course, and thus Vera complied.

"It smells like a painting."

"Exactly, like the oils and pigments used to create it. To lose that scent takes years, and during those years, the painting will acquire the odor of coal smoke if it hung over a fireplace, perhaps a hint of tobacco if the portrait graced a gentleman's study. I've come across paintings that smelled of lavender or tallow, based on where they'd spent the previous twenty years. Then too, I'm almost certain this canvas is linen."

"Dirk occasionally painted on linen."

"But hemp was the preferred type of canvas in France for much of the last century, and most French artists still use it. I prefer hemp myself, finding the fibers less troublesome than linen."

Vera stalked away, not in the mood for a discourse on the merits of hemp versus linen. "I can't sell forgeries."

"I'm delighted to hear it, Mrs. Channing, for I could not be associated with such an endeavor." Mr. Dorning prowled after her, and though the gallery was flooded with late morning sunshine, he conveyed the sense of a thundercloud rolling across an unsuspecting landscape.

"I was under the impression," he went on," that my task here was to restore older paintings to better condition, not appraise forgeries or support their sale."

Vera stood before a bow window that overlooked the side garden. Paddocks of lush summer grass stretched beyond the scythed lawn, and where the paddocks ended, the overgrown hedgerow shaded a stream and a walking path. On the far side of those trees, the ground turned into a mire for most of the year.

That progression—from garden to bog—was like this conversation.

"I do need to have a substantial number of paintings cleaned and restored," Vera said, hoping to stick to the path of truth. "If I can sell some of the more valuable items, that's all to the good."

"*Must* you sell them?" Mr. Dorning asked, propping a shoulder against the window frame.

He had the rangy, muscular dimensions of a plowman, and yet, he knew art. The combination was disconcerting and intriguing. Dirk had been a compact, tidy man of economical movements, quicksilver emotions, and grand ideas. Mr. Dorning was lanky of frame, and his mind seemed to prowl along logical, even shrewd, paths.

Why else would he be asking about Vera's finances within twenty-four hours of meeting her?

"My step-daughter, Catherine, is fourteen," she said. "Her antecedents are irregular. Dirk never married her mother, though the lady lived with him here as his hostess. I suspect Catherine's mother was married to somebody else, otherwise Dirk would have sanctified their union."

"You suspect? You aren't sure?"

That frown did not bode well for Mr. Dorning's continued interest in working at Merlin Hall. "Catherine is not at fault for her parents being unable to marry, Mr. Dorning. She's a perfectly lovely girl, and she needs a more-than-lovely dowry. Dirk promised me the Hall was full of treasures, but in several years of trying, I haven't found those treasures. You give me cause to doubt they exist."

Mr. Dorning was surrounded by art, and yet, he studied Vera. "And if I cannot find your treasures, will you expect me to clean up the forgeries so you can pass them off as part of Dirk Channing's collection?"

Vera sank onto the bench before the window. Fine motes of dust danced in the slanting beams, and the warmth of the sunshine was pleasant.

While this discussion was most unpleasant. Why had she never pressed Dirk for specifics where his damned treasures were concerned?

"If I knew I could sell forgeries without risk of discovery, Mr. Dorning, I'd be tempted. Catherine needs generous settlements, and Alexander will require means to run this estate when he eventually controls it. Those who buy art are seldom pressed for coin. They can afford to pay for their pretty acquisitions."

Mr. Dorning remained standing at the opposite end of the bench. "Is there a but, Mrs. Channing?" His tone suggested there had better be.

"*But* neither child would be served by the scandal that attaches to forged art. Some former colleague of Dirk's from the Royal Academy would make a disparaging remark, another former colleague would agree with him, and then I could be brought up on charges. Dirk's memory would suffer from such a scandal, and thus I will not be a party to selling forgeries. Where the welfare of my children is concerned, I will be ruthlessly sensible."

Mr. Dorning folded his arms, which caused fine wool to stretch across broad shoulders. "The paintings aren't all forgeries. Dirk might have purchased the French painting on a whim, knowing it to be flawed, or out of pity, because the artist was a friend who needed funds. Many a painter works *in the style of* the more successful artists of the past, and those works are not considered forgeries."

Now he was being kind. Vera preferred his shrewdness. "I had hoped you'd set foot in here and be awed by the number and quality of the artistic wonders you beheld. You needn't loom over me."

He joined her on the bench. "I'm sure you have plenty of good quality work here. I'll do a thorough perusal while I'm waiting for my supplies to arrive. Is there more art elsewhere in the house?"

"Merlin Hall is awash in art, but good quality is not enough, Mr. Dorning. I need excellent quality art if I'm to see Catherine happily settled."

"Did Dirk ever paint you, ma'am?"

The question caught Vera off guard, perhaps because she spied Catherine emerging from the copse of trees behind the stable. Her bright gold hair was a beacon at even this distance, though Miss Diggory had claimed Catherine was feeling indisposed.

"My husband sketched, drew, and painted by the hour, Mr. Dorning, and I have not paged through his every volume and stack of scribblings to know if he rendered my likeness. I assume he did. I see a truant, though, trying to sneak back to the house undetected. Feel free to linger here as long as you need to, and then we can attack the attic. I must have a word with my prodigal daughter."

"Should the young lady be putting up her hair?" Mr. Dorning asked, gaze on Catherine as she stopped halfway across a paddock to pet a broodmare.

"Put up her hair? She's only fourteen."

"My sister Daisy started putting up her hair at fourteen. My mother bestowed that privilege in hopes of inspiring adult behavior."

Catherine was growing up. Vera had been trying to deny that reality for months. "What sort of behavior?"

Mr. Dorning rose. "Mama thought Daisy should remain indoors memorizing poetry when a beautiful summer morning tempted a girl out of doors. Sitting patiently for hours behind a dreary old desk when Daisy longed to move. Listening to the third retelling of some dusty old lecture about deportment when native curiosity compelled her to explore the natural world."

He bent low, as if he'd whisper in Vera's ear. "I daresay you were not the sort of girl who passed up a beautiful day to remain closeted with a translation of Seneca."

No, I was not, and look what became of me. "Why did you ask if my husband had ever done my portrait?"

He straightened. "Because you are an interesting subject, Dirk was a talented portraitist, and I have thus far seen no likenesses of you in Merlin Hall's public rooms. I would enjoy attempting your portrait."

Vera rose, the open, airy gallery abruptly feeling too private. "Sitting for a portrait takes hours I doubt I can spare, Mr. Dorning, and I did not retain you to create yet still more paintings to hang on Merlin Hall's walls."

If Vera knew one thing to be true, it was that allowing Oak Dorning to paint her portrait was a bad idea.

"I am considered quick," he said. "A sitting or two might be sufficient. If you don't want to hang the painting here, I could sell it for you in London."

Worse and worse. "I must be going. I would like to apprehend Catherine before she adds use of the maids' stairs to her list of charges. I'll see you at dinner."

"And you'll think about allowing me to do a study of you?"

Had Jeremy Forester made that request, Vera would have known his objective to be thinly disguised flirtation. Mr. Dorning's interest was expressed without a smile, without flattery. He was once again studying her features, probably deciding what to do about her too-strong nose.

Vera absolutely must refuse him, particularly if he was intent on the result being exhibited in blasted London.

"I might consider it," she said, "but you are not to pester me. Please excuse me."

Mr. Dorning bowed politely, and Vera all but ran from the gallery.

CHAPTER THREE

Oak used different pencils for sketching and for writing, and while he always had a sketching pencil and drawing pad with him, he lacked a writing pencil with which to make notes about the gallery's offerings. Rather than appropriate what he needed from the library, where Bracken might come upon him rifling a desk, he returned to his apartment and retrieved a sharpened pencil from a side pocket of his valise.

He was replacing the valise in the cedar chest at the foot of the bed when he realized that somebody had gone through his effects.

The bed was made, the hearth swept, and the curtains opened. Clearly, a maid had been in the room, but would a maid open and retie the flaps over the valise's side compartments?

Having an abundance of brothers meant Oak had learned to guard his privacy. He'd attempted at one point to use some statues in his father's conservatory as models for a series of nude drawings. Sycamore, his youngest brother, had found the sketches and helped himself to the best two. Oak had drawn them again, and Sycamore had again helped himself.

The next time, Oak had drawn his youngest brother's face on the body of a satyr, but endowed the satyr with microscopic reproductive apparatus. Sycamore had left that image by Mama's place setting at the dinner table.

Mama, bless her, had passed the drawing to Papa. His lordship had harrumphed, slid the sketch into his pocket, and offered the blessing. After supper, Oak had received the dreaded summons to join Papa in the estate office.

Papa had returned the drawing with a few terse words of advice: Satirical sketches could be very lucrative, but if Sycamore had to work a bit harder at his purloining, those sketches might be entirely unnecessary.

Out of necessity, Oak had become proficient at identifying when somebody had done a clumsy job of trying to replicate a complicated knot.

In the case of his valise, no attempt had been made to hide the invasion of privacy. The snoop was either foolish or arrogant, possibly both, but he or she was not a thief. Oak found nothing missing, not a pencil, not a cravat pin, not the green and brown dog whelk seashell his father had given him on his eighth birthday.

Perhaps the maid had been nosy.

Oak forgot about that conundrum as he returned to the gallery and spent the next several hours studying Dirk Channing's collection of paintings. At some point, a tray laden with sandwiches appeared, but Oak didn't stop to eat until Jeremy Forester sauntered in sometime during the afternoon.

"You could rest for a day," he said. "Pretend travel left your artistic sensibilities fatigued. May I?" He gestured toward the tray.

"One-half of one sandwich," Oak replied, setting aside his pencil and paper. "I'm hungry." Famished, in fact. He took the tray over to the padded bench by the window and straddled the bench. "Is today not a day for lessons in the schoolroom?"

"Today's a lesson day," Jeremy replied around a mouthful of beef sandwich. "The terror was allowed to run tame for too long. He needs to catch up, so I am ever and always selflessly dedicated to his instruction. He's copying his Bible verses at present, and thus I am at liberty. What do you make of the great master's collection?"

"You mock Channing?"

Forester took the far end of the bench and stole a sip of Oak's ale. "I mock most everything, including myself. I've always thought art something of a racket, though I dare not admit that to other members of my family. Who's to say if a piece is good or bad? People buy what they like. What pleased some old Italian count two hundred years ago looks clumsy to me now, but mine is not an educated eye."

"Some of what's in here is lovely," Oak said, tearing into his first sandwich. "Some is intriguing, some is clearly an attempt to replicate the style of a bygone master. Channing included a few of his own works in this display, and yet, they are not his best efforts. I can't make sense of this gallery."

"He might have hung the best in the master suite," Forester replied. "God bless a cook who isn't parsimonious with the butter. Mind if I have a strawberry?"

Oak liked strawberries, but not enough to arm-wrestle for them. He dumped half the contents of the bowl onto his plate and passed the rest to Jeremy.

"I doubt Mrs. Channing wants me working on her late husband's paintings. They are too new to need restoration and of too much sentimental value to be for sale. I haven't inspected the library yet. I'm assuming some of the older works are in there?"

"A half-dozen grim, dark fellows in ruffed collars and odd hats scowl down from the walls. Some ladies in outmoded fashion smile at them, and there's a little boy with a dog. The terror occasionally whines for a dog. Might I have another sandwich?"

"You had your own lunch, Forester. Have you been in the attics?"

Forester produced a mock shudder. "Not even to track down the terror when he's in a rebellious mood would I venture into Merlin Hall's attics. The footmen have a dormitory on the attic floor—the maids' dormitory is across from the housekeeper's apartment below-stairs, by the by—but the attics are mostly full of covered furniture and such."

Meaning Forester had stolen at least a peek.

Oak started on a second sandwich. "Will Miss Diggory join us for supper?"

"She and Catherine usually do. Catherine drives the poor woman to distraction. The Channing offspring have more than the usual complement of stubbornness. Suppose they get it from their father. Catherine has the Channing name, but she's from the wrong side of the blanket. I mention that not because I am the judgmental sort who holds the sins of the mother against the child, but because one wants to know where to step lightly."

"Or not step at all. What of Miss Diggory?" And what of the *father's* sins?

"Miss Diggory is a good egg. She'd have to be, else she'd have strangled Catherine. She and I would both be eternally in your debt if you'd offer our charges some rudimentary drawing lessons. You can't be cataloging paintings the livelong day, after all."

Actually, Oak could, easily, but he considered a small boy trapped indoors behind an unforgiving wall of Deuteronomy, and a very young lady feuding with her own body.

"I like the role of drawing master," he said, picking up the tankard of ale mostly so Jeremy wouldn't help himself again. Public school bonhomie was one thing, unwarranted presumption another. "If Mrs. Channing has no objection, I'll spend some time instructing the children."

"Splendid," Jeremy said, rising and thumping Oak on the back, which resulted in ale sloshing over Oak's hand. "I'll tell Miss Diggory, and you will be remembered fondly in our prayers." He snatched up the remaining half a sandwich and went munching on his way.

Oak took his time finishing his meal, and may the kitchen be eternally blessed, somebody had included two generous squares of shortbread with the repast. He wrapped one in a linen table napkin and took the other and the last of his ale with him on a circuit of the gallery.

Dirk Channing had assembled these paintings for reasons, and displayed them knowing how unimpressive several were. The collection made no sense, the house having plenty of other rooms where a professional artist could have displayed works of more sentimental worth than aesthetic quality.

Wherever Channing's treasures were, they weren't in the gallery.

Oak took his ale back to the bench by the window, set down his tankard, and gave in to the urge to do a little sketching. The light was wrong, the pencil wasn't as sharp as he preferred, and he hadn't proper paper to work with, but the compulsion to capture Verity Channing's likeness would not be denied.

~

VERA'S AFTERNOON had gone completely awry, though she had enjoyed the time spent with Catherine. For once, they hadn't been arguing or trading veiled barbs. Catherine had claimed to be seeking fresh air to combat a megrim, a plausible excuse for truancy. When Vera had suggested they experiment with upswept coiffures, no more mention had been made of the headache.

Or of playing truant.

"You simply walk into the dining room as if it's another family dinner," Vera said, passing Catherine a paisley silk shawl of blue and gold. "If anybody comments on your appearance, they will do so to offer a compliment."

In the cheval mirror, Catherine's expression was doubtful. "Mr. Forester might tease me."

"Then I will turn him off without a character." Vera meant that, oddly enough. A man who made his living instructing young people either exercised some tact where those young people were concerned or found a different profession.

"You mustn't be harsh with Mr. Forester, Step-mama. He claims he's making great strides with the terror."

The silk shawl shimmered in the early evening sunlight, setting off the highlights in Catherine's tidy chignon. She looked like a young lady—a very young lady—rather than like a girl adopting womanly airs. Oak Dorning had seen the young lady yearning to put up her hair, while Vera had seen only the difficult adolescent.

"Mr. Forester offers himself compliments easily enough, doesn't he?" Vera said, adjusting the drape of the shawl. "I wish he would not refer to Alexander in such disparaging terms."

"He means no harm." Catherine turned this way and that, considering her reflection. "Does this gold make my eyes look pale?"

"That shawl brings out the highlights in your lovely hair. As for your eyes... Come with me."

Catherine trailed along behind Vera as they made their way from the nursery suite to Vera's apartment on the floor below.

"Will that artist fellow be at dinner?" Catherine asked ever so casually.

"Mr. Dorning? He should be. He's a polite sort, and he won't know that you're trying something a little different with your hair. Ladies try different coiffures from time to time, even widowed ladies."

"You don't."

"I've been too busy lately to tarry at my vanity. Come along." Vera led the way into her bedroom, the one place in the entire house she'd made over to suit her own tastes. She opened her jewelry box and withdrew a mother-of-pearl brooch rimmed in gold. "Your father would want you to have this."

Catherine looked at the brooch then at Vera. "I couldn't. Papa gave it to you." And oh, what a conflict that roused in Catherine's eyes.

"He gave me many such trinkets, Catherine, but you were too young for him to dote on in that regard. We will go through my collection of mementos and divide up the pieces according to whose coloring is flattered by each piece. This one, for example, is better suited to your fair complexion and light hair. Hold still."

Catherine stood docilely as Vera affixed the brooch to the shawl, creating a graceful gathering of the silk around slender shoulders and an accent to balance the knot of pale hair at Catherine's nape.

"That does nicely, doesn't it?" Vera said, stepping back. "Brings out the blue of your eyes. We must find you some combs too." And ribbons and all the accoutrements of fashion to which a young lady was entitled.

Next, they'd be shopping for the fabric to make Catherine's first full-length dresses, and heaven knew that was an expensive undertaking. A riding habit would likely require the services of a London tailor, and that would entail another tidy sum...

Catherine stood before the cheval mirror. "I do like the brooch, Step-mama. It's not too much. I don't want to look foolish, like I'm a little girl playing dress-up."

"You haven't been a little girl for some time, Catherine. Let's go down to dinner."

"Already?"

"You can admire yourself at endless length later. I, for one, am hungry."

Catherine looked down at her house slippers, plain buff footwear, no buckles or bows. "You're sure I don't look silly?"

Vera wanted to hug the girl hard, to tell her that she was beautiful —for she was, without regard to silk shawls or gold brooches. Catherine had a forthright courage, a sturdy intellect, and a good sense of humor. She strived to be fair, and she was protective of her brother.

Next to those qualities, what mattered the length of a young lady's nose or the curve of her damned eyebrows?

"You look splendid," Vera said. "You might feel nervous or shy, but I assure you, Catherine, nobody can see that. They will see the shawl and the brooch, and perhaps notice your coiffure in passing. If you take the attitude that a few small changes to your dress and appearance are of no moment, nobody else will dare make an issue of them."

And if they did, Vera would deal with them summarily.

"Miss Diggory might."

"She had best not. By day, you can continue to adopt the less complicated wardrobe suitable for the schoolroom, but if you prefer to trouble a bit about your appearance for dinner, that is your prerogative."

Catherine squared her shoulders and raised her chin. "I like having a prerogative." She smiled, and a pretty girl was transformed into a lovely young woman. "I am hungry, too, though. Let's be off, shall we?"

That smile... that smile was a revelation. Dirk had done portraits of Catherine's mother, and clearly the woman had been beautiful. She'd also been warmhearted and willing to bear censure in exchange for a place in the household of the man she loved.

When Catherine smiled like that, she exuded charm and good humor, and an attractiveness that was perilously adult. Fortunately, she had time to learn how and when to use that smile and what effect it could have on others.

Vera went first into the dining room, where—predictably—Jeremy was hovering by the sideboard, while Miss Diggory was sipping a glass of wine by the hearth. Mr. Dorning stood near her, suggesting Jeremy had handled the introductions.

"Let's do sit down," Vera said. "Mr. Dorning, I don't believe you've met my step-daughter. Miss Catherine Channing, may I make known to you Mr. Oak Dorning. Mr. Dorning, Miss Channing."

Vera had never formally introduced Catherine to anybody, much less to a gentleman of some station in life. Oak Dorning was an earl's son, and while he was the proverbial younger son, well away from any pretensions to the title, men of even his standing were a rarity in rural Hampshire.

Miss Diggory's eyes lit with veiled amusement, while at the sideboard, Jeremy looked ready to offer one of his signature humorous and not entirely kind quips.

Mr. Dorning, however, caught the hand Catherine had raised uncertainly toward her gold brooch.

"Miss Channing." He bowed politely. "A pleasure and an honor. May I be so bold as to observe that you have your father's keen blue eyes? Do you share his interest in art?"

"Mr. Dorning." Catherine dipped an easy curtsey. "The pleasure is mine. I do like to draw, and I understand you are here to restore some of our older paintings."

Oh, well done, Catherine. Well done, Mr. Dorning.

Mr. Dorning held Catherine's chair for her, leaving an apparently flummoxed Jeremy to do the honors for Miss Diggory. Mr. Dorning assisted Vera when he'd seen Catherine seated halfway down the table.

"Thank you," Vera murmured. "Thank you very much."

He took his place at Vera's right, which put Catherine to his right along the middle of the table. He and Catherine launched into a discussion of Spanish versus Italian Renaissance painters, during which Catherine showed herself to be surprisingly knowledgeable and witty. Miss Diggory offered an occasional opinion, while Jeremy remained mostly silent.

Vera held her peace as well, enjoying her wine and enjoying the sense that in Oak Dorning she had acquired an ally. Not in all regards, of course, and not for more than the short time he'd be with them at Merlin Hall.

But at this difficult moment, when being a step-mother to an orphaned girl on the verge of young womanhood could have gone terribly awry, Oak Dorning had proved to be an unlikely and perceptive ally.

Vera caught his eye and smiled, and he ever so subtly smiled back.

～

TO OAK'S RELIEF, the entire table withdrew to the family parlor. The men sipped port, and the ladies gathered around a pot of gunpowder. A book of fashion plates came out, and Oak sought refuge on the piano bench.

"Do you play?" Forester asked, draping himself over the piano, glass of port in his hand.

"Enough not to embarrass myself. You?"

"Haven't for years. Suppose I ought to practice while I'm immured here in the shires, but that would require finding time away from the terror."

Oak was increasingly offended by the nickname Jeremy insisted on using for his only pupil. "Why call the lad that?"

"You haven't met him, though I will remedy that oversight tomorrow directly after luncheon, if that suits. He can't draw worth a farthing, mostly because sitting still is beyond him. He seems to have inherited his papa's mercurial temper, but none of the family talent."

Oak began a little minuet in the key of G, a parlor piece, not grand enough for the dance floor. "In my experience," he said, "children, boys especially, tend to live down to our expectations. If we berate them and criticize them at every turn, their attention wanders, they fidget, and their memory fails them. If we praise whatever constructive impulses they exhibit, they try harder."

Forester took a sip of his port. "You're an expert on naughty little boys now? Do we conclude *you* were one, or perhaps you've sired one or two?" He wiggled his eyebrows on the word *sired.*

"I easily could have been a naughty boy. I was not the oldest, nor the spare. I hadn't my brother Hawthorne's affinity for livestock and farming, nor my brother Willow's genius with canines. I wasn't clever with sums and legal whatnot like Ash, or naturally sociable like Valerian. I was entirely devoid of my brother Sycamore's charm and guile. The role of brat was ever available to me, and I regret to report that on occasion I fulfilled it."

But upon reflection, Oak hadn't fulfilled that role so very often, a testament to his parents' and tutors' fundamental decency toward a lot of rowdy fellows.

"Perhaps I should call the boy *brat.*"

"You might try calling him Master Alexander."

Across the parlor, the ladies laughed, and Oak once again wished he'd secured Mrs. Channing's agreement to sit to him for a portrait. Her humor was subtle, but never far from the surface, and her affection for her step-daughter was probably plain to all save the girl herself.

Families were messy and complicated. Thank heavens painting was a straightforward undertaking.

Forester settled onto the end of the piano bench, his hip subtly pushing Oak off-center. The last time another male had tried to arse-shove Oak from his seat, he'd barely been breeched.

"So, Dorning, what do you make of our Young Miss? I haven't seen her with her hair up before. Makes quite a difference."

"I think she is sweet, smart, and lucky to have Mrs. Channing for a step-mother. Somebody has seen to her education and ensured she has some confidence, which is always a lovely quality in a young lady."

"You don't mention that she's pretty. Not gorgeous like her step-mama, of course, but she'll turn heads. Her mother was apparently a beauty too."

A note of speculation had crept into Forester's gaze as he regarded the three females sipping tea and comparing fashion plates.

"Drink your port, Forester, and find yourself some practice pieces to work on when Alexander and I are off sketching tomorrow."

Jeremy finished his drink and set his glass on the music rack, then picked up a pile of sheet music sitting on a stand beside the piano.

"I'll look for duets," he said. "Music is much more fun when it's a social occasion too. I prefer to play the top parts. What about you?"

The question was vaguely challenging and slightly sexual, also stupid in the manner of much male banter.

"Either part suits me well enough, provided I have a chance to look over the music before I'm called upon to perform it." Oak brought his minuet to a quiet cadence and rose. "I will leave you to your practice."

"Fetch a fellow another drop of the grape, would you?" Jeremy said, passing Oak his empty glass. "I will endeavor not to wreck anybody's hearing."

Another small ploy, putting Oak in the role of servant. His brothers had mercifully outgrown all but the most endearing of boyish traits. A cuff on the back of the head from a sibling meant *I love you.* An elbow on the ribs was a gesture of affection.

Nothing sly or mean about any of it.

Oak brought Jeremy half a glass of port, then made a polite goodnight to the ladies. Traveling had, as it turned out, sapped some of his energy, and he wanted the peace and quiet of his rooms to consider the day's developments.

And to write a letter to Casriel, not that Oak missed Dorning Hall *or* his oldest brother.

"I'll light you up," Mrs. Channing said. "I want to ensure your rooms are properly kitted out and that we've remembered to fill your coal bucket." She gave Catherine a quick squeeze about the shoulders, which seemed to surprise the girl, then lit a lantern and followed Oak to the corridor.

"I must thank you, Mr. Dorning," she said as soon as the parlor door was closed behind them. "Catherine was nervous of her reception this evening. She's never put up her hair before, and you were a perfect gentleman to her."

"I was merely polite. She's an accomplished conversationalist."

"She gets that from Dirk. That man could charm anybody." Mrs. Channing started up the steps, her lantern cutting through the gloom of an old house after sunset. "If you're to take on art instruction for the children, we ought to adjust your wages accordingly."

"I like teaching young people to sketch and paint. I'm happy to add it to my duties."

Mrs. Channing paused at the top of the steps. "Do not give away your talent, Mr. Dorning. Unless you also have independent means and can afford to regard art as a charitable undertaking, you deserve to be paid for the exercise of your abilities. You've worked for years to develop the skill you have. Don't squander it on every widow who tosses her children at you."

"You feel strongly about this."

She resumed walking, the corridor darker than the lower floor had been. "Dirk felt strongly about it. People were forever asking him to do *a little sketch* or render *a quick impression*, as if his art were a parlor trick. His charm was useful then. He'd gently point out that even as a boy doing tavern caricatures, he'd expected to be paid for his work."

"I am not much of one for charm."

"Yes, you are." She stopped before the door to his apartment. "You charmed Catherine. She needs to know that not all men are as flippant and glib as Jeremy. He's quite bright in some ways, but a complete dunderhead at times."

Oak opened the door. "Aren't we all a bit foolish, at times?" He was, in fact, feeling a trifle dunderheaded himself where his hostess was concerned. He liked being able to nudge aside her sheer physical beauty to see the devoted step-mother and loyal widow, the prag-matic head of Merlin Hall's household.

And Forester *was* a bit of a dunderhead. Miss Diggory seemed to be of the same opinion, if her faint smiles and patient silences were any indication.

"What did you make of Dirk's gallery pieces?" Mrs. Channing set the lamp down on the desk and poked some air into the fire burning low in the hearth. The task was both entirely mundane and —when she did it—the epitome of domestic grace.

"Dirk Channing was well known for painting in series," Oak replied, using the flame from the lantern to light a branch of three candles. "I cannot for the life of me organize what's in that gallery into groups of series or even a coherent collection. It's an interesting conundrum." He set the candelabra on the mantel and turned to find Mrs. Channing regarding him.

"Interesting, as in why would a successful artist collect such trash?"

"Not trash, but not great works either. I spent most of today simply cataloging the gallery's contents, trying to find common threads or themes—and seeing none. Your late husband's tastes were varied and broad."

Oak had closed the door out of habit. Conserving heat was a priority in most households, and Mrs. Channing was a widow, not a sheltered young lady whose reputation determined her fate. Then too, she had mentioned wages, and that discussion ought to be conducted privately.

"Most of Dirk's friends considered me an example of his eclectic tastes in action," Mrs. Channing said, rearranging the decanters on the sideboard in order of how full they were. "I was neither a highly regarded courtesan, as Catherine's mother was, nor an heiress, nor connected to a titled or artistic family. I had little understanding of art, in fact, though Dirk addressed that lack. I don't know what he saw in me, and his friends were surely puzzled as well."

She spoke not as a woman who desperately missed her husband, but as somebody frustrated with a puzzle that should have a simple solution.

"On all sides," Oak said, "Dirk Channing was treated as the great artist, the visionary who shed light on the struggles that inspired the Irish Rebellion. He was the brilliant mind that held the Americans up as standing for John Bull's values more effectively than we English have ourselves. He did this amid controversy, of course, amid both criticism and acclaim. To have the honest regard of a woman who wasn't distracted by all that noise was likely a precious boon." A relief, even.

"He married me because I was a pretty girl and easily overawed." Mrs. Channing spoke with more asperity than Oak had heard from her previously. "More than one of his acquaintances made sure I knew that."

Oak crossed the sitting room to face her directly. "You are wrong, Mrs. Channing, and his friends were jealous of you. I promise you that Dirk Channing had the company of as many pretty women as he chose. Some of those ladies had the means to pay him to paint their portraits. Others were happy to remove all of their clothing for his artistic pleasure—or so the tale usually begins. Successful painters are besieged with the female form in all its glory and fascination. Dirk needn't have married beauty to have it on hand every waking and sleeping hour."

Had she never considered how much time the average artist spent in the company of models and actresses? Never wondered why most studios were equipped with at least a chaise?

"Has your artistic education exposed you to *the female form in all its glory and fascination*, Mr. Dorning?"

"My own masculine curiosity did that, but yes, I've spent hours sketching nudes, painting them, and studying them. We're odd creatures, when you take off our outer finery."

And this was an odd conversation. The naked female form had fascinated Oak in his youth, as it likely fascinated most young males. Then the female nude had become another challenge to sketch and paint. Something of the boy's natural fascination had been lost as the artist had gained analytical skill, something lusty and sweet.

"I might have some nudes in the attic," Mrs. Channing said, moving toward the door. "If they fetch a good price, I hope the lumber rooms are full of naked ladies and bare-arsed Roman soldiers."

Money again. Money and plain speaking. Coin of the realm apparently mattered to Verity Channing, and the refined company of the artistic community did not.

"If you want to raise cash fast, then sit for me, and I'll paint you as Diana or Persephone. We can split the proceeds." Classical subjects didn't particularly interest Oak, but they were becoming popular and thus lucrative. "My brothers own an exclusive gaming hell, which passes for a supper club. They will display any work I complete without charging me. Their clientele is wealthy and frequently given to ostentation. Such people pay handsomely to hang a goddess or a series of goddesses on their walls."

Oak would rather do an honest portrait of Verity Channing, but a classical rendering would be interesting too.

"That is kind of you," she said. "I will consider it, but I'm not keen on modeling for anybody. I like my obscure life here in the shires, and not all of Society is open-minded where artists' models are concerned."

True enough. "I wasn't proposing to paint you in dishabille, madam." Oak did not, in fact, like the idea of *anybody* picturing this woman naked, an oddly unartistic sentiment.

"I know," she said, coming close enough to pat his lapel. "You are wonderfully decent, Oak Dorning. I doubt you grasp how rare you are. Good night."

She kissed his cheek, patted his lapel again, picked up the lantern, and quietly withdrew.

~

VISITS to the nursery had become an occasion for Vera to dread, at least where Alexander was concerned, and yet, she did not want to linger over breakfast either. Mr. Dorning would inevitably arrive for his first meal of the day, and Vera wanted to put off that encounter, so up the steps she went.

Alexander had not taken well to the regular discipline of Mr. Forester's tutoring, and that was a troubling development. The previous year, while sharing a governess with Catherine, Alexander had been a lovely little boy who did as he was bid most of the time and never grew too fussy.

Catherine's governess had retired, Miss Diggory had joined the household in the role of finishing governess, and Mr. Forester had been hired in the capacity of tutor. Alexander had been sullen, moody, difficult and—to Vera, this was most troubling—*unhappy* ever since.

"Good morning," she said, taking one of the chairs in the schoolroom.

Alexander kicked his feet against the legs of his stool. "Morning, Mama."

Jeremy appeared in the doorway to the corridor. "Stand when a lady enters the room, boy. How many times must I tell you that?"

Alexander scrambled out of his seat. "But she's my mama."

"Don't be impertinent."

"I never had to stand when Mama came to visit before. When did she turn into a lady?"

Jeremy looked to be hiding a smile. "She has always been a lady. The question is, when will you turn into a gentleman, hmm?"

Bony little shoulders slumped.

"Mr. Forester, if you would excuse us for a moment? I'd like to explain to Alexander that a drawing lesson will be added to his curriculum."

Alexander's head came up. "*More* schoolwork?"

"Don't sass your mother, young sir. There will be consequences." On that ominous note, Jeremy left the room.

Rather than ask Alexander what sort of consequences followed impertinence, Vera closed the door. Writing out Bible verses never hurt a boy, and she must not undermine Jeremy's authority as an instructor.

"Drawing is an accomplishment that might come to you very easily," Vera said, resuming her seat. "Your papa was fiendishly good at it."

"Papa is dead." Alexander made no move to resume his seat, but stood, head down, hands behind his back, as if bracing himself for a scold.

"Alexander, I know scholarship doesn't appeal to you just yet, but

I admire your persistence. Mr. Forester says you're making progress, albeit slow progress."

Nothing, not a sigh, not a glance. Alexander stared at the floor with more resignation than any martyr had shown in the lions' den.

"Do you hear me?"

He nodded.

"Mr. Dorning will be your drawing instructor. He's also teaching Catherine while he's here, but I've asked that your lessons and hers be separate."

Alexander looked up, his expression dismayed. "Doesn't Catherine want to be my sister anymore? She never visits the nursery. She and Miss Diggory are always in Miss Digg's sitting room, and I'm not allowed in there."

"You're not? Who made that rule?" Vera longed to brush her hand over Alexander's brow, longed to sit him in her lap, even, but six-year-old boys loathed such coddling. Jeremy had been very clear on that subject.

"Mr. Forester says I'm not to leave the nursery without his permission. I will earn my privileges." That last was recited as if Alexander was quoting somebody.

"You will leave the nursery with Mr. Dorning," Vera said, hoping that fit with Mr. Dorning's wishes. "If you're to learn to sketch landscapes, you can't do that in the nursery. Besides, it's summer, and you should be outside from time to time."

Alexander resumed staring at the floor. "What about Mr. Forester's rule?"

"Mr. Forester answers to me."

"He says you tell him what to do."

Some other question lay within that observation, something Alexander did not want to ask directly. Vera knelt before him, desperate to see his eyes, the better to see into his soul.

"You are struggling with the changes I've made here in the nursery," she said, yielding to the impulse to put her hands on his shoulders. "I know that. You miss Catherine. You miss Mrs. Tansbury and her easy ways. It's hard now, Alexander, but I am proud of you for trying, and I know you will adjust in time. Please be patient and don't give up. Mr. Forester says you have the potential to be a very fine young gentleman."

Alexander stared past her shoulder. "What does that mean?"

"It means your lessons won't always be so difficult, and one day, you'll be glad you worked diligently to master your schoolwork."

"I miss Papa." He nearly whispered those words, as if afraid of being overheard. Alexander had barely been three when Dirk had died, but he likely did miss his papa, even if he couldn't recall him very clearly.

"I miss him too. I thank heaven every day that I have you and Catherine to remember him by." Vera straightened lest she hug her little boy and mortify him past all bearing. "Mr. Dorning will come for you after lunch, and you are to give him your utmost attention."

"Will he beat me if I'm slow?"

What on earth? "You have a vivid imagination, Alexander. Mr. Dorning is a patient man, and he says he enjoys teaching others about art. I'm sure he'll have no cause to take up the birch rod."

Alexander sent a look of dread to the front of the room, where the old leather-handled birch rod had been resting in the corner likely since Dirk's grandfather had been a lad.

Jeremy must have been indulging in dire threats indeed. "Will you come see me when your lessons are done for today?" Vera asked, straightening. "I'll want to know how your first drawing session went."

"I'm not to leave the nursery without Mr. Forester's—"

"You aren't to disobey your mama either, Alexander. I miss you. Before you took up scholarship with Mr. Forester, I saw much more of you." Perhaps she ought not to have said that, because Alexander's eyes clouded with confusion. When had he become so serious? So literal? She brushed her hand over his hair, still the silky fine tresses of a little boy. "When your lessons are through for the day, I will expect a visit."

This inspired no smile, no excitement. Alexander remained standing by his desk as if awaiting the headmaster's inspection of the classroom.

"You may sit, Alexander. I give you permission to sit."

He shook his head. "I'll just have to stand again when Mr. Forester comes back. Good day, Mama. Thank you for coming by."

She was being politely dismissed by a six-year-old boy. Jeremy had told her to expect sulks and pouts, tantrums even, but Alexander wasn't sulking or pouting, and he certainly wasn't having a tantrum. He was simply waiting for her to leave.

Vera found Jeremy in the corridor. "Mr. Dorning will come by for Alexander after lunch, and I'd like to see my son at the end of his school day."

"He's in a bit of a mood lately, Mrs. Channing. Not exactly on his best behavior."

Vera was in a bit of mood, and Jeremy's relentless, faintly damning good cheer wasn't helping. "Alexander was perfectly polite to me, though it's clear he is not enjoying his studies."

"Good," Jeremy replied, smiling. "He needs to learn that life is not a romp, and we must do many things we don't enjoy. If he's absorbing that lesson, we are indeed making progress."

That reply annoyed Vera. "We also need to learn that hard work earns us respect and respite, Mr. Forester. Please, have Alexander join me in my sitting room when his studies are through for the day."

Jeremy pursed his lips, as if considering whether to comply with her direction. "You want to know how he gets on with Dorning, is that it? Probably a good idea. Artists are an impatient lot, and Alexander is not a quick study. You're right that they might not get on so easily. I'll send him to you, but please don't spoil him with treats and sweets."

He's my son, and I'll spoil him if I want to. Vera kept that sentiment to herself, because Jeremy, as usual, had a valid point. Supper in the nursery was served early, and too many sweets immediately beforehand were ill advised.

"I'll expect Alexander in my sitting room this afternoon," she said. "And I hope you will convey to the boy that I found his manners quite impressive."

"Of course, ma'am." Jeremy bowed and sauntered into the schoolroom, closing the door behind him.

Vera stood in the corridor, wanting to eavesdrop, wanting to fire Jeremy Forester without a character, and wanting to rail at a husband who wasn't available to guide his son's education.

"Patience," she muttered. "Patience and persistence." Soft footsteps had her turning, hoping she hadn't been overheard. "Mr. Dorning, good morning."

"Mrs. Channing." He offered a bow and a smile. "Good day. Are we to inspect the attics this morning?"

He was all pleasant curiosity and gentlemanly good manners. No hint of a reaction to the fact that last night, she'd kissed him—a man she'd known barely two days. Should she be disappointed or relieved at his apparent indifference?

But then, a friendly peck on the cheek from a mature widow barely qualified as a kiss. "The attic steps are this way," she said, moving off toward the end of the corridor. "The footmen's dormitory takes up about a quarter of the top floor. The rest is for storage."

Mr. Dorning followed her up the narrow, curving steps. The attics were not draped in cobwebs—the housekeeper was conscientious and the maids diligent—but the air was warm and close, even so early in the day.

"Will we need a lamp or two?" Mr. Dorning asked as Vera used a key to open a plank door.

"There are dormer windows, but I'll send up candles if you need them." She always had to gather her courage before entering the attics. She hadn't grown up at Merlin Hall as Dirk had, and her memories of the attics were far from fond.

The key refused to fit the lock, or Vera's hands refused to function. Mr. Dorning stood patiently at her back while she fumbled and mentally cursed and eventually got the blasted key jammed into the keyhole.

"It won't open," she muttered.

"Allow me." Mr. Dorning stepped around her, which put them in close proximity. He twisted the key firmly, and the lock gave. "It merely wanted some strength. A good oiling will set it to rights."

He made no move to step away, and Vera smelled both lavender and meadow grass on him. In the narrow confines of the landing, she was very much aware of his height and muscle.

"I kissed you last night," she said. "I am not a loose woman, Mr. Dorning, but you seemed... I ought not to have presumed. It won't happen again."

He bent near. "I did not mistake a passing friendly gesture for a wanton invitation." He brushed his lips over her cheek. "No more than you would make that mistake should I offer such a gesture to you. Let's inspect the attics, shall we?"

CHAPTER FOUR

Verity Channing was a problem. Oak reached that conclusion not because she was beautiful—he had, as he'd told her, seen many beautiful women, some of them wearing nothing but a smile of invitation. She was not a problem because she was apparently comfortably fixed. He was an earl's son, and as such he frequently kept company with well-off gentry.

She was not a problem because she'd kissed him. He thoroughly enjoyed kissing—*quite* thoroughly—and a quick buss on the cheek would not have been remarked in the very churchyard, for heaven's sake. Not unless rural Hampshire society was far more censorious than its Dorset counterpart.

Verity Channing was a problem because Oak *liked* her. He liked that she troubled over her step-daughter's feelings, that she was protective of a by-blow many women would have refused to acknowledge much less raise. He liked that she dined at the same table with the tutor, governess, and whatever Oak was. He liked that she didn't put on airs and wasn't vain. He liked very much that she seemed oblivious to her own fine looks.

And he had, despite all sense to the contrary, liked that she'd kissed his cheek, perhaps in thanks, perhaps in welcome. He'd liked very much the unexpected spark of daring that had prompted her to make the overture.

And none of this *liking* would advance his ambitions where the Royal Academy was concerned, or land him the paying commissions on which he could build an independent career. His brothers—Willow, then Casriel, followed by Hawthorne and Valerian—were finding lovely ladies to marry and establish households with. Sycamore and Ash made an excellent livelihood from The Coventry Club, leaving Oak... sitting in a tree and sketching ferns.

He must focus on gaining entry into the Royal Academy, not on a lovely widow rusticating in Hampshire.

Mrs. Channing swept past him into the gloom of the attic, her faint floral fragrance blending with the scents of dust and old wood. Weak light filtered in through dormer windows, more light than Oak had expected in a mere storage room.

"I do not make a habit of kissing strange men, Mr. Dorning," she said, facing away from him. "You were kind to Catherine, and that touched me, and I still should not have... I should not have kissed you."

So they were to have a *discussion*. Very well. "Why not? Kissing is enjoyable, provided all parties to the activity do so consensually."

"Because..." She turned slowly. "One should not kiss strangers in the first place."

"One should not *be caught* kissing strangers, perhaps. What's in the second place?"

She drew a finger across the shelf of a sconce that held an empty oil lamp. "I haven't wanted to. Kiss any strangers, that is. Kiss anybody."

Oak pushed the door closed. "You have been in mourning." He took out a handkerchief, dusted off the top of a sea trunk, and gestured for the lady to take a seat, which she did. "Might I have the place beside you?"

"We're discussing kisses, Mr. Dorning. You need not stand on ceremony."

"And yet, you call me Mr. Dorning."

He was rewarded with a slight smile. "Oak, then. I loved my husband."

Oak waited, having the sense that Mrs. Channing was airing her thoughts on this topic for the first time.

"Dirk loved me too," she went on, "though he wasn't *in* love with me. We weren't daft like that. He was affectionate, kind, and patient. He courted me with all the decorum and respect a lady longs for, and that was balm to my soul. When a young woman is pretty, people assume she's also worldly, that she knows how to handle innuendos and advances. I was a complete gudgeon.

"My father inherited from his father," she said, "also from uncles and brothers, and thus Papa ended up with very large land holdings. He was a glorified farmer who had no idea what to do with a pretty daughter. My step-mother's notions on that topic were far from kind. Dirk was passing through the Midlands on a sketching tour when he came upon me having a good cry at our fishpond."

A good cry over what? "Did his age bother you?"

"Not a bit. We got into an argument about the proper technique for skipping a stone, and then he asked to meet my parents. He was a fit and handsome eight-and-thirty. I was eighteen and desperate to leave my step-mother's household. From many perspectives, the match was entirely appropriate."

The attic made a peaceful confessional, with morning sunlight slanting through the windows. The attic was also quiet enough that Oak could hear the slight hitches and hesitations in Verity's breathing as she recited the tale of her courtship.

"Was the match *entirely appropriate* from your perspective, Verity?"

"My friends call me Vera."

She had friends, then. Oak wanted to meet them, to ensure they were true friends and not merely local gossips.

"Was the match entirely appropriate from your perspective, Vera?"

She tugged at her cuffs. "For the first year, we were happy. Dirk took me to Portugal and Italy. Everywhere we went, he was lionized. I see now that we traveled only to the affordable places where artists tend to congregate. Of course, he'd have acquaintances in such venues, but to me, at that age... I was agog. I was the luckiest bride ever to swan up the church aisle."

How wistful she sounded. "That delusion could not last."

"Dirk had forgotten to mention that he had a daughter by a previous relationship. He'd forgotten to mention that the girl's mother, whom he'd adored passionately for a very long time, had been gone less than a year when he proposed to me. He'd forgotten to mention a great deal. I had to learn to have disagreements with my husband over more than just how to skip rocks. That was hard."

Oak's parents had had regular, loud disagreements, and their arguments had never worried him. Papa could shift from thundering to teasing between the first and second halves of a sentence, as could Mama. For their worst rows, they would repair to their private apartment, from which they would emerge an hour or so later apparently once again in charity with each other.

That a married couple had to *learn* how to argue hadn't occurred to him. "I take it your parents weren't prone to disagreements?"

"Step-mama brooked no rebellion. Not in me, not in my father or my brothers. She ended up nearly bankrupting the family, and nobody checked her self-indulgence. My brothers will be decades undoing the havoc she wrought. My settlements were very modest, with Dirk providing nearly all the funds. That's something else I learned only after I'd come to dwell at Merlin Hall."

Oak took her hand, lest she decide that counting the linen had become urgently necessary. "Were you resentful of Catherine?"

"Resentful? Goodness, no. I was furious with my husband. The girl had lost her mother, and he'd handled his own grief by taking extended sketching tours. Then he chose a bride just out of the schoolroom and jaunted away on a succession of honey months with that bride. I was seven when my mother died. If my father had abandoned me like that, I might well not have survived."

Vera's hand was cold, so Oak enveloped her fingers between his palms. "You and Dirk resolved your differences?"

"That took time. Dirk's friends were not at all the sort of people I was used to. He could get along with anybody, from duchesses to drovers. I was fit only for rural assemblies and informal dinners. I had much to learn. Then I conceived Alexander, and we found a sort of truce. Alexander was a happy, healthy baby. Dirk adored him and adored me for being the mother of his son. Dirk gave me two children to love, and for that I will always be grateful."

And that seemed to be all she had to say regarding the past. If nothing else, the conversation had underscored that Verity Channing might be comfortably situated, but she had no fat settlements to fall back on and no wealthy family to assist with the raising of her offspring.

"You have occupied yourself since Dirk's death with being a mother," Oak concluded. "You haven't allowed yourself any frolics."

She rose from the trunk and shook out her skirts. "I haven't *wanted* any frolics. Dirk's friends were a tiresomely frisky lot. Prone to dramatics in their personal affairs and not the kindest of people. They brought a great deal of drama to this house, and why men must... They can indulge themselves without imposing on a woman, you know."

She slanted a look at Oak over her shoulder, partly belligerent, partly curious.

He offered her a bland smile. "I have certainly engaged in self-indulgence." At sixteen, he'd done little else.

"So one needn't disport for the sake of a few moments of pleasure," Vera said, pushing back a Holland cover to reveal a stack of canvases leaning against the wall. "The widowers and bachelors in the immediate surrounds have nothing more than that to offer. They aren't about to take on two step-children, and while Merlin Hall is solvent, it belongs to Alexander after I die. I don't need a man to manage my property, and I am thus not interested in remarrying for practical reasons."

Oak remained on the trunk, enjoying the look of Vera in a brown dress with an outdated high waist. She'd probably had that dress since before her marriage, and the older style left more of her figure to the imagination.

"You don't want to remarry, and you don't want to frolic with somebody you'll have to curtsey to in the churchyard for the rest of your days, and yet, you kissed me."

"I did, didn't I? I'd forgotten these were up here."

She was changing the subject, flipping through the canvases one by one. They weren't framed, and there were at least a dozen in the stack.

"They should be stored elsewhere," Oak said, joining her. "Floors are prone to chills and drafts, and that's hard on the paint."

The paintings turned out to be landscapes, the majority depicting bucolic English terrain, with gently rolling hills, sunny skies, and fluffy sheep. Several were more dramatic, full of dark clouds and billowing trees pressed earthward by howling winds, and one was a nightscape, more eerie than peaceful.

"Dirk did not paint these," Oak said.

"How can you tell? He liked to do landscapes between his more violent works."

"Dirk Channing's style is said to convey more in white space than many artists do with a full palette. One reason for that is his brush-work. He was willing to ruin his brushes for the sake of creating a texture that changed how the light affected his pigments. Look here, at the sheep and the clouds. Both white, and both more or less the same brushwork."

Oak prosed on, though he was abundantly aware that Vera stood next to him in her comfortable old dress and that she'd eliminated the marriage-minded bachelors and the neighborhood widowers from consideration as lovers, but she had not eliminated *him*.

"Now that you mention it," she said, "this doesn't *feel* like one of Dirk's landscapes, though I'm sure he did this exact vista several times. The view is an easy walk from here."

"If this were a Dirk Channing painting, I could take a half-inch square from the sheep and from the clouds, and you'd know which one came from what part based on the texture and the subtle undertones in the white. The renderings here are lifelike, and the image is doubtless a good reproduction of the subject, but it's not a Dirk Channing."

Vera let the canvas fall back against the stack. "It's not a treasure either." She glanced around the attic, which held many such stacks of canvases. "Isn't there a fairy tale about some fellow who spins straw into gold? Great huge heaps of straw?"

"Let me paint you. That will result in some gold." Oak would like to do a series, especially now that he knew a little more of Vera's past. The squire's daughter had an instinctive sense for how a country estate should be run. The half-orphaned girl had a tender heart for children who'd also lost a parent or two. The widow had seen more of the world than she wanted to, and more of disappointment too.

Vera Channing was pretty, and she was more than pretty. Oak wanted to capture the *more*, as well as the lovely face and gracefully curved figure.

He also wanted to kiss her, and not only on the cheek.

"Who do you think did that landscape?" she said, resuming her perch on the trunk.

Oak forced himself to consider the sheep, the clouds, and the little stream running diagonally through the scene.

"Peter Denton has a tendency to structure his images with water. He'll put a millpond or a stream at a focal point, or place his subjects on the shore of a sparkling lake. He's also no great fan of textured brushwork, mostly because he hasn't a gift for the technique. He and Mr. Turner were reported to have great rows about texture when they were both probationers at the Royal Academy."

"Mr. Turner has great rows with many people. Dirk kept a cordial distance from him."

"Mr. Turner and I have not met, though I've spent hours in his gallery. This might also be the work of Hanscomb Detwiler. He's quick, accurate, and a good mimic, but he also lacks a sense of adventure when it comes to brushwork." The painting held other clues to the artist's identity—the specific blue of the sky, the manner in which sunlight was flatly reflected from the cottage windows—but Oak wasn't interested in the painting.

He was interested in the woman wearing the old dress as she sat on the dusty trunk. "Will you kiss me again?"

"I want to, but I'm trying to determine my motivations. Behaving impulsively is the province of artists, not their widows."

Oak took the place beside her. "I cannot afford to behave impulsively. I know what I want—a career as a respected painter—and like the neighboring squires and bachelors, I do not see myself becoming the unpaid steward-by-marriage at some country estate, no matter how charming the widow who owns it."

"Honest," she said. "I appreciate honesty."

"I thought you might. I certainly hope to be dealt with honestly." And that seemed to settle the matter. Neither of them was looking for a permanent attachment, and neither of them wanted a mindless indulgence.

They'd had their *discussion*.

"Would you like to kiss me?" Vera asked.

"Very much." More than kiss her too. She had to know that.

She rose and twisted the lock on the door latch. "Why don't we give it a try and see how it goes?"

Oak remained seated, the better to ignore the evidence of arousal this conversation was inspiring. "Will you regret this?"

"Will you?"

He considered that question, or tried to, as Vera stood before him. He would leave Merlin Hall in the autumn, and whether he painted her or not, he'd have created some canvases for Sycamore and Ash to hang in their club. He would travel to London to deliver those paintings in person and to renew acquaintances from his university days.

Nothing on that schedule precluded a few friendly interludes with a willing widow.

"No regrets," Oak said. "No complications and no regrets."

Vera stepped between his legs and looped her arms around his shoulders. "This is an experiment, Mr. Dorning. You will in some way be my first. Moderate your expectations accordingly."

"Oak." He took her by the hips and drew her closer. "An experiment, then."

She pressed a luscious, lingering kiss on his mouth, and desire reverberated through Oak like a thunderclap. Her hands winnowed through his hair, and he rose, the better to gather her in his arms and lose himself in her embrace.

Coherent thoughts tried to swim against the tide of pleasurable sensation. Some notions were irrational. *I've missed you so*, for example, made no sense at all, though missing the voluptuous joy of an erotic kiss made all the sense in the world.

And other thoughts were howlingly inconvenient: Oak would be Vera's first, as she'd said. Her first affair, her first intimacy as a widow, her first foray into a nonmarital relationship. She'd waited several years to take this step and had chosen him from among many options.

Oak was mindful of the honor she did him, and he offered her respect, liking, and desire in return. Even so, he could not ignore the plaintive, *foolish* voice in his head that envied the man who could take a permanent place at her side.

Vera made a soft, yearning noise in her throat, and a final conclusion managed to coalesce in Oak's mind: The experiment was a success. If the hypothesis had been that he and Vera could enjoy a shared kiss, the hypothesis had been proved gloriously true.

~

OAK DORNING KISSED AS THOUGHTFULLY as he did everything.

Whether he was instructing Vera about the protocol for extracting a gig from a muddy rut, quizzing her on Dirk's gallery collection, or explaining why a painting could not have been her husband's work, he did so in a calm, orderly, self-possessed fashion.

His kisses were calm and orderly too—at first. He gently cradled Vera in his arms, nothing too passionate or abrupt in his movements. His fingers on her cheek were slow and warm as he traced her jaw and brushed his thumb over her cheekbones. When Vera touched her tongue to his lips, he reciprocated, easily, not as if he'd devour her in the next half minute.

While Oak kissed deliberately, almost leisurely, Vera's response was anything but self-possessed. She had not been honest with him. She *missed* conjugal pleasure—missed it badly. No matter how angry she and Dirk had been with each other, how exasperated, they'd never brought those differences past the bedroom door.

Much thoughtful discussion happened in the marriage bed, much forgiveness and honest affection. An intimacy more precious than pleasure could accompany erotic satisfaction, and Oak Dorning would be a tender, considerate lover.

And *relentless*. The overtures that had started out as polite forays became subtly more intense, more maddening, for being offered by a man in complete possession of himself. Oak knew exactly what he was about, while Vera was fast losing herself in erotic anticipation.

"I don't want to make a fool of myself," she whispered, resting her forehead against Oak's shoulder.

He stroked her back, and ye gods, what a pleasure to be held by a man in his prime. That thought might have been disloyal, but Dirk himself had told her not to wallow in widowhood, but rather, to enjoy life while it lasted.

Some of his friends had assumed her enjoyment should begin before the ground had settled over Dirk's grave.

"I don't want to make a fool of myself either," Oak said. "An artist can be the subject of a caricature, a bon vivant who lives for pleasure, respects no authority, and dies young and disgraced, his potential never fulfilled. I refuse to be that fool, but I am..."

He nuzzled Vera's cheek.

"Tempted, Oak?" He was also aroused, enough for Vera to know that she wasn't the only one affected by an experimental kiss.

"I am *lonely*."

Whatever she'd expected him to say, it wasn't that. Men did not admit to loneliness. They made jocular references to their humors being out of balance, they flirted, or they sat in dim corners over-imbibing late at night. Dirk had had many, many lonely friends.

"Loneliness is part of being a widow." Vera had never admitted that to herself, though it should have been obvious. "Maybe the worst part." Loneliness could also—alas—be part of a marriage, even a fairly good marriage.

"I am from a large family," Oak said, speaking quietly, his hands moving gently on her back. "My brothers are my best friends, and they are lately scattered to the four winds. I am happy for them, but I hadn't thought... I am expressing myself poorly. I do better with paints."

Vera took his hand and led him to an old sofa draped in a Holland cover. "Had you never left Dorset before?"

She had missed home terribly as a new bride, only slowly coming to realize the enormity of the step she'd taken when she'd spoken her vows.

"I've left Dorset many times. I went up to university, took courses at the Royal Academy, accompanied my father on his botanical jaunts all over Britain. He even traveled with me to Paris during the Peace of Amiens, and I've longed to return."

Vera took the place immediately beside him, hip to hip, and he wrapped an arm around her shoulders.

"But it's different, isn't it," she said, cuddling into his side, "when you realize that the next time you go back to the place where you grew up, the place you love so well, you will go back as a guest."

They remained curled up together on the old sofa for a long, sad, sweet moment. The sheer bliss of adult affection blended with a touch of homesickness, and Vera felt tears threaten. Dirk would have told her to cry and be done with it, for surely joy would follow, but Dirk hadn't always been right.

Sometimes, heartache followed heartache, a winter that never ended.

Oak kissed her cheek, an invitation for Vera to turn her head and kiss him back. She did, and that somehow resulted in her being on her back, one foot on the floor, Oak crouched over her.

"I want your weight," she said. Wanted the feel of a healthy male lying between her legs, his arousal pressing against her sex through a frustrating abundance of clothing.

Oak rested his forehead against hers, then sat up and offered Vera a hand so she might do likewise.

"We must not be precipitous," he said.

Inspiring Oak Dorning to precipitous passion sprang up as Vera's dearest wish. "You sound as dazed as I feel," she replied, smoothing down his hair. "And you look a bit precipitous." He looked more than a bit luscious, slightly flushed, a tad undone.

He smiled crookedly. "I found treasure in your attic, Mrs. Channing."

Naughty man. "So did I. Frolicking won't solve loneliness, Oak."

"Maybe not, but I suspect one can find distraction from loneliness in a friendly frolic, and maybe passing relief, if one's expectations are reasonable and one chooses one's company carefully."

Vera patted the tumescence disarranging his falls. "One, one, one. What are you sketching around, Oak?"

He took her hand, kissed her knuckles, and laced his fingers with hers. "I cannot offer you much. I will certainly do the work you've hired me to do. I will instruct the children. Other than that, I plan on leaving for London in the autumn, there to pursue my artistic ambitions. I do not foresee that my path will bring me back to Hampshire in the near future."

"This honesty business can be taken too far, you know."

"Until I leave for London, might we be friends, Vera? Friends and lovers? Either status would be a significant honor and a pleasure, but you aren't looking for a mere bedroom convenience, and I don't see myself serving in that capacity very comfortably. But a discreet liaison, a friendship that includes passing intimacy while I'm at Merlin Hall... Does that suit?"

She could not tell if he was talking himself into such an arrangement, or trying to convince her of its merits, but he'd hit on a necessary distinction. She did not want a bedroom convenience, and she did not want to remarry.

She did, very much, want Oak Dorning.

She rose and kissed him, then gave him another pat. "I will leave you here to compose yourself, while I find someplace quiet where I can consider the past hour and your interesting offer. The first group of paintings requiring restoration are in that stack." She pointed to a Holland cover in the corner. "And I will see you at dinner."

He rose in one lithe movement, his smile mostly in his eyes. "Will you retire to your bedroom to have a short lie-down?"

"I'm not tired, if that's—"

He leaned in, glossed a hand over Vera's breast, and smiled. "Begone, please. I must *compose* myself, and with you looking adorable and very likely wearing nothing under those skirts, that I cannot do."

"You cannot?"

He waved a hand toward the door. "Have mercy, Vera."

"I believe I will have a short lie-down," she said, starting for the door. "And, Oak?"

"Madam?"

"In summer, I rarely wear more than a light petticoat under my skirts." She slipped through the door, closing it softly behind her, the sound of Oak's laughter following her down the winding steps.

～

OAK ENJOYED CHILDREN. He enjoyed the breathtaking honesty of the very young, the brooding complexity and shifting moods of the adolescent. He liked the openheartedness of little children and the amazing wisdom that often flashed through youthful innocence. He also enjoyed the out of doors, which he considered to have been his first studio.

He was not enjoying the company of Master Alexander Channing. The boy was an accomplished practitioner of the Grand Sulk and hadn't a word to say unless a direct question was posed to him. Oak concluded a short lecture on the need to study a subject before putting pencil to paper, while Alexander kicked his legs against the bench and stared at the garden's crushed-shell walk.

"Have you any questions, Alexander?"

He looked up to the corner of the manor where the nursery was housed. "What if I can't draw?"

"Life goes on," Oak said, though the question took him somewhat aback. "Nobody *must* draw, but everybody who aspires to a life of gentility should have some appreciation for art."

"My papa could draw *anything*. He was brilliant."

Brilliant might be in a six-year-old's vocabulary as an expostulation. Alexander wasn't using the word in that sense.

"My papa was brilliant at botany," Oak said. "He knew every tree, shrub, and flower in Britain. Knew which ones like bogs, which ones like shade, which ones are fit only for the conservatory. I can draw them all, but I will never have the knowledge he had of plants. I am not my father."

Alexander peered over at Oak and ceased the infernal drumming of his heels against the bench. "Was your papa ashamed of you, sir?"

The earl had despaired of his sons loudly and often, but Oak had never doubted that his father was proud of all his children.

"My papa was pleased with me when I tried hard to better myself, and he was disappointed in me when I slacked."

A silence ensued while Alexander shot another furtive glance in the direction of the nursery.

"We have a bog," he said. "It's in the woods, and it's *dangerous*. A quaking bog is always dangerous. Mrs. Tansbury used to say that."

Some children expressed themselves more effectively with action than words. "Can you show me where the bog is?"

"You want me to *take* you there?"

"I like to work out of doors," Oak said, rising from the bench. "I do better with landscapes when the vista is immediately before me. I would not want to ramble into this bog all unawares when I'm out searching for a pretty view to sketch."

"Mr. Forester will scold me if I go near the bog."

Good heavens, did this child have no natural confidence? "We'll stay far back from the quaking part, and I will tell Mr. Forester that you were showing me the general direction only for the sake of my safety. A considerate host would do as much for any guest." And someday, Merlin Hall and all its holdings would belong to this withdrawn, uncertain boy.

"Very well." Alexander quit the bench and trudged up the garden path. "We can go out the back gate. I must not get my shoes dirty or get any mud on my clothing." The child sounded as prim as an aging maiden auntie.

"If we reach muddy ground, I'll carry you piggyback."

"What does that mean, sir?"

"I'll carry you on my back, like a knapsack."

They reached the gate, and rather than scramble over it or undo the latch himself, Alexander waited with the patience of a tired bullock while Oak unfastened the latch.

"If you carry me through the muddy parts," the boy said, "then your boots will get dirty, and Mr. Forester will blame me. The mess will be my fault because I did not keep you from the muddy path."

Oak might have dismissed Alexander's whining as the imagined martyrdom of a schoolboy with little aptitude for his lessons, except that Alexander sounded as if he was stating facts, not complaining of his lot.

"I was raised in the country, lad. I know how to clean my own boots."

Alexander puffed along at Oak's side as they headed off on a worn dirt trail. "Would you teach me how to clean my boots, sir? Mr. Forester gets ever so unhappy with me when my boots are dirty."

Since when was a tutor in charge of a boy's wardrobe? "Life in the country means boots occasionally get dirty. I'll be happy to show you how I tend to my footwear. Which way is the bog?"

"This way." He tromped off in the direction of the stream, his gait again putting Oak in mind of the elderly.

This child had no mischief. He had little *wind*, in fact, huffing and puffing though he wasn't at all stout. He had his father's fair coloring, and English children tended to be pale, but Alexander's pallor was more marked than that, and summer was well under way.

"I am probably not very good at drawing," Alexander said, pausing as they reached the stream. "I am a slow top."

"I am a slow top at Latin. I never understood why, if nobody speaks the language, so much time must be spent learning it. Why bother studying a dead language when there are living languages that are so much more useful?"

Oak wanted to linger for a moment by the stream. Water and sunlight were always an interesting combination, and the summer verdure was reaching its zenith. In a few weeks, the undergrowth would begin to yellow and die back, the birds would sing less exuberantly. A few weeks after that, he would head off to London.

"You mustn't say that about the Latin to Mr. Forester, sir. He says Latin separates the gentlemen from the heathens. I could help you with the Latin, if you like. Mr. Forester says I'm passably good at memorizing when I make an effort."

"That is very kind of you, Alexander." And not all children were kind. Not all *people* were kind. "Your mother would be proud of you for your generous spirit."

"She's not." Alexander stared at the dark water flowing sluggishly past. "She says she is, but Mr. Forester says she's ashamed of me. I must try harder."

Those words were not a ploy to gain pity; they were weary determination at the age of six. "Mr. Forester is sometimes mistaken, Alexander." More than that, Oak could not say when he had no idea whether the boy applied himself to his studies or reserved all of his mulish tendencies for the schoolroom.

Alexander trooped down the path. "We've almost reached the bog. When there's been a lot of rain, you must be even more careful, because it's not a bog you can always see. It's underground in places."

Something lurked underground with this child. Losing a father had to have been difficult, and the transition from a governess to a tutor might have added to Alexander's challenges. He was an unhappy child, and unhappy children did not make enthusiastic scholars. Surely Forester grasped that?

"We're not drawing, sir," Alexander said. "Mr. Forester told me you were to be my drawing teacher."

If Oak put pencil to paper, he'd draw Vera Channing peering at old, indifferently done canvases. He'd draw her plain brown dress draping around the curve of her hips. He'd draw her smile as she'd patted his falls, and he'd draw her luscious, perfect mouth rosy with his kisses.

Perhaps a sortie to the fleshpots of Mayfair should have preceded this assignment in Hampshire.

"Before we can draw well, Alexander, we must learn to see. Let's take a moment here and compare what we see."

"I see the woods, sir. I see the bog up ahead, where the ground is all bracken and dead ferns. I see trees and the sky."

"That's a very good start, Alexander. How many different colors can you count in the scene before us?"

By gradual degrees, Oak drew the boy into the task of *seeing*. The lad was astute and noticed similarities and contrasts many others his age would not have spotted. Very likely, he had his father's talent, though much hard work would be needed to turn talent into ability.

"You have a keen eye," Oak said, ruffling the boy's hair.

Alexander flinched at that presumption. "Thank you, sir. Must we return to the nursery now?"

"Do you have a pony?" Ponies could make inspiring subjects for a first attempt at a portrait.

"No, sir."

"Then let's return by way of the mare's pasture. Equestrian art is a significant specialty, and some portraitists make a living painting only horseflesh."

"Did you have a pony, sir?"

"Of course."

"Even though you were slow at Latin?"

"What has that...?" Oak let the question remain incomplete. Perhaps Alexander did not have a pony because he was a slow scholar, but if the boy could look forward to his riding lessons, he'd be that much easier to motivate in the schoolroom.

How could Forester not grasp that?

"I did the best I could at Latin," Oak said. "My brothers didn't have my talent with art, but they had more ability with Latin. My parents asked us only to do our best. They did not expect perfection."

Alexander stood beside the mare's pasture fence, peering between the boards at the livestock corralled within.

"Mr. Forester says a smart boy doesn't tolerate errors. I am not a smart boy."

And Jeremy Forester was apparently not a smart man either. "You are a young boy," Oak said. "You have years to learn what you need to know. Tomorrow, we'll start sketching."

"Yes, sir."

Oak scrambled over the fence and hopped to the ground, leaving the boy on the other side.

"Shall I use the gate, sir?"

"Climb up," Oak said. "I'll set you on your feet."

Alexander made an awkward business of clambering to the top of the fence, and when Oak caught him under the arms and lifted him to the ground, the boy felt too slight for his age.

Alexander made an anxious inspection of his sleeves and knees. "Did I get dirty?"

"Not in the least. How many different colors do you see among the mares and foals?"

Alexander applied himself to that task, his judgment astute enough to distinguish between the cream white of a chestnut mare's stockings, the silver white of a filly's blaze, and the pinkish white of an old pensioner's muzzle.

When Oak returned Alexander to the nursery, he made it a point to tell Forester that his pupil had been obedient and attentive at all times and that their walk hadn't taken them anywhere near boggy ground thanks to Alexander's good sense.

"I look forward to tomorrow's outing," Oak said, though that was not exactly true. He would much rather be closeted with Vera among the castoffs and restorations than spend another hour in the company of an anxious, frail boy who never smiled.

Perhaps it wasn't entirely a bad thing that a departure for London was only a few weeks off. A friendly liaison of limited duration wasn't meant to create emotional entanglements, and wading into the challenges in Vera Channing's nursery had entanglement painted all over it.

CHAPTER FIVE

Alexander fidgeted on the opposite wing chair, as if he'd rather be anywhere but perched on that cushion. He looked tired to Vera, but then, the afternoon was well advanced. Not that long ago, he'd taken occasional afternoon naps, an indulgence that would likely mortify him now.

"You used to take sugar in your tea," she said. "When did that change?"

"Sweets are to be earned, Mama."

She put a small lump of sugar into his cup anyway. The patient note of instruction in his voice, aimed at the female who'd given him life, grated on her nerves.

"Sweets are to be savored, Alexander. How did your first art lesson go?"

"Quite well, thank you."

Clearly, the boy did not want to be in Vera's private parlor, did not want to spend time with his mother, and did not care to discuss his art lesson—or anything.

"What did you and Mr. Dorning do?"

"We talked about colors and seeing what's before one, and we talked about shapes." He spared Vera a shy glance. "I climbed a fence."

As a young girl, Vera had climbed fences without number. Also trees, haystacks—very dangerous, that—and many a hill. Her family hadn't had tutors or governesses—her brothers had gone to the vicarage for a few Latin lessons in the colder months—and the whole business of managing a nursery was more fraught than she could have imagined.

"Did you climb any particular fence?"

"We walked across the mare's pasture. Did you know there are many different shades of white, Mama? There is white with pink, white with silver, and white with blue or yellow. All kinds of white." He took a slurp of his tea. "And sunlight can be white, when it lands on water or glass. Mr. Dorning used to sit for hours staring at sunlight and trees and clouds. He asked if I had a pony."

"Would you like a pony?" Catherine had a mare, a sweet old thing who only cantered in the direction of the barn and then never for more than a dozen yards.

The momentary gust of enthusiasm—over the color white, of all things—dropped from Alexander's sails. "I must earn my rewards, Mama."

Another small scold aimed at an adult too silly to grasp a basic tenet of childhood. "Did Mr. Forester tell you that?"

Alexander nodded.

Whatever Mr. Forester was accomplishing, he certainly hadn't taught Alexander anything about polite conversation.

"Would you like a biscuit, Alexander?"

"No, thank you, ma'am."

Good God, when had her company become such a tribulation to her son? "Would you like to be excused?"

The kicking resumed. "Yes, please, Mama. Thank you for the tea."

"One more question, Alexander. Did you enjoy the time spent with Mr. Dorning?"

Alexander looked at his tea cup, sitting half empty on the saucer on the tray. He looked at the door and at his hands. Then his gaze went to the window, where late afternoon sunshine slanted through the glass, sending dust motes dancing on warm, golden beams.

"Can Mr. Dorning be my tutor?"

"For art, while he's here, he can be. Mr. Forester will continue to instruct you in other subjects." Vera broke a biscuit in half and passed the larger portion to her son. "What did you enjoy about your time with Mr. Dorning?"

Alexander took the half-portion. "Mr. Dorning explains things. He isn't mean. He doesn't walk too fast for me to keep up, and he doesn't call me *boy*. I don't feel stupid because he knows more than I do. He said you are proud of me."

"I absolutely am."

The vehemence in Vera's tone must have surprised Alexander, because for the first time since this interview had begun, he looked her straight in the eye.

"You are proud of me?"

"Of course I am. You work hard at your studies, day after day. You are making progress, as I said this morning. You do not give up, and you never complain. Of course I'm proud of such a son."

The half biscuit disappeared into his pocket. "I'm a slow top, but Mr. Dorning said he was a slow top at Latin."

"I haven't a word of Latin, so you aren't as slow at it as I am."

"You're a *girl*, Mama. You needn't trouble over Latin." Another jarring touch of condescension colored that explanation. "May I be excused now?"

"You may, though I will continue to monitor your progress with Mr. Dorning."

He bowed like a little automaton. "Good day, ma'am. Thank you for the tea."

Alexander didn't exactly scamper from the room, but he certainly didn't dawdle either. When he opened the door, Oak Dorning was standing on the other side, his hand upraised as if to knock.

"I told Mama about all the colors of white, Mr. Dorning." This was offered somewhat nervously, for no reason Vera could discern. "I explained about what you said."

"We had a thorough discussion of undertones, didn't we?" Mr. Dorning replied. "We also had a nice ramble by the stream, and I hope tomorrow we can continue our conversation about seeing what's before us."

"You didn't go near the bog, did you, Alexander?" That bog had occasioned some enormous nightmares for Vera.

"We did not," Mr. Dorning said. "Alexander described its location, the better to ensure my safety, and we ventured nowhere near it, nor will we ever. I'll see you tomorrow after lunch, Alexander."

"Yes, sir." Alexander flung a bow at Mr. Dorning and scuttled through the door.

"The tea is still hot," Vera said. "Perhaps you'd like a cup?"

Oak left the door open, which meant he wasn't planning on taking liberties—alas—but the open door also meant he wouldn't risk starting talk among the staff, which Vera appreciated.

"Thank you," he said, taking the chair Alexander had vacated. "A cup of tea and a biscuit can right most of the ills of the world."

What a contrast between the pale, diffident boy and the handsome, muscular man. The child was fair, Oak Dorning was darkhaired. Alexander's eyes were the blue of a bachelor button, Oak Dorning's eyes were nearly the color of blooming myrtle, an unusual shade indeed. More to the point, the child had been uneasy, anxious, and ready to bolt. The man was relaxed, subtly confident, and ready to do justice to the tray.

"How is the resident scholar?" he asked, draining the last of Alexander's tea.

"I hardly know," Vera replied. "He's grown quite serious. He was always a quiet child, perhaps overshadowed by his older sister, but in recent months, Alexander has become nearly withdrawn. My brothers had only enough schooling to do sums and read the Bible, so I must defer to Mr. Forester's judgment regarding Alexander's curriculum. I am very likely being the overprotective mother every boy dreads, but I am worried for him."

Vera refilled Alexander's cup, though by rights everybody should have his own tea cup. To use Alexander's cup for Oak Dorning was familial, more than simply informal.

"He needs a dog," Oak said. "My brother Willow could send you a runt or an old hound. Willow knows dogs the way some hostesses know Debrett's."

"A *dog*? For Alexander?" Vera's father had had hounds, working dogs such as most yeomen kept. Had those canines presumed to set a paw in Step-mama's house, she would have shrieked down the heavens.

"A dog will get him out of the house regularly," Oak said, "give him somebody to talk to, and afford him a responsibility far more rewarding than memorizing the second Latin declension."

"I hadn't thought of a dog, but I suppose... He said you'd asked him about a pony. How do you take your tea?"

"A dash of honey will do. I ought not to have asked him about a pony. As a boy, I had a succession of trusty mounts, but I also had a herd of brothers. We thundered all over the countryside, playing Vikings and cavalry and brave explorers of the Nile, while some old groom sat on a cob nearby and napped. Alexander has no friends to ride with. Ergo, a dog comes to mind."

Alexander has no friends to ride with... "When you were a boy, how much time did you spend in the schoolroom?"

She passed him his tea, and their fingers brushed. He appeared not to notice.

"Mornings were spent in the schoolroom," he said, "from breakfast until the midday meal, around one of the clock. After our nooning, we were free to entertain ourselves. In fact, we were expected to entertain ourselves."

"You had no lessons in the afternoon?"

"No lessons in the afternoon, no lessons on Saturday, no lessons for much of the summer, and that was sufficient preparation for public school, even for me, and for university, and I am not particularly academic. Might I have a biscuit or two?"

Vera set two on a plate and passed them over. His fingers brushed hers once more, and again Oak appeared to take no notice.

"Mr. Forester keeps Alexander in the schoolroom the livelong day," Vera said. "He claims Alexander is behind in his studies."

Oak dunked a biscuit in his tea. "The child is six years old. How can he be behind?"

Vera rose because this conversation was not what she'd expected over a private cup of tea with a man she'd kissed passionately.

"I was a girl once upon a time," she said, pacing over to the window, "and therefore, I have some sense of how to go on with Catherine. More to the point, I was a girl who had a loving mother for my earliest years and then an unloving step-mother, so my judgment is informed by my experience. Alexander is a boy, and Mr. Forester seems quite confident regarding the proper course of a boy's education."

"Mr. Forester seems quite confident of a lot of things."

"While I am not confident. I've never raised a boy, never been a boy. Mr. Forester came well recommended, and his confidence was one of the reasons I hired him, but Alexander is miserable."

Saying it aloud made the reality worse. The waning day was glorious as only the English countryside in summer could be glorious. Birdsong drifted through the open window, and the scent of roses wafted up from the garden.

While Alexander had been positively gloomy for a child who ought not to have a care in the world.

"Alexander does seem subdued," Oak said. "What time of year did his father die?"

Vera returned to her seat, the better to serve Mr. Dorning more biscuits. "Why do you ask?"

"My mother was his lordship's second wife. The first countess fell ill in early July, declined rapidly, and Papa was in mourning by the first of August. My older sister explained this to me, because I was mystified as to why Papa always traveled in high summer when Dorning Hall was at its most beautiful. He'd often take one of us children and disappear to the Lakes or go poking along the Devon coast. He pretended these were botanical excursions, and they were, but he was also dodging sad memories."

A sense approaching vertigo assailed Vera, though she was on a comfy cushion in her own sunny parlor. "Dirk died in midsummer. He wasn't ill for long, and like your father's first wife, he declined rapidly. Would a boy who lost his father at the age of three even grasp what time of year the death occurred?"

"Of course, though the child might not be able to tell you why he's in a brown study at that same time of year. Get him a dog," Oak said, holding up his plate for more biscuits. "A pup will take him out of the house and possibly get him out of the doldrums."

This time, Vera didn't let her fingers touch his. "A dog, not a pony?"

"A pony would necessitate more instruction, and I gather Alexander is getting a bellyful of that just now. Will Mr. Forester take a holiday at any point?"

"Not until Yuletide, when he calls upon his uncle in London."

Oak stole a biscuit off Vera's plate, though she'd served him two more on his own plate. "My riding horse should arrive when my supplies do, tomorrow or the next day. I'll take Alexander up before me a time or two, and you'll know if he has an aptitude for the saddle. Most children seem to, given a decent mount."

"That is kind of you." Vera regarded her empty plate, then regarded the man who'd purloined her biscuit. "Why did you steal my sweet?"

He took a bite of that biscuit, and watching him devour it stirred an odd feeling in Vera's belly.

"Because, Vera Channing, you've ignored my every touch and smile. I'd descend to winking and ribald innuendo, except that you're worried for your son, and I am not a randy youth."

"You're not?"

"I'm a randy adult male." He finished the biscuit and dusted his hands over his plate. "At least, I seem to be prone to randy-ness around you."

And now Vera was fascinated with his hands, which would never do. She took one of *his* biscuits and broke it in half, then brushed at her bodice as if to dust the crumbs away.

"Randy-ness can be a sore affliction," she said, smiling blandly. "Tell me what you think of the paintings to be restored."

A pause followed, a bit goggling on his part, pleased on Vera's. Alexander's situation was troubling, but Oak Dorning had provided a reasonable explanation for that.

"Come with me to the gallery," he said, rising. "I'll show you what I've found."

"Did you find treasures, Mr. Dorning?"

"Possibly, or a clue to where the treasures might be hiding."

~

ARTISTS, for all they might live a life ruled by creativity, had to develop a sense of composition if they were to paint successfully. Within any one frame, colors, shapes, intensities of light, themes, and symbols all had to balance, to come together in a pleasing, well-thought-out impression. The whole had to work as an image, as a message.

Oak had fallen asleep struggling to solve the riddle of the composition that was Dirk Channing's personal gallery. Whatever Dirk's message had been, Oak could not divine it. The paintings made no sense as a grouping, and many of them made little sense as individual renderings.

Channing had been noted for always creating his works in series, but his gallery was a hodgepodge, no two paintings belonging together.

"I went back to our young mother," he said, coming to a halt before the frame. "I asked myself why Dirk Channing, who was an exceptionally sophisticated producer and consumer of art, would have a painting like this in his collection. The image is historically inaccurate, the subjects are mundane, the brushwork pedestrian. Nothing about this work impresses, except as a painting that in every way falls short."

Vera stood beside him, frowning at the lady and her two children. "You're saying an amateur could have done this?"

"Exactly. Why would Dirk not only keep a work this unimpressive, but also display it?"

"Because they look happy?"

Well, hell and damnation. Vera sounded so wistful as she posed that suggestion.

"I'll paint you all the happy parlor pieces you want, madam, but I suspect Dirk hung this work because it is such a clearly inferior effort. I've mentioned that the age of the canvas can often be deduced by examining it from the back. Take a look at this one."

Oak had first turned the painting over to confirm his hunch regarding its recent origins. He took it down now and held it so the back faced Vera.

"The canvas is new," she said. "I seldom heat the gallery, in part to protect the paintings from smoke, but that canvas can't be ten years old."

"I'd like your permission to take it out of the frame."

"Of course you may, but why dismantle the frame?"

Oak rehung the painting. "Because the frame is another clue. It hasn't been glued. If you take a close look at the corners, the frame is held together exclusively by hardware, and not much of it."

"So taking it apart won't be difficult." Vera moved away, on to the next painting. "This one's no better, is it?"

She peered at the landscape, an unremarkable rural scene with the requisite sheep, cows, undulating fields, and distant manor house. The only aspect of the composition to draw the eye was a pair of riders, a man and a woman, side by side on a lane in the bottom right corner of the frame. The lady's habit—a flowing, scarlet ensemble—

was the brightest element of the whole and thus placed awkwardly from a compositional standpoint.

"Nobody wears skirts that long anymore," Vera said, "and I've never seen an entirely red habit, despite the fashion for women's riding attire to mimic military styles. Let's have a look at the back."

"It's new," Oak said. "As new as the one next to it. Most of the paintings in here are new, and I believe they are framed so poorly because the frames were meant to be dismantled."

Vera crossed her arms, regarding the room wall by wall. "Why do that? Dirk's professional standing mattered to him. He had to know that I'd eventually resume entertaining, and people—the neighbors at least—would see this lot of tripe."

"I can't answer that. Perhaps he expected that his friends would raise the very questions I'm bringing up now. Perhaps he wasn't thinking clearly when he established this gallery. We might have more answers after I pry apart a frame or two."

"Do as you wish. The paintings are apparently worthless." Based on her grim expression, the lack of value bothered her exceedingly.

"You have some very nice old works in the attic, Vera. I can have them cleaned up and on their way to Town within a week. You'll want to wait until the Little Season to auction them, though a sale next spring would bring better prices still."

She crossed the room to perch on the bench before the window. "Because in spring, everybody is refurbishing the properties they let out for the Season proper, but the sooner I can invest funds for Catherine, the more she'll have as a dower portion. A year or so ago, I tried sending three paintings to Mr. Longacre to sell in Town—that landscape," she said, nodding in the direction of a trite rural scene, "and the two garden studies on either side of it. He couldn't find buyers for any of them, and now you're telling me to wait longer still to try again."

She had picked the best of the lot to send to Longacre, but the best of this collection would be beneath Longacre's notice.

"As soon as my supplies and equipment arrive," Oak said, "I'll get to work. Have you given any more thought to a portrait?"

While Vera gazed out at the bucolic countryside, Oak remained on his feet and found his attention drawn to the nape of her neck. Was there a more enticing aspect to a woman's body than that delicate, vulnerable, pale, sweet...?

He wanted to taste her there, to sniff and nuzzle and nibble and kiss. He wanted to know the exact texture of her skin, the scent and warmth of her.

"How soon can you take apart that painting?" Vera asked.

"I can start on it in the morning."

She rose. "Let me know what you find."

The door was open, and Vera headed straight for it, only to be met by Bracken. "Madam, the mail has arrived. You have more correspondence from London, so I brought it to you straightaway."

He sent Oak the kind of look Oak's mother had reserved for Papa's hounds when they presumed to accompany his lordship through the front door.

"Thank you, Bracken. Mr. Dorning, I'll see you at dinner." Vera hurried out, sorting the packet of letters.

Bracken remained, and Oak braced himself to be scolded by the senior-most member of Vera's staff. Gawping at a lady's neck with the door wide open was badly done, but then, Oak had never before harbored an attraction to a woman with whom he shared a dwelling.

Greater discretion was in order—much greater.

"Your trunks have arrived in Bathboro, Mr. Dorning," Bracken said, "as has your horse. I can send a groom with a cart to fetch both."

I *can* send, not I *have* sent. "Would you rather I handle this errand myself?" The day was sunny, the track would be dry and as navigable as cart tracks ever were.

Bracken was not the cheery, affable sort of butler Oak had grown up with at Dorning Hall. Nor was he the dignified, slightly aloof creature guarding the doors of most Mayfair establishments. He was more fierce and didn't care who remarked that quality.

"I understand that your early afternoons are spoken for," Bracken said. "Mr. Channing often took Alexander with him for trips into the village."

Oak was not Mr. Channing, nor did he wish to step into Mr. Channing's shoes. He did, however, want to get his hands on his supplies as soon as possible.

"Mr. Forester might disapprove of my kidnapping his pupil for such an outing."

"Mr. Forester will rejoice to have the time free, though he will pretend otherwise."

Ah, well. At least Oak wasn't alone in earning Bracken's disdain. "Mrs. Channing will permit the outing?"

Bracken's scowl became one degree less thunderous. "I shall inform her that you decided to extend Master Alexander's first art lesson into two sessions. She will not object."

She would not be given a chance to object, in other words.

"Then you have my thanks for your suggestion, Bracken. I am eager to retrieve my supplies and my horse, but I would not want to shirk my responsibility to Master Alexander."

The scowl faded into a mere frown. "Of course not, sir. You will be sure that Master Alexander wears his jacket, of course."

"Of course. And his cap, at least as far as the bottom of the drive."

"Very good, sir." Bracken nodded—he did not bow—and withdrew.

Oak sent word around to the stable to hitch up a stout cart and went to the nursery to collect his charge.

"This is most irregular," Forester muttered when Oak informed him of his plans. "The boy needs routine if he's to learn discipline. I can understand a ramble in the garden—landscapes and all that—but Bathboro is hardly worthy of artistic study."

"Alexander," Oak said, "please fetch your jacket and cap."

The boy remained unmoving beside his desk.

Forester waved a hand toward the door. "Do as Mr. Dorning says, boy. And if I hear that you gave Mr. Dorning the slightest trouble, that you so much as gazed longingly at a mud puddle, there will be consequences."

"Yes, sir." Alexander scampered for the door with more energy than Oak had seen him display previously.

"Boy!" Forester barked.

Alexander came to an abrupt halt and turned slowly. "Sir?"

"Make your *bow*, Alexander. You *bow* before taking leave of other gentlemen."

Alexander bowed correctly to Oak and to Forester. "May I fetch my jacket now, sir?"

"You may." As Alexander disappeared into the corridor, Forester heaved up a sigh. "That child has all the scholastic aptitude of a turtle and the memory of a gnat. You do him a disservice by introducing an element of frolic to his day, Dorning."

Oak wanted to like Jeremy Forester. He and Forester were of an age, of a similar station, both trying to find a way forward in life and not particularly succeeding. But Alexander did not like Forester, and most children were good judges of character.

"Do I tell you how to teach Master Alexander his sums?" Oak asked.

"Any fool can teach sums, Dorning. One plunks an abacus down before the pupil, moves some beads around, drills the basic concept, and it's taught. What's your point?"

"Are you an artist?"

"God spare me from such a fate."

"I *am* an artist, and I well know how to teach my craft. If Master Alexander is to develop artistic skill, he must learn to see his world with fresh eyes, to *notice*, to visually analyze what others see but ignore. The best way to teach that lesson is to put him in situations where he is keenly interested in novel surroundings. When he has exercised his powers of attention naturally, I can use that experience to encourage him to the same end for artistic purposes."

I am an artist. Oak had never said those words before, not as a bald statement of fact. *I enjoy art. I find art interesting. I am drawn to artistic pursuits.* All so much dithering that implied, *Please don't disapprove of me because I love my art.*

For he did. He absolutely did. Surely the Royal Academy would see that.

"Take the boy, then," Forester said, huffing out another sigh. "Corrupt him to your heart's content, but don't be surprised if he's so fidgety tomorrow that I'm compelled to take the birch rod to his hopeless little backside."

"He's six years old, Forester. You don't actually use that thing on him, do you?"

Forester smiled. "Mostly as a threat, and thank God it's effective in that capacity. The boy has a stubborn streak."

Mostly as a threat. Oak disliked the sound of that, but then, he wasn't a tutor combatting the unscholarly impulses of a little boy. He was an artist.

"I will have your pupil back in two or three hours," Oak said, pausing at the schoolroom door, "but might you consider addressing him as Master Alexander? You insist on proper deportment from him, you should at least show him the courtesy of proper address, shouldn't you? Children learn by example."

Forester picked up the old birch rod in the corner and whipped it through the air a few times. "*Master* Alexander. When he masters something—anything—I'll happily refer to him as such. How's that?" *Whip, whip.*

That was an infantile display of contrariness, but Oak had made his point. Alexander met him in the corridor, and it was all Oak could do not to put the little fellow on the polished bannister and show him what long staircases were truly meant for when a small boy's day needed some excitement.

Perhaps another time.

～

"MR. DORNING HAS TAKEN Master Alexander with him into Bathboro," Bracken said, setting a tea tray at Vera's elbow.

"He has?" Vera occasionally took Alexander to the village, though not since Jeremy had joined the household.

"Mr. Dorning's effects have arrived from Dorset, and he was eager to retrieve them. I gave him to understand that you would support this plan." Bracken stepped back. "I hope I did not misguide the artist in residence?"

Yesterday, Oak had taken Alexander for a walk without asking anybody's permission. Why shouldn't he take the child into the village?

"I can't imagine Mr. Forester was pleased with this development." Vera did not particularly want any tea, but rather than hurt Bracken's feelings, she poured herself a cup and dutifully sipped.

Bracken withdrew a wilting pink rose from among a bouquet on the mantel. "Mr. Forester predicted that the end times would soon be upon us if Master Alexander was permitted fresh air for an entire summer afternoon. This calamity is not to be confused with the apocalypse that will occur if the boy fails to translate Caesar's Gallic letters by Yuletide."

"Were you eavesdropping, Bracken?"

"Checking the oil in the lamps in the nursery corridor, ma'am." He tossed the fading rose into the dustbin and peered at the full coal bucket, though the day was too mild for a fire to have been lit in the parlor's hearth. His next dilatory tactic was to fuss with the folds of the drapes pulled back to let in the afternoon sun.

Vera was very much aware of the stack of letters in the middle of the blotter and equally aware that Bracken was hovering.

"You don't think much of Mr. Forester, do you, Bracken?"

He moved to another set of drapes. "I believe it more the case that Mr. Forester doesn't think much of me. His opinion of a butler is of no moment, but he had best remain respectful toward you, madam, or to quote a particularly dull-witted pedant, there will be consequences."

Vera had no idea who the pedant—oh. *That pedant.* "Exactly what kind of consequences does the pedant refer to?"

"That's a matter for discussion between you and Mr. Forester, madam. Please do have a sandwich or two, lest Cook be offended." He bowed and withdrew after a pointed glance at the tray.

Vera nibbled on an egg sandwich while she went through the correspondence. A single invitation, much to her relief. Only one invoice, from the thatchers who'd repaired a tenant's sheep byre. Vera unlocked her strong box and counted out the requisite coin, for skilled laborers preferred cash to bank drafts.

And—predictably—Richard Longacre expressed hopes that she might journey to London for Lady Montclair's summer reception. Vera would just as predictably decline and took out a sheet of paper preparing to pen her reply.

"Oh, excuse me, Mrs. Channing." Tamsin Diggory stood in the doorway. "I hadn't realized you were in here. I've misplaced my penknife and thought to borrow one from the desk."

Vera folded up the little note and tucked it under the rest of the stack.

She opened the desk's center drawer and found three penknives in a tray. "This one looks sharp." She passed over a pewter-handled blade. "Would you like some tea or sandwiches? I haven't much of an appetite, and Bracken will be disappointed if I send the tray back with food on it."

"Can't have that," Miss Diggory replied, choosing a sandwich and taking the seat opposite the desk. "I never know what to make of that man. If he's ever smiled, it was in the dark of night long, long ago."

"He lost a wife and child to smallpox. Dirk shared that confidence only after we'd been married for several years, and you must never refer to it. Bracken's lot has been difficult, and he has been unfailingly loyal to me and to the Hall. Tea?"

"Please. It's as well I found you here, for I've a request."

Tamsin Diggory was pleasant company. She had the gift of a light, cheerful touch with everybody, from the servants, to the governesses and companions she socialized with on her days off, to elderly ladies looking for assistance crossing a muddy churchyard.

And Tamsin was pretty, having the classic blond, blue-eyed coloring of the Saxon maiden. She'd disclosed her age as five-and-twenty. Old enough to claim some common sense, as she'd said, young enough not to take life too seriously.

"And what is your request?" Vera asked, retrieving a spare tea cup and saucer from the sideboard. "Have the charms of Hampshire in summer paled? Are you ready for a holiday?" Tamsin and Jeremy had begun at Merlin Hall within a fortnight of each other, though Catherine's adjustment to a new governess had been swift and easy compared to Alexander's ongoing discontent.

"No holiday quite yet," Tamsin said. "Catherine is now putting up her hair."

"I thought it was time. Catherine more than agreed."

"As do I, but the decision was yours to make and mine to accommodate. We will end lessons a little earlier in the afternoon so Catherine has time to change for dinner."

"Gracious. That didn't take long." The topic was a happy one, and yet, Vera knew a pang of loss. Must Catherine be so pleased to put childhood behind her?

Tamsin helped herself to a lump of sugar. "I suspect she'll lose interest in the preening and fussing once she finds a few hairstyles she likes, but she has mentioned letting her hems down the rest of the way."

"Of course." Except that figure of speech actually referred to making up a young woman's entire first adult wardrobe rather than turning a few seams. "I have some fabric in the attic suitable for starting that project."

"Might we plan a trip into Winchester, perhaps?"

To buy more fabric, to order slippers, gloves, bonnets, and other fripperies necessary to properly ornament a lady. To acquaint Catherine with the process of procuring her needs from a shop.

"Next month," Vera said. "Start making a list, and I will do likewise."

"Excellent." Tamsin chose a second sandwich, having finished the first. "That was not the only question I wanted to ask you, though. With Mr. Dorning underfoot, I thought we might put him to use of an evening."

Vera glanced up from stirring her tea. "I beg your pardon?"

Tamsin grinned. "That came out wrong. What I meant was, Mr. Dorning is clearly a gentleman and can be relied upon to act as one where Catherine is concerned. I thought we might try adding a hand of cards to the after-dinner routine. You have a foursome, if Mr. Forester and Mr. Dorning are both pressed into service, and Catherine can get some experience with polite play before she starts socializing as an adult."

Well, of course. Cards were an essential skill for anybody of sufficient station to circulate in society.

"This is all happening rather quickly," Vera said. "If you'll be on hand to partner Catherine, I don't see that much could go amiss, though."

"Me?" Tamsin chose a square of shortbread from the tray. "I would far rather have my evenings at liberty, if you please. I thought *you* might sit down with the gentlemen over a hand of cards, while I enjoy a long soak in a hot bath."

The tea wasn't sitting well with Vera, or perhaps the conversation wasn't. "I am happy to play a few hands for the sake of Catherine's social skills, but you must also take your turn, Tamsin."

"Oh, very well." She chose another piece of shortbread and rose. "I will do my best to be agreeable and ladylike, as ever, but if Mr. Forester is too unbearable, I will kick him under the table."

Whatever did that mean? "I'll see you at dinner."

Tamsin left, though she'd forgotten her penknife.

Vera tried to focus on her ledgers. A household the size of Merlin Hall generated endless ledger entries, each one less interesting than the one before. When the ledgers failed to distract her, she turned to her social correspondence, penning a polite refusal to the Bonners' invitation to dinner and dancing.

Soon, she'd have to accept such invitations for Catherine's sake, and when invitations were accepted, they should also, eventually, be reciprocated. The whole business was tiresome for a farmer's daughter who longed to spend her afternoons reading in the orchard.

Vera rose, the small of her back aching from the hard seat of her writing chair. She stretched and went to the window, realizing that half the afternoon had passed, and she had little to show for the time she'd spent at her desk.

A commotion drew her attention to the bottom of the drive. Oak Dorning sat on the bench of a small farm wagon, a sizable bay horse tied to the back. Large trunks filled the bed of the wagon, and right next to Oak sat Alexander.

His cap was off, and in his small hands he held the reins to the single horse pulling the wagon, a massive chestnut gelding worthy of a wheeler's honors.

Vera was too much of a countrywoman to be frightened by the sight of Alexander learning to guide a ton of horseflesh, and she trusted Oak to keep her son safe in any case, but as a mother...

Ye gods, they were *both* growing up. Alexander *and* Catherine, before her very eyes. Five years from now, Catherine could well be married and starting her own family, and Alexander might be off to public school.

Oak caught sight of her in the window and waved. Vera waved and smiled back. When Alexander—aided by Oak—brought the horse to a stop at the foot of the manor house steps, he looked up and smiled at his mama for the first time in months.

Vera vowed, then and there, that Alexander would enjoy more trips to the village, and to hell with Caesar's letters to the Galatians, or whatever Jeremy thought was so dratted urgent in the schoolroom.

And she would see about getting Alexander a dog—and possibly one for herself as well.

CHAPTER SIX

"A moment, Alexander," Oak said as a groom came forward to take the cart horse's reins. "We must attend to the dust of the road."

"The dust of the road, sir?" Alexander's voice had lost yesterday's hesitant quality, and his gaze was no longer downcast.

Oak lifted him off the wagon bench and set him on his feet. "Our boots." Oak flourished a handkerchief. "When it rains, a fellow contends with mud. When it doesn't rain, the problem is dust. The ladies take a dim view of either on their carpets. Hold still." Oak dusted off Alexander's toes, then did the same to his own footwear. In the normal course, Oak would not have bothered, but why give Forester a pretext for criticizing the child?

"Mama saw me at the ribbons," Alexander said, bouncing up the steps to the front door. "She smiled at me."

"She did, indeed. You should be very proud of yourself, Alexander." The horse, a stalwart behemoth named Atlas, had probably traveled from Merlin Hall into the village weekly for years and would have trotted the distance with no guidance from a driver.

"May we drive into the village tomorrow, Mr. Dorning?"

"Tomorrow, we will see how Charlie has recovered from his travels. A quiet hack will do, and I will take you up before me if you're amenable."

"What's a menable?"

"Amenable means agreeable, willing. I will walk with you up to the schoolroom if you're amenable to having my company."

Alexander preceded Oak into the foyer, where they were greeted by an unsmiling Bracken.

"I took the ribbons, Bracken!" Alexander announced. "All the way back from Bathboro. Is that many miles, Mr. Dorning?"

"A vast distance," Oak said, ruffling the boy's hair.

"Have we lost our cap, Master Alexander?" Bracken asked.

Alexander's hand went to the top of his head, and all the animation in him turned to worry. "My cap! I have lost my—"

Oak pulled the cap from his jacket pocket. "Right here." He passed the cap to Bracken, then knelt to unbutton Alexander's jacket.

"I can do that myself, sir."

"My apologies," Oak said, undoing the final button. "But now that the task is complete, let's find your mother so she can fuss over you."

Bracken took Alexander's jacket. "Mrs. Channing is in her private parlor. We'll have your trunks sent up to your rooms, Mr. Dorning."

"My thanks." Oak extended a hand to the boy. "Come along, lad, and prepare to endure a thorough maternal hugging."

"Mama will hug me?" Alexander took Oak's hand and pulled him toward the steps.

"And you will allow it. You will even hug her back a little, gently, because the ladies can be delicate."

This curious, energetic version of Alexander was a very different little boy from the silent, sullen child who'd trudged down the front steps two hours earlier. Oak felt a peculiar sense of accomplishment for having coaxed the livelier child from the shadows in the schoolroom.

"Mrs. Channing." Oak stopped several paces from her desk and bowed. Alexander, who was still hand in hand with Oak, did likewise an instant later.

"Mama, I took the ribbons. I steered Atlas all the way home from Bathboro, and he never put a foot wrong. Mr. Dorning said I am a natural whip."

Vera had come around from behind her desk and held out her arms to her son. "You are a brilliant whip. I saw you with my own two eyes. Come here."

Alexander grinned at Oak and scampered across the carpet as his mother knelt to indulge in the predicted affection.

"Tomorrow we will hack out on Charles II," Alexander said when Vera let him go. "What color is a lark's song, Mama?"

"I hardly know. The color of happiness, maybe?"

"I asked Mr. Dorning, and he said there is no wrong answer to such a question, because we each hear that song differently according to our moods. Then *he* asked *me* what color a nightingale's song would be, but that's difficult, because they sing most often in the dark, don't they, and how does one show a color in the darkness?"

Oak assisted Vera to rise.

"Mr. Dorning, my son is becoming a philosopher."

"Master Alexander is very bright," Oak said. "He notices much and thinks deeply, but now I must accompany him back to the school-room, or Mr. Forester will fear his pupil was kidnapped by brigands." Oak again held out a hand to the boy, who was all but skipping around the room. "If you'll excuse us, Mrs. Channing?"

Alexander caught Oak's hand and came to a stop. "Must I return to the schoolroom, sir?"

"Alas, yes, for all good things must end, but I can see that you arrive to your destination in the style to which a skilled coachy is enti-tled." He swung Alexander up onto his back and scissored the boy's legs around his waist. "Grab me about the neck and off we go."

"When you've delivered your charge, Mr. Dorning, I'd like a moment of your time, please."

"Of course. Alexander, let's be off."

Oak trotted from the room, jostling the boy on his back some, but not too much. A piggyback ride wasn't supposed to be a serious undertaking.

"You won't tell Mr. Forester I nearly lost my cap, will you?" Alexander asked when Oak set him on his feet in the schoolroom.

"Of course not. You were too busy steering Atlas to notice I snatched it from your head before the wind could toss it into the bushes. I'll look forward to tomorrow's outing, Alexander."

"I will too, sir." Alexander sat at his desk, once again the unhappy lump of little boy he'd been two hours ago.

"Alexander, have you Bible verses to copy for today?"

"Yes, sir. Twenty verses a day, without fail, except on the Sabbath, when I am to do forty."

Bloody hell. If anything was likely to put a child on the path to ignoring divine guidance, that would do it.

"Why not start on today's verses, and I'll let Mr. Forester know you're back at your labors."

"Yes, sir."

Oak left Alexander paging through the Bible on the table at the front of the room, pencil in hand, foolscap on the table beside him. Alexander stood on a box for this effort, much as Oak had stood on boxes to study his father's maps.

But Bible verses could not hold a candle to maps in terms of sparking a small boy's fancy, and the schoolroom had neither a globe nor an atlas. Oak left the scholar to his verses and departed, intent on tidying himself up before he rejoined Vera in her private parlor. He was thus rounding a corner in the direction of the back steps when he heard a soft rustling of fabric and quiet sigh.

"All I need is five minutes," Jeremy Forester said. "I can pleasure you thoroughly, Tamsin. You know you want it."

His voice held the half-wheedling, half-boasting tone of a man importuning a woman for favors she was reluctant to give—or perhaps unwilling to give so lightly.

"All you think about," Miss Diggory replied, "is getting under somebody's skirts. If Mrs. Channing knew what a strutting cock you are, she'd sack you in a moment."

"If she knew what a tease you are—Tamsin, come back here. You can't leave me in this state."

"Alexander has returned from the village," Miss Diggory said. "I saw the cart being led around to the carriage house. You'd best get back to the schoolroom and put your mind on dusty old battles until your breeches aren't fitting so snugly."

The sound of a smacking kiss followed, then soft footsteps retreated down the corridor. A door opened and closed, probably Jeremy seeking to steal a few moments of privacy.

Did Vera know her governess and her tutor were canoodling in the corridors? Should Oak tell her? Why or why not? Oak begrudged no pair of consenting adults their diversions, but what if Catherine should come across the couple in an amorous mood? For that matter, what if Catherine should come across her mother kissing a penniless artist in the attics?

Such questions were as complicated as the conundrum of the color that best depicted a nightingale's song, though much more vexing.

Oak stopped by his room to comb his hair, retie his cravat, and trade his riding jacket for the lighter-weight attire suitable for the indoors. If he hadn't been prompted to locate the dog whelk seashell in the bottom of his valise—seashells made good rudimentary sketching projects—he'd not have noticed.

But he did retrieve his papa's lucky shell, and thus he did notice. Though nothing was stolen, somebody had once again gone through his things, and that, he most assuredly ought to discuss with the lady of the house.

~

"YOU MISSED DINNER," Vera said, setting the tray on a deal table and closing the door. "This will be your studio?"

Oak had chosen to establish himself in a room on the northern side of the house, a former game room was Vera's best guess, for the space came with a wide balcony such as gentlemen might use for a late-night cigar.

"I'll do most of my work here," Oak said, wiping his hands on a rag. "I need the ventilation if I'm to properly clean the older works, and a northern exposure means the sun doesn't create shifting shadows throughout the day."

His space was orderly, compared to the studios Dirk had used. A half-dozen unframed canvases from the attics leaned against the wall beneath the deal table. A midsize worktable sat against another interior wall, while a pair of worn reading chairs had been arranged on a rug beside the hearth. An easel stood near the French doors, and the windowsill was lined with brushes and tools in glass jars.

"This room has no art of its own," Vera said.

"The better to help me focus on my work. Will you keep me company while I eat?"

She had missed him at dinner and been aware that Catherine had missed him too. Jeremy Forester lacked the will, or possibly the ability, to sustain a polite conversation at a table of females.

"I ought to abandon you to your art," Vera said, "as you abandoned me to Catherine's sighs and Miss Diggory's long-suffering smiles."

Oak fetched the tray and set it on the low table between the pair of chairs facing the empty hearth. "Did Mr. Forester abandon you as well?"

"No, more's the pity. I've come to realize that his version of conversation is a series of quips." Vera sank into a chair. "That's your fault. Until you showed up, I found him witty, if a trifle sarcastic."

"You brought me lemonade." Oak took the other chair and sipped from the tall glass Cook had sent along with the food. "I hadn't realized how thirsty I am."

"Wine seemed presumptuous for a plate of sandwiches. I should let you get back to your tasks."

"You should stay and bear me a few minutes company, or I will happily labor through the night and be of no use to anybody tomorrow." He bit into a sandwich, and Vera took a moment to study the details of his temporary studio.

The little painting of the mother and children had been removed from its frame. The canvas sat on the worktable, propped against a tall glass jar.

"That's a pleasant scene," Vera said. "Not without charm, for all you pronounce it inadequate. The mama clearly dotes on her offspring."

"Did you want more children?"

Not a question anybody had been brave enough to ask Vera before. "I have five brothers. That Catherine and Alexander are so far apart in age, no siblings between them, isn't what I had planned, but then, I hadn't planned on becoming a widow before I turned thirty."

"You can remarry," Oak said as he reached for the second half of a fat ham-and-cheddar sandwich.

That Oak would remark, between the lemonade and the sandwich, on Vera's ability to remarry was disappointing. Perhaps a friend would make that observation, but coming from a prospective lover, it implied a disinterest at odds with shared intimacy.

"I am content as I am," she said, "and finding a husband is problematic. What of you, do you intend to marry?"

The question caught him with his lemonade halfway to his mouth. He studied Vera over the rim of his glass, expression unreadable.

"I must establish myself professionally before I contemplate matrimonial ambitions. I had a drawing lesson with Catherine today."

What sort of answer was that? "She mentioned her lesson at supper. *In detail*. Mr. Dorning this, and Mr. Dorning that. I believe her recitation put Mr. Forester off his feed, which amused Miss Diggory, and that bothered Mr. Forester all the more."

Oak dusted his hands over the empty plate. "Our Mr. Forester has undertaken a flirtation with Miss Diggory."

"A moment, please." Vera rose and fetched a lamp from the sconce in the corridor. Upon her return, she closed the studio door—flirtation was under discussion, after all—and used the lamp to light a branch of candles on the mantel and another on the worktable. "Tell me about this flirtation."

"I nearly came upon them in the corridor. Forester was trying to persuade the lady to grant him intimate liberties. I believe kisses were exchanged. He sought more."

"Was Miss Diggory upset? She was her usual cheerful self at dinner."

"Miss Diggory had the situation in hand. She seemed amused more than anything else, but I was not in a position to assess her expression. I heard this exchange, I did not see it."

"I am unhappy with Jeremy for accosting Tamsin where anybody could happen upon them. To the wrong sort of observer, that behavior compromises the lady's good name." Without being able to say why, Vera knew that Oak would never be so cavalier. He'd do his exchanging of kisses behind closed and locked doors and away from large windows.

"I was intent on using the servants' stairs," Oak said. "I would not have come upon them otherwise."

"My servants gossip, for which I don't blame them." Vera set the lamp on the deal table. "A footman who came upon that scene would mention it to his brothers or cousins over darts. A maid would tell her aunt in the churchyard. The news would spread to other households, and by this time next month, Miss Diggory could be enduring untoward remarks from louts on market day."

And Vera did not want Tamsin, a decent and pleasant young woman, to suffer such a fate. Neither did Vera look forward to scolding Jeremy, a grown man who ought to know better.

"I can say something to Forester." Oak rose and crossed to the worktable. "I'll tell him he was observed and that another lapse in discretion could cost him his post—which it should. If I am ever that indiscreet, you should sack me too. Come have a look at our mystery painting."

"You wouldn't mind having a pointed word with Jeremy?" Vera asked, joining Oak at the worktable. "I could not raise the topic without blushing furiously, while you can probably make a casual comment and convey an entire lecture."

"Consider it done. If Forester takes me into dislike for offering a friendly warning, no matter. I'll be gone in a few weeks."

Why must he remind Vera of that? Why did she *need* reminding?

Oak withdrew a folding knife from his boot and turned the canvas over. Vera moved the candles closer.

"You won't hurt them, will you? The young mother and her children?"

He smiled, a crooked, piratical smile. "She's safe, as are the children." He opened the knife, a casual gesture that spoke of familiarity and skill.

Oak Dorning was not Dirk, and Vera liked the differences she'd seen so far. Dirk would never have carried a knife in his boot, but then, Dirk had been an artist dwelling in the country from time to time. Oak Dorning was a countryman born and bred.

Dirk would have either ignored a tutor importuning a governess, or made a great drama out of it, depending on his mood. Oak Dorning considered that matter a problem best handled through a quiet aside between the fellows, and Vera's relief to have a man take responsibility for resolving a masculine sort of household issue was inordinate.

"The more you criticize this little scene," Vera said, peering over his shoulder, "the more I like it."

"I will put her back in her frame by noon tomorrow, but have a look here." He held up the painting, which was now a canvas stretched across a rectangle of wooden supports. "It's as I thought. There's another canvas under this one."

By virtue of prying gently at tacks in a pattern that made little sense to Vera, Oak soon had the canvases free of the wood framing. He carefully peeled the French lady from the painting beneath, then laid the second work on the table.

"*That* is beautiful," he said, moving the branch of candles closer. "*That* is exquisite. My brother Sycamore would likely bankrupt himself for the pleasure of owning this painting."

"That," Vera said, her belly doing an uncomfortable flip, "is *Catherine's mother*, and because she hasn't a stitch on, nobody must see this painting. Not ever."

The painting was lovely. A woman lay sleeping amid a tangle of ruby and violet quilts, candlelight playing over her bare breasts and exquisitely curved flank. One foot dangled from the bed, one hand was flung back against the pillow. A half-full bottle of wine on the bedside table and a dark form behind her suggested a lover slept at her side.

So daringly low were the covers that even the curls between her legs had been alluded to with shadows and brushwork.

"Everything about this work is masterfully done," Oak said, taking up a magnifying glass. "The composition, the palette, the lighting. Notice the contrast between her pale skin and the jewel tones of the covers. Look at how the light reflecting off the wineglass and the candle against the mirrored sconce balance each other. This is a side to Dirk Channing nobody has seen before, and it might well be his best work."

"She's smiling," Vera said, reluctantly fascinated. "Having a lovely dream."

"She *is* a lovely dream, and thank all the benign powers, Dirk signed this." Oak straightened and set aside the quizzing glass. "Catherine's mother will bring a fine sum, Vera, and if the rest of the gallery holds work of similar quality, then you have found Dirk's treasures."

The wine in the bottle had the garnet hue of Merlot, Dirk's favorite for a bedside glass.

Vera leaned close enough to the painting to verify that the signature was, indeed, Dirk's.

"I cannot sell or display this painting. Catherine is already laboring under the stigma of irregular antecedents. Imagine she's at a house party over in Surrey a few years from now. Dirk has friends there who'd extend such a courtesy to her. In walks some Town swell who has seen this painting in your brother's gambling hell. Being somewhat connected with the artistic set, Mr. Town Dandy recognizes the connection between Catherine Channing and the woman who served as Dirk's model. Anna Beaumont was Dirk's hostess for years and, at least among the gentlemen, was accepted as such."

Oak was no longer studying the painting, he was studying Vera. "This painting is not some sordid bit of rhyparography. This could well be the making of Dirk Channing's legacy, and the financial security you seek."

"I believe you," Vera said, gaze again on the painting. "She is in love, that woman, and the man who painted her loved her back, but this is not art for public consumption. Maybe in thirty years, but not... not now." And why had Dirk kept these works hidden until after he no longer had to answer to the truth of them, no longer had to face the fact that he'd rendered the love of his life in shocking verisimilitude to her role at Merlin Hall?

Oak scrubbed a hand through his hair. "I applaud your protectiveness toward Catherine, but I am exasperated that so beautiful a work, so perfect a work, should be hidden away."

So *valuable* a work. He didn't need to emphasize the point. "The painting is exceptional, which is all the more reason London's artistic sophisticates will demean it. I've seen how they behave, and the results are neither kind nor honorable. By all means, find whatever else is lurking in Dirk's gallery, but speak of this to no one."

Oak moved the candles away from the painting. "Are you jealous of her, Vera?"

"Envious, maybe." Even in shadow, the woman's dreaming, utterly pleasured smile was the central message of the painting. "She is well loved, in all senses. If Dirk ever did a portrait of me, he'd have caught me adding needlework to some seat cushion or tallying my ledgers."

"I beg leave to doubt that assessment." Oak took Vera in his arms, the embrace having nothing of desire about it. "Though a woman can be lovely and tempting even when she's working at her ledgers."

Vera allowed herself the pleasure of his embrace, the comfort of it. She'd gone years without the simple bodily joy of adult affection, and that Oak could offer her a hug—no innuendo or arousal in evidence—raised him further in her esteem.

He bore the faint scents of linseed and turpentine, good smells to Vera. His rangy frame and muscular build were novel, a contradiction to the cliché of the artist as a fussy, pale, excitable creature given to flights, inebriation, and sulks. Oak was wonderfully solid and delightfully *male,* and his embrace was a haven at the end of a trying day.

"Will you come to bed with me?" Vera asked, stepping back.

He took her hands in his. "Nothing would please me more. Just give me another half hour here to—"

A tap sounded on the door.

"Who could that be?" Vera asked, putting two yards between herself and the man she intended to spend the night with. For good measure, she picked up the empty tray.

Oak opened the door. "Come in," he said, his tone pleasant.

Bracken remained in the corridor. "Excuse me, madam, Mr. Dorning." He held a tray complete with a porcelain teapot. "I thought Mr. Dorning might be hungry, having missed his supper."

"Very thoughtful of you," Oak said, "and never let it be said food went to waste when a Dorning was in the room, but Mrs. Channing kindly provided me a snack."

"I'll leave this with you nonetheless," Bracken said, setting the tray on the worktable. "Madam, I can take that down to the kitchen for you."

Vera passed over the empty tray. "Thank you, Bracken. Are we locked up for the night?"

"Of course, madam. I bid you good evening." Bracken bowed slightly and withdrew.

"Bless the fellow, he brought a meat pie," Oak said, closing the door and surveying the offerings. "A pint of summer ale and what looks like an apple torte."

"Oak, he brought a warning."

Oak left off inspecting the tray. "A delectable one, if so. For whom is this warning intended?"

"I don't know, but as soon as he asked the kitchen to prepare a tray for you, somebody probably told him I had asked for one not thirty minutes earlier. Bracken came up here to interrupt whatever we were about."

Oak braced his hips against the worktable. "All Bracken interrupted was a conversation. Is that a problem?"

"I don't know. On the one hand, Bracken is the self-appointed guardian of Merlin Hall, and I would never question his loyalty."

By candlelight, Oak looked tired, worn, and a little rumpled—abundantly kissable, in other words. The studio, however, afforded no chaise, no cot, no place to accommodate a couple's frolics. Perhaps that was by design?

"I am not at all offended that Bracken has an eye on your safety, Vera, but I chose this room for more than its northern exposure and windows."

"You did?"

"The door locks." Oak brandished a key from an inner coat pocket. "The only other key is on your set, according to the housekeeper. Catherine's mother will be safe from discovery and so, in a passionate moment, would we be safe from discovery. While I enjoy a quick tup against the wall, that's hardly the sort of first impression as a lover I want to make on you."

"Give me an hour," Vera said. "You do know where my rooms are?"

"I do. The next hour will be the longest of my adult life."

Vera left him in his studio, smiling and looking devilish. She went straight to her room and prepared for bed, though all the while, she was plagued by a question.

What on earth was a tup against the wall?

~

OAK FINISHED the food Bracken had brought and locked the studio. He returned to his room in a state of semi-distraction. On the one hand, his body anticipated a tryst. His mind, however, was caught up in the conundrum of Dirk Channing's treasures.

What if another spectacular nude hid beneath every mediocre painting in the gallery? Vera refused to sell them, for reasons Oak understood, but then what was to become of Channing's best work? The problem wasn't one Oak could confide to anybody at the Academy, save perhaps to Richard Longacre.

Longacre had been a friend to Channing and had recommended Oak for Vera's restoration work. Writing to him would not do, for letters could fall into the wrong hands, but a jaunt into London might present an opportunity to discuss the matter in person.

Oak took particular care with his ablutions and still had another half hour before he could join Vera. He sat down to sketch, a habit he'd found more satisfying than making a written entry in some journal at the end of the day.

He sketched Alexander holding the ribbons, the boy for once smiling and energetic. He sketched Bracken, exploring why vigilance on such a man took the appearance of unrelenting disapproval. Something in his eyes, something about the way his mouth suggested clenched teeth...

By the time Oak put down his sketch pad, well over an hour had passed. Vera would think ill of him for that. He thought ill of himself too.

He traversed the corridors swiftly, seeing not a soul. The night porter would doze in his nook near the front door, but Vera did not require a footman to remain on duty through the night as well.

Oak opened Vera's door without knocking and found himself in a sitting room. The gracious formality of Merlin Hall was nowhere in evidence here. A green velvet upholstered sofa sat across from the hearth, a deeply cushioned reading chair angled at the end of the sofa. The walls held sketches, mostly of Catherine and Alexander, but also two of Dirk. One with each child.

The floor was covered by a green, white, and gold Turkey carpet, the draperies were also green. A maroon afghan lay draped along the back of the sofa. This room would flatter a redhead wonderfully, but where was the book, embroidery hoop, or pair of knitting needles that suggested Vera actually spent time here?

A landscape hung above the mantel, perhaps a rendering of the farm where Vera had been born. The opposite wall held more land-scapes. They bore Dirk Channing's signature brushwork, but none of the verve and daring of his wartime images and none of the complexity of his portraits.

Vera had chosen the calmest and least passionate of her husband's works to keep in her private space. Why was that?

Oak crossed the room to the only other door and tapped quietly. "Vera?"

Nothing, not a peep. He pushed the door open and entered her bedroom, which was illuminated by only a banked fire. If there was art on the walls here, he'd have to inspect it on another occasion. The room was dominated by a four-poster bed, and the contour of the quilt suggested somebody was in that bed. The hangings were drawn back as was typical in summer.

"I lost track of the time," Oak said, removing his jacket and draping it over the chest at the foot of the bed. "Started sketching away the remains of the day and fell into the puzzle of Bracken's eyes. Alexander has Dirk's chin."

Vera remained unmoving and silent on the bed. Perhaps she was unhappy with a lover who'd made her wait.

"Vera?" Oak sat on the chest to pull off his boots, then shed his waistcoat and shirt and laid them over his jacket.

The lady was apparently asleep. Should he wake her, go back to his own room, leave a note—assuming he could find writing paper and a pencil?

In a few weeks, he'd be in London, and this opportunity to share something special with a lovely woman would be gone. He folded his breeches and stockings on top of his waistcoat, leaving his handkerchief on the bedside table. The steps were on Vera's side of the bed, so Oak had to more or less hike himself onto the mattress.

Even the rocking of the bed did not awaken Oak's sleeping beauty, suggesting the lady was exhausted.

Oak was not exactly bursting with energy himself. Perhaps a short nap was in order. One wanted to make an excellent first impression, complete with cuddling before and after, rather than a peck on the cheek and inconsiderate snoring.

He leaned over to kiss Vera's brow, then sank into the sweet embrace of the clean sheets, soft pillows, and a comfortable mattress. Ye gods, was there any pleasure on earth to compare with that moment when a tired head met a welcoming pillow?

Well, yes, of course there were pleasures greater than that instant of bliss. Far greater. To distract himself from those pleasures, Oak mentally critiqued the painting he'd unveiled that afternoon. How had Dirk Channing handled the pillows in his portrait of Catherine's mother? Pillows were usually covered in damnably white linen, meaning they had to appear white without *being* white. Dirk had managed that feat by imbuing the pillowcase with pink and gold undertones, to pick up on the candlelight and the purple velvet covers.

Contemplating the image of the woman naked and replete among the bedcovers added to the pleasant sense of arousal Vera's proximity created, though in Oak's imagination, the woman who had been so well pleasured that she smiled in sleep became Vera.

And then she became dreams of Vera, and then she became deep, much-needed sleep.

~

THE FOREMOST SCULPTOR in London sat snoring by the fire in one of the club's many comfortable reading chairs. Richard Longacre, who occupied another such comfy chair, knew the poor fellow craved the warmth of this cozy room because the rheumatism in his hands grew worse by the year.

Near the door to the reading room, a brilliant and handsome young portraitist stood, conversing with his companion. The gifted Mr. Endymion de Beauharnais was rumored to have connections to the late French empress, though in fact he'd been born Andrew Hackett, in the hamlet—a generous characterization—of Hogtrot. He and his friend—neither as attractive nor as talented as de Beauharnais, but of an exceptionally charming demeanor—pretended they were off to find deeper play at the tables around the corner on St. James's Street.

Artists, no matter how talented, handsome, or charming, could not afford deep play.

De Beauharnais—Diamond to his familiars—was, in fact, escorting his cheerful associate to a discreet set of rooms on a quiet street in Bloomsbury, where the pair would spend the rest of the night in each other's arms.

The charmer waved to Richard, probably thinking himself daring and naughty. The portraitist made no such friendly display. To Richard, their attempts at discretion were laughable, almost touching. Half the club's membership indulged in sexual adventures, if not outright orgies. The other half had done so in their youth. If being an artist wasn't to make a man wealthy—and all too often, it did not—then the artistic lifestyle ought to at least afford him some wanton pleasure.

Or so the usual self-absolving reasoning went.

"You're here a bit late, aren't you, Longacre?" Stebbins Holmes sank into the seat opposite Richard's. "Kitchener maundered on for three bottles of port about the pathetic state of art and the demise of discipline in the Academy apprentices."

Stebby, unlike some of the club's other senior members, had not let himself go to pot. He was trim, dapper, and his white hair was always tidily queued back, an old-fashioned affectation a sought-after children's portraitist could carry off.

"If Kitchener doesn't moderate his appetites," Richard replied, "he will soon be swilling port in Saint Peter's company."

"Even if he does moderate his appetites, he won't last much longer. Old boy never had any discipline, of all the ironies."

What the old boy likely did have was a progressive case of a very nasty disease. He'd soon step down as head of the Academy's admissions committee. Holmes was the logical successor, though when did logic and artistic organizations ever accommodate each other?

"I've done something you should know about," Richard said.

"Regarding?"

"Channing's widow."

"Ah." A single quiet syllable. Holmes had been one of Dirk Channing's many mentors, then his advocate and his friend. He had seen Dirk's potential as a young man, had seen both the talent and the ambition that would keep that talent safe from a fate such as old Kitchener faced. Dirk had frittered away neither his time nor his health, and he'd been generous in his encouragement of younger artists.

A bloody bedamned paragon, except for his long-term liaison with the formerly respectable Anna Beaumont, for which his peers hadn't censured him.

Ancient history. Not relevant to the present conversation. "Mrs. Channing wrote to me asking if I knew of anybody willing to travel out to Hampshire to restore some older works. Not Channing's paintings, but works he collected."

Holmes crossed his legs at the knee, another Continental affectation. "So Dirk left the pretty widow without means, did he? Not very sporting of him. Why hasn't she remarried? Many a man would pay well to gaze upon that much beauty across the breakfast table each morning."

Verity Channing wasn't simply pretty, she was lovely. The outer woman and the inner woman resonated in a way few artists could have captured on canvas. Dirk had taken all that loveliness to wife little more than a year after Anna Beaumont's death.

"The boy inherited the property," Richard said. "Mrs. Channing isn't homeless, and I doubt Dirk left her in dire difficulties. As long as she avoids Town extravagances, she's doubtless managing adequately."

Holmes remained silent until a waiter had finished collecting dirty glasses from around the room. The fellow then malingered by adjusting the wicks on the lamps on the wall sconces, until he ran out of excuses and had to take his tray and leave.

"Why is Verity Channing bothering with a lot of second-rate portraits?" Stebby mused. "And why now? Are you soon to leave for Hampshire?"

"Of course not. I have too many committee obligations to leave Town, and restoring castoffs is work for somebody who needs the money."

Richard needed money, and he *liked* money. His duties for the Academy brought in no coin, directly. Even more than money, though, he liked having information in his grasp that let him control others and predict their behaviors better than they could themselves. Collecting that information was best done in Town.

"So what is this thing you've done?" Holmes asked. "I am too old to stand as anybody's second on the field of honor, but I'm quite good with a eulogy or a funerary toast."

"Have you crossed paths with a fellow named Oak Dorning?"

"Of course. He's an earl's son, has taken classes at the Academy, gets along with most everybody, and—lest we neglect the details—wields a paintbrush with no little skill. He has family in Town—a pair of brothers running The Coventry Club—while the earl prefers to rusticate. Lord Casriel married a widow, I believe, though I can't recall who, which suggests she was neither merry nor wealthy. Has a biblical name. Oak Dorning is exactly the sort we ought to admit to the Academy, once he's exhibited a few noteworthy works or taken some prominent commissions."

Richard was not the only club member who liked to collect information. "Mr. Dorning would probably agree with you, but for now he's consigned to Verity Channing's attics, where he will grow bored to flinders dusting off old works in preparation for sale. When his assignment is finished, he will remove to Town."

Holmes was quiet for a time. He presented himself as a spry, dapper old gent, still young at heart, but he was venerable enough to nod off late in the evening.

"Richard," he said quietly, "what are you about?"

"I am trying to do two people a favor. Mrs. Channing needed skilled labor, Dorning needed paying work. The association will be mutually beneficial."

"I know you," Holmes said. "I'm not always sure I like you, but I know you, and you are ever motivated by self-interest and the interests of the Academy, which you would like to turn into your private fiefdom, of course. Perhaps insanity runs in your family. In any case, you are up to something where Mrs. Channing is concerned."

And Holmes would eventually figure out exactly what, hence this little tête-à-tête before the dying fire. Holmes liked to air his speculations before a younger audience, and such was his influence that the younger audience often listened to him.

Ergo, the need to avoid the near occasion of Holmes's speculations.

"If Dorning should come across anything odd in the Channing collection," Richard said, "if he sees a previously unknown work of Channing's hanging in the servants' hall, he'll bring that news to me before he tells anybody else."

"So you're spying. I thought you were attracted to Verity Channing. If I were twenty years younger—even ten—*I'd* be attracted to her in more than an artistic sense. You might consider asking her if Dirk's drunken mutterings were based on reality or on his endless supply of grandiose dreams."

"Verity Channing is quite attractive, I'll grant you, but she is utterly safe from my romantic advances." And that was the absolute truth.

Holmes rose and stretched. "She's safe from your advances, but is she safe from *you?*"

He sauntered on his way, an old fellow who could view the intrigues and follies of life at a benign distance. The sculptor snored by the fire, his mouth slightly open. Richard remained in his comfortable chair, mentally composing a chatty, slightly gossipy note to Dorning.

A well-bred young man who sought to curry favor with Academy members would answer in the same vein, reiterating his thanks for the post, of course. Another such exchange while Dorning bided in the country, a few subtle suggestions, and Dorning would become Richard's spy in truth.

CHAPTER SEVEN

For a year after Dirk's death, Vera had endured the waking ritual of drowsing in bed, knowing the day must be begun, and knowing that leaving her bed meant confronting some great sadness. A sanguine intention to rise and see to the tasks at hand was sent toppling into the ditch of grief as she faced the realization again—and again and again—that Dirk was gone forever.

Vera had loved her husband, she hadn't always liked him. He had doubtless held her in dubious regard from time to time as well, but particularly after Alexander's birth, they had learned to rub along in charity with each other. Dirk's intimate demands on her had slowed considerably after the first year of marriage, while his affectionate displays had become more frequent.

And Vera had missed that, missed the cuddling and talking, the walking hand in hand, the friendly good-morning and good-night kisses. She missed the smiles and casual familiarities that she and her husband had shared.

To awaken in a man's embrace was thus lovely, a fragile dream to be cherished until cruel reality once again intruded. Birdsong pierced the predawn chill beyond the window, but under the covers, all was marvelously cozy and content.

Very cozy, in fact.

Exceedingly cozy.

Vera's waking mind registered the fact that she *truly* was in a man's embrace. She lay on her side, facing the window. Her companion was ranged along her back like a heated blanket, his arm draped around her waist.

He was not Dirk. This fellow was appreciably taller and leaner. He smelled of lavender soap rather than the Continental fragrances Dirk had favored. He apparently slept without a nightshirt, and without being able to say why, Vera was pleased to find him in her bed.

The mists of sleep thinned the last increment, and Vera recalled inviting Oak Dorning to join her in bed.

"You're awake," he said, making no move to shift away.

"As are you." An understatement, given the length of hard male flesh pressed against Vera's bum. "Have we become lovers?"

"We have not." Soft lips pressed against the side of Vera's neck. "Not yet. You were far gone in sleep when I joined you. I was tired, and here we are."

"I can't remember when I've slept so well." Vera recalled many occasions when Dirk had roused her from deep slumber, not a word spoken between them for the duration of the coupling. She'd accommodated him, sometimes without entirely waking, and regarded that variety of lovemaking as a wifely obligation easily dispatched.

"I slept soundly too," Oak said, lacing his fingers with hers. "I dreamed of you. You were tangled in green and purple quilts, trying to thrash loose but exhausted. I so wanted to peel the covers away and reveal the bare glory of you as the Creator fashioned you. I wanted to let you sleep, too, though, to rest."

"Green and purple quilts? That feels good." His hand trailed over Vera's hip and around her bottom in a slow, kneading caress. She abruptly wished to be free of her nightgown and in the next instant wished that sunrise was hours away.

"Shall we make love, Vera?" Oak asked, nuzzling her ear. "Shall we begin our day with mutual pleasuring?"

He was as hard as an andiron, and yet, he *asked* for her participation. That question solved a riddle in Vera's mind relating to those silent couplings she'd shared with her husband. She liked lovemaking, liked the closeness of it.

Dirk's husbandly presumption had undermined any true intimacy, though, and left a vague residue of annoyance where only affection ought to have been.

"We can make love," Vera said. "The household will soon be stirring, though. We'd best hurry."

She wanted to use her toothpowder and halfway had to use the chamber pot. When Dirk had indulged in morning copulation, his goal had been quick satisfaction, not languid lovemaking.

Oak Dorning, given the chance, would be a very different sort of lover.

His touch on her flank disappeared. "Is a hurried moment how we're to begin?" He eased her cotton nightgown aside and kissed her nape. "The sun isn't even up yet, and I locked the bedroom door before joining you under the covers, Vera."

Thank goodness for that bit of caution. "A sip of water would be appreciated," Vera said, struggling to sit up.

Oak sat up as well and passed her the glass of water he'd apparently poured for himself before climbing into bed.

"Having second thoughts, Vera?"

She was thirsty, as it happened, and draining half the glass gave her a moment to consider Oak's question. He sounded amused, and sitting with his back against the pillows, his dark hair tousled, he looked delectable.

So why wasn't she devouring him? "I thought I was ready for this. Ready to be the self-possessed widow indulging in a discreet liaison."

He took the glass, had a sip, and set it aside. "But?"

"But I have stretch marks. I want to use my toothpowder before I kiss you. I loved sleeping with you, but all I can think now is what if you're seen leaving my rooms? An astute maid might find a short dark hair on my pillows, and then—"

He scratched his chest, which was dusted with those short dark hairs. "And then?"

"And then I'm somehow less loyal to my husband's memory? I don't know what comes *and then*. I wasn't raised to frolic with handsome fellows passing through on the way to London, and I didn't expect to be widowed seven years after I spoke my vows."

He slouched down onto his side to regard her, stashing a pillow under his arm and propping his head on his palm.

"I thought the fact that I was passing through on the way to London was half my charm."

It wasn't. A tiny part of his charm, perhaps, but also part of why Vera hesitated. "I'm making a hash of this."

Oak surprised her by taking her in his arms and situating her against his side. She went into his embrace willingly, even gratefully.

"Here is what I think," he said, smoothing a hand over her hair. "I think too many of us go a-romping without taking into consideration whether we truly want to romp, or whether romping is simply foolishness or a consolation for more elusive joys. Men do this, you know. Swagger about, waving their pizzles around like the boom of a ship caught in the eye of the wind. That's my father's analogy, by the way. He once told me he remarried in part to simply have done with the foolishness."

Foolishness. This discussion didn't feel foolish. It felt honest and intimate. "I'm supposed to be in my romping years," Vera countered, thinking that was quite the strangest admission she'd ever made. "Dirk always said I took life too seriously."

"Dirk." Oak kissed her temple. "He was born to a founding member of the Royal Academy. His uncle was a court painter to old George. He was talented, charming, and well placed to line up commissions from an early age. He arrived on this earth at a time when a Grand Tour was still possible and thus had the further benefit of directly observing the greatest masterpieces on the Continent. He was never without paying work, never without friends and supporters. To his credit, he was generous to his peers and kind to those in need of encouragement, but what would such a man know of life's sorrows?"

Well, yes. Dirk had been lucky. Very lucky. "He lost his Anna. She was his muse."

"And he married you within a year. Perhaps he was incapable of dealing with life's most serious challenges, while you haven't had a choice."

That was a conclusion worth pondering—some other time.

"What of you?" Vera asked, brushing dark curls from Oak's brow. "Have you had serious challenges to deal with?"

~

THE PLEASURE of awakening in female company was a wonderful rarity, and Oak's male body rejoiced at the possibility of impending intimacies. Of course, he usually awoke in the same state of reproductive rejoicing even when he was alone. Ignoring his arousal, however, had never been so difficult.

Vera was nearly naked, her braid a frazzled rope, and her body... Blessed Saint Luke, her body was the feminine ideal, and she seemed oblivious to her own endowments. She nestled against Oak's side like a stray kitten given shelter before a toasty hearth.

Oak longed to take her hand and wrap it around his cock, but how selfish would that be? Instead, he kissed her fingers and placed her palm on his chest.

"You ask if I've faced serious challenges. The answer is no." Ignoring a cockstand was not a serious challenge. Not at all. "I was ridiculed for pursuing art, of course, until my father asked me to illustrate his botanical treatises. My brothers stopped teasing me then, though I caused some consternation at university. Losing my mother was sad, but she hadn't been happy for some time and rather washed her hands of us several years before her death."

"She abandoned you?"

"We could not afford to reopen and staff the dower house, so she removed to Bath to be with friends." Mama's departure had only felt like an abandonment, an echo of Jacaranda's departure years earlier.

"So you're a happy fellow, not a care in the world?" Vera's hand drifted across Oak's chest, the caress nearly soothing until she happened to trail her fingers across his nipple. She apparently didn't realize the effect on him, for she did it again a moment later.

"I am a happy fellow." A happy, increasingly frustrated fellow. "But I cannot continue to impose on my brother's generosity. Hence, I am on my way to London." The third time Vera's touch glanced across his nipple, he shuddered.

She peered at him. "Are you well?"

"I'm sensitive," he said, taking her hand and glossing the tip of her index finger in a delicate circle. "There. That arouses me." A stupid statement of the obvious when made to a married woman.

"It does?"

Oak pushed the covers down, baring himself in all his morning glory. "Quite."

Vera stared at his unrepentant cock, her expression puzzled. "Touching you here..." Oh yes, she touched him again. "Affects you there."

There was a nod in the direction of his breeding organs. "Afraid so. You needn't—"

Ye bare naked cherubs. She used the same fingertip to touch the head of his cock. "Men are as soft here as the nose of a horse. I've always wondered about that."

"Have you now?" All three words were coherent. A feat of articulation, given that she was circling the tip of his cock in a maddeningly lazy caress.

"I saw little of Dirk in this state. He was a dressing-gown-and-lights-out sort of fellow, which was fine with me. This has to be the most peculiar bit of human anatomy. I think he was self-conscious about his age."

Oak would pity Dirk Channing his self-consciousness on some other, more saintly, day. "Vera, I'm not objecting, but if you are intent on continuing..." The words petered out as arousal became the defining beacon of Oak's existence. He groped for his handkerchief on the bedside table, nearly knocking over the water glass in the process.

"I've never done this," Vera said, reversing direction to circle him the other way. "Never toyed with a man's parts." She sounded as if she was mixing her pigments, trying for a particular shade of blue and coming so, so close to the desired result.

"Indulge yourself," Oak replied. "I'm not far from indulging myself too."

He expected she'd withdraw her attentions at that warning. Instead, she slipped her hand down to sleeve his shaft.

"What about this? Do you like this too, Oak?"

He wrapped his hand around hers, showed her exactly *how* he liked it, and lasted less than a half-dozen strokes before pleasure cascaded through him. He made a mess on his belly and scented the air with evidence of his satisfaction, but holding back any longer simply hadn't been possible.

Vera took the handkerchief from his limp grasp and tidied him up, then sat back, gaze on his softening member.

"I haven't done that before," she said. "Did I do it right?" Again, she put him in mind of an artist turning a critical eye on an experimental composition.

"If you did it any more right, I'd be the first man to expire from an excess of bliss. Come here." He wrestled her down against his side—not that she resisted—and wrapped an arm around her shoulders. "You have quite undone me."

"You smile like the woman in that painting you found. All naughty secrets and lovely dreams." Vera remained covered from neck to knees in her nightgown, though she was smiling a naughty smile too.

"You are pleased with yourself," Oak said, "and well you should be."

She turned her face against his shoulder and drew her toe up his calf. "I want to discuss what just happened, Oak."

"Talking is about all I'm good for at the moment."

"Why was I married for seven years without realizing...? What is a tup against the wall?"

The first rays of sunshine hit the vanity opposite the window, reflecting off scent bottles and dotting the wall with jewels of color.

Oak realized that his notion of an intimate friendship with Vera would not travel along the rutted path of his expectations. She was a woman with experience, true, but not as much experience as Dirk Channing's wife ought to have had.

Oak tossed back the covers, hopped off his side of the bed, and stretched. "Absent drawing paper and pencil, it's easier to show you the basic idea." He crossed the room and beckoned.

"You aren't wearing a stitch," Vera said, looking equal parts fascinated and appalled.

"Clothing would be more of an impediment than anything else. The general concept is easily demonstrated."

Vera cast a longing glance at a dressing gown hanging on her bedpost, then crossed the room to his side. He took her by the shoulders and positioned her between him and the wall.

"The general idea is"—he hoisted her against the wall, and she gave a little *yeep*—"wrap your legs around my waist and your arms around my shoulders."

She clutched at him. "And we make love like this?"

"The angle can be satisfying to both parties, though this position also challenges the strength of a man's legs." Already, Oak's body was taking a more than theoretical interest in this tutorial, and his leg strength was improving by the moment.

Vera studied him, and because he'd braced her back high against the wall, she was at his eye level.

Footsteps pattered by in the corridor, probably a maid bringing a pot of tea up to the nursery floor.

"I want to know more about this," Vera said as Oak let her slide down the wall to regain her feet. "I want to discuss it at length, but now is not the time. You must be going, and please, for the love of heaven—"

"Don't let anybody see me."

Oak hadn't had a woman's help dressing since he'd been a small child, though Vera made a very competent valet. He wanted to linger long enough to provide her the same courtesy, to make the encounter more reciprocal and less a matter of her hustling him on his way after sexually servicing him.

Vera passed him a comb. "How will I face you at breakfast?"

"With a smile, I hope." Her question reminded him that he'd been wrong about her. He'd assumed that a beautiful woman married to a worldly artist would be erotically sophisticated.

Vera grabbed him in an unexpected hug. "I'm miserable at this frolicking business. I'm sorry. I'll get better at it."

Oak hugged her back, overcome with an odd protectiveness. "A lady should never apologize for stating her honest misgivings, Vera. If you're disinclined to share another encounter with me, you simply say so. I hardly acquitted myself like a legendary lover, did I?"

She rested her forehead against his cravat, then stepped back. "We'll talk about that. I must sort out my thoughts first. You've put me in a considerable muddle."

Oak took her dressing gown down and draped it around her shoulders. Then he bowed with a sweeping, courtly gesture of his hand.

"Until breakfast, Mrs. Channing."

That made her smile, which was his cue to depart. He waited by the sitting room door to make sure no more footsteps pattered by in the corridor, then slipped back to his own rooms.

Truth be told, he was in rather a muddle too. He should have been content with the encounter—he was sexually satisfied, wasn't he?—but instead, he was unsettled, displeased with himself, and not entirely sure why.

~

BREAKFAST WAS NOT the ordeal Vera had anticipated. Oak Dorning appeared just as she was perusing the offerings on the sideboard, and the only other person in the room was Tamsin Diggory.

An ally of sorts.

"Good morning, Mrs. Channing." Oak bowed. "Miss Diggory. We're to have another beautiful day, from the looks of the sky. Miss Catherine and I should have our drawing lesson in the garden, methinks. What hour would suit you, Miss Diggory?"

With a few mundane words, Oak Dorning turned the meal into the start of just another placid morning, except that Vera was left to wonder how many of these potentially awkward breakfasts he'd managed with the same calm assurance.

Might I have the butter? Smile.

How I adore eggs served good and hot. Glance.

Oak was handsome, ambitious, and talented. Why shouldn't he have the savoir faire to smile at his lover over the teapot? Except that he and Vera weren't quite lovers, which only added to Vera's sense of disquiet.

It was soon agreed that Catherine's art lesson would follow Alexander's. By the time Jeremy and Catherine joined the table, Vera had started on her second cup and was feeling more self-possessed.

"I'm off to pay a call on Mrs. Treeble," she said. "Miss Diggory, if you'd like to accompany me, I can time the outing to coincide with Catherine's drawing lesson."

"That would suit wonderfully," Miss Diggory replied.

Catherine set down her fork. "But then I can't go with you."

Oak was at the sideboard, making a second raid on the eggs. "I can schedule your lesson for later, Miss Catherine. The garden is just as worthy of sketching in the late afternoon as at midday."

Jeremy took a sip of his tea and patted his lips with his table napkin. "Catherine wants to steal a moment with young Tom Treeble. I've seen how he looks at her in the churchyard."

Catherine blushed rose pink, Miss Diggory frowned, and Vera wanted to slap Jeremy for his lack of consideration.

"A gentleman," Oak said mildly as he resumed his seat, "would not remark the occasion of another fellow's unrequited longings, particularly not those of a young lad whose masculine pride is in its tenderest beginnings. Pass the honey, please."

Jeremy set the honeypot at Oak's elbow. "A *gentleman* doesn't pine for his ladylove in public like the veriest moon calf either. Catherine would turn any man's head, but that doesn't mean she should have to put up with Master Treeble making sheep's eyes at her over his hymnal, hmm?"

Catherine apparently did not know what to make of that assertion, while Vera found it badly done. Catherine had just put up her hair for the first time. Sheep's eyes and lovelorn looks should be a good way off and turning any man's head some distance after that.

"I'll take both Catherine and Alexander with me," Vera said. "You can use a few hours at liberty, Jeremy, and I will enjoy the company of my children."

Jeremy stirred his tea. "I will refrain from informing the terror that he's to have another interruption in his studies until the hour is upon him. He's been exceptionally distractible lately, but I can hardly fault him for that. Mr. Dorning's arrival has caused all manner of upheaval. I'm sure things will soon settle down."

Oak drizzled honey into his tea. "I'll be off to London before you can list my many shortcomings, Forester, and perhaps by then you will have begun addressing your charge politely rather than making snide references to the child before his own family." Oak let the last of the honey drip from the wooden whisk. "*Hmm?*"

He smiled faintly at Jeremy and set the honeypot in the center of the table.

Catherine was frankly goggling. Miss Diggory's expression had gone carefully blank. Vera was astounded to find a duel being fought at her breakfast table, but also pleased. A man raised with a herd of brothers wouldn't bat an eye at Jeremy's sarcasm and verbal sniping, while Vera hadn't known what, if anything, to do about it.

And Jeremy *was* sniping—at a small boy with no means of defending himself.

She took a final sip of tea and rose. "I'm sure Mr. Forester means only to poke affectionate fun at Alexander—my son is anything but a terror, after all—though I do agree with Mr. Dorning. If we expect Alexander to adopt the manners of a gentleman, we ought to take every opportunity to set a polite example for him. Wouldn't you agree, Miss Diggory?"

"Of course, Mrs. Channing."

Oak rose, as a gentleman did when a lady left the room. "Well, that's settled. Master Alexander and I can have our drawing lesson when he returns from escorting the ladies on their call. Miss Catherine, you and I can meet before supper, if that suits." Oak turned a mildly inquisitive gaze on Jeremy, who shoved to his feet.

"I'll enjoy my free time," Jeremy said. "Have a pleasant outing, Mrs. Channing."

"I'm sure I will." Vera would have made a grand exit, except that Oak touched her arm.

"Might I have a word with you regarding the paintings to be restored, Mrs. Channing?"

"Now, Mr. Dorning?"

"Now would suit."

"Very well." And blast the luck, he looked as if he did, indeed, have nothing more than paintings on his mind. Vera accompanied Oak from the breakfast parlor up the steps to the floor where he'd organized his studio.

Breakfast had gone reasonably well, for a public encounter after a near tryst, but the near tryst still puzzled Vera. She was attracted to Oak Dorning, she liked him better the more time she spent with him, and she truly wasn't looking for an entanglement.

So why had she been so missish about taking him as a lover? Why was she out of sorts now?

"I spent some time in my studio before breakfast," Oak said, "and I wanted you to see the fruits of my labors." He unlocked the door and bowed her through before relocking it.

The windows were open, though a faint odor of turpentine and linseed yet lingered in the room. The portrait of Anna Beaumont as an odalisque lay on the worktable, another unframed canvas beside it.

"Have a look," Oak said.

He'd apparently dismantled another of the mundane paintings cluttering up the gallery walls and again found a more worthy work beneath—more worthy and more shocking.

"God in heaven." Anna again lay among tangled covers, and this time her entire body was revealed, but for an ankle draped with a ruby quilt. The composition was such that her mons occupied the main point of interest, dark curls contrasting with pale skin, wild brushwork erupting from long, smooth strokes.

"That painting is brilliant," Oak said, "though it goes beyond what can be displayed as an artful nude."

"Well beyond." Anna's breasts were entirely on display, pinkish-taupe nipples peaked, her fingers brushing the fullness of one breast. Her other hand was flung back against the pillow, and in this painting, no lover hovered in the shadows on the other side of the bed.

"She looks as if she's been pleasuring herself," Oak said. "The scene has an air of repletion, as if in the next moment, she'll drag the covers up and indulge in a nap full of erotic dreams."

"Pleasured herself?"

He leaned closer to the canvas, studying the drape of the quilt over the lady's ankle, a subtle suggestion of a silken manacle.

"As you pleasured me earlier today. Onanism, self-gratification, manufriction, manustupration, masturbation." He lifted the painting and held it at eye level, the painted surface parallel with the floor. "Self-pollution, to use the preacher's vocabulary."

Vera knew exactly one of the terms he'd tossed out. "Women do that?"

Oak set down the painting. "Dirk Channing wasn't much of a lover. I'm sorry. Yes, women do that. Some men do it a lot. There's no harm in self-gratification and much pleasure, which might be the message the painting is trying to convey."

"That is not a message most people want to hang on their walls." And why—why, why, why—had Dirk hidden these works in his own home? What was Vera supposed to *do* with them?

"Some people collect erotica, and for works of this quality, they'd pay a handsome sum. Much more than they'll pay for the leavings of your attics, Vera."

"I cannot sell such, such... I don't know what to call them." The painting upset her, not only because of its subject matter. "Dirk might have created a few more dashing scenes of battle or restful Hampshire landscapes. Those I could sell, but these..."

"These are *art*," Oak said, as if that decided the matter in all its particulars. "They will be respected as such. Are you concerned that he painted images like this of you?"

Vera's imaginings came to an abrupt, determined halt. "Dirk *could not* have painted images like this of me. I wasn't... We didn't... He wasn't a strutting young buck when I married him. He had a daughter to raise, an established reputation to safeguard. Our marriage was cordial."

And compared to the passion Dirk had shown his Anna, cordial was second best. A make-do compromise undertaken to provide Catherine a mother and Merlin Hall a hostess, leaving Vera with...

What?

Oak propped his hips against the worktable and folded his arms. "I suspect half the works in your gallery are hiding images such as these, Vera. They are worth a fortune to the right buyer."

"But the instant they leave Merlin Hall, they destroy Catherine's chances of a decent match, to say nothing of what they'll do to Dirk's reputation." *Or my own.*

"To those who appreciate art, this caliber of painting can only increase his stature."

"And to those less sophisticated?" Vera asked, thinking of her step-mother. "To those who regard modesty as the defining womanly virtue? I regret to inform you, those folk outnumber your connoisseurs by a fair margin, Mr. Dorning.

"And setting aside the Puritans for a moment," she went on, "Dirk's associates at the Academy will fall upon these paintings like a pack of jackals. One will claim they are forgeries, another will claim they are inferior compositions. The third will assert—quite confidently and in the most public venue possible—that they are inferior *and* forgeries. They do so, all of them, while assuring each other they hold Dirk's memory in nothing but highest esteem and his scheming widow in the lowest contempt."

She looked away from the painting, unable to bear the combination of beauty and betrayal it represented.

Oak uncrossed his arms and went to the window, wedging it open another two inches and propping a tall jar beneath the raised pane.

"You will have to decide, Vera, whose opinion matters." He took off his jacket and laid it over the back of a reading chair. "This is great art, however the small-minded might view it. I will continue exploring the gallery, but don't be surprised if we come upon images of you in similar situations."

A breeze stirred through the room, bringing with it the fresh scent of the countryside in high summer. Vera's neighbors, who generally regarded London as the seat of all wickedness, would never grasp the aesthetic subtleties of nude paintings, much less nude erotic paintings.

They might silently tolerate a naked Roman, provided he sported a few strategic fig leaves. Amazons of old were permitted to bare an occasional breast, and satirical prints could be filthy as long as they were humorous, but an erotic *portrait*?

Vera would no longer be troubled with invitations if word of these paintings got out.

"This is all just a discussion of art to you," she said. "Of canvases and asking prices. I cannot claim that degree of disinterest. I never posed for Dirk unless I was fully clothed, never sat for him in anything less formal than a morning dress. He could not have included me in his collection of... naked ladies."

Oak undid his cuffs and slipped the sleeve buttons into his pocket. "I could draw you without your clothing easily. Artists are imaginative, and Dirk surely had opportunities to observe you. Perhaps he walked in on you at your bath or came upon you with Alexander at the breast. What Dirk didn't observe with his eyes, he explored with his hands, or I hope he did."

Not very carefully, he hadn't. "See what's lurking in my gallery before you turn to the restorations, please, but you will find no risqué renderings of me. I'm sure of that."

Oak turned back his cuffs and propped his fists on his hips. "Would it be such a terrible thing, Vera, if your husband had paid artistic tribute to his desire for you?"

She hadn't an answer to that. Either way—if Dirk imagined her as a houri and if he never had—she had grounds to be upset.

"Explore the gallery. I'll see you at supper."

"As you wish, but before you go, I'd like to deal with one other matter."

A gentleman did not typically remove any article of his attire before a lady, and thus the sight of Oak, his wrists exposed, his chest and arms clad in a shirt and waistcoat, affected Vera. She'd seen him naked and aroused, but was still susceptible to this minor display of dishabille.

With Dirk? Vera shut that line of inquiry down before her mind could form an answer. "What other matters have we to discuss, Mr. Dorning?"

He crossed the room to stand before her, and Vera was assailed by the memory of him hoisting her so easily against the wall. Perhaps the hardest part of a discreet liaison was not exchanging pleasantries over the breakfast table, but managing this unexpected inner tumult.

This *desire*.

"I passed a very agreeable night in your bed," he said, "and woke to even more agreeable activities, but I neglected to so much as kiss you. Not well done of me."

"Oh. Well. We managed to find other—"

He pressed his mouth to hers, a nearly chaste kiss, except that it was lip to lip, and he touched her nowhere else. Why did that make her yearn to *be* touched?

He lingered near for a moment, close enough that Vera could feel the heat of his cheek next to hers, close enough that she could pick up the fragrance of his lavender soap beneath the painterly scents in the room.

"Enjoy your visit with the neighbors," he whispered, just as Vera would have put her hands on his arms and commenced to kissing him properly—or improperly.

She stepped back. "I'll see you at supper."

He held the door for her, and she abruptly wanted him to close it, lock it, and tup her against the wall.

"Have a pleasant day, Mrs. Channing."

"You too, Mr. Dorning."

She walked past him into the corridor, and he quietly closed the door behind her. The soft snick of the lock said he'd work in his studio for the next several hours. Vera was halfway to the main staircase when it occurred to her that Oak had said *some men* pleasure themselves a lot.

Perhaps he was one of them, and perhaps that was part of the reason why he worked behind a locked door. The thought had her smiling before she reached the steps.

~

JEREMY HAD LEFT the table at the end of supper claiming he had lessons to prepare. Miss Diggory had pleaded fatigue, and thus Oak was ending his day with Vera and Catherine in the family parlor.

Catherine sat at the pianoforte and did justice to a Haydn sonata. Vera occupied a wing chair and worked at some piece of embroidery. No fire burned in the hearth owing to the mildness of the evening, and thus the room was illuminated only by candles.

Oak had taken the end of the sofa, where he sketched—what else was he to do in such a pleasantly domestic situation?—and wondered if Miss Diggory and Jeremy were canoodling in their stolen hour. That Oak's imagination had been pulled in canoodling directions *all day* left him annoyed and mentally weary.

"A bit slower on the adagio," Vera murmured. "Take your time with it, Catherine."

Catherine reduced the tempo of her playing, and the music was better for it.

"How did your social call go?" Oak asked, for want of anything else to say.

"Quite well," Vera replied. "Mrs. Treeble's nephew, a little fellow by the name of Samuel, has come to live with her. He and Alexander got on splendidly. Catherine and Tom Treeble graciously agreed to mind the younger boys in the garden, so Mrs. Treeble, Miss Diggory, and I could enjoy a quiet conversation."

"She's your nearest neighbor?"

Catherine brought her slow movement to a conclusion, though she had played only as far as the exposition of the first theme.

"That's as far as I know well enough to attempt in front of other people," she said, leaving the piano bench. "I very much enjoyed paying a call with you, Step-mama. Perhaps we can do more socializing before the summer's over." She snitched a piece of shortbread from the tea tray. "Mr. Dorning, good night. I will dream of skies full of rainbow clouds."

She curtseyed and left Oak alone with Vera.

"Rainbow clouds?" Vera asked.

"The undersides of clouds are particularly interesting from an artistic point of view. Catherine and I were fortunate enough to observe a parhelion, which prompted a discussion of the challenges of capturing natural light on canvas."

Oak's pencil paused above the page. The undersides of a woman's bare breasts were also fascinating. Vera's figure would move Venus to envy, and yet, the exact contour of her breasts told Oak that she had indeed breastfed her only child.

Vera held her embroidery hoop up to the light of the candelabra on the mantel. "What is a parhelion?"

"A sun dog, a windgall. A little fragment of a rainbow that parallels the sun, especially in early morning or early evening. The sailors say a sun dog presages high wind. The farmers claim it's a harbinger of rain."

"Either way, it portends trouble. Mrs. Treeble is a pleasant sort."

The subject had changed—or had it? "And you had a friendly chat free of the company of children?"

Vera rolled up her work and stashed it in her workbasket, the movements more forceful than mere linen deserved.

"More or less. Mrs. Treeble had to remind me that Dirk referred to me as *his maid of the shires*. She used the term three times, as if goading me to put aside my mourning attire."

"Put aside your mourning attire—half-mourning at home, I might add—and do what?" Pity the age that had not yet discovered firelight, for it rendered Vera's complexion luminous, and her hair... Painting her hair by firelight accurately would be impossible. Perhaps with a thousand tiny brushstrokes in myriad colors, viewed at a distance...

"Put aside my mourning and resume being some sort of ideal of rural innocence, despite having a six-year-old child, mind you. If Tamsin hadn't been with us, I would have shortened the call considerably. Mrs. Treeble didn't mean anything by her prattling, and that made it all the worse." Vera rose and took up a candle snuffer from the mantel. "I am being ridiculous."

Oak wished she hadn't moved, but added a few quick strokes to the page anyway. "What is ridiculous about resenting a label you never chose, one that no longer fits, if it ever did?"

"I am not a paragon of rural innocence. As a girl, I used to hold the mares in the breeding shed. They stayed calmer for me than for my brothers, who were occupied handling the stallion. I had no idea women were banned from such activities until I mentioned this to my husband. He was equal parts fascinated and appalled."

She brought the snuffer down over four candles in succession, dousing one of the three candelabra in the room. Shadows deepened, and Oak realized he was in the presence of a complicated emotion with old roots.

"I'm surprised your step-mother allowed you to assist with breedings."

"Mares are valuable, foals bring in money. Step-mama knew nothing of the particulars beyond that, would be my guess. A maid of the shires should have known nothing of it too."

Oak rose and set aside his sketchbook. "If you ever were a maid of the shires, you are no longer. You are a widow of substance and means." *Shall I join you again tonight?*

The moment was wrong to ask that question, and yet, Oak could not assume he was welcome in Vera's bed.

"Why is it," Vera said, taking the snuffer to a second set of candles, "that a woman is defined only as she is related to men or to an absent man? I am a sister, a step-daughter, a widow of some fellow gone these three years. I am entitled to dwell in this house only because I am Alexander's mother. The property belongs to him—a six-year-old—and I have a life estate only because Merlin Hall has no dower cottage."

"You are angry." Vera's ire was evident in her movements and in her tone of voice, and yet, something lay beneath the obvious air of annoyance.

She looked around the parlor as if wondering who'd put out most of the candles. "Perhaps I am angry. I have been thinking of those paintings."

The nudes. She was clearly uncomfortable even saying the word. "And?"

"And I realize that I am put out with Dirk for creating them in the first place—they aren't salable, they aren't practical. But I am also put out with Anna for being a woman who'd pose for those images. A woman who was that... that... self-possessed. She was no maid of the shires, and she didn't care who knew it."

Oak retrieved his sketch pad, took Vera by the wrist, and moved her closer to the last lit branch of candles. "Look at this."

She accepted the sketch pad with a frown, then peered at what he'd drawn. "Mr. Dorning, you have quite the imagination."

"You're not angry."

"I am..." She brought the drawing closer to the light. "I am speechless. I want to say, 'Who is she?' Except she bears a resemblance to me. Not a version of me I see in the mirror."

He'd drawn her naked, curled up in the corner of a sofa, a crocheted shawl revealing as much as it concealed. Her hair was coming down, soft tendrils complementing the tassels and drape of the shawl, sturdy calves and bare feet clearly in evidence, along with the curve of her haunch and the profile of one lush breast.

"I wanted you to know that an artist can render an image for which no model has posed. Anna might never have sprawled naked in bed while Dirk sketched preliminary studies in the corner. She might have had no idea those paintings were created. She might have forbidden him to paint her thus, and that's why the paintings are hidden."

"You're saying Dirk could have rendered similar portraits of me?"

"He might have, but the point is, you are as lovely as any odalisque, and you must not envy a dead woman because your late husband imagined her as an erotic model."

Vera lowered the sketch. "You sound very stern. Almost angry yourself."

Oak was not *almost* angry, he was angry—for her, for what she deserved from the man who'd taken her to wife, for what Oak was in no position to give her.

"I am frustrated," Oak said, managing a smile. "The condition is normal for men in my position."

Vera passed him back the sketch pad and moved toward the door. "You are doomed to more frustration, I'm afraid."

She was rejecting him. Well, that was... that was... probably wise of her. He'd finish his restorations and be on his way. What need had she of an all-but-itinerant artist without means? Oak hadn't seen this coming, and he should not be disappointed, but he was.

Oh, he was. Bitterly, howlingly. He was disappointed to a profound, undignified depth. "I apologize if I've in any way given you offense, Vera. That was not my intention."

She paused, back to him, hand on the door latch, then slowly turned. "Given offense?"

"If you are putting an end to our intimate dealings, I will understand, and you need not speak of the matter further." Those were the required words, spoken in the required civil tones. Oak wanted to shred his sketchbook and toss the pieces into the fire, except there was no fire and what would such a tantrum yield anyway?

Vera crossed the room and kept coming until her arms were around his waist, and her cheek was pillowed against his chest.

"You are such a gentleman. I have no wish to end our intimate dealings, but as of shortly before supper, I am indisposed."

He embraced her without conscious thought. "Indisposed. As women are regularly indisposed?"

She nodded, and Oak would have bet his dog whelk shell she was blushing. He let the sketchbook fall to the wing chair and stroked her hair, all of his frustration muting into a peculiar tenderness.

Women paid a high price for the ability to bring forth new life. Unfairly high, often mortally high. "Are you in pain?"

"Crampy. Nothing of significance."

He wanted to cosset and cuddle her, bring her tisanes and rub her back—or whatever a devoted swain did in such circumstances.

"I am not well versed in the miseries that afflict women of child-bearing age," he said. "My sisters delighted in inflicting upon their brothers more awareness of lunation than any boy can bear, but about the details... you must enlighten me."

"I am fortunate that the indisposition is usually of only four or five days' duration and rarely more than a nuisance in terms of discomfort."

She was minimizing her pain as Miss Diggory had tried to minimize Catherine's. "What helps?"

"Nothing... Well, a touch of the poppy if matters grow dire, but then one has a headache and a muzzy mind, and it's easier simply to endure. That feels good."

Oak rubbed her back, wanting to gather her in his arms and take on her pain for himself. He was being ridiculous, of course, but maybe Vera hadn't had anybody to *be* ridiculous on her behalf before.

"Shall I carry you up to your bed?"

She drew back and smiled. "Gallant of you, but I'm quite capable of walking. Will you light me up?"

"I will." He retrieved his sketch pad and took up the remaining candelabra. When they reached Vera's apartment, he came into her parlor with her and went so far as to light the candles in her bedroom.

"Shall I undo your hooks?"

The offer pleased her, if her smile was any indication. "You shall. How was Catherine's drawing lesson?"

"She is immensely observant, more observant than the average bothersomely astute adolescent. I suspect she has quite a bit of talent."

Oak assisted Vera to undress, a service made more intimate by the fact that he was simply trying to be helpful rather than hasten a woman from her clothes in the interests of sexual expedience. That insight occurred to him as he passed Vera her dressing gown and watched her belt it—loosely—about her waist.

"I have neglected Catherine's artistic education," Vera said, taking a seat at her vanity. "Perhaps your lessons will help address that oversight."

Oak began searching through Vera's hair for pins. "Have you considered a finishing school for her? Some of them have very competent drawing masters." He set the pins in a green ormer shell on Vera's vanity. The mother-of-pearl lining the shell's inner surface caught the candlelight and cast a bright reflection into Vera's folding mirror.

Oh Lord, the compositions that came to mind when he was with her.

"I have not thought that far ahead," she said. "I hate to think of Catherine leaving Merlin Hall."

Oak found the last pin, and Vera's braid slipped down over her shoulders. "She's young. You have a few years to consider other options." He set about undoing the braid and tucked her hair ribbon —lavender, a mourning color, but one that suited her—into his pocket.

He spent the next few minutes brushing out and rebraiding her hair, then using the warmer on the sheets while she made use of the privacy screen. The excuses to linger were used up one by one, and the poor woman likely needed her rest more than usual. When Vera climbed under the covers, Oak hung the dressing gown on the bedpost, kissed her brow, and drew the quilts up around her shoulders.

"Sweet dreams, Vera."

"To you too."

He picked up the branch of candles and prepared to leave, but her voice stopped him at the door. "Thank you, Oak."

"For?"

She sat up, her braid a rope over her shoulder in the dim shadows. "For pinning back Jeremy Forester's ears at breakfast, for noticing Catherine's talent, for not being horrified by my biology. Or by my moods. For being you."

"The pleasure is mine." He bowed, carefully, because he held the candles, and withdrew.

The corridor was blessedly quiet, as was the whole house. Oak made his way to his rooms, oddly at peace with the day. Somewhere behind a locked door, Jeremy Forester and Tamsin Diggory were probably engaged in a happy tumble, a shared moment that signified nothing, provided it bore no consequences.

Oak would have been doing likewise, had Vera allowed it, but her situation meant that instead they'd talked, they'd spent time together, they'd shared a different sort of intimacy. The romping was all quite lovely, and Oak hoped to do a lot of it with Vera, but the other...

The other was precious, and fascinating, and would haunt Oak's heart long after he'd made the trek to London, there to knock on the Academy's door until they admitted him to their numbers.

CHAPTER EIGHT

"Dorning says you have inherited a bit of your papa's talent."

Mr. Forester sauntered along the crushed-shell walk, swinging his walking stick at the fading roses. He connected with a bush, scattering pink petals all over the earth and the walkway.

Catherine resented the interruption, but she did not resent an opportunity to converse with Mr. Forester more or less privately. He was interesting, almost as interesting as the way bright sunlight turned the side of a blade of grass white.

"Mr. Dorning is a talented instructor. I wish Step-mama had come upon him earlier."

"Do you?" Mr. Forester gazed out across the garden, his mind clearly focused on something other than a passing discussion with a mere girl. "I'm not surprised. Your mind is a good deal brighter than the terror's, and you are ever so much more pleasant to look upon."

Catherine sat a little straighter and wished she'd put up her hair that morning. "You aren't to call Alexander *the terror* anymore, are you?" That had been decided at breakfast three days ago. Catherine wanted to verify with Alexander that Step-mama's directions were being followed in the schoolroom, but hadn't found the opportunity.

"Whatever I call him, he remains a moody and indifferent scholar, doesn't he? May I join you?"

A gentleman asked such permission of a lady. "You may. Is Alexander at his drawing lesson?"

"Yes, and thank the benevolent powers for that." Mr. Forester took a seat a mere foot from Catherine, splayed his legs, and ranged an arm along the top of the bench. "The little blighter about drives me barmy."

That was an insult to Alexander, also a confidence of sorts. "Perhaps you drive him barmy too. He's a small boy. You're a grown man. If you don't like being his tutor, maybe you should look for another post."

Mr. Forester's smile blossomed into a grin. "I love a woman with a temper. Perhaps you inherited that from your papa too."

"I simply made a suggestion, Mr. Forester. And if I have a temper, I suspect that's of my own making. Papa was ever sweet and patient with me."

Mr. Forester closed his eyes and leaned his head back. "As Mr. Dorning is sweet and patient with you?"

The question hinted at unkind conclusions, perhaps about Catherine herself, more likely about Mr. Dorning.

"Are you jealous because he's an earl's son?" Not that Mr. Dorning ever mentioned his family's title. Catherine had looked him up in Debrett's, and though he was far down along the succession, his brother was the present Earl of Casriel.

"I am absolutely jealous of him," Mr. Forester replied, opening his eyes, "but not because of some dusty old title he probably longs for in his secret dreams. I am jealous because he'll be off to London in a few weeks and because until we are rid of him, he gets to spend an hour each day with you."

Mr. Forester slanted a look at her that she could not fathom. Was he gauging her reaction to his remark, sorry he'd been so honest, or teasing her?

"Mr. Dorning is unfailingly proper with me, I assure you." He had the knack of... Catherine did not know what to call his knack. He was always going on about light and perspective and compositional elements, but he'd not peached on her about taking a bit of air without Miss Digg's permission. He'd acted as if putting up her hair was simply what one did before dinner. He spoke to her as if she was worth educating, not an extra duty imposed between the tasks he'd rather see to.

Mr. Forester set the bottom of his walking stick on the ground between his knees and batted the handle from hand to hand. To lounge with his legs spread like that was not quite seemly, but the occasion wasn't exactly a royal garden party either.

"The proper ones are the fellows who bear the most watching, my dear Catherine. Has he tried to kiss you yet?" Mr. Forester aimed a considering glance at her mouth, as if her lips had become somehow different in recent days in a way that would prove whether she'd been kissed.

"He certainly has not attempted to take any liberties whatsoever, nor will he."

"Then perhaps Master Alexander is not the slowest top in the household. I don't suppose you were sketching Dorning's handsome countenance?"

Catherine held up her sketch pad. "I was trying to sketch the roses, because the canes and leaves are a complicated pattern, and that is my challenge at present. To render accurate representations of what I see." Which required seeing in a way Catherine hadn't been taught to see previously. *Paying attention.*

Jeremy Forester was paying attention to her. Catherine wasn't sure how she felt about that. She was uneasy, and also flattered.

"If I had an hour to spend with you privately each day," he said, "I'd not be wasting it on dreary old sketches and blown roses. You're nearly fifteen. Girls get engaged and even have babies at that age." His gaze brushed lower than her mouth, over her *person.*

"Are you flirting with me?"

He rose and bowed in a mockery of politesse. "Perish the thought.

I'd be getting far above myself should I presume to that degree. If Dorning in any way oversteps, you will apply to me to address the matter. He could do with a sound pummeling, and I'd delight in delivering it to him."

Pummel Mr. Dorning? Catherine did not know if Mr. Forester was daft or in earnest. "Nobody need pummel anybody." She stood and gathered up her sketching pad, penknife, and pencil.

"Where are you off to, sweet Catherine?"

"You ruined the bushes I was sketching. I must find another subject."

"I ruined...? I am abjectly sorry. You must allow me to aid you in your search. Come, take my arm, and we will investigate the garden." He crooked his elbow at her and appeared to be entirely serious.

Catherine took his arm and allowed herself to be escorted up the walkway as if the occasion were, in fact, a royal garden party. The experience was a tad unsettling and also lovely.

Quite, quite lovely.

~

"IS THIS ALL OF THEM?" Vera asked, turning in a slow circle to survey the eleven paintings Oak had arranged about his studio.

"Everything I found in the gallery. I'd be surprised if more lurk in the attic or in the frames hanging in your private apartment, but it's possible. Eleven is a very odd number for a man who always painted in series."

Half of the compositions were not of Anna. Three were of a blond woman Vera didn't recognize, two were renderings of a brunette with an impressive bust, and one was of the brunette and the blond in an embrace that was not remotely sisterly, given where and how the women touched each other.

"I like this one best," Oak said, nodding at the entwined women. "Never have I seen purple and orange harmonized so effectively, and all it took was some greenery, a few hints of red and yellow—*et voilà tout*—a wildly daring palette becomes all of a piece."

"Are you blind to the wildly daring subject?" Vera could hardly look away.

"They are loving each other," Oak said, taking the place at her side. "A common enough theme across all of the arts. In addition to the palette, the composition, the brushwork, and the very effective use of natural light, what makes this painting glow is that we're not seeing one person caught in a moment of private pleasure. This is a moment between lovers. The whole relationship—the tenderness, yearning, frustration, and joy—is present in one image."

Vera set aside her shock and focused not on hands, genitals, and breasts, but on the subjects' expressions.

"The smiles are different," she said. "Not like Anna's dreamy secrets, but like... like..."

Oak regarded her with patient humor. "Like I look at you?"

Vera sank onto one of the two venerable wing chairs before the cold hearth. She was assailed by memories collected over the past few days.

Oak taking down her hair at night.

Oak holding her chair at breakfast, then performing the same courtesy for Catherine and Miss Diggory.

Oak engaging Catherine in a lively argument about Mr. Turner's brushwork.

One recollection in particular stood out. Oak had accompanied the household to divine services and patiently endured the inevitable round of introductions in the churchyard afterward. He'd bowed over the hands of all three spinster Davies sisters, raised his voice to accommodate Grandfather Stiles's poor hearing, listened with apparent interest to young Howard Frampton's artistic aspirations, and—when Alexander had begun to shuffle from foot to foot at Vera's side—he'd casually hoisted the boy onto his hip.

"Note the change in perspective," Oak had said quietly to

Alexander. "When you are eye to eye with a subject, the scene is different."

Alexander had peered about as if he'd suddenly found himself cast ashore on the fair isle of Lilliput. All the while, Oak conversed politely with Vera's neighbors, even bowing slightly to wish Grandmother Stiles a good day.

When the time had come to return to Merlin Hall, Oak had suggested that he and Alexander walk the distance. To a man in his prime, two miles was a pleasant ramble. For a six-year-old boy...

"Alexander, are you up to that challenge?" Vera had asked.

"Yes, ma'am." He'd nodded so vigorously his cap had come down over his eyes.

"That settles it." Oak had straightened Alexander's cap and put the boy on his feet. "Let's mind the mud puddles, and off we go. Do you know any tramping songs, lad? A good rousing hymn might do in deference to the Lord's day."

They'd ambled out of the churchyard, Alexander marching along as if he, too, considered a two-mile hike a mere ramble. The sight of the man and boy in earnest discussion as they struck off across the green had brought an ache to Vera's throat.

Upon returning home from services, Vera had heard her son before she'd seen him. She'd been sitting at her desk, trying to pen a polite note to Richard Longacre, when through the open window, she'd caught a snippet of song.

THERE'S many men get store of treasure
yet they live like ignorant knaves:
In this world they have no pleasure
the more they have, the more they crave.

OAK DORNING HAD A FINE BARITONE, though the lyrics he'd sung—with Alexander's descant kiting above the melody—were from a drinking song Vera's brothers were fond of. She'd watched as man and boy strode up the drive, Alexander's cheeks ruddy, his singing more robust than musical. Dirk had died too soon to have any moments with Alexander such as this, a Sabbath hour stolen to teach his son a hearty tune, an hour wandering the countryside on a summer day.

Vera had missed moments such as this, but watching Oak keep a pace that Alexander could manage, she vowed that she'd do better at appreciating her children, and appreciating Alexander especially.

And now, surrounded by Dirk's art in Oak's studio, Vera was hard put to appreciate her late husband at all.

"I grant you," she said, "the paintings are lovely. They are fine art, and they deserve to be appreciated as such, but I cannot sell them, and thus they must be stored out of sight."

Oak lowered himself into the second wing chair, and as often happened when another man's hands would have been idle, he took up a sketch pad and pencil.

"I could frame those paintings such that the signature is obscured. Nobody would know who created them save for the purchasers. Turn your chin half an inch—yes."

Vera had grown accustomed to Oak's sketching habit. Over the past week, he'd sketched while she'd read to him in the late-night privacy of her bedroom. He'd sketched while they talked about her neighbors and family. He'd sketched while he'd acquainted her—by image and anecdote—with his many siblings.

"The signature is half of what makes any painting valuable," Vera replied. "If you obscure the signature, you diminish the value."

"Not necessarily. The signature is the easiest part of a painting to forge. Another half inch to the left... Thank you. I would utterly adore doing your portrait, and I assure you I would render my subject fully clothed."

"May I tell you something?"

His pencil stilled. "Of course."

"You asked if I was concerned that Dirk might have painted similar portraits of me, not fully clothed."

Quiet patience was one of Oak Dorning's many strengths. He regarded Vera with a steady composure that helped her complete her thought.

"Now that you've raised the possibility," she went on, "I am almost certain Dirk painted nudes of me. I'd awaken and find him studying me, though I always slept in a nightgown. He did come upon me at my bath more than once, and when another husband might have withdrawn, he found excuses to linger before leaving me my privacy. I never thought anything of it, because he seemed to think nothing of it. We were married, after all."

Oak shifted forward so Vera sat knee to knee with him.

He took her hand. "Your privacy is not a detail, Vera. I will never render a woman on canvas who resembles you without first gaining your agreement. Particularly if my objective is a nude, for me to abuse your trust by failing to obtain permission to create your likeness is unthinkable."

"Thank you." How she loved holding hands with him, loved the quiet decency he brought to every undertaking. "Oak?"

"Vera?"

"I am no longer indisposed." This admission, which had been a topic of casual exchanges with Dirk on any number of occasions, caused Vera to blush. She hadn't planned such an announcement, but Oak's smile said he was glad she'd made it.

"One did not want to admit to counting the days," he said, "or the minutes. May I come to you tonight?"

He always asked, he never presumed. "Unless you want me climbing into your bed at the midnight hour, you had better come to me."

"I would love for you to climb into my bed at any hour." He kissed the corner of her mouth, which of course made her want to be kissed properly, so she remedied his off-center aim, and that resulted in Oak scooping her into his lap.

"I have another confession," she said, snuggling into his embrace.

"You cannot wait until tonight. I sympathize with your plight. Truly I do. That is why the door is locked."

Vera was sitting in his lap, and the evidence of his *sympathy* was physically apparent. "I will wait until tonight, as you have waited for the past five days, but I admit that I have been glad for the pause, Oak."

"Anticipation and all that rot?"

"Maybe, but also... you are an attentive lover when lovemaking is not on the agenda. I have enjoyed that." Lapped it up like an alley cat coming upon a defenseless dish of cream.

"I'm a competent lady's maid?"

He was trying to make the moment light. Vera would think later about why that should be.

"You are an attentive *lover*," she said. "You act as if you enjoy my company over a meal, over cards, or when we're like this. In the middle of the morning, trying to figure out what to do with Dirk's paintings."

Oak went quiet, his cheek resting against Vera's temple. "I do enjoy your company. I hope the feeling is mutual."

Had she said something wrong? "It is. It very much is."

He rose with Vera in his arms—how easily he did that—and set her on her feet, though he kept his hands on her shoulders.

"Vera, you could send me to Coventry, refuse to so much as acknowledge me at the breakfast table, and I'd finish the work you've tasked me with and be on my way. You don't owe me a consummation to our dalliance."

The word *dalliance* rankled, even in such a gallant context. "I want a consummation, sir."

"Good." He kissed her cheek. "As do I. Perhaps tonight we can talk further about what to do with Dirk's naked treasures."

Vera disliked the sense that she was being dismissed. "I'm distracting you, aren't I?"

He dropped his hands from her shoulders. "Distraction is a mere nuisance, an off-key piano played in the next room. Far more accurate to say that you render me witless, and in your presence, I cannot keep my hands to myself, given our plans for the evening."

She leaned close and took a sniff of him, merely because she could. "I don't want you to keep your hands to yourself."

"Yes," he said, "you do, unless a tumble on a worn and itchy hearth rug appeals to you."

Vera's gaze went to the carpet. "It's not *that* worn."

"Out," Oak said, taking her by the arm and guiding her to the door. "Out, out, out, or I will accomplish nothing this whole day save daydreams of you."

What a lovely, lovely thing to say. "Until tonight, then. And I've decided we will simply return Dirk's naked ladies to storage."

Oak looked like he wanted to argue, so Vera patted his bum and slipped out the door, closing it softly behind her. She heard male laughter, then the metallic snick of the lock.

Discipline was a fine quality—in moderation. Vera told herself that her discipline was equal to the challenge of attending to necessary tasks for the rest of the day, though they had best be simple tasks. She had never finished her note to Richard Longacre, so she turned her steps in the direction of her private parlor, intent on completing that courtesy.

The encounter with Oak had been unsettling, not only because of the paintings he'd found, but also because of the man Vera was discovering beneath the artist. The artist was talented, ambitious, hardworking, and determined.

The man was decent, kind, honorable, good-humored, casually virile, and perceptive. Vera nearly hated the artist, precisely because she was falling in love with the man. The artist would hie off to London, never to be seen again, and he'd take a piece of Vera's heart with him.

Not what she had planned where Oak Dorning was concerned, but she was looking very much forward to nightfall nonetheless.

~

CATHERINE WAS a talented artist whose gifts had been neglected. Oak became more aware of this each time he instructed her. She had an instinctive eye for composition and a quick, accurate hand.

"You truly have inherited your father's ability," Oak said as he assessed her pencil portrait of Jeremy Forester. "Your mama will have to find you a permanent drawing master when I leave."

Forester had agreed to sit for her after lunch, while Oak had been busy with Alexander. The boy demanded to go outside now if the day was fair, and he dawdled and dodged when the time came to return to the schoolroom. Oak regarded both developments as positive steps toward typical childhood behavior.

With Catherine, Oak was more at sea. "You have caught Forester's capacity for humor and his restlessness," he said. "What else were you attempting to portray?"

Catherine selected a cherry from the bowl on the table and popped it into her mouth. "I'm not sure. Mr. Forester is not that well known to me."

They were in the kitchen, where the best still lifes were assembled. The ubiquitous pears and apples were out of season, so Catherine had chosen a bowl of cherries for a study Oak would have her do in pencil, pastels, and watercolors.

And oils. She really should be given at least a passing acquaintance with oils.

"Cherries will be difficult," she said. "Why must I work with fruit at all? It's not as if fruit is inherently fascinating."

"Fruit doesn't fidget," Oak said, "even if the project takes hours. Fruit doesn't drop its petals or scratch its nose. Fruit does not require pleasant conversation by the hour, as you start over, change your mind about a pigment, or realize you've sketched an element of the composition all wrong. Fruit doesn't mind if you need to heed nature's call, and yet, the challenges of its contours and colors are formidable."

Catherine munched her cherry, then went to the slop bucket and spit out the pit. "You talk to me like I might be an artist one day. Women aren't artists."

Oak snorted. "Tell that to Mary Moser and Angelica Kauffman. They were both founding members of the Royal Academy. Tell that to Anne Seymour Damer, whose sculptures have been exhibited at the Academy for decades. If you want depictions of violence that exceed even what your father was able to convey in his battle scenes, find some of Artemisia Gentileschi's biblical subjects."

"Who?"

"Precisely. Just because you haven't heard of her doesn't mean she didn't set the world on its ear in a less narrow-minded day."

Catherine slid into the seat across the table, her movements conveying neither a child's casual slouch nor a young lady's self-conscious deportment. She had an inherent grace that would serve her well in adulthood.

"Papa set the world on its ear. He said if England is determined to conquer the world, the price of that conquest should be made apparent. Nobody *likes* his battle scenes, but they gawk at them endlessly."

"Art can inform," Oak said, helping himself to a cherry. "It can make people think, can bring joy or sorrow. Perhaps you won't become an artist, but if you wish to paint as your father did, I can show you the basics of working in oils."

Vera might object. She probably should object, in fact.

"If I remind you that women don't work in oils, Mr. Dorning, will you lecture me again?"

"Possibly, if your point of view is in want of the salient facts."

"I like your lectures." She held up the portrait of Forester as if trying to determine whether she liked *him*. "I was trying to convey that Mr. Forester isn't as clever as he thinks he is."

And how had Catherine come to that conclusion? "Put a hint of fear in his eyes."

"How?"

Oak took the drawing and added a few lines around the eyes, a bit of shading beneath the brows.

"Oh my. That is Mr. Forester to the life." Catherine studied the portrait, frowning. "How does one know, Mr. Dorning, if one is being flirted with?"

Forester apparently needed a severe lesson in manners. "If the flirtation is competently done, the lady can be sure that humorous banter has taken on harmlessly amorous undertones. If the flirtation is of the bumbling variety, the lady is left feeling uncertain, insulted, or angry. Did Tom Treeble try out his flirtations on you, Catherine?"

She set aside Forester's portrait and opened her sketchbook to a clean page. "Something like that. The whole business strikes me as silly. Papa was a flirt, and you flirted with the Davies sisters after services. Everybody knows you don't mean anything by it, so why flirt at all?"

The questions one half-grown female could ask... "I was merely passing the time with new acquaintances." Oak considered what Catherine had not told him, considered the sketch, and considered the slight awkwardness between Catherine and her step-mother. "If a fellow's attempts to flirt are unwelcome, Catherine, you simply tell him so."

"Tell him he's a bumbler? Are you much acquainted with young men, Mr. Dorning? They do not cope well with unflattering truths."

I am a young man. Except in Catherine's eyes, Oak was apparently among the doddering ancients.

"You say something along the lines of, 'Mr. Treeble, I hope you aren't attempting to flirt with me. I have no patience with that sort of foolishness, and I have always admired your great good sense.'" Oak had raised the pitch of his voice to a clipped falsetto, though, really, why should a young woman have to offer false flattery to get a fellow to desist with his melting glances and bad puns?

Catherine peered at him over the top of her sketch. "That is very good. I will practice saying that in the mirror. What if I want him to flirt?"

When had an art lesson become something else entirely? "Catherine, might you have this conversation with your mother?"

Her pencil moved more quickly over the page. "That's twice you've referred to Step-mama as my mother. She's not my mother, and while I love her and am grateful to her, I am not her daughter."

"Is that what Miss Diggory tells you?"

"Yes. Aunt says the same thing. My mama was Papa's muse, while I am his by-blow. Merlin Hall is not my home. I am here at Step-mama's sufferance, and should she send me off into service as a *governess*,"—Catherine's expression conveyed endless dread—"I will have nothing to say to it."

Oak took the sketch of Forester and added some lines about the mouth and nose. "Catherine, Merlin Hall is most assuredly your home. Do you know why your step-mother is selling some of the older works?"

"Because they are cluttering up the attic."

"Because she wants you to have a considerable dower portion. Because she wants to be able to afford finishing school for you."

Catherine looked up, gaze narrowed. "Step-mama *told* you that?"

"She did. She has no use for the money herself, having a life estate here at Merlin Hall. The funds will go to assure your security." And why the hell would Tamsin Diggory imply that Catherine was destined for a governess's life?

"By-blows don't go to finishing schools, Mr. Dorning." Spoken in faintly amused, condescending tones.

"My beloved niece is a by-blow, and her mother was a tavern maid. Tabitha will start her second year at school in the autumn, and she's having a grand time. We miss her very much at Dorning Hall." Oak missed her very much. Casriel's pining for his daughter went beyond mere missing. "You and she would get on famously."

Though, of course, they'd never meet.

A beat of silence went by while Catherine's pencil made short, sharp strokes on the paper. "Why do you want to go to London so badly?" she asked.

Oak had expected more questions about flirtation, or perhaps—this was an art lesson, at least in theory—a query about the differences between oils and watercolors.

"You wield your verbal arrows with the skill of an Amazon, Catherine Channing." Oak put the last touches on Forester's eyes. "I am bound for London because the Royal Academy is there, impressive commissions are more likely to be found there, and all the best exhibitions are held there."

Financial independence lay in London, professional recognition, a commercial and aesthetic demand that Oak could supply. It wasn't a stretch to say that Oak's self-respect dwelled in the capital. Among his siblings, he was an oddity, an affectionately tolerated eccentric. Among fellow artists, he could maunder on about brushwork and light and balance, and they would maunder right back at him.

Catherine passed over the drawing she'd been working on, and it was not of cherries in a ceramic bowl on a wooden table.

"You can paint anywhere," she said, "but if you go to London, I can't tell you the things I tell no one else. Nobody reassures me that I can stay here. Nobody else has ever said this is my home. I don't want you to go, and Step-mama and Alexander have been happier since you came here. You should stay."

She gathered up her effects and would have left Oak sitting at the table, reeling from her broadside, but he had the presence of mind to hand her the sketch of Jeremy Forester.

"Catherine, if Jeremy ever missteps with you, you must promise to tell your step-mother. Not Miss Diggory, not your aunt, not Bracken. Tell your step-mother."

"I'd rather tell you."

"I won't be here." Though he admitted that he wanted to bide at Merlin Hall. He wanted to stand by, fists at the ready, should Forester overstep with a fourteen-year-old girl. Oak wanted to drop in on the schoolroom and assure himself that Forester was instructing his little charge more than he was intimidating him. Oak wanted very much to be Vera's lady's maid for the rest of her days and her lover for the rest of her nights.

Foolishness, all of it. He was at the Hall to restore a few old paintings. Anything else was... Oak didn't know what it was. An unlooked-for boon. A harmless frolic. Temporary madness.

Catherine gave him an unnervingly adult perusal. "Right. You'll be in *Lon-don*, but will you be *happy* in stinky old London, far from the fresh air you adore and from people who like you? I'm not sure I could be."

She left, her sketching pencil tucked behind her ear, her sketch pad in hand.

∿

"THE WORK IS GOOD," Richard Longacre said, pulling back draperies to let afternoon sunlight strike Endymion de Beauharnais's latest creation. "Almost too good to be one of old Shackleton's portraits."

De Beauharnais remained silent, very likely seething at the near insult. He excelled at seething, but thank heavens he was even more adept at mimicking other painters' styles.

"Let's have a drink to celebrate another success," Richard said, changing the angle of the portrait's easel, the better to illuminate the brushwork. "You never disappoint, de Beauharnais. That has become a rare quality among today's younger talents."

Richard poured two glasses of excellent brandy and passed one over to his guest. De Beauharnais accepted the drink, probably because he was unable to afford such fine libation at his own quarters.

"To your talent," Richard said, lifting his glass. *And to your ambition.*

"And is my talent sufficient to gain me admittance to the Academy, Longacre?"

Richard sipped his drink, needing the moment to marshal his strategy. De Beauharnais was useful only to the extent his objective could be withheld from him, though that objective must appear to dangle ever closer to his grasp.

Richard offered a genial smile. "Your ability is quite the talk of the Exhibition Committee. They are unanimous in their willingness to invite you to contribute to next year's showing."

De Beauharnais tossed back half his drink at once, an abomination against the cult of Dionysus, if not against basic manners.

"I exhibited this year, Longacre, and last year and the year before."

"And you shall exhibit next year. I promised you admittance to the Academy, my friend. I also cautioned you that such a promise cannot be quickly kept. Every flatulent, wheezing pensioner who ever sketched a royal princess's lapdog thinks he should be the next academician, and his cousin, nephew, or brother-in-law has announced the same conclusion to all of polite society. One must proceed delicately."

In fact, one usually had to proceed for decades, producing the right art for the right people, in the right style, before Academy membership was a possibility. Young men with no connections, no wealth, and questionable personal habits stood little chance of admission, no matter their talent.

Life was so unfair.

"You are using me." De Beauharnais offered not an accusation, but a sadly amused conclusion. "You will never allow me to become even an associate, no matter that I paint better than three-quarters of the current members, including you."

"You are discouraged," Longacre replied, adding more brandy to de Beauharnais's glass. "Rheumatism has left me intimately acquainted with discouragement, but with your abilities, you must persevere. Nobody lives forever, particularly not a lot of profligate old painters and sculptors. Your talent is enormous. We simply need to keep you in coin until the right moment comes along, and you can take your proper place in the art world's pantheon."

Flattery was an art demanding every bit as much skill as forgery.

A light, sincerely complimentary hand was needed, along with a dollop of ruthlessness.

"I am done with your schemes, Longacre," de Beauharnais said, taking a more moderate taste of his brandy. "I am talented, I am hardworking. Everybody comes to you for suggestions when they seek to hire an artist. You consign me to your dirty little projects when you could instead refer paying commissions to me."

Richard set aside his brandy, fished a quizzing glass out of the library's desk drawer, and moved to stand before the general's portrait. The old boy would have to spend a few weeks gathering dust and the scent of mildew in the attics, but he'd serve his intended purpose more than adequately.

"I did refer you a paying commission just last week. Mrs. Hambleton Finchley must have a portrait of her twin daughters as they prepare to leave the schoolroom. Bring Tolliver along as your assistant for the commission contemplates that expense. Your fee will be timely and handsomely paid, and she'll have you back next summer to paint her favorite hunter or canary."

Tolliver might someday be useful. No reason not to toss a few coins his way.

"Mrs. Finchley left a card just yesterday," de Beauharnais said. "I'm to call on her."

Richard peered very closely at the brushwork that constituted the subject's powdered wig in the "Shackleton" portrait. Shackleton, a court painter in the previous century, had been a conservative talent, happy to paint within the conventions of his day. For the most part, de Beauharnais had copied Shackleton's style quite well, though the brushwork was just a touch too extravagant—too modern—for perfection.

Not that the buyer would notice.

"Mrs. Finchley is a highly social creature," Richard said, studying the signature again. "Her daughters will make their come outs just as next year's Summer Exhibition opens. Choose a study of her twins as your submission to the exhibit, and you will find more commissions readily in hand."

"The signature's perfect, Longacre. You need not pretend otherwise."

"The whole work is exquisite," Richard said, examining the embroidery on the subject's ornate frock coat. "Utterly impressive, de Beauharnais. You truly do have a gift."

He would render a likeness of the Finchley twins that would convey whatever lovely qualities they had without unduly obscuring their imperfections. Of all the ironies, de Beauharnais was an honest, compassionate portraitist.

"I have a gift," de Beauharnais replied, beginning a circuit of the library, "but I do not have money. The Finchley commission is all well and good, but it's not sovereigns in hand. Town has emptied out for the summer, and you've yet to pay me for yonder general."

The general was a great-uncle to a wealthy maiden lady dwelling in the north. When Richard had informed her that a long-lost Shackleton portrait of her great-uncle had been unearthed in a late friend's effects, she had been more than willing to pay for such a treasure. The friend's effects had, in fact, included a workmanlike portrait of the old fellow done by some obscure hand. De Beauharnais's forgery was thus an exercise in copying content from one source and style from another.

And he had executed that challenge brilliantly.

"I will pay you, my friend. You are pockets to let?" Richard asked, shifting to study the rings on the general's hand.

"I am perpetually pockets to let, and you know it. London is too bloody expensive, and appearances must be maintained."

That, they did. "I do have another little project, if you're interested."

De Beauharnais held his drink up to the window light. "Not another Shackleton, pray God."

"Something more modern, something I won't have to put in an

old frame. A painting that will allow your talent a greater chance to shine."

De Beauharnais paused before the portrait Dirk Channing had done of his young daughter, Catherine. The painting had been a gift to Richard, perhaps an apology. The girl was about eight, a darling, smiling little child climbing onto the lap of a mother who'd already gone to her reward at the time the painting had been finished.

The mother was present mostly in shadow, her skirts evident, not her features. She grasped the climbing child with graceful hands, and the little girl was ecstatic to be scrambling up into her mother's embrace.

Perhaps Channing had been unable to look upon the thing.

"You want me to copy this?" de Beauharnais asked, peering at the signature.

"Dirk Channing was talented," Richard said, putting the quizzing glass in his pocket and joining de Beauharnais before the portrait. "Channing was not an old man when he died, alas. I have several of his better works."

"Channing is barely cold in his grave, Longacre. I knew him, I attended his funeral. Copying a Channing isn't like copying some relic from the last century."

The token show of reluctance was part of de Beauharnais's dance. Perhaps Tolliver found that appealing in bed. Richard found it tiresome.

"You are certainly free to decline my business at any time," Richard said. "I understand your reservations, and I know I am fortunate to be able to call upon you."

Just as de Beauharnais was fortunate not to be in Newgate awaiting the hangman's kind attentions. Forgery was a felony, and nobody back at Hogtrot Hall was of sufficient standing to intercede for de Beauharnais should he be taken up by the magistrate for forgery—or for buggery.

Such charges were nearly impossible to prove without witnesses. One of the participants had to confess to the deed, and confession itself could result in a death sentence. Fortunately, the scandal of the charges alone would be ruinous.

Fortunately for Richard.

"Replicating Channing's style will take considerable skill," de Beauharnais said, "considerable effort. He was said to ruin his brushes in a single session, some of them sable and quite dear, and he was fanatical about details—as you are, de Beauharnais. You attended Dirk's funeral." Half the extant artists in the realm had. "I have a work I'd like you to study in detail before you begin, but you doubtless saw other examples of Channing's art when at his home."

"I was a guest at Merlin Hall on two occasions, a protégé of sorts. Channing was happy to instruct those who had ability, and all he required in return was adoration and flattery. At the time, I was eager to provide both, particularly when I was also receiving free meals and a comfortable guest bed."

"Then you've met Channing's widow?"

De Beauharnais studied Richard as closely as he'd been examining Channing's rendering of a child's smile.

"Mrs. Channing was substantially younger than her husband, and prettier than she knew. I liked her, but I was merely one of a regiment of houseguests, and she was taken up with making Channing's life exactly as he wished it to be."

"She's still pretty," Richard said. "Prettier than ever. Channing called her his maid of the shires, but she had another side, not so maidenly. Did you know she modeled for Channing?"

De Beauharnais took a considering sip of his brandy, then put the drink down unfinished on the desk. "I suppose modeling is a cross an artist's wife must bear, particularly if she's attractive."

"Verity Channing is beautiful, but she also had a delightfully naughty streak, though is it naughty if a man is painting nudes of his own wife?"

"You want me to paint a nude of Verity Channing?"

"Nudes—plural. Channing did a whole series of nudes earlier in his career—I have one you should inspect—and Mrs. Channing doubtless came in for the same thorough study on his part."

De Beauharnais considered the painting on the wall, then consulted his watch, a plain little piece that had doubtless been given to him by some doting auntie.

"Such a painting will cost you, Longacre. Cost you enough that I needn't accept another of your projects ever again. They are beneath my talent, in the first place, and in the second, you have graduated from taking modest advantage of some old beldame with a work purporting to be from a bygone era, to ruining a young widow who never did anything to harm you."

"You don't know that," Richard said. "You don't know how Verity Channing has comported herself, toward me or toward anybody else. She's a jumped-up dairy maid who got her hooks into Dirk and will be comfortably situated into old age for her efforts."

De Beauharnais snapped his watch closed. "Isn't that precisely what women are taught to do? Find a fellow and make the best possible life with him, hoping all the while that his babies don't kill her? I rather admire the ladies for their courage, fellows in general being an unreliable and difficult lot."

"You don't even like women. Stop being contrary."

"I like women quite well, better than I like most men." His gaze went to the happy child, who'd been half orphaned as Dirk had painted her likeness. "Pay me for the general."

Richard opened the desk drawer and counted out the agreed-upon sum plus a bit more. One could be generous in victory.

"I will cheerfully part with five times that amount if you can complete the Channing study in two weeks' time. That will be enough to tide you over for the rest of the year, and I promise the Finchley referral won't be the last I send in your direction."

De Beauharnais slipped the coins into an inner coat pocket. "Before I agree to this project, explain exactly what you want me to do."

"The objective is simple, almost beneath your talent. I have a nude Channing did of his favorite model, a woman named Anna Beaumont. The work is lovely, semi-erotic, and exquisitely rendered. You simply substitute Verity Channing for Anna Beaumont."

"Your mother was a Beaumont. Was this Anna a relation?"

"My cousin. I introduced her to Dirk, in fact. Come, I'll show you the study, and you can let me know what you think."

CHAPTER NINE

For Vera, the hours had developed leaden feet, putting her oddly in mind of her wedding day. She was to take a lover, a notion that would have astonished her prior to meeting Oak Dorning. A soft tap on the bedroom door nearly startled her out of her slippers, so immersed was she in contemplation of what was to come.

"Come in."

Oak opened the door and remained at the threshold. "Am I too early?"

Vera took a moment to behold the sheer masculine wonder of him. At Merlin Hall, the evening meal was informal, and thus Oak was in his usual garb—breeches, waistcoat, jacket, cravat. He might have been a country squire ending a long summer day. His collar was without starch, his cravat without lace. His boots were serviceably clean rather than gleaming with the champagne polish favored by Town dandies.

You do not belong in London. Vera knew the London art crowd. She'd seen them fawning over Dirk like flies swarming over rotting fruit, each sycophant more elegant and witty than the next. Most of them had smiled through their lies and wielded more talent with an insult than with a paintbrush.

They had competed in their attempts to insult her whenever Dirk was out of earshot, and when she'd complained to Dirk, he'd patted her hand and told her not to take offense at a jest.

"Your timing is perfect," she said, meaning the words in a larger sense. In another year, she might have resigned herself to solitary widowhood. A year earlier, and misplaced loyalty to Dirk's memory would have prevented her from enjoying this moment.

Oak closed the door, his movements unhurried. "You said earlier today that the pause of this past week was enjoyable for you. That you liked being cosseted a bit."

The day had grown chilly, then rain had moved in. Vera's hearth thus held a fire. Oak put aside the screen and began poking air into the desultory blaze.

"I did like the cosseting, and I liked cosseting you too."

He straightened and set the poker back on the hearth stand. "I hope I haven't imposed."

Vera slipped her arms around his waist and leaned against him. "Dirk wanted attention. You enjoy companionship. The two needs are very different. I was happy to attend my husband, and now, your companionship is also a joy."

His arms came around her, and Vera tucked closer. Oak wasn't aroused, not evenly slightly, which she was probably not meant to notice.

"Are you having second thoughts, Oak?"

"If there's a child..."

She was pleased he'd acknowledge the risk. "I will tell you, of course, and I will not require that you marry me." Would it be so bad, though, to be married to her? Merlin Hall was a comfortable home, the children adored Oak, and even old Bracken seemed to be thawing toward him.

"*I* will require that I marry you. No offspring of mine will suffer the needless stigma of illegitimacy, and I would never leave you to raise yet another child on your own."

That was a stirring declaration... of *duty*, and some of Vera's hopes for the evening deflated. She wanted this liaison with Oak to be more than a tawdry tumble, and perhaps it was, but the unromantic realities were intruding anyway.

A forced marriage was nothing to look forward to.

"I am not likely to conceive this soon after my courses. When Alexander was born, the midwife had a very blunt conversation with me and an equally blunt conversation with Dirk." Vera eased away enough to untie Oak's cravat. "I suspect my mother, had she survived, would have had those discussions with me prior to my wedding."

She slid the cloth from around his neck and began unbuttoning his waistcoat. She'd been Dirk's valet, and he her lady's maid, as was typical of couples of modest station. Those marital courtesies had never taken on sexual overtones.

The sight of Oak in her bedroom after dark, the warmth of his body heat beneath Vera's palm, felt anything but courteous.

"Don't stop," he said. "I'm not shy."

She knew that about him, knew him to be entirely comfortable in his own skin. "I *am* shy, you daft man. Dirk liked that about me. I do not like it about myself."

And why was Dirk's ghost choosing now to haunt her? To make every word spoken and gesture exchanged a comparison with a mostly happy marriage fading into obscure memory?

"You are modest," Oak said, drawing a pin from her hair. "You are not shy, any more than lavender is the same shade as pink. They are both soft, lovely colors, but quite distinct." He held the pin up, so the firelight caught the gleam of onyx, then slipped the pin into his pocket. "Let me take down your hair."

Vera settled on the stool before her vanity, glad that Oak was for once not being so polite. He'd brushed out her hair several times previously, but tonight he stopped halfway through the job and pressed his lips to her nape.

"The scent of you here is like a winter sunset, brilliant hues that portend approaching night."

She shivered, though Oak's hands on her shoulders were warm. Her hair was half up and half down, and the mirror reflected a wanton creature who bore no resemblance to a staid widow.

The luminous, exotic woman in the mirror frightened Vera a little, and intrigued her too.

Oak gathered a skein of her hair and tipped her head back—she watched him do that in the mirror, watched his hand wrap itself in her hair. He commenced a voluptuous spree of kissing that included her mouth, her eyelids, her brow, her throat, and the ticklish place below her ear.

At some point in the midst of this bouquet of kisses, he slid a hand between her dressing gown and her nightgown and palmed her breast. That single caress, and the gentle pressure to her nipple that followed it, sent sensation rampaging through her.

When Oak desisted, Vera leaned against the hard column of his thigh, her heart thumping, her body abuzz while he stroked her hair.

So this is desire. This roaring bodily need, this desperate yearning of the heart. Vera had desired her husband, but not like this. God in heaven, *not like this.*

And this was Oak Dorning too. The polite sketcher of domestic scenes was nowhere to be found, replaced by the artist rendering uncompromising truth with a storm of color and passion. The artist lurked behind the gentleman's fine tailoring and exquisite manners most of the time, but the artist would join Vera in her bed, and she rejoiced to meet him there.

"I need a braid," she managed, drawing her unbound hair over her shoulder. "My hair becomes a disaster without a braid."

Oak backed away from the vanity, and Vera felt as if her every prop and stay had been taken from her. Simply sitting on a padded stool took effort as she watched Oak shrug from his jacket and waistcoat, then undo his cuffs and pull his shirt over his head.

"Lock the door, Vera. I locked the parlor door, but the bedroom door should be locked too."

"Finish undressing. Then I'll lock the door." For she refused to miss a moment of his unveiling.

He braced his hips against the clothes press and pulled off his boots and stockings. Vera had never envied her husband his ability to paint, but oh, she longed to capture the image of Oak clad in only his breeches. His musculature was as heroic as any Canova masterpiece, from tanned arms to flat belly and all across a chest sprinkled with dark hair.

He stood and looked right at her as he undid the buttons of his breeches, then he let the flap of fabric fall open as it was designed to do.

He was aroused now. He was gloriously, unabashedly aroused. The male endowments Vera had seen on Greek statues and painted in the classical nudes hadn't a hint of the grandeur of Oak Dorning possessed in anticipation of lovemaking.

He let her stare, then stepped out of his breeches and draped them on the clothes press. He walked past Vera to flick the lock on the bedroom door, then extended a hand to her.

"You are overdressed for the occasion, Verity."

"You want me *naked?*"

"Do I *ever.*"

But I always wore my nightgown with Dirk. She kept that inanity behind her teeth. Dirk was dead and gone. For the first time since losing him, she could regard his death as not entirely a sorrow. He'd had a fine life, made great art, and had many friends. She'd been lucky to be his wife.

But her life had *not* ended with his passing. Not nearly.

Oak watched her, his smile patient, as if he knew exactly what he asked of her.

"Braid my hair, please," she said. "Then you will assist me to disrobe." Never before had she given orders in the bedroom, though why not? Why not state what she needed and desired, the better to see those needs met?

Oak made short work of tidying up her hair, and then she was standing beside the bed as he unbelted her dressing gown and drew it from her shoulders.

"The nightgown, too, Vera. I wouldn't want it to get torn."

"Torn?"

He gathered up the two sides of her décolletage in his fists. "Rent asunder and flung who knows where."

Like my wits. "No tearing needed. Would you see to the candles?"

"Soon." He hung the dressing gown over its customary hook on the bedpost. "I want to *see* you. I want to know the shade of your breasts by firelight—rose alabaster, perhaps. I want to see the curve of your hip and learn the exact line of your belly as it flows down to your mons. I want to know if your second toe is longer than the first and which hip is higher."

"You are *not* painting me."

He undid the bow holding her nightgown gathered at her décolletage. "And you are *not* the blushing maid of the shires, if you ever were."

She studied him for a long moment, seeing in his eyes both desire and a challenge. "I am not the blushing maid of the shires, and I am not a coward either." She drew the nightgown over her head, threw it at him, and stood before him, allowing him to inspect her more closely than she'd ever inspected herself.

~

OAK'S BODY knew exactly what the next steps should be.

He should toss Vera onto the bed—gently, of course—then fall upon her in a mad passion and thrust his way to glory. Recent self-indulgence meant he probably had enough restraint to ensure Vera traveled with him on that lovely road.

Probably wasn't good enough. Not for the goddess standing before him, as naked as she'd arrived into the world. As the past week had rolled along, Oak had gradually come to appreciate what taking a lover would mean to Vera, how it would mark a turning point in the progression from wife, to widow, to an independence few women ever negotiated.

She was, in essence, leaving home, as Oak had left home. When she'd tossed her nightgown at him, she'd tossed him a challenge: *Be worthy of my courage, for you'll not have an opportunity like this again.*

"Never," he said, "has the need to sketch so thoroughly challenged the desire to copulate." Vera was sturdy, as countrywomen were sturdy, with defined musculature on her legs and arms. But ye gods, she was also curved. Her hips flared generously from her waist, and her belly wasn't quite flat, but rather echoed the contours of Renaissance nudes. Her breasts were full and pale, and indeed, rose alabaster would have done them justice.

The whole of her was lovely, and Oak had the ungallant thought that if Dirk Channing hadn't painted his wife nude, Channing had been an idiot.

"What?" she said, chin coming up.

Oak draped her nightgown across the foot of the bed. "You kept your nightgown on when you slept with your husband?"

"I did, and he blew out the candles."

Oak took a step closer. "You asked him for those sops to modesty?"

"No. If he'd expected differently of me, I would have accommodated him. He was my husband."

"He was a fool," Oak said, sending up a prayer that Channing was at least resting in peace. "My guess is, he was self-conscious about his own less than youthful appearance by the time you came along. He pretended to defer to your nonexistent maidenly vapors rather than risk coming up short before his lovely wife."

"He was proud. Most men are."

Oak was ready to have done with any mention of the late, great, *vain* Dirk Channing. "You loved him. You did not care if he was a picture of manly vigor. You wanted only to please him and build a life with him. He could have held you through the night, skin to skin, but instead—nightgowns and nightshirts. He was a brilliant artist, and he was an idiot."

For an older husband to yield to the limitations of vanity was understandable. Male sexual prowess did not fare well in close proximity to self-consciousness. For an artist to deny himself the sheer beauty of Vera unclad, though, was harder to understand.

Oak didn't bother trying. Not now. He turned Vera by the arm so the firelight illuminated the long lines of her legs, the exquisite geometry of her back, the delectable swell of her derriere.

"She maketh me to rejoice in my soul," Oak murmured, misquoting some old line of poetry. He could gawk at her until the sun rose and sketch her naked form until the shire was blanketed in snow. But he could make love with her for the rest of his life. "Shall we to bed, Verity Channing?"

"I liked sleeping with you," she said, climbing the step beside the bed. "I look forward to sleeping with you again. Should we have warmed the covers?"

"We'll warm them well enough." Oak banked the fire, extracted a handkerchief from his coat pocket, and blew out all the candles save one that he left burning on the bedside table. The moment to join Vera under the covers had arrived, and yet, Oak hesitated.

"Why me, Vera? I assume various friends of Dirk's have called upon you. The neighborhood probably has its share of merry widowers. Why me?"

She held up the blankets, and Oak took the place beside her. His arm went around her shoulders, she tucked up against his side, and the fit was so sweet and right, they might as well have been a married couple years past their vows.

"Because you are who you are."

What did that mean? Vera's hand drifted across his belly, and

Oak lost track of the question. "Touch me, please. However you like, wherever you like."

She wrapped her fingers around his shaft. "Here?"

"A fine place to start." And—if he didn't get himself under control —also a place to finish.

The demented woman made a study of him, mapping his every male attribute with hands and fingers, and a few locations with her lips too. She was relentless in her curiosity, and as Oak battled to keep his desire in check, he realized yet again that he was becoming the lover of a woman of considerable courage.

Dirk Channing had put his pretty young wife on a domestic pedestal and promptly forgotten not that she was a woman—they'd had a child, after all—but that she was a *person*. A person with needs, with a vigorous intellect and a vivid imagination. A person full of curiosity and passion, full of dreams and hopes, and exceptionally bold caresses, given half an opportunity to indulge them.

And heavens above, *her tongue*. "Vera, if you keep that up, I will not be *able* to answer for the consequences, because I'll be a panting heap of mortified, wilting male."

"You'll spend?" She eased away from her mischief and lay back down beside him.

"I will spend."

She cuddled up, her fingers trailing idly across his nipples. "Am I too bold?"

He hated the uncertainty behind the question and loved the trust it embodied. "No, love. I am too frail. Kiss me so I can kiss you back." He wrestled her over him, ready to seek happy revenge for her earlier explorations.

Vera looked about, as if surprised to find herself atop a naked male, then she pulled the covers up and folded down over him. The kissing progressed from sweet, to playful, to passionate, and all the while, Oak let his hands wander over feminine perfection.

Without Oak planning the moment, Vera slipped her body over his cock and went still.

"I didn't—" She mashed her nose against his shoulder. "I wasn't, that is, I hadn't intended... I want you so."

"Hush." He stroked her hair. "You should have what you desire. I want only to please you."

That simple truth seemed to be what she needed to hear. The mood shifted from the slightly awkward erotic teasing of new lovers to a profound, unlooked-for intimacy. Vera moved slowly, and Oak let her set the pace.

When she raised up on her arms, he kept his eyes closed rather than allow himself the visual provocation of her breasts. She sped up, and he vowed to expire of unsatisfied passion before he took control of the timing from her.

Eternities passed during the next few seconds, while Oak grasped the spindles of the headboard in a desperate grip, and the bed ropes creaked in a soft rhythm.

He had formed the thought, *She needs me to make this happen...* When Vera abruptly came at him like a female tempest battering herself against the Channel cliffs. She bucked, she rocked, she flailed, and quite thoroughly *pounded* him, until Oak was blasted free of his self-restraint and cast loose upon the gale.

The result was the most disorientingly thorough pleasure he'd ever known. He clung to Vera and she to him, fused by passion and wonder, then fused by the sheer inability to move.

And why would he want to move, when bliss itself defined him? Vera's heart thumped against his as she sprawled on his chest. Her braid was an itchy rope against his neck, and his balls were humming, a peculiar novelty.

Vera moved enough to extricate her braid from between them. "I have no words."

That was all right, then, if she had no words too. "Rest," Oak said. "We've earned it."

"Handkerchief," she muttered, reaching to the nightstand.

Oak gave the nipple hovering above his mouth a friendly nip. "I did not do justice to your breasts. Remiss of me. I promise to remedy the oversight."

He sounded and felt drunk. All out to sea on long overdue satisfaction and something else, something dangerously tender and unique to Vera.

She lifted her hips, and he slid free of her body, even that small, sweet friction causing a surfeit of sensation. She tucked his handkerchief between her legs—lucky handkerchief—then flopped to the mattress beside him.

"Come here, you." He got an arm under her neck and drew her against his side.

Vera was soon breathing in a soft, relaxed rhythm, while Oak lay awake, the fog of pleasure gradually lifting to reveal a landscape as beautiful as it was unfamiliar. Tenderness toward Vera bathed him in light, while the mocking voice of common sense painted jagged peaks on the near horizon.

What fool had spoken to Vera of an intimate friendship? What fool had thought he could romp with this woman and go whistling off to London with his heart whole?

Oak drifted off to sleep, wrapped around his lover, not an answer in sight.

~

"CATHERINE IS QUITE TAKEN with Mr. Dorning," Miss Diggory said. "That distraction aside, she continues to make progress with all of her subjects. She is particularly adept at mathematics and might benefit from time spent with Mr. Forester."

Vera met with Miss Diggory once a week to discuss Catherine's studies, though the reports had taken on a sameness.

"If Catherine is excelling so consistently, might she be in need of a more challenging curriculum?" Vera asked.

Miss Diggory poured herself another cup of tea, which was a bit presuming, though only a bit. "She's at a difficult age, Mrs. Channing. The purpose of her studies now is to keep her from boredom, for a bored young lady finds trouble. She can read, write, and sketch. She has parlor French and some basic geography and natural science. Even those subjects aren't the usual for a girl in her position, but she does well in them, so I continue to provide her material beyond what she needs."

Who was Tamsin Diggory to say what a young woman in *Catherine's position* needed? Richard Longacre had recommended Tamsin personally, and she was an agreeable addition to the household. That did not mean her judgment was flawless.

"I am contemplating sending Catherine off to school," Vera said. "She has sufficient intellect to fare well academically in such a setting, and she's—"

Miss Diggory was shaking her head. "I went off to school, Mrs. Channing, while—if I may be blunt—you apparently did not. That is the last experience you want to inflict on your step-daughter."

"You are confident in this opinion. Why?"

"Because young girls left to their own devices are a petty, nasty lot. Catherine's lack of breeding would be thrown in her face at every turn. Even the instructors would make passing references to it, and her life would be a misery. I saw this with my own eyes, time and time again. She belongs here, with you, with the neighbors who've known her since birth. Trust me on this."

A month ago, Vera would have been glad to have such firm guidance. She'd had the benefit of Oak Dorning's companionship, though, and last night she and he had become lovers. The person she'd always known herself to be would not have taken a lover, and yet, she had, and she was glad of it.

She'd risen from her bed and donned familiar half-mourning, but in her heart little of mourning remained.

Not today, anyway. "Catherine will face censure her entire life because her parents weren't married," Vera said. "I cannot protect her from such mean-spiritedness much longer, and you are right: If she grows bored here, she'll get up to mischief. Tom-Treeble-mischief, possibly."

Miss Diggory wrapped a pair of tea cakes in a table napkin and slipped them into her pocket. "Perhaps Tom Treeble—in a few years —will be more of a solution than a problem. Find her a lad with some acres, and she'll be happy enough."

"Miss Diggory, I hope you aren't pilfering tea cakes when Catherine is on hand."

Tamsin looked up, her expression not that of a governess found in a slight misstep, but of a naughty schoolgirl who'd broken a rule and resented being caught. The mulishness was fleeting and out of character, but Vera trusted the evidence of her eyes.

Now—after waking up in Oak Dorning's arms, after hearing him describe her hair as a blend of mahogany, garnet, ironwood, night, and gold—she could not discount what she'd seen. Oak claimed to sketch what he saw. Vera lacked that skill, but she could do a better job of seeing what was before her eyes.

"I'm sorry," Miss Diggory replied. "I thought Catherine might appreciate a treat. She and Mr. Dorning ramble all over the property looking for subjects, though if you ask me, he ought to be sitting her down before a proper easel and helping her refine her skill with watercolors."

Catherine's first set of watercolor brushes had been put in her chubby little hands at the age of three, according to Dirk. Oak claimed she was ready for oils.

"Because Mr. Dorning's skill as an artist eclipses that of the rest of the household put together, I will trust his judgment regarding Catherine's instruction with paints. Please don't mention a finishing school to Catherine. It's not a plan I'd act on anytime soon, but it's one I'd like you to keep in mind."

Miss Diggory took another tea cake onto her saucer. "If you think she needs a challenge, perhaps Mr. Forester could supervise her education in mathematics. It's not as if instructing one six-year-old boy fills his day, and Catherine has a natural aptitude for the subject matter."

"You don't enjoy maths?"

She shuddered. "A lot of squiggling and scribbling, numbers everywhere. If a girl has enough math to not be cheated in the shops, she has enough math."

You sound like my step-mother. That insight popped into Vera's head, the solution to a riddle. Tamsin Diggory was pleasant, soft-spoken, good-humored, and she came well-recommended. Catherine got on well enough with her.

Vera had been slow to warm to Miss Diggory, attributing that reticence to the fact that the household hadn't had a proper governess before. Old Mrs. Tansbury had been a glorified nursery maid who'd loved books and children. The truth was, Tamsin and Jeremy shared a faint streak of insolence, and that was not a quality Vera wanted her children emulating.

"I'll have the kitchen send a tray up for Catherine when she returns from her art lesson," Vera said. "And as always, I thank you for your efforts to educate her. I do believe she'll need a professional drawing master, though."

"And is the handsome Mr. Dorning applying for that post? He's pleasant company at the card table, and I think Mr. Forester enjoys having another fellow at supper."

"Mr. Dorning will soon be leaving for London. His assessment of Catherine's abilities is both informed and disinterested." Not quite true. Oak clearly liked Catherine and enjoyed teaching her. He was equally well disposed toward Alexander, which did not seem to characterize Jeremy's attitude toward his sole charge.

"Will you be sorry to see Mr. Dorning go?" Miss Diggory watched Vera over the rim of her tea cup as she posed the question.

Vera's first reaction to that query was horror, for Miss Diggory's tone implied that she knew exactly who had been in Vera's bed for most of the night. Except *nobody* knew. Oak had been discreet, as he would always be when a woman's reputation was at stake. He'd not come to Vera until the footmen were all abed, and he'd left for his own quarters before the maids had stirred.

So Tamsin Diggory was speculating, or insinuating, or trying to start mischief. The conclusion was disappointing, suggesting that one of the mean girls at Tamsin's finishing school had been Tamsin herself.

And this was the person with whom Catherine spent most of her waking hours? Perhaps Richard Longacre wasn't as good a judge of people as Vera had hoped.

"I will miss Mr. Dorning when he leaves," Vera said, "as we all will. You are correct that he's good company. He's also a perfect gentleman toward Catherine, a good influence on both Mr. Forester and Alexander, and he makes you smile over a hand of piquet. I'm very much indebted to your uncle for recommending him."

"Uncle Richard recommended him? I suppose that makes sense." Miss Diggory rose without being excused. "I'll return to the schoolroom and look for some French poetry Catherine might enjoy. If you're giving Mr. Forester charge of her mathematics lessons, please let him know. I would rather be spared his grumbling when he's asked to take on that responsibility."

Vera hadn't made that decision, nor would she be manipulated into it. Bad enough if Catherine was developing a girlish tendresse for Oak, worse yet if she turned her nascent wiles on Jeremy.

"Miss Diggory?"

She paused by the door. "Ma'am?"

"Your grumbling is no more attractive than Jeremy's. You are paid a generous wage to look after one reasonably pleasant young woman who deserves every advantage in life I can give her. I will instruct Mr. Forester to take on Catherine's math curriculum, but I expect you to help her with it."

Miss Diggory's expression became a blank mask. "Yes, ma'am. Of course, ma'am." She curtseyed and lifted the door latch. "Oh, I did have one question, if I might ask it?"

"Of course."

"I went searching for a penknife the other day and thought I might find one in Mr. Dorning's studio. Did you know he keeps those chambers locked unless he's working there?"

"Of course he does. Some of the pigments needed to render a subject in oils are dangerously toxic. Mr. Channing was adamant that any room used as a painter's studio, whether his own or a guest's, be kept locked when not in use. Mr. Dorning is exercising the basic prudence I expect of any household member."

This was a fabrication, or an improvisation, more like. White pigments, some of which were lead-based, were powerfully toxic. Dirk had kept his pigments locked up, but never his studio, for who would have dared intrude on that holy ground uninvited?

Miss Diggory dipped a hint of a curtsey and withdrew, leaving Vera to sip cold tea and ponder the exchange. Tamsin had developed a curious inability to keep track of her penknives. Her understanding of mathematics apparently bordered on rudimentary, and she wasn't able to provide Catherine a curriculum that challenged her in any subject.

Bracken came in to clear the tray a moment later.

Vera was tempted to ask him what he thought of Miss Diggory—and Mr. Forester, for that matter—but Bracken's immense dignity prevented such informality. She would instead ask Oak for his opinion, and he would give it.

That too, was a shift Vera could lay at his handsome feet. She took greater notice of her surroundings thanks to Oak Dorning's observant company, and she considered ideas that Dirk Channing's meek, devoted helpmeet would not have entertained.

Perhaps Tamsin Diggory had been a poor choice. Perhaps Jeremy Forester wasn't the ideal tutor for Alexander. Perhaps Richard Longacre was a fine source of artistic guidance, but not as knowledgeable when it came to finding staff for a nursery.

He'd been a friend to Dirk and to Vera, but she honestly did not know Longacre all that well.

What she did know was that she'd miss Oak Dorning sorely for the rest of her quiet, rusticating widowhood.

~

"OAK WANTS the traveling coach sent up to Hampshire." Valerian announced that development as if Oak had requisitioned every fungible asset Dorning Hall possessed. "He's now trafficking in art, purveying the widow's castoffs. He sent me a sketch of her."

Grey watched Valerian, the Dorning sibling with stores of self-possession equal to any social challenge, the king's man, the consummate solver of human conundrums. Valerian paced the carpet in Beatitude's private parlor like a mare in anticipation of foaling.

"He sent me a sketch of the Channings as well," Grey said, sanding the letter he'd just finished. "The little fellow stood on one side of his mama, the girl on the other. Quite charming."

Valerian halted before Grey's desk. "You describe a family portrait, Casriel. It needs only the addition of a doting step-papa to be complete."

Beatitude had come to the same conclusion, though the prospect of Oak as a husband and step-father had not distressed her as it was clearly distressing Valerian.

Valerian tossed himself into the chair opposite the desk. "We did not send Oak to Hampshire to become some widow's..."

"Plaything? I have never been a plaything, myself, but Oak is unattached, in full possession of his wits and his health, and embarking on a career in the arts. Plaything-ing might go with that territory."

"That is distasteful."

"The lady is Dirk Channing's widow. A connection with her would stand Oak in good stead."

"Who is Dirk—? Wasn't Channing the battle-scene painter? He romanticized the Irish uprising and made the Americans look brave. How did you come upon this information?"

"The same way I come upon most information pertinent to my own siblings—through Beatitude's good offices."

Valerian scowled. "Her ladyship's in-law's cousin's neighbor's parson's wife has been spying?"

"What a vulgar choice of word, Valerian. My countess is conscientious in her correspondence, and she wanted to chase down the rumors of untoward doings at Merlin Hall."

Valerian shoved to his feet. "What sort of name is that for a country manor, and what sort of untoward doings?"

"As it happens, the rumors are quite old, having nothing to do with the present Mrs. Channing. The previous lady of the manor was more in the nature of a concubine whom Dirk Channing regarded as his muse. She either would not or could not marry Channing, and the girl in Oak's family portrait is the fruit of that irregular union."

Valerian moved to the window, gazing out on a rainy morning trying to turn up sunny. Oak loved rain because it did interesting things to light. He'd walk around out in the rain, intermittently gazing straight up at the sky and sketching in pencil.

Who would have thought a brother exhibiting such daft behavior would be missed every single time Dorset's weather turned rainy—and often when it didn't?

"The widow is raising her husband's by-blow?" Valerian asked.

"Apparently so, and Oak described the relationship as loving."

Valerian lowered himself to the window seat. "We must like her for that, mustn't we?"

"Afraid so."

"Oak will like her for that. What else do we know of her?"

"She's the daughter of a wealthy squire, country born and bred, never made a come out. Hasn't any use for London Society and is quite, quite pretty."

Valerian pulled a folded paper from an inside coat pocket and studied the bottom half of the page. A red wax stain made a half circle across the top of the paper, suggesting a letter from Oak.

"He doesn't sketch her as pretty," Valerian said, brows knitting.

"He sketches her as *lovely*. You can't tell from these drawings which is the step-child. That will matter to Oak."

It mattered to Grey, whose daughter Tabitha called Beatitude Mama, though they were no blood relation. "He sketches Mrs. Channing as *loving*."

Valerian put the letter back in his pocket. "Oak draws what he sees, to hear him tell it, but Emily says there's a difference between a portrait and a likeness. Oak usually draws a very accurate likeness."

"Probably the result of all the botanical work he did for Papa."

Valerian was on his feet again. "No, it's the other way 'round. The botanical sketches were accurate because Oak drew them. Now he's making little portraits on his letters, *portraying* rather than copying onto paper what he sees with his eyes. This is serious."

"Oak is overdue for a serious encounter." Beatitude had made that suggestion. Grey hadn't wanted to hear it.

"Oak cannot afford a serious encounter with this woman, Grey. She's a widow, and they are a canny lot, but how can she have missed that he's determined to take his place in London, while she apparently wants nothing to do with Town?"

Grey dumped the sand from his letter back into the tray in the corner of his blotter. "Sometimes, the person who seems out of reach is the very person we're meant to hold most closely in our hearts."

"You refer to my dearest Emily. She was more than out of reach. She was beyond my dreams."

"No, she wasn't. I refer to Beatitude. I was determined to marry money, she hadn't any to speak of, and yet, I could not imagine sharing my life with any woman except her. I had confused money and wealth. I wanted money, I needed wealth."

"Wealth, Casriel? We're still notably without means, as titled families go."

"Our circumstances are improving, but even without means, we are wealthy in the things that matter. We are respected, we are healthy, we are more or less in charity with one another, except for Sycamore, who glories in the role of sibling *provocateur*. We are finding the spouses we are meant to share our lives with. The only thing we lack, at least as far as our bachelor brothers are concerned, is common sense."

"Oak is very sensible. He simply keeps most of his conclusions to himself."

Grey folded the letter he'd written and used a spill from the jar on the mantel to carry a flame from the hearth to the wax jack.

"Is that a letter to Oak?" Valerian asked as the wax dripped onto the paper.

"It is."

"You are letting him know the traveling coach will be along directly?"

Grey blew out the taper, leaving a hint of smoke and beeswax on the air. "Alas, no. Beatitude has requisitioned the coach to do some shopping in Dorchester—or she's about to. I am helpless to deny her, so Oak must apply to Sycamore for the use of his traveling coach."

"You'll leave Oak stranded in the wilds of Hampshire?"

"For as long as possible."

"Devious," Valerian said as Grey pressed the family seal into the warm wax. "I like it."

~

IN DORSET, Oak had lived with a growing sense of frustration. His dreams had all pointed to London—success as a portraitist was possible only in London—though he'd lacked a plan for getting there.

Then Casriel had gone up to Town in search of a countess and come home matched with his heart's desire. Willow had found his dear Susannah in London. Sycamore was thriving in London, and Ash appeared to have found a way to support himself in the capital as Sycamore's conscience and business associate.

Oak had concluded that the first step in any plan to succeed in London had been to simply *go to London*. From Winchester, he could travel to the capital in a long day, if the roads were dry and the post chaise teams sound. He told himself regularly that he should set a departure date, pack up Vera's attic paintings, and be on his way.

Pursue the dream he'd cherished since boyhood.

In London.

Noisy, stinking London, where Verity had no desire to be, ever.

He'd tried to explore why she was so averse to the metropolis, but the conversation was invariably waylaid by desire. Somebody started kissing somebody else, hands grew busy and inventive, and doors were locked. For the past week, Oak had been sharing Verity's bed for the most of every night, though she occupied his thoughts nigh constantly.

And here he was again, sauntering into her bedroom at the end of the day, helpless to waste what little time they had left together.

"How does Alexander seem to you?" Vera asked, untying his cravat.

"He seems like Alexander. Serious, shy, intelligent, and unusually complicated for such a little fellow." He put Oak in mind of himself as a boy, in fact. "Why do you begrudge me the pleasure of undressing you, Verity Channing? By the time I join you of late, you are in your nightgown and dressing gown. I am denied the experience of unbuttoning, unlacing, and unwrapping you."

And he wanted that experience, wanted to look forward to it at the end of every day.

Her hands paused. "And I never start my day with the sight of you as you don your finery. Never hear you using your toothpowder behind the privacy screen, never see you making the odd faces men make when they shave. I will never see you at your bath, never ambush you some rainy morning as you lounge about in a banyan and pajama trousers."

She drew the jacket from his shoulders and hung it over the back of her reading chair. When she would have unbuttoned his waistcoat, Oak caught her hands.

"Come to London with me."

She shook free of his grasp and started on his buttons. "And live with you in an unsanctioned union? How would that reflect on my children, Oak? How would that reflect on me?"

"I didn't mean—" What *had* he meant? "You could stay at my brother's town house. I can have Will or Grey or Valerian come up to Town. A sister-in-law or two will make your visit plausible, and I'll stay with Sycamore and Ash if I can't find my own quarters. Nothing unsanctioned about it."

Though his brothers would think he'd run mad, and they'd be half right. Oak wasn't traveling all the way to London to once again be the butt of fraternal humor.

Vera finished unbuttoning his waistcoat and started on his shirt. "Assuming your siblings are willing to drop everything, travel to London, and idle about Mayfair while I find excuses to tryst with you, what then? I have no real friends in London, you must pursue your aspirations, and I am responsible for this property. Harvest does not happen without management on hand, Oak. Alexander and Catherine need a mother, and as to that, I'm not sure Miss Diggory and Mr. Forester are the best staff I can find for my nursery."

"Neither am I."

Vera drew off his waistcoat and hung it over his jacket. "Why do you say that?"

"Because they are involved in a not-discreet-enough liaison, not mere stolen kisses. I nearly walked in on them canoodling in the guest room across from my studio." He held out his hand, and Vera removed a sleeve button from his cuff. "I thought a cat had got stuck behind a closed door, but no cat makes that sort of thumping and groaning."

She undid the second sleeve button. "Dear heavens. I want to scold them, but..."

But Oak was involved in a fair amount of thumping and groaning with Vera, and the two situations weren't that different. That admission made Oak want to kick heavy furniture and paint battle scenes.

"I don't begrudge anybody shared pleasure with another willing adult," Oak said, "but the business requires discretion."

Vera put his sleeve buttons on the clothes press. "Something like that. I've asked Mr. Forester to tutor Catherine in mathematics. If he's blatantly accosting Miss Diggory, I'm less comfortable with that arrangement. Am I being ridiculous?"

Vera appeared more confident in the role of lady of the manor than she truly felt. Oak had come to this realization only gradually, as their late-night visits shifted from an immediate, mutual devouring, to this cozy domesticity followed by mutual devouring.

"Miss Diggory might be doing some of the accosting," Oak said. "For Forester's sake, I hope she is. The issue isn't that they enjoy each other's company, it's that I've become aware of it."

He tugged off one boot then the other, and Vera set them at the foot of the bed. His stockings came next, but he kept his breeches on and took a seat in the reading chair.

"Alexander does not like to return to the schoolroom," Oak said, patting his knee.

Vera cuddled into his lap without further prompting. The weight of her, the feel of her in his arms, settled some unrest that talk of canoodling and skulking had agitated.

"I see that," she said. "I watch him pelting across the garden at the beginning of his outings with you, then see him trudging back to the house an hour later. He becomes a different child, and yet, Mr. Forester says he's making progress."

"Shall I question Alexander about his studies?" Oak asked, stroking Vera's back.

"Please. I have already become that great superfluity in a boy's life, his mother."

Oak kissed her cheek. "You are not superfluous to him or to me. I'll have a word with him and report back. Is the vicar coming to luncheon tomorrow?"

They chatted about the local parson and his wife, about Catherine's talent, about what sort of puppy Alexander might like. All the while, Oak was aware of a pleasant, humming arousal, a quiet joy to be ending the day yet again with a woman he esteemed and desired.

The closeness Vera offered him in these domestic discussions called to him, every bit as much as the intimate pleasure did.

And that was.... That was lovely, though why in the bloody hell did these delights have to be mere passing pleasures?

Rather than dwell on that frustrating topic, Oak introduced Vera to the experience of sex against a sturdy wall, sex on all fours, and then—what desperation had come over him?—sex in a reading chair.

CHAPTER TEN

Vera lay in Oak's arms, torn between the peace that follows passionate lovemaking and the turmoil that had been growing since she'd first kissed him. Oak offered her an intimate friendship, and for a man intent on the worldly sophistication of London, perhaps that was an offer easily made, a bargain cheerfully kept.

For Vera... inventive lovemaking was only a small piece of what Oak's version of friendship yielded her. He was attentive to the children, kind, and patient; he brought a level of learning and graciousness to conversation at meals; he made a fine impression on Vera's neighbors. He was affectionate—ye saints and angels, was he affectionate—and Vera had missed the profound pleasure of an undemanding, caring touch.

"I can hear your thoughts," he said, his fingers trailing over her arm. "You are already up and about, taking the day by storm."

The cool, sweet notes of a mistle thrush's song warned of approaching dawn. Vera wanted to close and lock the window, climb back in bed, and pull a pillow over her head.

"You give me much to think about."

He slipped an arm around her waist. "Happy thoughts, I hope."

Well, no. Not exactly. She would not burden him with foolish entreaties to stay on at Merlin Hall, but she could share with him other thoughts.

"Those paintings you found, of Anna and the other women, they explain some of the behavior Dirk's friends exhibited toward me."

"Bad behavior."

"Dirk told me not to read too much into harmless banter. The fact that they reserved their overtures for when Dirk was absent suggested much of it was disrespectful."

"They treated you the way a fool treats any woman who takes off her clothes for money, and they assumed that you—like Anna— were of that ilk." Oak rolled to his back. "I was fortunate to have Stebbins Holmes as teacher for my live-model classes. He tolerated no crudeness toward the models, no vulgar jokes. If a woman was willing to disrobe for a young man's edification, her generosity was to be respectfully appreciated, or old Stebby sent the miscreant packing."

"You never drew live male models?"

"Less frequently, as every male artist has his own form to study, doesn't he? Why didn't you insist Dirk put his foot down when his friends overstepped?"

Vera remained on her side, facing the window, her back ranged along Oak's warmth. She loved the pleasure of lying close like this, but she also preferred not to have Oak watching her face in the predawn gloom. He saw much, sometimes too much.

"I did not know if they were overstepping, Oak. My brothers were often ribald, but not if they knew I could overhear them. Perhaps standards for wives were different, I reasoned, or perhaps standards for artists' wives were different. Perhaps a bumpkin such as I ought not to be so prudish. I learned to avoid our guests once the brandy started flowing and to stay off the back stairs if I was alone."

"And you are still avoiding Dirk's friends. Is this why you've tucked yourself away in the countryside, because you dread the company you might encounter in London?"

Another bird joined the first, a robin perhaps, given the more pedestrian nature of its song.

"I've been to London, Oak. The stench alone should drive people away. Beggars everywhere, maimed soldiers among them. Prostitutes exhibit their wares right outside the theaters. Children go hungry while fine coaches nearly run them down in the street. Even if Dirk's London friends hadn't propositioned me and tried to make free with their hands, I would dislike London."

Some change came over Oak. Vera could not see it, but she sensed it.

"They *touched* you?"

"They touched me, some of them with blatant impropriety that I was to regard as a friendly compliment. One of them lay in wait for me in the attic, and that was a very near thing. I wasn't to mind being groped and patted when it was *all in good fun.*" Vera forgot who'd used that term. Some fawning acolyte of Dirk's who'd been genuinely surprised when she'd slapped him. "Others asked me to model for them, and they meant model in the nude. They intimated that Dirk wouldn't mind, that Anna had happily dropped her clothing for anybody with a notion to sketch her thus."

Oak was listening. Of that much, Vera was certain.

"I'm sorry," he said. "I am profoundly sorry, and I apologize on behalf of every man who so egregiously mistreated you."

The apology was sincere, and yet, it did not help with the anger these memories engendered—anger at the presuming louts, at Dirk and Anna, and at Vera herself.

"I gather Dirk's relationship with Anna was far more mutually permissive than anything I could have imagined when I married him. I didn't like that he would treat any woman that way. Didn't like the idea that Anna was property that could be shared around. Anna apparently thrived under Dirk's roof. She was a free spirit; I am a squire's daughter. I wanted domesticity, peace, and calm, and I concluded Dirk wanted that of me too. When he married me, he was no longer a young man gleefully shocking the world with his talent and his radical notions."

Vera faced the approaching day, angry at the dawn itself. That tears should well now surprised her. This was old business, long since grieved and put aside.

Oak sat up, his back against the headboard. "Vera, for the love of God, Dirk had a *daughter* to think of. What was Catherine to conclude about men who importuned her mother, about a father who regarded such behavior as harmless diversion?"

"Catherine was doubtless kept in the nursery, away from all the late-night mischief. Mrs. Tansbury was devoted to her."

Oak climbed off the far side of the bed. "The girl was seven when her mother died. Seven-year-olds overhear servants, they peer out of windows, they lurk in conservatories and trees and follies. If Catherine is reluctant to trust you, perhaps that's because her own mother wasn't much of a mother to her, nor Dirk much of a father."

He came around to Vera's side of the bed and crouched so he was at her eye level. "Why are summer nights so short?" he asked, smoothing back her hair. "When I'm with you, there are never enough hours. This is a topic that wants more discussion, and yet, I must away to my own room."

If he saw her tears, he was politely ignoring them.

"We will talk more later. I believe I'll start my day with a soaking bath."

He brushed his fingers over her brow, tucking a loose lock of hair behind her ear. "I've made you sore. Bad of me. I do apologize."

Vera *was* a trifle sore in intimate locations. That wasn't why she wanted an excuse to linger in her bed rather than impersonate a cheerful woman at breakfast.

"You'll be leaving for London soon, won't you?"

Oak rose and appropriated Vera's dressing gown, though it barely reached his calves. "I've done what I can with the older paintings, and they will earn you some coin. The nudes... I recognize the blond model, Vera. Hannah Stoltzfus still takes an occasional sitting and runs a political salon on Tuesday evenings. My brother Sycamore is among her acquaintances."

Vera sat up. "Is that a euphemism for something more intimate?"

Oak brought her nightgown to her. "With Sycamore, one is better off not asking. He will reply with more honesty than any brother deserves, and he'll do it in public. My point is, Miss Stoltzfus is semi-respectable. She could display at least two of the nudes without any negative reflection upon you, Dirk, or Catherine. She could sell them for you."

Vera rose and regarded the messy bed. After Oak left, she'd inspect the sheets and pillows for dark hairs and open more windows to air the room. She'd wash out the handkerchief crumpled on the bedside table and otherwise erase any evidence of Oak's presence.

Perhaps Dirk and Anna hadn't been *entirely* wrong to rail against society's conventions.

"I'll think about it," she said. "The potential for coin is tempting, but if Dirk painted two nudes, people will speculate that he painted others, particularly given his relationship with Anna." The total number of nudes came to eleven, and for some reason, that number bothered Vera.

Oak took off the dressing gown and wrapped it around her shoulders. His warmth and scent enveloped her, a pleasant bit of consideration she doubted any other man in the whole of England showed his lover.

"People speculate no matter how careful we are," he replied, tugging the lapels together. "You might as well have the money, Vera, and it will be a goodly sum. Those are exquisite works of art."

Oak was an exquisite work of art, utterly unselfconscious of his nudity. Vera watched him dress, handing him this or that article of clothing, passing him sleeve buttons when he was once again in a country gentleman's finery.

"You did not answer my question," she said. "When are you planning to leave?"

He borrowed her hairbrush, but she took it from him and did the honors.

"Are you eager to be rid of me?" he asked, smiling slightly.

"No." She set the brush on her vanity. To a casual observer crossing paths with Oak in the corridor, he was simply up and about early, dressed and ready for the day.

He took her hands in his and drew her into his embrace. "I am not eager to go, truth be told. Alexander loved our ride yesterday. Catherine is taking to oils like a foal to spring grass. And the time I spend with you..."

He kissed her brow and snuggled her close. Vera waited, waited for him to offer to stay through the winter, to paint away the months in his airy studio, to let London wait just a bit longer.

She waited in vain. "Be off with you," she said, stepping back and trying for a smile. "The sun will be up all too soon." Though benighted London had sat on the banks of the Thames since Julius Caesar had been in nappies, and would likely blight the same location for centuries to come.

"I've asked my brother to send along the traveling coach," Oak said, "in order that I may safely transport your paintings. When the coach arrives, I'll need a day or two to pack up, and then I'll be on my way."

"I will miss you."

"And I will miss you. You must decide what to do with the nudes that remain here at Merlin Hall. I can return them to their hiding places, if you like."

"A sound course."

Awkwardness arose, a new and painful addition to Vera's vocabulary of emotions where Oak was concerned. She had sense enough to know the awkwardness would get worse as the time for his departure drew nearer, so she busied herself belting her dressing gown.

"I'll likely miss breakfast," she said. "And please do have a word with Alexander. He seems to trust you."

Oak's expression said he knew he was being dismissed. He did not know that Vera was likely to climb back into bed and cry at length when he'd gone.

"I'll see you at luncheon." He kissed her cheek and withdrew, closing the bedroom door softly.

Vera did dodge breakfast, and if the vicar and his wife hadn't been on hand, she would have dodged luncheon too.

~

WHERE WAS a meddling brother or two when a fellow needed sorting out? That Oak could miss Hawthorne's fists, Valerian's scathing common sense, Cam's irreverence, or Casriel's lordly over-simplifications was a rude shock.

That he'd also miss Ash's brooding questions and even Willow's canine analogies suggested matters were beyond dire. Fortunately, the hour had come to instruct young Alexander, and for Oak, time out of doors was usually an effective tonic for low spirits.

Though why should Oak's spirits *be* low?

"I would rather not ride today," Alexander said when he emerged onto the back terrace. "If you don't mind, sir, that is."

"Saddle-sore?" Oak asked, pushing away from the balustrade. The pain of new acquaintance with the saddle was often worst not the day after a ride, but the day following that.

"Yes. That's it. I am saddle-sore. Might we sketch Charles this afternoon?"

Alexander never wanted to work in the house. Even on rainy days, the boy would rather sketch in the stable or sit bundled in a blanket beneath a porch overhang while discussing how light was affected by a cloud cover.

"Let's have a ramble," Oak said. "Lunch with the vicar and his wife has left me needing to move about. We can finish up in the stables." He had enjoyed the luncheon with the vicar, a jovial old fellow married to an equally cheerful wife. Oak also liked the time spent with Vera's son, liked listening to how Alexander's busy little mind made sense of the world.

"I won't be late again returning to the nursery, will I? A gentleman is punctual, sir."

Oak did not enjoy Alexander's tendency to chronic fretfulness. "Is that more of Mr. Forester's tripe?"

Alexander's gaze across the garden was oddly adult. "I am not to insult my elders."

Oak ruffled his hair. "I believe you just did, and rather deftly. Let's see how the stream is getting on, shall we?"

Alexander no longer trudged at Oak's side, huffing and puffing, and in the usual course the boy no longer remained silent either. Today, he was both trudging and silent.

"Alexander, if you were a small boy's tutor, how would you go about the job?"

"I wouldn't. Tutoring is the worst post in the world. Mr. Forester says he must have committed some great sin against the universe to deserve the fate of teaching me."

From some window or other, Vera was doubtless watching Oak cross the back garden with her son. Oak wanted to turn and wave, to see her caught by the afternoon sunlight, to point her out to Alexander.

He kept on walking. "But if you had to teach a young boy, a good little fellow, though without much education, how would you go about it?"

Alexander tromped along in silence until they reached the gate at the foot of the garden. "I'd ask him what he likes to learn about and start there. If he likes horses, we'd learn about horses. If he likes books, we'd read books. If he's fond of butterflies, then we'd study butterflies."

"What about Latin?"

"Butterflies have Latin names, according to Miss Digg, and so a little boy who loves butterflies already has a reason to study his declensions, doesn't he?"

Alexander was very much his mother's son. He was smarter and more sensible than he appeared, and also less confident than he should be.

"Do you like butterflies, Alexander?"

"Yes. They are ever so pretty, and they can fly anywhere they want to. Nobody traps a butterfly in a schoolroom. Nobody flogs a butterfly for being stupid."

What the hell? Oak took his time latching the gate closed. "Which one is your favorite?"

"The green hairstreak can hide among the leaves. Nobody can see him unless he wants to be seen."

Worse and worse. "What about the Adonis blue or purple emperor?"

"They are bright, and that makes them easy to catch. Some people stick pins in butterflies and collect the carcasses. I wouldn't do that."

Oak wouldn't do that either. "How do you study the butterfly well enough to draw him if you don't collect a specimen to sketch?"

They'd reached the gate by the stream. Alexander clambered over, waiting for Oak on the other side. Oak unlatched the gate and stepped through, then refastened the gate. On a different day, he would have vaulted the obstacle, but the morning's discussion with Vera had stolen such ebullience.

"If I wanted to draw a butterfly," Alexander said, "I'd catch him in a glass jar and make sure he had leaves and whatnot to keep him comfortable. I'd sketch him as best I could, then I would thank him for his patience and let him go. Mr. Forester says talking to animals is a sign of a weak mind."

Mr. Forester is an idiot. "Well, then, my mind is complete mush, for I confide all of my troubles in Charles, and he has never given me bad advice. I've suggested to your mother that you should have a dog."

Alexander came to a halt. "A dog? For me? *My own dog?*"

"I've written to my brother Willow, who raises dogs, in hopes of securing a canine companion for you. Willow not only speaks to dogs, he can hear their replies."

They had reached the stream, which in high summer was more of a soggy, meandering burn than a watercourse.

"Nobody can hear a dog talk," Alexander said, picking up a stick and pitching it into the slow-moving current. "That's silly."

How many times had Oak's brothers told him that drawing flowers was silly? "Do you know when Catherine is sad?"

"Yes. She looks out of windows a lot and twiddles the ends of her hair. When Miss Digg scolds her for that, Catherine doesn't care. If she pouts and makes faces when she's scolded, she's not sad, she's in a taking."

The ground was too damp to sit on this close to the bog, so Oak perched on the log where he and Catherine had become acquainted.

"You know when Catherine's sad because you watch how she behaves. She doesn't need to say, 'I am sad,' but you know. It's like that with dogs and horses and all manner of things. Watch closely, and you can see what they aren't saying."

He hoisted Alexander to sit beside him, though the boy jumped right back down. "Is that what you do, sir? You watch and study and see who people are?"

"Something like that." Oak pushed away from his makeshift bench, unwilling to deny Alexander more activity when the boy had so little time out of doors. "Let's have a look at the bog, shall we?"

"Do I have time, sir? We haven't sketched Charles, and I must not be late."

I will find this boy a pocket watch when I'm in London and send it to him for a Christmas token. Though Christmas tokens were usually exchanged only between family and friends, and when Oak left Merlin Hall, his departure would be permanent.

"We have time. What color would you use to paint the water, Alexander?"

The child took to the question with his characteristic earnest enthusiasm. The peaty quality of the stream, the low summer volume, and the afternoon sunlight created hues of amber, burgundy, bronze, sable, and gold, and Oak was able to use those observations to point out that black in a painting was seldom truly black, just as white was usually not quite white.

"And this stream flows under the bog?" Alexander asked, stopping on the edge of the path.

"That's hard to say. Sometimes, a quaking bog forms as a pond recedes or spreads; sometimes, we don't know what created it or whether it's more extensive in summer, spring, or fall."

"Or winter," Alexander replied. "Bogs don't always freeze just because you see ice. Mrs. Tansbury says bogs are never safe."

"Mrs. Tansbury is right. We'd best be getting back if we're to say hello to Charlie."

Oak, much like his pupil, did not want to return to the house, did not want to explain to Catherine how to mix a carmine hue rather than scarlet or mulberry or strawberry. He wanted to find Vera and...

And what?

"Charlie's coat has the same color brown as the peat water does when it's in shade," Alexander said as they approached the geldings' paddock. "The sun gives him golden highlights too."

"Because we groomed him so thoroughly the other day, and he hasn't yet found any mud to roll in."

Charles went on cropping the lush summer grass, indifferent to his observers. Oak was struck by the recollection that Charles did not like Town. If he wasn't galloped—hard—every morning, he developed vices and became unruly. He was a country horse, but because he was the only horse Oak owned, into Town he would go.

"If Charles rolls in the mud," Alexander asked, climbing the fence rails, "do you beat him?"

What in seven schoolroom purgatories could prompt such a question? "Of course not. Horses roll to itch their backs, to put dirt between them and the flies, and because it's fun. Try it sometime. Get down and roll in the grass or roll down a hill, then get up and shake all over."

Alexander, perched on the top rail, was nearly eye to eye with Oak. "You are jesting. Mr. Forester says you frequently jest."

Oak wanted to grab this solemn little boy and show him how to roll down a hillside. Wanted to find him a few good climbing trees where he could have solitude when his little world needed pondering...

Wanted to tickle him and hug him and toss him into the air... As Oak had been tickled, and hugged, and tossed.

"I am not jesting when I say that I believe you should have a dog. Mr. Forester's opinion on that subject doesn't signify, so you need not air it with him. Come along." He lifted Alexander off the fence rail and set him on his feet.

"I am not to tell Mr. Forester that you might talk Mama into getting me a dog?"

"You are not."

"Am I late, sir?"

"No. Why?"

"Because you are walking almost as fast as Mr. Forester walks."

Oak tossed Alexander into the air, then carried the boy piggyback to the garden.

"If you were a dog," Alexander said as Oak passed through the gate, "you would be telling me you were unhappy without speaking human words. Why are you unhappy, Mr. Dorning?"

Oak could lecture the boy on the intrusiveness of asking about other people's private feelings, he could make a joke, he could...

"I will soon have to leave Merlin Hall, Alexander. My work here is nearly done. I will miss you, and I will miss your family."

Alexander squeezed him silently about the neck the whole way up to the terrace. When the boy's grip eased up, Oak set him on his feet.

"You are in no danger of being late," Oak said. "None at all."

Such a thunderous, conflicted expression met Oak's announcement. Alexander's blue eyes were full of recrimination and consternation, and Oak knew in that moment what it was to betray a child's trust.

"Mr. Forester said you'd never stay at a pokey little farm like Merlin Hall. Merlin Hall isn't a pokey little farm. It's a lovely place to live. Even I know that. You should stay here."

Before Oak could offer consoling lies—*I'll write to you, I'll visit, you must come see me in London*—Alexander pelted into the house at a dead run. Oak hoped the boy slowed down before he reached the schoolroom, lest Forester lecture him about gentlemen never proceeding at more than a dignified stroll.

Rather than return to the studio, Oak perched again on the balustrade overlooking the back garden. The walk with Alexander had helped clarify at least one source of Oak's low mood.

He'd asked Vera outright to come to London with him, and her reasons for refusing were many and sound. He'd been a fool—a selfish fool—to ask her. He was an equally selfish fool to expect her to ask him to tarry here at Merlin Hall. The Little Season wouldn't start for weeks, and many families ruralized through the whole winter before returning to Town.

As the cold stone seat on the balustrade grew uncomfortable, Oak realized that he'd been watching Vera in hopes she'd issue an invitation for him to stay on at Merlin Hall, and no such invitation would be forthcoming.

By this time next week, he could be in London. Why wasn't that cause for rejoicing?

When Oak retrieved his mail from Bracken, he found a letter from Richard Longacre. Longacre had recommended Oak as a portraitist to no less than three young mothers in search of portraits of their offspring. Oak had only to express his acceptance of the commissions, and the work would be his upon his arrival in London.

More cause for rejoicing. For elation and ebullience, and happy letters sent to all siblings.

Oak instead went back to his studio and asked Bracken to send up a bottle of brandy.

~

VERA WAS WEARY, despite getting adequate sleep. The predawn conversation with Oak weighed on her soul, and the thought of bidding him farewell put a constant lump in her throat.

The effort of pretending that Oak Dorning was simply an artistic fellow biding for a few weeks at the Hall to do some restoration work took another sort of toll. Vera listened for his tread outside her parlor door while she tried to focus on her accounts. She took her weekly cup of tea with the housekeeper and pretended an enthusiasm for menus she barely glanced at.

She joined Catherine and Miss Diggory in a session of choosing fabric for Catherine's first full-length dresses and barely contributed to the undertaking other than to suggest that Catherine avoid yellow, no matter how enthusiastically Miss Diggory rhapsodized about buttercups and daffodils.

This painful, yearning quality had never characterized her life with Dirk Channing, though Dirk had been moody, impulsive, self-absorbed, and occasionally petulant.

Oak was none of those things. He was simply intent on pursuing his profession in the location where he was most likely to succeed. As an earl's son, with family in Town, he'd thrive in London, and Vera would become a fond, distant memory to him.

She slit open the top letter in the stack of correspondence she'd been ignoring for the past half hour. Richard Longacre politely inquired regarding her health and asked for her impressions of Mr. Dorning's talents. He finished up with some reminiscence about Dirk and a drinking contest in Venice and added the usual postscript: Should Vera be of a mind to visit London, Longacre would happily arrange lodgings for her and serve as her host. Lady Montclair's reception was simply not to be missed this year, and all of Vera's *old friends* would be there.

Longacre had been making that offer since a year after Dirk's death. A second postscript followed the first: Longacre hoped that

Miss Diggory and Mr. Forester were proving adequate to the positions they'd taken on.

They were not, if Vera were honest. She struggled to say exactly why—her concerns were only that, not outright objections—but neither Jeremy nor Tamsin was quite what she wanted for her children. If she sacked either the tutor or the governess, would Longacre be offended?

A tap on the parlor's open door had her looking up and expecting to see Bracken with a tea tray.

Oak stood in the doorway, a bit tousled and tired.

"May I have a moment of your time?" he asked.

"Of course." She took up another unopened letter, mostly to occupy her hands. "Have a seat."

"I have begun a painting," he said, taking the chair opposite Vera's desk. "I didn't plan on starting it, and I'm here to offer my excuses for dinner. Forester cast aspersion on Merlin Hall in Alexander's hearing, and I realized you have no landscape on the premises that includes the Hall."

"You are painting Merlin Hall?"

"Consider it a present to Alexander, whose home this is. I haven't painted anything for some time, and this project seemed…"

He fell silent, staring at his hands. Brown paint ringed his left thumb, and a pink streak crossed the back of his left hand.

"Is this a farewell gift?" Vera said, slitting open the letter she held.

"Something like that. Alexander and Catherine are wroth with me for leaving."

I am wroth with you for leaving. Though that wasn't exactly true. Vera was wroth with herself for falling in love with him and wroth with him for being so dear—and so determined on his objectives.

"People leave, Oak. The children need to learn that lesson and need to learn that they can carry on despite the sorrow." A miserable lesson to inflict on Catherine and Alexander, both of whom had lost a parent much too early in life.

Vera scanned the note and set it aside.

"Is something wrong?" Oak asked.

"That." Vera nodded at the epistle. "Hera McIntrye, who believes herself to be the last word on the proper artistic rendering of flowers in all media, has reminded me that Lady Montclair's exhibit should feature a posthumous work of Dirk's. Miss McIntrye's father is an Academy associate, and when they visited here, she was a difficult guest."

Oak rose and picked up the note. "'*I understand London can be overwhelming to those raised in less sophisticated surrounds, but the duty to preserve Dirk Channing's legacy should transcend our petty insecurities, don't you agree?*' She's been sending you this kind of sanctimonious rubbish for three years?"

"She's worse about the Summer Exhibition. Her father was among those who disrespected me, and I suspect that she and he laughed about that all the way back to London."

Oak returned the letter to Vera's desk. "I don't like this. I don't like that Forester insults Alexander's home while carping at the boy ceaselessly over gentlemanly deportment. I don't like that Miss Diggory has done nothing to encourage Catherine's artistic talent. I don't like that I'm leaving you here alone to deal with nasty letters, but Longacre has promised me three commissions as soon as I can make my way to London. The subjects are children, and I'd be a very poor talent if I could not do artistic justice to children."

"*Three* commissions?"

Oak resumed his seat, looking miserable. "Longacre has done much for me, Vera. He's the reason I'm here at Merlin Hall. I owe him, now more than ever. He's arranged for me to lodge with another portraitist, a fellow I know from the Academy classes. I get on well with de Beauharnais. He's serious about his art, exceptionally talented, and not given to dramatics."

"I thought you'd stay with your brothers, Ash and what's the other one's name?"

"Sycamore. Cam, though he'd answer to Beelzebub in a certain mood. I love my brothers, and I miss them, but to become their free lodger, using their parlor for my studio... Longacre's plan is better."

Despite the miasma of her own misery, Vera admitted the enormity of the challenges facing Oak. Dirk had never bided in London for twelve consecutive months, simply because sunlight was at a premium in the metropolis. Coal smoke, river fog, tall buildings, gloomy weather in every season... All of these factors and more meant rooms with adequate light and proper exposures were few and dear.

Oak needed not only commissions, he needed a studio, a store of supplies, introductions, and means to subsist through the winter before polite society returned to London in the spring.

"Longacre apparently enjoys helping others find a path in life," Vera said. "I would not have thought that of him, given how testy he and Dirk could be with one another, but Longacre recommended both Tamsin and Jeremy."

Oak looked around at the parlor's appointments, his gaze settling on an oil painting of flowers above the hearth.

"Neither Miss Diggory nor Mr. Forester is well suited to their duties, and that painting is not a Dirk Channing."

Vera glanced over her shoulder at the painting of a bouquet of irises beginning to wilt. "Longacre did this, though he claims rheumatism has stolen most of his talent. He sent it as a gift after Dirk's death, and I felt obligated to display it. Last year I prevailed upon Longacre to make an initial attempt to sell some of the gallery's lesser specimens. He was unable to find buyers for the first three paintings I sent him, and you've helped explain why."

Oak rose and moved closer to the painting. "His hands must truly be afflicted. The whites are too flat, the shadows inconsistent with the light source." He brushed a finger over a rendering of a rose petal. "Here, here, and here, where the open window to the left of the flowers should result in light on this side and shadow on the other..."

He fell silent, apparently lost in the assessment of qualities only he could see.

"Oak?"

"Hmm."

"I'd like to sack Jeremy and Tamsin." Vera had come to that conclusion in the past five minutes, and only because Oak, too, found both parties lacking.

Oak perched a hip on a corner of her desk. "Then sack them. Alexander positively loathes Forester, and I gather Catherine isn't that impressed with Miss Diggory. Forester intimidates the boy, and Alexander clearly grasps the difference between a bully and competent tutor."

A bully. That single word illuminated much that Vera had been pushing into her mental shadows.

"I was bullied. By my step-mother, by Dirk's so-called friends." Vera rose and headed for the door. "You've put your finger on the problem. Jeremy hasn't the knack of inspiring respect. I don't respect him, and I gather he has little respect for me."

Oak stood, but did not follow after her. "Vera, wait."

She halted two steps short of the door. "If I don't do this now, I will lose my nerve."

"I'm not suggesting you keep Forester on. I'm suggesting you consider the terms on which you let him go."

"He bullies my son," she said, stalking back across the carpet, "and worse, I've let it go on. I told myself Alexander had to adjust, that all boys mourn the loss of a dear governess when a proper tutor takes over. I did not want to offend Alexander by intimating that he wasn't smart enough to work with a tutor. I've handled this all wrong."

And that was an old, familiar feeling, of being inadequate, the wrong person for the job, wanting. Vera had felt that way as Dirk's wife and as the only daughter in a family of boisterous and unruly brothers. The same sense of being inadequate plagued her as Oak's lover.

He'd sought an intimate friendship, and here she was, in a welter of heartache over a man bound for London.

"Forester is not the right tutor for Alexander," Oak said, "though you do yourself no favors if you make it plain the fault lies with Forester."

"But it clearly does. Alexander is six years old. He's not incorrigible or dull-witted. He simply lacks confidence."

"Forester lacks skill," Oak said, "though if you turn him off without a character, he will trot back to Town, pouting and smarting. He will intimate to Longacre and to all and sundry that you were an impossible employer and Alexander a spoiled brat."

Vera sank into the chair before her desk. "I don't want that. I want Forester gone, and Miss Diggory with him. Longacre meant well, but he chose poorly."

"I will inquire of my family regarding replacements," Oak said. "The countess in particular and my sister Jacaranda know everybody. By Michaelmas at the latest, you can have a new governess and tutor at Merlin Hall."

"I want those two gone now, Oak." Before Oak abandoned her for London, which was cowardly of her.

"Then you tell them that you're planning a holiday for the children, perhaps a trip to the Lakes, and that both Tamsin and Jeremy are free to take holidays of their own. When they have left the household and some time has passed, you send them additional severance. You suggest to Jeremy that Alexander is benefiting from more time to mature before he resumes his studies, and you cannot in good conscience keep Jeremy from seeking another post. Wish him best of luck and enclose a character of sorts."

"And Tamsin?"

Oak again propped a hip against a corner of the desk. "The same basic approach. Turn her loose, then follow up with a letter indicating that Catherine has benefited from a pause in her studies. You are researching finishing schools, and Miss Diggory must consider herself free to pursue other opportunities. Send along enough severance, and they will both recall you fondly."

"And how can I write characters for a pair who honestly aren't well suited to instructing children?"

"Damn with faint praise. Forester performed his duties conscientiously, which means with a complete lack of imagination. Miss Diggory was patient with an adolescent's temperament, which means little education occurred. Give it some thought, and the words will come. I have faith in you."

He leaned down, kissed her cheek, and headed for the door.

"Oak?"

"Mrs. Channing?"

"Thank you."

He ran a paint-stained hand through his hair. "It's the least I can do."

Then he left Vera alone with Longacre's letter and much to think about.

CHAPTER ELEVEN

The bedamned traveling coach arrived, not from Dorset, but from London. When the matched grays trotted up the Merlin Hall drive, who should descend but both Ash and Sycamore.

Oak was so glad to see his brothers, he didn't even pummel them for spying on him. Sycamore had become an elegant man-about-town —the transformation was obvious before he'd set his booted foot over Merlin's Hall's threshold—while Ash was still Ash: quiet, faintly amused, hard to read. Both brothers set about charming Vera, and that was...

That was what Vera deserved. To be flirted with and flattered, entertained and appreciated. The decision was made that Ash and Cam would bide at Merlin Hall for two days, giving the coachy, grooms, and horses a chance to rest. Then Oak would depart with his brothers for Town.

Finally. At last.

"So why," Cam asked, when the ladies had left the supper table for a pot of tea in the parlor, "don't you look ebullient to be storming the great citadel of art and culture?"

"London is not a citadel," Oak retorted, glad that Forester had pleaded fatigue rather than join the Dorning brothers for a round of port.

"The heart is a citadel," Ash said, "and Mrs. Channing has captured yours."

Oak stared at his drink, idly noting the garnet, amber, and gold highlights created by the candlelight.

"Why did I ever think I missed my siblings?" he mused. "For weeks, nobody has presumed to announce my inmost thoughts to the world, nobody has insulted my attire, nobody has joked about my calling. You are under this roof a mere six hours, and already you declare me lovesick."

"Five hours," Cam said, glancing at the clock on the dining room mantel, "and you don't deny the accusation. The widow is damned pretty, but you've been sketching the damned pretty ones since you went up to university. I like her."

Ash sat back, crossing an ankle over one knee. "Oak likes Mrs. Channing, too, and she likes Oak. She doesn't want him to hare off to the big city. Why isn't marriage under discussion?"

That Cam let the question hang in the air, rather than heaping his unhelpful observations on top of Ash's query, meant Oak would have to answer.

"I am an artist," he said. "I've bent my entire being, from boyhood on, to achieving artistic success. Am I to throw it all away now, without testing my mettle in the only arena that matters?"

"A paintbrush-wielding gladiator," Cam murmured. "I'm having trouble picturing it."

So was Oak, truth be told. "If I take your club away from you, Cam, what's left? Who are you?"

Cam sent Ash a look. "I am your tired brother, that's who I am, and I'm a damned fine-looking fellow with pots of money and all the best connections. You should invite Mrs. Channing to Town. She's welcome to the use of my rental on Hillman Street. This time of year, nobody seeks a house in London, but one doesn't want to let the servants go, because they need their wages."

"Vera doesn't exactly have pots of money," Oak replied, sipping his port. "You'd have to make it plain she was a guest, not a renter."

Another look passed between his brothers, and Oak realized his mistake. He should have scoffed at the notion of Vera traveling to Town, should have snorted with disdain. Vera did not want to travel to Town, had no reason to travel to Town. None at all. She'd been very clear about that.

Oak had made mistakes, plural, for he'd not even acknowledged Ash's question about marriage.

"Vera has bad memories of London," Oak said. "Channing's friends were less than respectful toward her. She was a rural inno-cent, and they were artists orbiting her worldly husband. His previous relationship was irregular."

Actually, Oak's mistakes were up to three, because he ought not to have referred to his employer as *Vera.*

"Hence the lovely Miss Catherine," Cam said. "She has all the makings of an original. I like her too."

"That's your problem," Oak said. "You like everybody, but about whom do you truly *care,* little brother?"

Ash ran a finger around the rim of his glass. "Got you there, Cam."

"I care about you," Cam replied, rising. "Though heaven alone knows why. You look at Mrs. Channing the way Casriel looked at the fair Beatitude when he was being all muttonheaded about marrying money. Doomed love is not an attractive accessory to any man's turnout. At least Ash has channeled his unrequited passion into a becoming touch of *weltschmerz,* as the Germans say. That reminds me. I know the Forester fellow. We had the same German tutor during my ill-fated terms at Oxford."

Ash's smile faded, and he took another sip of his brandy.

"You know Jeremy Forester?" Oak asked.

"In my brief penance as a university scholar, my path crossed with his. He was sent down more than once and was heartily disliked by the tavern maids. He tried to take by force and guile what he could not purchase with coin."

This description, unfortunately, fit all too well with what Oak knew of Forester. "And yet, he lectures a six-year-old about gentlemanly deportment. What about Forester's academics? Did he apply himself there?"

Cam picked up his drink. "Hardly. His nickname was Slow Top. He lacked the artistic ability to follow in his uncle's footsteps and lacked the discipline to become any sort of scholar. I pity the little fellow shut up in a schoolroom all day with Forester for a tutor."

Slow Top. "Who is his uncle?"

Cam sauntered toward the door. "Your patron saint, Mr. Richard Longacre, RA. What a coincidence. Make my excuses to the ladies, please. I need my rest if I'm to be on my most charming behavior at the breakfast table."

He blew Oak a kiss and went on his way.

"He's worse in Town," Ash said, getting up to close the door. "More flamboyant, more reckless. The club is a stage for him, and he seldom misses a performance, though all that London savoir faire takes a toll on a mere lad from Dorset."

"The club is thriving?"

"Handsomely."

Oak finished his drink, for he did not intend to make his excuses to the ladies. "So why does Sycamore seem as restless and unsettled as ever? Has he a lady friend?"

"Our baby brother has many lady friends. A different one each week, and they all adore him regardless of his fickle ways."

"I adore Verity Channing."

Ash returned to the table and saluted with his drink. "An understatement, I'm guessing, and she appears to hold you in high regard as well. So, like the dunderheaded Dorning that you are, you will turn your back on her and spend the rest of your life regretting the decision."

This was progress of a sort, because Ash seldom commented on his own situation. "Have you mended fences with Lady Della?"

The whole family had been certain Ash would offer for Lady Della Haddonfield, perhaps Lady Della had been similarly persuaded. Ash had apparently been of a different mind.

He peered into his brandy. "Her ladyship and I have reached a truce. She avoids Town, and when she must be in Town, I avoid her. Like you, I have had little to offer a woman in material terms—she's an earl's daughter—and she deserves a man who can..." He set his glass down, still half-full. "You will excuse me. Not that Cam is a good example, but I, too, will seek my bed rather than inflict my tired company on the ladies."

"Does Longacre ever come to the club?" Oak had no idea what prompted that question.

"Attendance is supposed to be held in confidence," Ash said, "but yes, he does. All of fashionable Society waltzes through the doors of The Coventry, and most of them are lighter in the pocket when they waltz out. Longacre spends his time where the rich and reckless spend theirs, the better to curry commissions from them for his protégés."

"You don't like Longacre?"

"At The Coventry, we like everybody, Oak, provided they pay their debts and can hold their liquor. I'm for bed."

Which meant, no, Ash did not like Longacre. Oak walked with his brother to the foot of the main staircase. "Why didn't Casriel send his traveling coach?" he asked.

"He was cryptic, saying only that we were to take our time delivering you Cam's coach. Cam wasn't having any of that, and so here we are, very likely exactly as Casriel intended we be. It is good to see you, Oak, and you look as if the fresh air of Hampshire is agreeing with you."

"It is."

Ash, who was notably reserved, wrapped Oak in a gentle hug.

"Then perhaps you should stay here. Good night." He ascended the steps without looking back.

Oak was tempted to sit on the stairs and ponder his brother's behavior—had Ash been trying to *console* him?—but Vera waited in the family parlor. Once he had her alone in her own bedroom, he'd again ask her to come with him to London.

And this time, he'd ask as sweetly and persuasively as he possibly could.

~

TO VERA'S RELIEF, Miss Diggory escorted Catherine up to bed almost as soon as Oak joined the ladies in the parlor. He made excuses for his brothers, and that, too, was a relief.

"I know not who was more smitten with whom," Vera said, pouring Oak a cup of tea. "Catherine or Miss Diggory, with Sycamore or Ash. Mr. Forester was quite subdued at supper."

Oak took the wing chair angled at the end of the sofa where Vera presided over the tea tray. "Sycamore knew Forester—or knew of him—at university. Did you know Forester is related to Richard Longacre?"

What had that to do with anything? "Tamsin is as well, a niece or great-niece, maybe a cousin once removed. Jeremy and Tamsin have no blood relation, but are connected by family. Longacre mentioned that when he recommended her."

The tea had gone tepid, and the parlor was acquiring a chill. Summer nights could be like this—not cold enough for a fire, not warm enough to be comfortable.

"You're cold," Oak said, rising to unfold an afghan from the back of his wing chair. "You need not stay up to keep me company." He draped the wool around Vera's shoulders and resumed his seat.

"Is that a way to tell me that because your brothers are here, you'll keep to your own rooms tonight?" Vera sounded testy to her own ears.

Oak swirled his cold tea. "I apologize for the ambush, Vera. My brothers should have sent a note. They should have sent the coach without coming on an inspection tour themselves. This is part of the reason I wanted so desperately to go to London."

Vera was heartily sick of hearing about London. "I admit I am somewhat nonplussed to have uninvited houseguests. That is ungracious of me."

Oak shifted to sit beside her on the sofa. "That is human of you. Some of my siblings are polite, in the usual sense, but they all have ways of prying. And a pair of London bachelors would not be your first pick for houseguests."

"True enough."

The parlor door was open, but Bracken had already come around to dim the lamps in the corridor. Except for Oak and Vera, the household was abed.

"You seek distance from your family by going to London," Vera said. "But you have two brothers and a sister there, don't you?"

"Just the brothers. Jacaranda and her family are in the country for the summer." He set down his tea cup without having taken a sip. "I won't lodge with my brothers in London, and they will be busy with their club. We might meet in the park for a hack some morning, or share a meal at the club, but they won't be in my pocket, nor I in theirs. At Dorning Hall, I saw family at every meal. I would take my sketch pad and pencil with me on long hikes just so I had an excuse to find some solitude."

Vera had not envisioned Oak as having to seek solitude from his own family, though memories of her step-mother's hovering presence made the concept understandable.

"You love your family," she said, "and they clearly love you."

"I love them to distraction, and damnation to any who speaks ill of my siblings. There are a lot of them, though, and they are loud."

London is loud. To say that would be needlessly combative. Oak had been to London, he knew the difference between a city's noise and the relentless bustle of a full house.

"I will miss you." The words came out without Vera planning to say them. That feeling—of missing Oak—had already started in her heart. "I watched you bantering with your brothers over dinner, telling stories on each other, and I realized how little I know of you and how much I like what I know."

Oak tucked an arm around her shoulders. "You like me?"

"I rather do."

"I like you very much, Verity Channing. Have you decided what to do with the Stoltzfus paintings?"

I like you very much. Was Oak being polite? Trying to spare Vera's feelings? His arm around her shoulders spoke of affection, his abrupt change of subject shifted the conversation to their impending separation.

"I am inclined to keep those paintings here where they can't get into any trouble."

"But?"

"But I need the money, Oak. Even if I have only five years to invest the proceeds for Catherine, that's some interest on the principal. As it is..."

Oak rearranged the afghan more snugly around her. "As it is...?"

"Merlin Hall is solvent. We've had good harvests, and I have good tenants, but that is not a plan for my old age, that is not a plan for the bad years, and every shire has bad years. I don't want those paintings, and selling unused assets makes sense."

"You're selling the paintings I restored. They will bring something."

"Not much, not compared to what Dirk's nudes could bring. Catherine cannot be presented at court, but she can learn to move in London society. That will take significant investment and enormous luck, but I feel I owe her the attempt."

"And Tom Treeble?"

Vera would miss much about Oak—his patience with the children, his presence at meals, his presence in Vera's bed—but she'd also miss his pure companionship. He had an ability to talk through problems with her, to offer insights that never quite rose to the weight of sermonizing. He'd become the friend he'd offered to be, and that was...

That was exactly what Vera had needed without even knowing it.

"Tom Treeble might well be her choice, but, Oak, I want her to *have* a choice. Dirk came along, the first man to more than smile at me, and I leaped at the chance to get away from my step-mother's household. Catherine knows Merlin Hall belongs to her brother, and she might well be desperate to get away from me too."

Oak took Vera's hand, his grip warm. "Come to London with me and bring the children. Use the trip as an excuse to send Forester and Miss Diggory packing. Sycamore has offered you free lodgings at one of his houses—he believes real estate is a sound investment, given how London is growing—and yet, he can't rent the better properties this time of year."

"I don't care for London, Oak. You know that." Though Vera had been hoping he'd renew his request.

He kissed her knuckles. "Polite society is long gone from Town, and soon what few families remain will head for the grouse moors and house parties. You'll be safe, and I'll be on hand to escort you and Catherine to the shops, if that's where you'd like to go. She and Alexander should see the museums, too, and have an ice at Gunter's."

Every child should have that experience on a pleasant summer day. "Gunter's is well worth a visit. I went there myself more than once."

"And you prefer vanilla ices," Oak said.

"How do you know that?"

"Because vanilla is exotic and rich and suits you. It's my favorite as well."

He painted a different picture of London than Vera had seen, one devoid of dinner parties that ran too late, free of half-drunken men leering at her as if she were a streetwalker.

"Richard Longacre has been after me to come to London for

years. I don't think he'll cease importuning me until I make the
journey."

Oak leaned his head back against the cushions and closed his
eyes. "Is he sweet on you?"

Vera's first inclination was to laugh, but Oak saw what others
missed. "I don't know. He and Dirk had a friendship punctuated by
frequent loud quarrels. Longacre was some relation to Anna, and I
gather that was a source of unspoken tension. I never pried, lest I find
myself in the midst of an explosion of temper."

"Longacre sent me to you, and he sent you Miss Diggory and
Forester. He writes to you fairly often, and I expect he's mentioned
his plans to you any time he'll be traveling in the area."

Vera thought back to various polite letters, seeing a pattern she
hadn't noticed before. "He does. He travels through Winchester
when he's bound for Lyme Regis. Was I supposed to invite him to the
Hall for a visit?"

"Not as long as you were in mourning, you weren't."

"I've been out of first mourning for two years."

"So come to London with me. Bring the children. We'll see the
sights and rid you of the staff that isn't working out. You can interview replacements from the London agencies in person and be on
hand to negotiate prices for your paintings."

The reasons to go were piling up, obscuring the reasons Vera
never wanted to set foot in Town again. Oak was too polite to note
that she was unlikely to have free lodgings and a well-placed escort
ever again. Longacre had offered to serve as host, but he hadn't
offered particulars, and he wasn't an earl's well-connected son. Then
too, the children should see the capital, and a trip would make
sacking Jeremy and Tamsin much easier.

"For me to travel to London with you will solve nothing, Oak. I
will still have to part from you, and I still dread that day."

He kissed her temple. "As do I, but I will treasure the memory of
sharing a vanilla ice with you beneath the maples at Gunter's." He
rose and began blowing out candles. "May I light you to your room?"

He always found a way to ask permission to join her at the end of the day, however obliquely.

"You may."

They walked through the darkened house arm in arm, and Vera's sense of heartache crested higher. She wanted more nights like this, quiet conversation, affection, a sweet loving to end the evening, and the peace of shared slumber after that.

Maybe London wasn't so bad after all, and maybe it had changed in the years since she'd been utterly miserable there.

~

OAK WAS TUCKING the last of the nudes behind its mundane disguise when somebody thumped loudly on his studio door.

"Mr. Dorning, you have to let me in!" Alexander shouted that demand.

Oak unlatched the door, and Alexander barreled into the room. "You must make Mama take us with her. You must. Catherine and me both. Please."

Oak closed the door. "Alexander, what is this about?"

"I will not stay here with Mr. Forester. He'll beat me and make me go without supper, and I will run away! I hate Latin and I hate the Bible and I hate sums."

A basically sweet little boy was moved to blasphemy. Oak locked the door, lest Forester join the discussion uninvited. "Let's discuss this on the balcony, shall we?"

"I don't want to discuss anything. I want to go to London with M-Mama."

The look of horror that came over Alexander's face at the quaver in his voice was the embodiment of misery. Shame, anger, fear... Oak took the boy by the hand and led him to the balcony.

"Have a seat," Oak said, folding himself onto one of a pair of wrought-iron chairs. "Who told you that your mother was traveling to London?"

Alexander sniffed, his gaze on the parkland that rolled away from the Hall's back garden. "She is leaving Merlin Hall, and it's your fault."

"No, actually, it isn't. Not entirely. Your mother has been receiving invitations to visit in the capital for some time. My brothers and I merely make handy escorts. What would be so terrible about biding at Merlin Hall in her absence?"

A memory surfaced, of Alexander unable to sit on a log, unwilling to go for another hack on Charlie, though the boy loved to be in the saddle.

"Mr. Forester. That's what would be so terrible. Him and the bloody birch rod."

Blasphemy *and* profanity. "He birches you?"

"Sometimes twice a day, and if I cry, I get extra stripes. I hate him."

I hate him too. "And he told you if you complained, he'd just pile on more stripes?"

Alexander nodded. "A gentleman accepts his lot without complaining. I never wanted to be a gentleman, and if Mr. Forester is a gentleman, then I would rather be a highwayman instead."

Oak passed Alexander his handkerchief. "Blow."

Alexander honked and folded the linen neatly before offering it back to Oak, who set it aside.

"I truly will run away, sir. I hate him and he's mean and he says mean things about Mama and Catherine and Miss Digg. He even said mean things about Papa, and Papa's dead. We're not supposed to speak ill of the dead." Alexander made *speak ill* one word, though his ire conveyed clearly enough.

"Running away is, on rare occasion, the sensible thing to do," Oak said. "I am running away from the place where I grew up, if my actions are viewed from a certain perspective."

Alexander's brows drew down. "Did somebody beat your arse too?"

Do not smile when a small boy is desperate to be taken seriously.

"Not recently, but I was lonely and needed to make my way in the world. I did not see a way to do that at Dorning Hall." Oak had seen Grey and Beatitude awash in domestic bliss, Hawthorne married to the lovely widow, and Valerian falling for the prettiest heiress in the shire.

He'd scarpered, though at least he'd bolted in the direction of his lifelong ambitions.

"Did you run away to Merlin Hall, Mr. Dorning?"

"I am on my way to London. I stopped here because I love art and wanted to help your mama by restoring some of the older works your papa collected. I will sell them in London, because Merlin Hall doesn't need them anymore."

"I will run away to London, then. Catherine says Papa knew everybody in London. Nobody will beat me in London."

Oak longed to hug the boy tight and never let him go. In London, a lone child would be snatched off the street and sold into a hell no one should endure.

"Alexander, what problem are you trying to solve by running away?"

"Mr. Forester." Said with a universe of disgust. "He's a *big* problem. He says I'm a slow top, but you were a slow top at Latin, and Mama doesn't know any Latin at all."

"I agree with you that he's a problem and that he has failed you as a tutor and as an example. You try hard to learn, and if your progress is slow, your tutor is partly responsible. Do you know who has the power to make Mr. Forester go away for good?"

"God could send the Angel of Death to strike him down. Cook says Mrs. Tansbury could give him the bloody flux with one of her tisanes. He'd probably beat me for that too. Mr. Forester would, not God."

And when had Cook said that within a child's hearing, and more to the point, why? "What else did Cook say?"

"That if Mr. Forester kisses Catherine the way he kisses Miss

Digg, Cook will do him an injury. Bracken told her to cease gabbling, but Mrs. Hepplewhite agreed."

This conversation, which had to have taken place in the servants' hall, could have been overheard by only a stealthy little eavesdropper.

"You sneaked into my room when I first arrived at the Hall, didn't you?"

Alexander turned to brace his back against the balcony railing, hands in his pockets, feet crossed at the ankles. The posture was strangely adult, doubtless one Forester had frequently adopted.

"I had to make sure you were truly an artist. Merlin Hall belongs to me, and Mama and Catherine have nobody else to protect them. What if you were a bad man come to steal from us?"

What a question and what a lot of responsibility for one small boy. "What did you find in my satchel?"

"Sketch pads, pencils, erasers, drawings of people who look like you—good drawings. I wanted to study them. You have a seashell too."

So you came back and had another look. "I spied from time to time when I was a small boy, Alexander. I hid in trees and eavesdropped on the gardeners. I am ashamed of myself for that."

"A gentleman doesn't spy?"

"He seldom spies. Your justification—to protect your mother and sister—is noble, though you can't protect them if you tear off to London. We need not discuss spying again if you understand that prying into people's privacy is not nice. For me to eavesdrop on the gardeners was wrong."

Alexander met Oak's gaze for the first time in this entire conversation. "Did you get a birching?"

"I deserved punishment, but a guilty conscience was a heavier burden than a smarting backside. I suspect my papa knew that. Might we return to the topic of Mr. Forester?"

"I hate him. I don't care if that's a sin. I can barely sit down to eat my porridge, and Mr. Forester thinks that's funny. He offers me a pillow, and I want to hit him."

"So do I, and I'm not the person he's been tormenting. Don't hit him, though. He'd probably strike you back and make up some story about how you attacked him first. Bullies are like that. But bullies can be sacked, Alexander."

"He says I'll never learn anything if I let Mama coddle me."

Oak propped his boots on the railing, and leaned back in his chair. The day was beautiful, his brothers were on hand to see him safely to London, and Vera might even make the trip with them. Life was good, truly it was. Or it should be, but at that moment, nothing in Oak wanted to decamp for London.

"Mr. Forester was dishonest, Alexander."

"A gentleman never lies." Alexander was grinning, the first truly happy expression Oak had seen from him.

"Exactly. A gentleman is kind and honest, no matter how inconvenient that might be. Being a highwayman is much easier. I want you to understand something, though. Just as Mr. Forester tried to make you feel stupid, he tried to make your mother feel like she had no authority in the schoolroom. But here's the thing: Mr. Forester was wrong about you being stupid—you're quite bright—and he's even more wrong about your mother's lack of authority. He never told her he used the birch rod on you, and she will be furious with him for both the harsh discipline and the lying."

"Mama is never furious."

"Yes, she is. She simply doesn't show it." Or sometimes, she didn't admit to herself that she was angry. "You must tell her what you've told me."

Alexander whipped around, giving Oak his back. "She'll say I'm whining."

"You are not whining. You've been brave and uncomplaining— the opposite of whining. Your mother can toss Forester out on his ear. She deserves the opportunity to do that before you abandon her for any misguided flights."

Alexander gave him a puzzled look over his shoulder.

"Before you run away," Oak said, "and leave Merlin Hall without your protection." The words hurt. No small child should be made to feel as if an entire estate depended on him, but neither should Alexander go on believing he lacked all consequence.

"Will you come with me to talk to Mama?"

That Alexander would ask mattered in ways Oak was reluctant to examine. "Yes, I will come with you. We'd best be about it now, before Forester starts looking for you and tries to air his version of events first."

"He's with Miss Digg. I was supposed to be copying my verses, and they are supposed to be discussing Catherine's mathematics lessons, but Miss Digg locked her sitting room door. Catherine says I'm not to ask why. She seemed angry about it."

I am angry about it. "Let's find your mother." Oak rose and bent to gently hug the boy before Alexander could scuttle back into the studio. "You are a wonderful little fellow, and on whatever heavenly cloud is reserved for great artists, your father is very proud of you. I am proud of you."

Alexander, for the briefest and most precious of moments, hugged Oak back, then scampered away.

~

"ALEXANDER and I have something to discuss with you." Oak sounded more serious than Vera had ever heard him. "The matter is somewhat pressing."

Everything was pressing lately. If Vera was to leave for London, she'd best give the order for the maids to start packing, but she hadn't. Tamsin and Jeremy had to be dealt with, and she hadn't decided on a strategy for those hurdles either. The household hadn't been without family in residence for years, and instructions should be left for Cook and Mrs. Hepplewhite, and how would Bracken feel about a remove to London?

In the middle of all those questions loomed the real problem: How to part from Oak Dorning?

Alexander clutched Oak's hand, and Oak stood beside Vera's son as if that was normal, as if Alexander had every right to cling to his hand.

Would that he did. "Please have a seat," Vera said. "My lists can wait." Not that she'd started on them.

"I would rather stand, Mama, if you please."

Oak was trying to convey some message to Vera, about forbearance or urgency. She could not tell which.

"Then you may stand," Vera said, "and you have my complete attention."

Alexander sent Oak an unreadable look and dropped his hand. "Can't you tell her, sir?"

Oak shook his head. "Courage, lad. Your mother has loved you since before you drew breath. She will love you when she's wearing wings and playing a harp."

That was true. That was absolutely true, and even as that thought went flitting through Vera's mind, another more ominous truth chased it off.

"Alexander, is there a reason you are reluctant to sit?"

Another glance at Oak, then a nod. "A gentleman doesn't... That is, Mr. Forester... My bum..." Alexander knuckled his eyes. "He birches me all the time. For nothing. For forgetting things he never taught me, for a sum being off by one. He birches me for crying when he birches me. I hate sums. I hate Latin." A shuddery breath followed. "I hate everything, and I'm going to run away, but Mr. Dorning said I must speak to you first. I must not leave you without my protection, but, Mama, I cannot stay if you are leaving Merlin Hall."

Of all the reasons Alexander might have had for interrupting Vera's morning, she hadn't seen this one lurking among them—or had she? Vera's belly became a pit of sick foreboding, while Oak sent her that steady, searching look.

Alexander's dignity must be protected every bit as fiercely as his safety, and Vera must effect that miracle without dissolving into rage or tears herself.

"Is your bum sore?" she asked.

Alexander nodded. "I sleep on my belly, but I don't like that. Mr. Forester keeps asking me if I want a pillow. He's not being nice, he's being mean when he asks."

"He will soon be unemployed," Vera said, rising and coming around the desk to take a chair beside Alexander. "I never gave him permission to physically discipline you. It never occurred to me that he'd use a birch rod on a six-year-old."

Alexander bristled. "I'm almost grown up."

Oh dear. "True, but because you *are* almost grown up, how would Mr. Forester's means of chiding you work next year, when you are even taller and stronger than you are now? One of these days, you might have planted him a facer, and because you are faster than he, he would soon be unable to best you. Is the schoolroom merely a place to demonstrate pugilism?"

"You mean I could birch him right back?"

No, no, no. Fisticuffs and violence were no way to resolve anything, but Vera again caught Oak's eye, and he seemed marginally less stern.

"Mr. Forester would never see it coming," Vera said, brushing Alexander's bangs from his forehead. "The poor man would be smarting into next week if you gave him a birching. I'm glad you told me about this, Alexander."

Alexander bore her touch easily for once. "I'm not peaching?"

"Of course not. You are telling the truth. I hope you will always tell me the truth. And I am being absolutely honest when I tell you Mr. Forester was wrong to beat you. I was wrong to trust him with your education."

And good God, what if Alexander hadn't had Oak Dorning to confide in?

"You were wrong, Mama?"

"Yes, I was wrong, and I am sorry. Mr. Forester is no longer your tutor. You will help me select his successor when we are in London."

Alexander's smile was painfully hesitant. "*We* are going to London? Will Catherine come, too, and Bracken and Mr. Dorning?"

"Mr. Dorning is making his home in London, and he and his brothers will escort us there for a visit. We shall leave tomorrow."

Oak's smile was subtle. "Will we, now?"

"We shall, and Mr. Forester will take himself off elsewhere at first light."

Alexander looked from one adult to the other. "Do I have to go back to the schoolroom now?"

"No," Vera said, rising. "I must have a discussion with Mr. Forester, and you and Mr. Dorning will take your art lesson."

Oak touched her arm. "I would rather be with you when you talk to Forester."

Vera would rather not be alone with Jeremy Forester either, but after tomorrow, she'd be back to fighting her domestic battles without Oak at her side.

"How hard can sacking one arrogant puppy be?" she asked. "His pride will be less affronted if I speak with him privately." The dread Vera felt at that prospect was probably nothing compared to the dread Alexander had hidden every day for months.

She would rage and sob about that later.

"Not hard, but not pleasant," Oak said. "Forester will be easier to deal with if his disgrace has no audience, you're right about that, but make him heed your summons, Vera. Don't accost him in the schoolroom. Let Bracken and your biggest footman know what's afoot and station them right outside the door. Have a bank draft for the total sum of his wages and severance in hand when you confront him."

"Carry the birch rod too, Mama. Swing it around right near him before you actually swat him on the arse with it."

Oak ruffled Alexander's hair. "Language, lad."

"Should I have said on the bum?"

"Better," Vera said, though tears were threatening. "Away with you both. Enjoy the lovely day, and please don't say anything to Catherine about London. I want to tell her myself."

"Yes, Mama. Come along, Mr. Dorning. We can sketch Charlie."

They left the room, though Oak paused long enough to toss Vera a wink and a salute. Her son did not offer her a stiff little bow, and that—that—finally inspired Vera to tears.

CHAPTER TWELVE

"What do you mean, you're leaving Town?" Oak asked. "Longacre gave me to understand we were to share these quarters."

A pair of porters brought Oak's trunk in from the baggage coach and continued up the steps. Endymion De Beauharnais waited until they were out of earshot to reply.

"I'm leaving London at the end of the week for home," he said. "I've missed my family. You're here to keep an eye on the place. Don't fret about the rent. I've paid my share through the end of the quarter."

De Beauharnais was something of a dandy, always dressed with a touch of flamboyance, as if he feared that his impressive talent and great good looks weren't enough to get him noticed. His penchant for style was not merely a matter of public display, though. If he lounged by the fire in the evening, he did so wearing a pair of fantastically embroidered slippers. At the breakfast table, he wore a silk banyan of the richest, most vivid blue.

He was a splendid specimen with an eye for beauty, but today he was attired from head to toe in chocolate brown, and even his waistcoat was a subdued creation of beige with mere dashes of red and gold embroidery.

"But why leave now?" Oak asked as the porters trooped back down the stairs and out the door.

"You have a nose," de Beauharnais replied. "Town in summer is an assault upon the olfactory senses. Most anybody who can has decamped for the shires, and I haven't seen my parents for months. They write the most plaintive letters, as if I'm off to war rather than kicking my heels in Town."

The porters returned with the last of the trunks, this one holding Oak's easels and supplies.

"To the top floor with that one," Oak said, for the jewel in the crown of these bachelor quarters was a garret with north-facing windows that did excellent service as a studio.

"What of Lady Montclair's reception?" Oak asked. "Will you miss the summer's premier gathering of patrons and artists just as your star is rising? Longacre speaks of you most enthusiastically, and I'm surprised he sent me any commissions at all when you're on hand."

De Beauharnais wandered into the front parlor that opened off the foyer. The furnishings were comfortable without descending into bachelor-shabbiness, another reason to like the place.

"Longacre is sending you commissions already?"

"Three. Children's portraits, which I will enjoy, but which you are also quite capable of painting."

De Beauharnais watched the scene beyond the window, a pleasant London side street in a not-too-expensive neighborhood that was nonetheless an easy walk to both Mayfair's mansions and the hum and bustle of the Strand.

"Do you have letters of engagement for these commissions, Dorning?"

"Only for the one."

The porters tromped down the steps, the older of the two stopping in the doorway to the parlor. "That's the last of it, guv. We'll be off to The Coventry, and good day to ye."

Oak tossed him a coin. "My thanks, and regards to my brothers if you should see them."

Sycamore, may he be damned to the circle of hell reserved for scheming siblings, had insisted on escorting Vera and the children to their temporary lodgings, and Ash had abetted him. *Run along to your studio. Surely you have some painting to do.*

Only Vera's understanding smile had allowed Oak to make a civil exit.

When the porters had closed the front door, de Beauharnais sent Oak a brooding look over his shoulder.

"Dorning, don't take this the wrong way, but be careful where Longacre is concerned."

"He likes to manage matters," Oak said, "for which God be thanked, because the Academy's more tedious business doesn't see to itself. I feel sorry for an artist whose health makes painting impossible, but Longacre seems to deal with that challenge philosophically."

De Beauharnais had modeled for his classmates, and Oak had occasion to know the man was as exquisite without his clothes as he was wearing them. The Creator had fashioned in Endymion a male ideal, one who could have easily made his way as a model, art instructor to wealthy young ladies, or ornament at large. He was that stunning and had that much ability.

And yet, he was leaving London just as his talent was gaining notice. "De Beauharnais, are you well?"

De Beauharnais tossed himself into a wing chair. "I am quite in the pink. Why?"

"Because your usual taciturn nature has taken a turn for the melancholy. I am overjoyed to be back in London at last, prepared to make my mark here professionally, and delighted to renew old friendships, while you are nearly gloomy. What is this about?"

De Beauharnais fiddled with the undone bottom button of his

waistcoat—ivory from the look of it. How did an artist of limited means afford ivory buttons?

"You always have paid closer attention than most."

Oak took the opposite wing chair, feeling abruptly travel weary and out of sorts. "I have rearranged my entire life to be in London at long last. I can finally have the company of people who will not think me odd for stopping to stare at the reflection of sunlight on a mud puddle. I need not explain why a sunset is such a challenging subject, and neither must I make excuses for staying up all night to finish a project. I am at last among those of like precious faith, as it were, and now you decamp without a real explanation. If you're pockets to let, I can cover the rent."

Vera had paid him in full and added a generous sum for the landscape of Merlin Hall.

De Beauharnais parted with one of his rare, startlingly warm smiles. If Oak ever painted de Beauharnais's portrait, he'd do it to try to capture that smile.

"One forgets that people like you exist, Dorning. Don't let the capital wear the decency out of you. As it happens, I am for once well fixed, but I'm frankly disgusted at what I had to paint to earn my latest commission. I made a compromise that I will be ashamed of for the rest of my life. It's time to go home to the people who know me as plain Andy Hackett and paint some landscapes."

"They will be gorgeous landscapes." De Beauharnais occasionally preferred men as intimate partners, though Oak had also known him to enjoy the company of women. A man's personal appetites were nobody's business, but any fellow who indulged an attraction to his own gender took a risk.

Perhaps those risks explained de Beauharnais's plans. "Is there anything I can do to help?"

De Beauharnais rose, bent down to hug Oak about the shoulders, and ambled for the door. "Bless you for offering, but no. I've made a mistake. I must consider how to atone for the wrong I've committed.

Do you know if Mrs. Channing intends to bide in Town permanently?"

The subject was being changed. A friend did not try to unchange it. "She has lodgings here as long as she's inclined to stay, and the children are with her. They will see the sights, and I hope to spend some time in Mrs. Channing's company as well."

A pained expression crossed de Beauharnais's features. "She always struck me as a sweet woman."

"She is, though she's nobody's fool."

"Verity Channing was Dirk's fool. I think he regretted marrying her, but realized that even he could not take a woman to wife, then set her aside simply because she was too good for him. He missed his Anna, he saw an available distraction from his grief, and so he charmed an unsuspecting young woman into a life she never anticipated."

Oak rose, uncomfortable to be discussing Vera in her absence. "Perhaps Channing's great battle scenes were so effective because they reflected his internal reality in addition to the horrors of actual war."

"If you insist on being that insightful, Dorning, I truly must seek a ruralizing respite. I never made that connection, and I was a guest under Dirk's roof twice, for weeks at a time on both occasions. Let's mount a raid on the larder, shall we?" De Beauharnais threw a companionable arm around Oak's shoulders. "And tell me of your first commission. We will open a good vintage and celebrate that milestone."

This was what Oak had come to London for. The company of his fellows, talk of art, and yet more talk of art.

"I am to paint the twin daughters of a Mrs. Finchley. She's some wealthy cit's wife, and her daughters will make their come outs next year."

Because Oak was ambling down the passage side by side with de Beauharnais, he felt rather than saw a change in de Beauharnais's posture.

"Mrs. Finchley? The cloth heiress who married some baronet's eldest?"

"Sounds about right."

"Longacre tried to engage me for that job. Take Tolliver as your assistant, and don't spend the commission until it's nestled comfortably in your bank account."

"Tolliver chatters." Tolly was like a sparrow, never still, never silent, and he never seemed to finish his projects. He also had a penchant for patting Oak's bum that had ceased to be friendly or funny years ago.

They reached the steps to the kitchen, and de Beauharnais descended first. "Take Tolliver. He'll guard your interests, and he honestly makes a good assistant." De Beauharnais stopped in the middle of the kitchen, hands on hips. "I will miss him."

"I will miss you," Oak said, "but you will be back, and then we need not have any more of these gloomy conversations. I see an undefended wheel of cheese in the window box. Where do you suppose Cook has got off to?"

"Market, by way of the nearest pub, bless her. She and Polly do like their afternoon pints. Bread is in the box, and that ham has a contribution to make to the contentment of English manhood."

They were soon seated at the worktable, tankards of summer ale and a platter of sandwiches before them.

"I am hungry," Oak said, biting into a sandwich. "I don't always realize when my belly's empty, but my disposition sours and my head starts to ache if I go for too long without eating. If you were a small boy, what part of London would you most enjoy seeing?"

De Beauharnais tucked a table napkin into his collar. "I thought Dirk's son was still in leading strings."

"Alexander is six, and a very serious little fellow. Catherine is fourteen, artistically talented, and as delightfully awkward as a female can be at that age. She is ferociously honest and damnably perceptive. Mrs. Channing is devoted to them both, though with Catherine the situation is a bit delicate."

De Beauharnais picked up a sandwich. "You like the children?"

"Children are easy to like."

De Beauharnais frowned at his food. "Mrs. Channing is easy to like, and I never believed the rumors about her."

The bite of sandwich Oak had just swallowed got stuck in his throat. "I beg your pardon?"

"I came upon her once on the maids' stairs. I was trying to get back to my rooms without anybody noticing my escape. Harry Carlson had Mrs. Channing against the wall on the landing. She struggled against his advances, by no means inviting them, and Carlson has been accounted Byron's better-looking twin. I believe he not only offended her, he frightened her."

Oak tried to wash the ache from his throat with a sip of ale. "Carlson was lurking on the maids' stairs, and he made advances to another man's wife?"

"I sent him packing, gave the lady my handkerchief, and promised her discretion. I mentioned something to Dirk, and he merely laughed, but Carlson departed on urgent business the next day."

"Where is Carlson now?"

De Beauharnais put his sandwich down untasted. "Like that, is it? You'll call him out and avenge the honor of another man's widow for a slight from years ago? I thought you more sensible than that, Dorning."

Oak thought *himself* more sensible than that. "Carlson is a hound, but if he implied in any regard that Verity Channing encouraged his advances, then he's a lying hound who deserves to be held accountable."

De Beauharnais untucked the table napkin from his collar, took a sip of ale, and sat back. "Dorning, are you *entangled* with Mrs. Channing?"

A gentleman would never intimate that a lady had been free with her favors, and yet, Oak did not want to deny his attraction to Vera. The night before leaving for London, he had beat the stuffing out of Jeremy Forester for mistreating Alexander, though a few of those blows had been for abusing Vera's trust too. Bracken had seen Forester off the following dawn, and reported that Forester planned to impose on friends in Manchester for the remainder of the summer.

Administering justice on Vera's behalf had felt wonderful. Still, Vera would not be best served by gossip, so Forester's remove to distant parts was a relief.

And De Beauharnais's question required an answer.

"I am not entangled with anybody," Oak said. "I am here in London to embark upon the next phase of my artistic endeavors. What rumors did you allude to regarding Verity Channing?"

"The usual." De Beauharnais set aside his ale and folded the table napkin into precise eighths. "That she was another Anna Beaumont, that she was loyal to Dirk but not necessarily faithful, that she had appetites an older husband could not entirely satisfy."

The food in Oak's belly curdled. "Who would say such things?"

"They weren't said overtly, Dorning. You know how men talk once the port starts flowing, a quip here, a clumsy jest there. I paid it all little mind."

Perhaps at the time, that had been true, but de Beauharnais had lost the demeanor of an old friend happy to share a schoolboy raid on the larder. His gaze had gone bleak, and he wasn't partaking of the food.

"What aren't you telling me, Diamond?"

"I hate that name."

"*Andy*, I have known you since university, and I consider us friends. What the hell aren't you saying?"

De Beauharnais rose. "You are being fanciful, Dorning. Not at all like you. Must be the foul miasmas off the river going to your head." He strode for the door, attempting an air of casual humor that fell flat.

"De Beauharnais—*Hackett*—Verity Channing came to the capital largely because I offered her my escort and encouraged her to make the journey. I have introduced her to my brothers, and I am fond of her children. I consider her a friend. If you do not tell me what the hell has put you in this odd mood, I might have to beat it out of you."

The threat was actually a form of flattery. Oak engaged in fisticuffs with only his brothers, whom he loved dearly.

"I might like that," de Beauharnais said, pausing at the doorway. "I might enjoy that thrashing very much. All I can tell you, Dorning, is to watch your step with Richard Longacre and take Tolly with you to any commissions Longacre sets up for you. Welcome to London."

～

"SO WHAT DID you do about the moony-eyed tutor?" Sycamore Dorning asked.

Vera had sent the children up to their rooms with the maid-of-all-work, a cheerful soul who introduced herself as Sissy Banks. Ash Dorning had made his farewells, claiming a need to stretch his legs after hours in the coach.

Sycamore was ostensibly showing Vera about the premises, though any fool could see the town house was lovely and commodious.

"I informed Mr. Forester that I'd decided to take a holiday of indefinite duration and could not in good conscience ask him to wait for our return." Oak's plan had worked wonderfully, obviating the need for harsh words and harsher judgments. Vera's character reference for Jeremy Forester had noted his punctuality and self-confidence, which any mama ought to read as faint praise indeed.

Miss Diggory's character had merited slightly warmer words, but only slightly.

"That sounds like something Oak might have cooked up," Sycamore said, peering at the spines of bound volumes on the library shelves. "Polite, not quite dishonest, expedient."

Vera missed Oak already, which boded ill for her return to Merlin Hall. She wanted to sit down with a strong cup of tea and a few biscuits, put her feet up on a pillow, and stare at nothing for a good twenty minutes. She was back in London, in part because Oak was here, but not entirely.

"Have you something in particular you wish to say to me, Mr. Dorning?" For he did seem to be lingering beyond the requirements of a polite host.

"Forthright," he said, turning his back on the books. "I like that, and I will take the liberty of returning the compliment. My brothers and I were raised in Dorset."

Oh no, not this speech, not here, not now. *Not ever.* "And in Dorset," Vera said, stalking off across the Axminster carpet, "young men are safe from the wiles of scheming widows. Alas, not so in Hampshire, where an unsuspecting fellow can be set upon by the likes of me, who was so underhanded and devious that I waved actual paintings at your virginal artist brother. Is that what you were about to say?"

Finely arched brows drew down. "I doubt Oak is a virgin. The quiet ones generally get away with the most mischief, I always say."

"I like your brother, Mr. Dorning. I like him, I *respect* him, and I owe him more than mere wages for the work he did. I don't know what rumors you've heard, but I would never attempt to manipulate or take advantage of—"

Mr. Dorning was holding up a hand. "This conversation has gone off in quite the wrong direction. It might surprise you to learn that in Dorset, we have our share of merry widows, merry wives, and merry maids. We have merry lads, too, come to that, and probably a few merry sheep, but I digress. My brothers are comely fellows with plenty of charm and good manners. I tell you in all modesty that the Dornings are well liked. We don't put on airs, and we do look after our tenants and neighbors."

Vera crossed her arms. "Do you look after one other?"

"Ma'am?" Sycamore looked genuinely puzzled.

"I'm sorry. My memories of London are unhappy, and I underestimated the effect on my mood of coming back here. I am tired and out of sorts." *And I miss Oak.* "Please continue."

"I am the youngest brother," Sycamore said, ambling along the bookshelves. "My station in life required that I keep track of my older siblings. They mistakenly referred to that as spying on them, but no matter. I have a forgiving nature; I overlook their error. In the course of my keeping track, I had reason to learn that every one of my older siblings had a sweetheart or two. I have a niece as a result of one of those forays into romance on the part of my oldest brother."

"Tabitha," Vera said. "Oak misses her."

Sycamore came to a halt beside a statue of some winged goddess holding a wreath aloft. "He *said* that to you?"

"Why wouldn't he?"

"Because Oak doesn't talk about such things. He goes off and sketches dragonflies. He does miniatures of Hawthorne's children and shows our solemn little Greta how to draw flowers. He doesn't maunder on about private matters."

Since when had missing a loved one become a private matter? "He admitted to missing you, Mr. Dorning, and to being lonely. I don't think telling you that violates a confidence."

Sycamore peered at the head of his mahogany walking stick—a unicorn. "You make my point for me," he said. "My brothers all had their youthful romances. Some of them had several youthful romances at once, but not Oak. He was in love with his art, with light and water and colors and all manner of whatnot. When Ash took a fancy to the vicar's daughter, Oak drew him a little sketch of her. When Hawthorne became infatuated with both of the Dunsworth twins at once... I digress yet again. Oak does not become smitten, but he is smitten with you."

"That is not my fault." *And I am smitten with him too.*

Sycamore propped his walking stick against his shoulder. "Mrs. Channing, you insist on seeing accusation where I intend only deepest respect. Oak does not fall in love with mere mortal women, and yet, he has fallen for you. He is head over ears for you, ergo, you must be a woman of immense character and heart."

Vera sank onto the sofa before the fireplace. "I believe you mean to compliment me, though your flattery doubtless presages a warning."

Sycamore took the place beside her without being invited. It was his house and his sofa, true enough, and yet, Vera suspected he was presuming by nature. Perhaps he'd had to be.

"You wish for me to convey a warning? Very well, for I am nothing if not agreeable in all things and womanhood's most humble servant. Oak has not been in love before. He will without doubt make a hash of the whole undertaking. He will no more acquit himself sensibly in this regard than I could paint a recognizable portrait of my own foot, though I assure you I am possessed of two handsome feet."

Vera began to like Oak's brother, in the manner one could like an enthusiastic puppy or nosy neighbor. "You are keeping track of something that is none of your business, Mr. Dorning."

"Oak would do the same for me, if he ever stopped painting long enough to recall who I am. The point of my overture is to assure you that you have an ally in me. My resources are substantial, and if you should ever have need of a friend, please consider including me on that honored list."

He looked both earnest and embarrassed to make that offer. "You are very like Oak, Mr. Dorning. You don't strut about declaiming heroic poetry, but you are a good man."

"Then you take my point? About Oak having little experience in matters of the heart? He won't mean to miss the mark, but we all do."

"And is your experience so vast in matters of the heart, Mr. Dorning?"

He rose and tugged the bell-pull. "I've learned from my brothers' examples, and I learn from watching my customers at The Coventry Club. The capacity of the human heart for foolishness is unbounded. You are far from home, and my brothers are all handsome dunderheads. I mitigate damage as best I can."

He extended a hand to Vera as she got to her feet. "You are very sweet, Mr. Dorning, but after a spot of sightseeing and maybe some shopping, I will return to Merlin Hall, and Oak will bide here in

London. Your fears are for naught, though I appreciate very much your good intentions."

He kept hold of her hand. "It's Oak you should appreciate. He has five other brothers just like me, only worse. Our two sisters are as formidable as the lot of us brothers put together, and we've collected a few in-laws to round out our forces. If you are Oak's friend, then we are at your service, Mrs. Channing."

He bowed over her hand, then—the handsome bounder!—kissed her cheek. "Oak can't take his damned art to bed at night, can't kiss it good morning, can't enjoy an ice with it, or canoodle with his art on a rainy morning. I've always thought Oak dedicated, I never considered him a fool. You are proof that my faith in him has been justified."

He withdrew, swinging his walking stick and whistling.

The maid appeared with a tea tray as soon as Mr. Dorning had departed. Vera fixed herself a cup, put her feet up on a hassock, and stared off at nothing for a good twenty minutes.

And all the while, she missed Oak.

                        ~

"I MIGHT HAVE to revise my assessment of London," Vera said, leading Oak up the steps of her temporary home. "The children are having a wonderful time."

Oak was not having a wonderful time. Between sittings for the Finchley twins, de Beauharnais's sour mood, and Cam and Ash providing Vera an escort more days than not, Oak's London sojourn was starting off on a decidedly not-wonderful foot.

"Are *you* having a wonderful time?" Oak asked as they reached Vera's bedroom.

She paused, hand on the door latch, her smile mischievous. "I'm about to."

"As am I." Thank God, at long last. Though Cam and Ash would exact a price for taking the children to see the menagerie on the staff's half day.

Vera continued into her sitting room. "Alexander adored Astley's, and if Catherine ever runs away from home, I will find her in the Academy's exhibition rooms. What of you? Is Town living up to your expectations?"

Oak closed and locked the door. "I'm settling in. I have a paying commission to work on, and that is a significant step." Though the Finchley twins were difficult young women. Rather than regard their portrait as the indulgence of a loving parent, they seemed bored and resentful toward the whole undertaking.

As was—how could this be?—Oak himself.

"Come," Vera said, holding out a hand to him. "Making love in the middle of the day feels naughty, and I haven't felt naughty since we left Merlin Hall."

Oak by contrast hadn't felt *right* since leaving Merlin Hall. London in summer was hot and smelly, true, but it was still London. Still the thriving epicenter of British culture, and still where Oak needed to be.

He took Vera's hand, followed her into the bedroom, and closed and locked that door too. "This is a lovely house."

"You sound surprised." Vera began untying his cravat. "Sycamore and Ash have two others. I gather they are slowly investing their profits in real estate, and Ash explained that your family also owns a shop that sells botanical remedies and fragrances."

She draped his cravat over the clothes press and started on the buttons of his waistcoat.

"My father was a passionate amateur botanist, and Dorning Hall has many acres devoted to his specimens and experiments. My brother Hawthorne, ably overseen by Casriel and assisted by Valerian, is turning Papa's passion into a business venture."

Vera stepped behind him to take off his coat, then his waistcoat.

"Your family is very enterprising," she said, laying his clothing over the back of the chair at the escritoire. "I admire that. My brothers will live and die on their acres. They will never see London and won't care that they've missed it. Sleeve buttons."

Oak held out one wrist then the other so she could undo his cuffs. "Vera, might I kiss you?" This whole business was going forth a little too predictably, even briskly.

She put his sleeve buttons on the blotter of the escritoire. "I was hoping you'd ask." She approached him and stepped into his embrace. "I miss you."

Some of the tension that had been hounding Oak since arriving in London eased. "I've missed you too. Sycamore took you to our shop, didn't he?"

"Ash did. How can you tell?"

She'd abandoned her usual floral fragrance for one of the Dorning blends. A meadow-y, grassy scent with a hint of lemon.

"My sister-in-law Margaret is becoming something of a *parfumier*. You're wearing one of her creations." Vera was also wearing too many clothes. And Oak would do something about that, soon. "Holding you feels good," he said. "Holding you..."

He kissed her cheek, and she kissed his mouth. "I have had such dreams of you, Oak Dorning. The nights in London are short, but also very long." She emphasized the last word with a glancing caress to his falls, behind which nothing much had grown particularly long.

What the hell is wrong with me? He was in London, finally being paid to create fine art, enjoying an afternoon tryst with a woman he adored, and life was going swimmingly—wasn't it?

"Boots off," Vera said, stepping back. "We have only so much time, and I have plans for you, sir."

Perhaps that was the problem, Oak mused, pulling off his boots. They had only so much time. They had hours for this encounter— time to make love, talk, nap, and make love again—but in the larger sense, their time was almost gone. Vera might still be in London on the staff's next half day, but what about the week after that?

"I have plans for you as well," Oak said. "May I see to your hooks?"

Vera turned and presented him with her nape. That she was

eager to be intimate with him was lovely, but must they be so rushed about their intimacy? Could true intimacy be rushed?

He peeled her out of her clothing, and punctuated the disrobing with a kiss here and a caress there. Vera was soon down to her shift, and Oak wore only his breeches.

He did not want to remove them, which made no bedamned sense at all. "Let's cuddle a bit," he said. "My mind is still wandering off to my last sitting, and that is not where it should be."

Vera treated him to a slow, thoughtful perusal. "I have realized something about my marriage."

Not something happy. "Tell me."

"Dirk was unfaithful to me."

Oak gathered her in his arms. "I am sorry. You re-created yourself to be the wife he needed and wanted, and infidelity was no sort of recompense."

"I don't mean he slept with other women, though he well might have. I mean he put art before all else, even the children. The other woman was his art, and she was a jealous and demanding mistress. Do you know, Dirk never took me for an ice at Gunter's?"

Oak hadn't taken Vera for an ice at Gunter's—not yet.

"We were in Town for months at a time," she went on, "and my children have seen more of London's sights in the past week than I saw in all the time Dirk and I lived here. He couldn't be bothered to escort me sightseeing, not when we were attending this supper or that lecture night after night, and he was painting by day."

She rested her cheek against Oak's chest. "I was so lonely here."

Oak was lonely, but he hadn't put that label on his feelings. Homesick, unsettled, at sixes and sevens.... the honest term was *lonely*.

"Come to bed with me," he said. "I have been lonely for you."

The next kiss was different, slower, more honest, more of an admission of longing and desire. Oak scooped Vera into his arms and carried her to the bed.

"We're not to christen the wall of your brother's home?" Vera asked when Oak came down over her.

"Maybe next time. I am abruptly in a tearing hurry to be out of my breeches." He sat up and dispatched with the last of his clothing. "Do you know why I am in such a hurry?"

"Because you've missed me."

"That too." He settled over Vera again, and now his flesh was as willing as his spirit. "I want to love you witless, then take you for an ice at Gunter's." He wanted to give her something Dirk had not, wanted to share with her an experience Dirk had denied her, however prosaic.

Vera still had on her chemise, but she scooted and wiggled and soon had it rucked up to her waist.

"I want to love you witless too, Oak Dorning."

The sight of her—braced on her elbows, naked from the waist down, legs splayed, chemise bunched around her middle and barely covering her breasts—was a composition of such perfection that Oak took a moment simply to drink in the picture she created.

The pinks and whites and in-betweens, the afternoon sun creating mellow golden light and soft shadows, the attitude of frank erotic welcome and unsatisfied desire... If he painted for the next hundred years, he could never do this version of Vera justice on canvas.

So he would do justice to her on the bed. Oak settled into her embrace, joining them as slowly as he could bear to. Vera set a deliberate, demanding tempo, but soon pleasure threatened to swamp Oak's control.

"Let go," Vera whispered. "Please."

He held out for another half-dozen slow, hard strokes, but his will was no match for her passion, and they were soon thrashing their way to glory. When the pleasure had burned down to embers, Oak levered up enough to let cool air eddy between their bodies.

"When I make love with you," Vera said, stroking his back, "I am thunderstruck, or lightning struck. I feel like that tree I saw as a girl at my grandmother's. Consumed by a fire from within."

"An apt analogy." Oak did not want to move, did not want to leave Vera's embrace. He eased away, used a handkerchief to keep the resulting mess from the sheets, and sat back. "Let me hold you."

They arranged themselves spoon-fashion under the covers, Vera fitting against Oak like the familiar treasure she was. She was soon breathing in an easy, steady rhythm, but Oak could not manage to join her in slumber.

His mind was busy, full of the Finchley portrait and of Mrs. Finchley's less than subtle attempts to inveigle him into her bedroom. Tolliver had accommodated the lady—his nickname was Jolly Tolly for a reason—and thank God the portrait was all but finished. Longacre had made no more mention of the other two subjects, and Oak had a sneaking suspicion those commissions had gone to other artists.

Then too, Mrs. Finchley hadn't paid him. She'd asked for an invoice and said something about her husband having the final say on all expenditures.

London in reality was not quite the portrait Oak had painted of it in his mind.

"You mustn't let me fall asleep," Vera murmured, rolling over to face him. "Richard Longacre has asked me to pay a call. He says he has some painting or other that I'm apparently supposed to gush over. Are you free tomorrow afternoon?"

Oak would rather avoid Longacre until the Finchley painting was done and delivered. He'd packed up the unfinished work to complete in his garret rather than be under Mrs. Finchley's roof without Tolliver's escort.

"I must work tomorrow," Oak said. "But I am free now. Shall we have that vanilla ice?"

"I would love to, but first, I fancy another treat, if you don't mind?"

She arranged herself in such a manner that she could lick her treat to her heart's content, while Oak fisted his hands in the sheets and prayed for self-restraint. By the time Vera had situated herself over him, he'd forgotten about Gunter's, portraits, and anything but making love to the woman in his arms.

The pleasure was explosive, with Vera giving no quarter until Oak was a panting heap of happy male beneath her, and she was curled onto his chest, her chemise *hors de combat* at the foot of the bed.

As Oak drew a sketch of Merlin Hall on her back, thunder rumbled in the distance. The sun still shone through the window, though the curtains stirred on a sudden breeze.

"The children will be back soon," Vera murmured, pushing up off Oak's chest. "The bad weather will send them pelting home. Ah, well. I had my treat." She stretched luxuriously, which presented her breasts to Oak in all their lovely perfection.

"I still want to share an ice with you," he said as the curtains whipped about on a warm gust. "I truly do."

Vera shifted off of him, and rather than come down beside him, she left the bed and closed the window.

"I'd like that, Oak, but today is apparently not the day for that outing." She retrieved her chemise and dropped it over her head.

And that was wrong. They should not have to leap out of bed and dress in haste, should not have to forgo their ice because of the blighted weather. They should be making love at the end of a pretty summer day, talking quietly of domestic matters while Oak grumbled a little about how the cat in the Finchley painting still wasn't quite right.

He shook himself free of that mental litany and climbed from the bed. Vera had disappeared behind the privacy screen, leaving Oak to dress himself. He borrowed her hairbrush to tidy up and was soon once again fully clothed.

Vera emerged from behind the privacy screen, dressed and needing only a few hooks done up before she was presentable.

Rain hit the window in a few hard spatters, then a steady downpour began.

"Stay until your brothers return with the children," Vera said. "I don't want you walking back to your rooms in this downpour."

"I'd rather Cam and Ash not find me here," Oak replied. "They will speculate about how you spent your afternoon, and they will interrogate me without mercy. If I'm elsewhere, they won't know we've been trysting. Besides, I like a good ramble around old London town, and rain does interesting things to light."

A hard rain turned London's streets into sewers, and the stench in summer was not to be borne. He'd forgotten that about London.

Vera hugged him, and he hugged her back. "I wish you could stay."

"I wish I could too."

He kissed her again, wondering how many more times they'd exchange those words. Vera accompanied him to the front door, insisting he at least take an umbrella. He complied to oblige her, but a mere umbrella was pointless against a summer cloudburst.

"Give my regards to Longacre," Oak said as Vera stood with him in the foyer. "I will call upon him soon myself."

"And you will take me for a vanilla ice," she said, kissing his cheek. "I will look forward to that, Oak. Very much."

She smiled, he smiled, and then he was out in the frigid rain, wrecking his boots, missing the mud of the Hampshire countryside, and wondering why in the bloody hell he'd ever thought London was where all of his dreams would come true.

~

YESTERDAY'S LOVEMAKING had been spectacular and harrowing, though Vera congratulated herself on having sent Oak on his way before she'd succumbed to tears. The fire of his passion had destroyed her from within, as lightning had destroyed her grandmother's tree.

Where a pleasant memory should have stood, Vera instead felt heartache, sorrow, and towering frustration.

Why in the name of everything dear must Oak be so determined to make his way in London? Why did she hate the place? For she still did. The noise and crowding were bearable, but the memories...

Vera nonetheless took herself off to call upon Richard Longacre, not quite sure why she dreaded the encounter. Richard had never been among those who'd offered insults to her face or her person, and he'd been a loyal correspondent since Dirk's death.

He admitted her into an elegant parlor, one so lavishly adorned in gilt-framed art that Vera felt as if she were at an exhibition rather than in a private home. Stern men in dark clothing, pretty ladies in elaborate brocades, bucolic landscapes, and the occasional storm-tossed sloop covered the walls, each frame nearly touching the ones beside, above, and below it.

The furniture was fussy as only relics of the last century could be. The harpsichord looked to be of Italian extraction, with elaborate carving on the side panels. The underside of the raised lid depicted some goddess or other reclining on billowy clouds, while winged cherubs flitted above her, strumming gilt lyres.

The music was open to a Scarlatti sonata, the notes as dense on the page as the bric-a-brac was on Longacre's sideboard and shelves. Snuffboxes, scent bottles, puzzle boxes, porcelain figurines, minia-tures... a whole curiosity cabinet was devoted to porcelain pipes.

To a more educated eye, Longacre's public parlor might be a jewel box in miniature.

Vera hated it for the ostentation alone. A single jeweled and enameled snuffbox was an elegant touch, a dozen was surely ridiculous.

"Shall I ring for tea?" Longacre asked, closing the parlor door. "I am overjoyed to see you in the capital at last, and I must say you are in great good looks."

His perusal of her was a little too obvious for Vera's liking, but then, Longacre was an artist, albeit retired, and they had not seen each other for several years.

"Thank you, and tea would be appreciated. You have quite a lot of art here." She offered that observation, because clearly Longacre was proud of this collection.

"My little acquisitions give me great joy," he said, tugging a bell-pull. "What do you suppose Dirk would make of these treasures?"

Vera had no idea what Dirk would have made of them. Oak would find the crowding alone appalling.

"Dirk never called upon you here?"

"Alas, no. Do you miss him?"

A friend might ask that question, though Longacre wasn't quite a friend. "Of course. Time helps, but Dirk was my husband, and he was still very much in his prime. Your note mentioned a painting you wished to show me." She injected a note of cheerful curiosity into her voice, though the change of subject was nearly rude.

Vera wished she'd waited until Oak could have joined her on this visit. Something about Longacre was off, just as his recommendations for staff for Vera's nursery had proved to be off.

"Has London brought back old memories, Vera?" Longacre asked, rearranging his snuffboxes one by one.

"Not many. I am content with my life in Hampshire, and I am much concerned with raising my children and running Merlin Hall." *About that painting?*

The tea tray arrived, and Longacre asked her to pour out. She obliged, though the point of the exercise was apparently to show off Longacre's elaborately decorated antique Meissen service.

When the requisite two cups of a pedestrian gunpowder had been consumed, Longacre rose.

"And now, my dear, if you'd accompany me to the library, I have something to show you." His tone was cordial, but something about the look in his eyes—assessing rather than inviting—made Vera's skin prickle. This painting was apparently the point of the visit, and thus she allowed Longacre to escort her down the carpeted corridor to another elaborately decorated chamber.

The library's oak wainscoting was carved with leaves and fruit worthy of a drunken apprentice of Grinling Gibbons; the ceiling sported an entire toga-clad pantheon apparently involved in a stag hunt. The manic quality of the composition suggested the artist had tried to imitate the great Antonio Verrio—tried and failed.

Perhaps Longacre had had a reason for not inviting Dirk to his home.

"Our masterpiece is this way," Longacre said after he'd closed the door. "An exceptional work, exquisite really, and one I'm sure the artist was very proud of."

An easel sat in the far interior corner of the library, where direct sunlight could not reach the painting. Vera approached, prepared to make complimentary noises about some old master's use of light and perspective and whatever.

She stopped six feet away from the abomination propped on the easel.

"I never posed for that," she said, heart hammering against her ribs. "I would never... Where did you get this?"

The woman depicted in the painting was Vera, right down to the exact shade of her hair and the exact curve of her jaw. She wore nothing, not even a quilt draped over one ankle, as she sprawled amid pillows and sheets. She held a golden goblet in her left hand and stroked her own breast with her right. Her eyes were half closed, her expression rapturous.

A pipe sat in a dish on the table beside the bed, a thin stream of white smoke drifting heavenward. Vera did not have Oak's eye for artistic details, but this painting looked very like Dirk's other nudes.

Very, very like them. It felt exactly like a Dirk Channing.

"Magnificent," Longacre said, taking the place at Vera's side. He stood too close, but she did not give him the satisfaction of moving away. "Utterly captivating and worth a very great deal."

"I did not pose for that painting."

"Oh, perhaps not, but your husband doubtless had both opportunity and imagination sufficient to create the likeness anyway. How I do envy him those privileges. There's a French comte, a fellow who somehow managed to salvage a fortune from all the madness, and he is particularly fond of red hair."

"You cannot sell that, and Dirk did not give it to you." Vera's voice betrayed her with a tremor, as she realized the signature was either Dirk's or an exact copy.

"Believe what you like, Vera Channing. I will sell that painting unless you pose in a similarly uninhibited manner for the artist of my choice."

Vera again felt like that lightning-struck tree, but the emotion that consumed her was rage. "I will do no such thing. Go ahead and sell that... that nonsense to your wealthy French friend."

Longacre drew a finger along her jaw. "Dirk said you have hidden reserves of determination. He loved that about you, while I don't find that quality at all attractive in a woman. Allow me to present you with a bit more context. You either model as I please to have you model, or I will ruin Oak Dorning. I had enough eyes and ears at Merlin Hall to know you've grown quite fond of our mutual friend."

Longacre stepped closer to the painting and took a quizzing glass from his pocket. He examined the area of the painting devoted to the woman's most intimate parts, then glanced assessingly at Vera's hair.

"You cannot ruin Oak Dorning," she said. "He is both honorable and talented and has committed no transgression that Society would censure him for. He has already taken his first paying commission, and many more are likely to follow."

Even as Vera's rage blended with a gnawing fear, she could also sense a puzzle. *Why* was Longacre doing this? Many women were willing to take coin to serve as nude models. What drove Longacre to violate her dignity this way?

"I can ruin anybody," Longacre said, offering her a pleasant smile. "Did you know Mr. Dorning has already slept with the woman who offered him his first commission? She hasn't complained about his prowess in bed, but she's none too impressed with his artistic skills. I doubt she'll pay him for either."

Oak would never, ever, not in a million, starving years...

"Mr. Longacre, do you truly mean to imply that in the history of portraiture, no artist has slept with a patron or subject? Not once? That this happens in only the most debauched situations?"

Longacre's smile disappeared. "Dorning can swive his way from here to Carlton House for all I care, and you're right—a good-looking young man like that, taking what's on offer, might not be remarked. But if I put it about that his work is inferior, that he has a particular disease so far gone that it affects his mind, that he cannot control his drinking... then his dream is over before it begins, and that would be a pity. He will never paint professionally unless you do as I say."

"Why?" Vera asked, turning her back on the easel. "You will ruin me or ruin Oak Dorning, and neither one of us has harmed you in any fashion."

Longacre gave her another flesh-crawling perusal. "Dirk Channing loved you. He bragged about your wifely devotion, but you were never more than a consolation to him. The woman he loved above all others, the one who made him an artist, was Anna Beaumont. For her devotion, he ruined her as thoroughly as I could ruin you—unless you pose for me like the harlot Anna became for Dirk."

"Pose for *you*?" Vera asked.

"Oh, no. For an artist whose skill far exceeds my own."

A tap sounded on the library door. Longacre admitted a butler holding a card tray. "Mr. Oak Dorning come to call, sir. He's in the guest parlor."

Longacre took the card. "Thank you. Please tell Dorning I will be happy to receive him in a moment. I will see Mrs. Channing out first."

So pleasant, so courteous, and so rotten.

The butler withdrew on a bow.

"I will see myself out," Vera said.

"Of course." Longacre also bowed to her politely. "Make your grand exit, shed a few tears because of the horrible imposition I'm making—though you bore Dirk a child, so you happily shed your clothes for him on countless occasions. Down a few glasses of cordial to soothe your nerves, then send me a note letting me know when you can sit for my artist. Take your time. I have much to do putting the finishing touches on Lady Montclair's exhibition. I think you'll approve of my choice of artist when you meet him, but don't be surprised if I want to watch the genius at work. I do so enjoy creative talent on display."

Vera stalked out, not even pausing in the foyer to gather up her hat and parasol.

CHAPTER THIRTEEN

Oak was sitting on the guest parlor's piano bench, peering at a complicated Scarlatti sonata, when Richard Longacre joined him.

"Dorning, a very great pleasure to see you."

The front door closed rather decisively as Oak rose and bowed. "Longacre, the pleasure is mine."

From the corner of his eye, Oak saw Vera Channing marching down the walkway. He'd hoped to catch her here and take her for that ice at Gunter's. The pace she set suggested she was late for her next appointment, but something else was wrong. She had neither bonnet nor parasol, which made no sense.

"How are you finding the great metropolis?" Longacre asked, taking a seat in an ornate wing chair. The whole parlor was over-stuffed with art, like an eccentric uncle's attic, and the quality appeared to be of that caliber as well.

"I am pleased to be in London," Oak said, taking the opposite wing chair, though he had not been invited to sit. "The change of scene is an adjustment, one I am happy to make. The Finchley portrait should be done in the next few days, and I thank you again for the commission." Oak stopped short of the obvious question: *Have you another commission for me?* Or would the work disappear, as de Beauharnais had predicted?

Something passed over Longacre's features, as if he'd detected an unpleasant odor and was too well bred to remark it. He rose from his chair, took a seat on the piano bench, and undid the bottom button of his waistcoat.

"Dorning, don't take this the wrong way, but Mrs. Finchley has a surprisingly discerning eye, and she was not that impressed with what she saw of your work." He began to play. The harpsichord was in good tune, suggesting somebody in the house used it regularly. "She was more complimentary of your amatory skills—appallingly complimentary, in fact."

Oak was tempted to point out that Tolliver had accommodated the curiously insistent Mrs. Finchley. Instinct warned him to take a different approach.

"What were her specific criticisms of the portrait?" Oak asked.

Longacre's fingers flew over the keys, filling the parlor with blazingly fast notes. "She said you made the girls look too much alike."

Oak had specifically insisted they dress differently, adopt different postures, and occupy their hands with different objects.

"What else?"

"From the mother of twins, that's criticism enough. She might well consider the liberties you took as compensation enough for the work you've done. This is not a good first impression to make on London Society, Dorning."

Nor was it an accurate impression. "Did you convey the details of my faux pas to Mrs. Channing? She apparently left here in something of a temper."

Longacre indulged in a cadenza of ascending parallel sixths, a barrage of arpeggios, a waterfall of parallel thirds, then a grand pause.

"I might have mentioned the situation in general terms," Longacre said. "Nothing more." He went off into another display of pointless bravura, then brought the piece to a crashing conclusion. "Come along, Dorning. I have something you will want to see."

Vera had mentioned that Longacre had wanted to show her a painting. Oak rose and followed his host down the hall to a garish caricature of a high baroque library. More gods and goddesses cavorted on the ceiling than in the combined pantheons of Greece, Rome and Persia.

"My little portrait is one of Dirk Channing's best, I think," Longacre said, closing the library door. "Over here."

Oak expected a battle scene, more of Dirk's screaming horses, expiring heroes, horrified drummer boys, and brave—spotless— commanding officers shouting orders from the saddle, while smoke and sunlight created an otherworldly sky.

This was not a battle scene.

"What do you think?" Longacre asked. "A bit shocking, but brilliant nonetheless. He did a matching version using Anna Beaumont as his model. They are different, but equally magnificent."

The painting purported to be a portrait of Vera in a moment either anticipating or following sexual repletion. Her splendid form lay exposed to the spectator's eye in intimate detail and her fingers trailed over a taut rosy-pink nipple.

Either Dirk Channing had got the color of his own wife's nipples wrong, or...

Oak stepped closer and was immediately assailed by the scent of linseed oil. He peered at the painting, noting a certain flatness to the white of the sheets and even to the undersides of Vera's breasts.

"Dirk gave this to you?" Oak asked, examining the signature.

"He did, perhaps as an apology for ruining my Anna. She and I were to marry, you know. The agreements had been signed."

"I did not know that." Did Vera know that? "It's an impressive work." *For a forgery.* "But why show it to me?"

"Because you will paint a few others just like it for me. She has already agreed to model for you."

Oak pretended confusion. "I do not aspire to paint nudes of decent widows, Longacre, no matter how lovely or willing the model." Before an artist took up that challenge, he had to establish himself with more mundane subjects.

Longacre clapped him on the shoulder, and Oak nearly reacted with a fist to Longacre's gut. "She's very pretty," Longacre said, "and while she might have played the proper widow in Hampshire, we in London know her to be quite willing to... Well, she's quite *willing*. Dirk was absorbed with his art, and Vera amused herself as best she could."

Oak studied the painting again, lest his disgust show on his face. The forgery was good, but especially in the shadows, the brushwork was a shade too flamboyant to be that of a man who'd come of age artistically in the shadow of Gainsborough and Reynolds.

"Did Mrs. Channing amuse herself with you?" Oak asked.

Longacre examined a showy gold ring on his smallest finger. "One doesn't frolic and tell, Dorning. You mustn't be jealous. Vera and I are friends of long standing. If you do a good job with the series I have in mind, she might permit you an occasional interlude. I'm not possessive, and she's no longer quite as dewy as I prefer my women."

I will kill you, and you will die a eunuch. Oak shifted his gaze to the hunt scene on the library ceiling.

"Have you any other of Channing's nudes? I was under the impression he preferred landscapes and battles scenes."

"He sent me one other, of Anna Beaumont. As I said, it matches this portrait of Vera. Some artists do that, paint the same study over and over, changing only a detail or two. In this case, Dirk changed models. He liked to paint in series, and I have wondered how many odalisques he might have secreted away at Merlin Hall."

"May I see the other one?"

This occasioned pursed lips and a slight frown. "If you're to paint Vera for me, then I suppose studying another Channing can only stand you in good stead." He opened a drawer beneath the reading table near the window and lifted out an unframed canvas similar in size to the painting that purported to be of Vera. "Have a look."

Oak had a thorough, close look. "And what will you do with the series you're commissioning from me? The paintings of Mrs. Channing?"

Longacre put the painting away. "You are refreshingly naïve, Dorning. I am not commissioning anything from you. You will paint a half-dozen nudes of Vera Channing, mimicking as closely as possible the style of Dirk Channing. I will do with them as I see fit. She is an exquisite subject without her clothes, and the continental market isn't nearly as puritanical as the English market."

Nor as familiar with Dirk's works. "Am I to understand that I'm painting forgeries for you?"

Longacre came around the table and patted Oak's arm. "You country fellows are always so direct. You are painting études for me, exercises in the style of Dirk Channing. If your conscience troubles you, don't append a signature to them."

Because even Longacre had sufficient skill to replicate a signature. "Why would I do this?"

"Because if you don't, I'll make sure everybody Dirk knew recalls just what a strumpet Vera Channing was, and I will similarly mention what a mediocre talent *you* are, Dorning." He ambled over to the painting in the corner and tilted his head. "I daresay you could use some practice, and what artist worth his salt wouldn't want a chance to paint more of this?"

Longacre had many allies in the art world; Oak had few. Longacre was powerful; Oak was all but a charity case. Longacre had been poisoning the well of Vera's reputation for years; Oak had known—and loved—the lady for a handful of weeks.

Before he pounded Longacre to dust, he'd discuss this situation with Vera. "This is not what I had planned for my first major London project," Oak said. "You will allow me some time to consider the matter."

"Consider away," Longacre replied, facing Oak and waving a hand toward the door. "I will be too busy to arrange the sittings until after Lady Montclair's reception. Run along, Dorning, though you really should be thanking me. Not every young man gets to spend hours in the same room with a naked woman as beautiful as Vera Channing."

Oak turned to leave, but stopped short of the door. "Why involve me in this? Why not paint her yourself if she's so willing?" He knew the answer well enough: Because once the paintings were done, Longacre would threaten blackmail, and if Oak refused to do the paintings, his fate would be artistic and social ruin.

"You ask why I don't take on this delectable project myself," Longacre said. "I would love to paint again, but"—he held up his hands—"rheumatism, young Dorning. My hands grew too soon old, but my eye is as sharp as ever, so don't think to do a poor job on these paintings."

Oak bowed, barely. "I will see you at Lady Montclair's reception."

"Bring Mrs. Channing," Longacre said. "Tell her to wear something pretty."

Oak withdrew, pausing only long enough to snatch up Vera's hat and parasol before showing himself out.

∽

VERA HAD REACHED a place after Dirk's death where crying was pointless. Grief became a leaden weight on the soul, a burden that had to simply be borne as she explained to Alexander—again—that his papa would not come back from heaven.

Ever.

The grief she experienced as she took down her favorite shawl was different. This sorrow was angry, and potentially destructive. She began packing by folding the shawl into the bottom of the trunk she'd unpacked only a week past.

"Excuse me, ma'am." Sissy Banks stood in the doorway. "You have a caller."

Vera was not in the mood to put up with Sycamore Dorning's

banter or Ash Dorning's faultless politesse, but she needed to thank both men before she left London once and for all.

"I'll be down in a moment, and we won't need a tray."

Sissy bobbed a curtsey and withdrew, her expression dubious.

Vera took a moment to assess her appearance in the cheval mirror. The woman gazing back at her was pretty enough, if a bit pale, but she was brittle. Hard. Determined. London had once again taken a toll on her, and she would be glad to be quit of the place.

She would not be glad to be quit of Oak Dorning, but that could not be helped. She tried for a smile, and the result was a grimace. No false good cheer, then. She marched into the parlor prepared to dispense brisk thanks to a Dorning brother and came to an abrupt halt when Oak turned to face her.

"You have my hat and parasol."

"I thought to catch you at Longacre's and take you for an ice."

Leaving London would be easy, an enormous relief, in fact, but leaving Oak Dorning... His gaze suggested he knew that Vera had started packing. Or, worse, he knew what Longacre had been about.

"And how did you find Mr. Longacre?" she asked.

"I found him pusillanimous and much in need of a good pummeling. What did he say to you, Vera?"

"That doesn't concern you, but I'll be leaving for Hampshire this afternoon. There's a coach departing from—"

He took a step closer. "I saw the painting, the one he claims is a Dirk Channing nude portrait of you."

"I know my husband's signature, Oak. You needn't be delicate."

Another step, and even though Oak was holding a frilly parasol and a lace-trimmed bonnet, he had the quality of an advancing storm.

"I know your *late* husband's signature too. Did you smell that painting, Vera?" He set the bonnet and parasol on the sideboard. "Did you examine how flat the whites were? How extravagant the brushwork in the shadows?"

"The portrait feels like a Dirk Channing, and that is all anybody will care about."

Oak touched her cheek. "That painting is a forgery, and not a very good one."

This mattered to him for some reason, while to Vera... "Nobody will believe it is a forgery, and unless I leave this vile, stinking, cesspit of a city, Longacre will make trouble."

"As he's been making trouble, apparently, for years. He tried to convince me that you were like Anna, dispensing favors in all directions, but now I wonder if Anna was like Anna, or if Longacre spread the same lies about her that he did about you."

Vera could not think when Oak was gazing down at her so sternly, when he was close enough to touch and cling to. She sidled past him and took a seat on the sofa.

"Richard was the reason Dirk's friends thought I was fast?"

"I am certain of it. Did you know Richard and Anna were engaged at one point?"

Oak came down beside her, and Vera wanted nothing so much as to throw herself into his arms. But that was no solution to anything.

"I knew they were distantly related, second cousins, maybe third, but I didn't know they were engaged. Why does that matter? Longacre has decided to ruin me, and I want to be far, far away when that happens."

Oak's touch on her shoulder was as light as a kiss. "What a coincidence. He's set about to ruin me too."

She caught his hand in her own. "I do not understand, and I am sick of feeling like a simpleton. Whether it's my ignorance of art, or my inability to see an enemy standing right before me, or the intrigues and schemes Longacre is weaving... I want to go home and never leave Hampshire again."

Oak wrapped her hand in both of his, his grip warm and firm. "Maybe that's what Longacre wants. Maybe his objective is to ensure that we both scamper away, trembling in fear of him and his vast influence in the art world. I am not inclined to oblige him."

"Oak, he will ruin you. You have waited years for a chance to take your place in London's artistic community. You have talent, your family here will support you, you deserve..." The damned tears tried to ambush her, but she won that battle by virtue of pure stubbornness.

"Longacre told you to either pose for more nudes, or he'd resume his nasty gossip. Did he also tell you he'd ruin me if you refused his coercion?"

"Exactly, but, Oak, if I do pose for him, he'll ruin you all the same."

Oak tugged her hand, and she sat back so he could wrap an arm around her shoulders. "Explain yourself."

"If I pose for whoever Longacre has recruited for this project, you will go happily on your way, painting this or that commission, submitting to the exhibitions, occasionally lecturing at the Academy, and making your way ever closer to admittance."

"My dream come true."

"And Longacre will make it a nightmare. Sometime soon, he will ask you to do a few canvases for him, and you will realize they are to be sold as forgeries. He will threaten to start talk about your brothers' club, to malign you, to support a rival if you don't accommodate him. You will have your membership in the Academy if and only if Longacre wants you to have it, and by that time, you will be as bitter, manipulative, mendacious, and scheming as he."

Oak was quiet for a moment, his lips against Vera's temple. The tears threatened again, because the moment was both so sweet and so bitter.

"He told me," Oak said, "if I did not paint a nude series of you, in Dirk's style, that he'd set about my ruin immediately—and yours, too, of course. I refuse to accommodate him, Vera."

Well, of course, Longacre would choose Oak to execute the portraits. Oak had the talent, and for Vera to model for him—a former guest at Merlin Hall—would appeal to Longacre's twisted sense of revenge.

Vera made one more try to reason with the man she loved. "You can either have eventual membership in his bloody Academy, Oak, or you can have a very hard road, with Longacre thwarting you every step of the way."

"You had that hard road," Oak said. "You didn't know he was thwarting you, which in a sense made it even worse. For that alone, I will see Longacre pay." Oak spoke calmly, and his thumb moved over Vera's nape in lazy circles. He was not ranting or hurling wild threats, he was planning a composition only he could see.

"He will ruin you," Vera said dully. "I am apparently already ruined, did I but know it, but you... You take him on at great risk to your ambition, Oak."

Oak planted a cheery little smacker on her cheek. "Longacre takes *us* on at great peril to *his* ambitions, Verity Channing. Did you know that your nipples shade closer to pinkish taupe than the pink of a blooming carnation? And here,"—he patted the juncture of her thighs gently—"the hair is the same color as the hair on your head, not three shades lighter, as Longacre's forger would have us believe. You take after a brunette rather than a redhead in that regard."

He'd seen both the forgery and Vera's naked form, *studied* both, which Vera should not have found amusing, but she did.

"What has that to do with anything?"

"Somebody forged the painting Longacre showed us. I suspect I know who, and he is doubtless neither the first nor the last to be so manipulated. Longacre believes himself the prince of some artistic fiefdom here in London, but he's been oppressing the peasants for too long."

"What are you planning to do?"

"I will do what countrymen have done in the face of tyranny from time immemorial, Vera. I will lead a peasant revolt and march on the capital, but I need your permission to do it. My plan now will impact you and potentially your children, and I cannot undertake it without your support."

"Peasant revolts seldom succeed, Oak. What are you asking of me?"

"First, don't let Longacre hound you back to Hampshire. Stay in

London a little longer. Second, plan on attending Lady Montclair's exhibition with me."

Vera subsided against him, her feelings in a welter of confusion. "Dirk asked me to marry him, and that was the last time he asked me for anything of substance. The rest was... he assumed, he politely demanded, he simply took. He did not ask." And Vera had learned to give, to do without, to argue on occasion, and to manage in a lonely marriage.

"I am asking for your trust," Oak said, "and your help, but you must do as you see fit. You have children to consider, and cleaning London's artistic house can profit you nothing."

Not quite true. If holding Richard Longacre accountable for his schemes benefited Oak, Vera would consider that a substantial profit.

"What weapons will you wield, Oak?" she asked. "London is not your home turf, and Longacre has been at his games for ages."

"I will use the same weapons artists have used since the first caveman dabbed ashes on the walls of his abode: I will use talent, truth, and courage."

Courage. *Oh, that.* "I am not very brave," Vera said.

"Verity Channing, you are the bravest woman I know."

She liked the sound of that, liked the utter conviction in Oak's words. What had cowering out in Hampshire earned her anyway, but more loneliness and a pair of spies in her nursery?

"Tell me what you have in mind. I will do what I can."

❦

OAK TIMED his first sortie for midday at a club frequented by those whose greatest artistic successes were in the past. The staff was discreet, the furnishings comfortable, and the capacity for gossip endless.

Stebbins Holmes greeted him with a friendly wave from a table by the windows. "Dorning, a pleasure. You are here in London at last and ready to take the art world by storm. Do have a seat."

Oak didn't bother perusing a menu. The meal would be steak, bread, and potatoes, washed down with port or ale. Yeoman's fare, of all the ironies.

"Longacre is attempting to blackmail me," Oak said, just as the waiter approached the table. The fellow's steps faltered, and he sent Holmes a bewildered look.

Holmes gestured him closer. "Steak for me and my guest, Timothy, and you will ignore Mr. Dorning's penchant for hyperbole."

"Longacre is also trying to blackmail Verity Channing," Oak said, before the waiter was more than three feet from the table. "We are not the first victims of his scheming. Why haven't you done anything to stop him?"

A mug of ale arrived for Oak. Holmes apparently preferred port. "We all have our little secrets, Dorning. One doesn't fly into the bows over petty dramas."

"Ruining Dirk Channing's widow, spreading falsehoods about her over a period of years—falsehoods that saw her repeatedly assaulted and nearly raped—is not a petty drama. It's contemptible, dangerous, and exactly how artists end up in unflattering caricatures."

Holmes took a sip of his port. "And do you know why the Society of Artists failed in my father's day?"

"Because everybody was too focused on petty squabbles rather than on advancing the cause of British art. I have eight siblings, Holmes, I know all about petty squabbles."

The food arrived, and a few more diners took tables nearby. Oak recognized two older fellows who lectured at the Academy and an Italian sculptor in London to execute some expensive commissions.

"Exactly," Holmes said, picking up a knife. "Internal strife can ruin an organization, and artists are an excitable lot. Richard has fallen victim to unfortunate medical limitations, and he works tirelessly for the Academy as a whole. We overlook his games for the sake of the greater good."

We, meaning Longacre's plots were common knowledge in some circles. Oak lost what appetite he'd had.

"Endymion de Beauharnais is leaving London," Oak said, loudly enough to turn a few heads. "He is one of the best talents to come along in decades, and Longacre's disgusting behavior is forcing him back to the shires. You allow that to go on."

Holmes sawed away at his steak. "A pity, but de Beauharnais is young. He has time to return to the fold when he's not so—"

"He will go to Paris," Oak said, "and he will make sure the French know why he's turned his back on London. From there, he will go to Rome and very likely the Americas. A man with that much raw ability need not put up with an Academy that tolerates extortion and corruption."

The Italian was gaping. Three waiters were assiduously perfecting the arrangement of cutlery at empty tables nearby.

"Longacre forces talented young painters to create forgeries," Oak said, which might have been slander, except it was the truth. "He's attempting the same game with me."

Holmes leaned across the table, his air of urbane humor deserting him. "Paint a few pictures for him," he all but whispered, "and he'll move on to fresh game. Richard is venal, but not stupid. He hasn't the talent to create his own reproductions, and one must nearly admire his ingenuity. I suspect if Anna Beaumont hadn't thrown him over for Dirk Channing, he might have been content to paint landscapes and flatter dowagers."

Oak did *not* lower his voice. "But instead of politely ceding the field where Anna was concerned, Longacre has been sulking ever since she threw him over."

"It's worse than that," Holmes said, glancing around. "He refused to release her from her betrothal agreements. If she'd married Dirk, Longacre would have brought suit. It's not the done thing, but a man can legally sue for breach of promise."

"A gentleman would not," Oak countered. "And this is your

version of supporting the greater good? Ignoring Longacre's tantrums and crimes?"

Holmes speared a bite of beef and chewed vigorously. "Dorning, you are not a bad artist, and I did have hopes for you, but London might not be the best place to pursue your ambitions."

Oak resisted the urge to dash Holmes's port in his face. "I point out to you that the Academy is harboring a forger, slanderer, and blackmailer among its ranks, and your reaction is to tell me to run along, because this criminal has the patience to winkle commissions out of women married to wealthy cits. Where is your honor, Holmes? Where is your artistic integrity?"

"Artistic integrity? Dorning, such a quaint concept has no place in—"

"Without our integrity, artists have little to offer but shallow decoration to cover the water stains in our grandmothers' parlors. You have disappointed me, Holmes, and betrayed your calling. I'll bid you good day."

Holmes set down his knife and fork. "It's not as if Anna Beaumont was a lady. She was just some country cousin Richard took a fancy to. Pretty enough, but Dirk had to have her, and she had to have him, and there was no reasoning with either of them. One feels sorry for Longacre as the losing party."

"The losing party," Oak said, "will be the Academy if you continue to ignore Longacre's behavior. And, Holmes?"

"Dorning?"

"Anna Beaumont was a lady. They are *all* ladies." He nodded rather than bow or offer his hand.

"Dorning," Holmes said, picking up his wineglass, "righteous fury becomes no one."

"Sheer complacence in the face of wrongdoing becomes us even less, and moral bankruptcy becomes us not at all."

CHAPTER FOURTEEN

Oak took a seat at a faro table, though in the afternoon light, The Coventry Club was deserted. "I need your help."

Sycamore and Ash, lounging at the same table, exchanged a glance. Oak had been watching his siblings exchange glances since his earliest youth, and those looks had never included him. He read this one easily enough: What has Oaky-dear got up to now?

Cam spoke first. "I thought you needed to conquer the Academy and storm London, paintbrushes affixed to your blunderbuss?"

"Shut your mouth, Cam," Ash muttered. "What do you need?"

Ash was something of a family conundrum. He was as smart with numbers as Cam, as canny with people as Valerian, as physically robust as Hawthorne, and as good at strategy as Casriel. London's matchmakers should have snapped him up and tossed him into parson's mousetrap long ago, but he remained quite single and quite self-possessed.

"I need..." Oak considered the pictures in his head. "Vera and I need allies."

Cam propped his boots on the corner of the table. "Has the fair widow mis-stepped?"

"No." Ash had spoken at the same time as Oak.

"Cam, you are overdue for a thrashing," Ash went on. "I will be happy to oblige you anytime you wish to step into the ring with me at Jackson's. You, yourself, said she is smitten with Oak."

"Ladies, when presented with a more attractive and youthful alternative, can get unsmitten," Cam said. "Sensible ladies."

Oak cuffed him on the side of the head. "Stop playing the brat. This is serious. Vera has done nothing wrong."

"You would not care if she had," Cam countered. "You are so lost to sense, you would dance naked in the streets of Mayfair for that woman."

"Of course I would, and you are jealous."

"I am. Utterly overcome. Envy is my middle name, and of *you*, of all the daft notions." Cam smiled sweetly, and in the midst of a very serious matter indeed, Oak smiled back.

"About damned time," Ash muttered, for no particular reason Oak could discern. "What do you need from us?"

"I need Cam's big mouth, and your discreet asides, Ash. I need gossip, the very thing Longacre has wielded so skillfully against Vera and has threatened to wield against many a talented young artist. Except that our gossip will be true. Dirk Channing likely felt sorry for Longacre's lack of artistic success, or perhaps Dirk had a guilty conscience because Anna Beaumont chose him over respectability. Longacre appeared to patch things up with Dirk, the better to spread lies about his former betrothed."

"Hell hath no fury like a hack revealed as a hack..." Cam muttered.

Ash hit him on the arm, a mere love tap compared to the pugilism Ash was capable of. "We are to put it about that Longacre is a liar?"

"We will let that be our little secret," Oak said. "For now, put it about that Longacre trades in lucrative forgeries."

"Does he?" Cam asked, his smile acquiring a feline quality.

"He absolutely does."

Ash's smile bore a close resemblance to Cam's. "Do go on..."

~

"I LIKE THIS ONE BETTER," Oak said, standing beside de Beauharnais before the finished work. "A touch of haste has inspired you."

De Beauharnais wiped his hands on a rag. "A touch of revenge. You really think she's better than the one I did for Longacre? I walked a line with that one, trying to make the crime obvious, but not too obvious."

"You succeeded. Your shadows are more restrained with this one," Oak said, comparing the newest creation with the work he'd had shipped in from Merlin Hall. "You had a better example to copy from. Dirk's rendering of Anna Beaumont simply wasn't as good as this treatment of Hannah Stoltzfus."

"I'm good," de Beauharnais said, as if coming to that conclusion for the first time. "What do you make of the Anna Beaumont portrait Longacre has?"

"It's genuine," Oak replied. "Dirk painted many such portraits. I found eleven different nudes at Merlin Hall, all hidden behind lesser works. One of them is a Sapphic duo and nothing short of spectacular. Channing is well known for painting in series—duets, trios, octets —but what artist paints a series of eleven canvases? Longacre got his hands on the twelfth canvas—Vera didn't even realize she'd sent it to him—and that gave him unholy inspiration where Mrs. Channing was concerned."

De Beauharnais rolled down his sleeves. "You should call me out, Dorning. Mrs. Channing should call me out."

"You've apologized," Oak said, gesturing at the fresh canvas, "and you created this. I could never have accomplished what you did with the Stoltzfus portrait, particularly not in so little time."

"I am good, aren't I?" De Beauharnais fished a sleeve button from his pocket and began fumbling with his cuff. "What a notion."

"You are not merely good, de Beauharnais, you are brilliant. That you doubt yourself is exactly why Longacre must be banished from the Academy. He sent you enough minor commissions to keep you dependent on him and kept you from more ambitious and visible work. You are not the only person he's abused like that."

De Beauharnais seemed to be having trouble with his sleeve button.

"Let me do that," Oak said, taking the little gold clasp from him. Oak fitted the sleeve button through the buttonhole of the cuff, then did the second one. When he would have stepped back, de Beauharnais caught him by the hand.

"I wasn't bound for home," he said, his grasp desperately tight. "I told you I was leaving Town, but that's not... I wasn't."

Foreboding gathered low in Oak's belly. "Andy?"

"You go at night," de Beauharnais said, gaze on the carpet, "to London Bridge. You tie your boots together at the ankle—tie them tightly with a complicated knot, so tightly you can't pull your feet out if you lose your courage. Sew your pockets full of rocks. I'm told it helps if you're drunk. A wool cloak is best, because it becomes heavy in the water. You put a coin in a little bag around your neck—for the watermen or the mud larks, whoever finds you—and then you jump. A few minutes later, all your troubles are over. Tolly's cousin went that way."

"No," Oak said, grabbing him by the scruff of the neck. "No, you do not. Not ever."

De Beauharnais eased away and turned his back, pulling a handkerchief from his pocket. "My uncle said I wouldn't last a fortnight in London. I lasted six weeks before Longacre started... started in on me. That was nearly a year ago. I couldn't see a way... Well, I saw one way."

Oak allowed de Beauharnais a measure of privacy—and himself as well, because as bad as Longacre's behavior toward Vera had been, this was worse.

"Longacre came after me when I'd been in Town less than a week," Oak said. "I suspect that was because you had pulled free of his clutches. As long as he had you to do his bidding, other newcomers were safe. You had enough talent for whatever Longacre got up to."

"I did four paintings for him," de Beauharnais said, facing Oak, "in addition to whatever commissions he sent me. I will write to the buyers of the forgeries and claim there has been confusion regarding the works they possess. That will likely land me in prison—one of the patrons is quite wealthy."

"No," Oak said, "it will not. I have a different suggestion. We will sort out Longacre, and he will take responsibility for any *confusion* he involved you in. And I assure you, before you came to Town, some other talented prey stumbled into Longacre's snares, and some others before that."

"We're not the only ones?" De Beauharnais wandered over to the Dirk Channing nude and ran a careful finger over the lady's pale flank. "You're sure of that?"

"Positive. I am equally certain we will be the last. Now tell me about the four forgeries."

~

IN THE DAYS leading up to the Montclair reception, Vera watched how a family with one foot in the countryside and one foot in the capital mobilized its resources. Sycamore's traveling coach made another lightning dash from Town to retrieve Trenton, Earl of Wilton, whom Oak knew as a connection through his sister Jacaranda's husband, Worth Kettering.

Kettering himself returned to Town, contending that his lady wife would disown him if he allowed a Dorning scheme to unfold without his supervision.

Other august parties were quietly recruited, including a marquess once thought dead on the battlefields of Spain—another of Worth Kettering's clients, as it happened—an enormously tall earl who counted among Willow Dorning's in-laws, and a half-dozen courtesy titles connected to the Dornings through the vast labyrinth of polite society.

Not a one of them had any claim to artistic expertise, but they had come when Oak needed them.

"I begin to see," Vera said, "that the world I thought so broad and sophisticated was really just Dirk's little corner of a littler corner."

"Little corners can be complicated," Oak replied, "and you look splendid."

Vera had dressed for the Montclair reception in a creation of burgundy silk, one she and Sissy Banks had spent endless hours stitching. Her shawl was deep lavender, as were her gloves, and the ensemble honestly made her feel more than a little self-conscious.

Also pretty and *daring*. "You chose the colors," she said, turning before the mirror in the foyer. "I would never have been this bold."

Oak had chosen a waistcoat of the same shade of burgundy as Vera's dress, and his boutonniere was a tiny lavender bouquet designed to match Vera's wrist corsage. Without saying a word, he proclaimed himself to be coupled with her, and splendidly proud of it.

"Are you nervous?" Oak asked as a coach clattered to a halt beyond the front door.

"Yes. Are you?"

He kissed her. "I am determined. Shall we?"

He winged his arm, and Vera's nerves settled. Oak knew exactly what he was doing, and more than that, he knew exactly what his honor and his art demanded of him. At Lady Montclair's reception, his air was cordial and good-humored, even as Vera sensed him reconnoitering the crowd.

"He's here," Oak murmured thirty minutes after they'd arrived. "Came alone, and there's Mr. Tolliver with Mrs. Finchley on his arm. Longacre looks surprised to see her."

And Oak sounded very pleased.

"Is Worth Kettering here yet?" Vera asked. Kettering was a solicitor. He had the ear of the Regent and invested the funds of some of the realm's wealthiest families—including his own.

"Kettering is busily flirting with the Marchioness of Hesketh, while that lady's husband looks amused. His lordship must be a client of long standing. And there's Jonathan Tresham."

Vera had had only one glass of punch, but already, her head was spinning. "I forget who he is."

"Tresham is a friend of Ash and Sycamore's. He's selling them The Coventry, and more to the point, he's one of the Academy's most generous patrons—oh, and also the heir to a dukedom. He's conferring with Her Grace of Walden, another generous benefactor of the arts. Let's give Longacre another five minutes to enjoy himself, and then we will put an end to his games. Shall we say hello to Stebbins Holmes?"

"Let's not," Vera said, setting down her empty glass. "I'm angry with him on my own behalf and on Anna Beaumont's."

And why hadn't Dirk noticed that Longacre was such a snake? But then, Vera knew why. The same art that made Oak such a keen observer had made Dirk oblivious to what was in front of his face. Made him all but complicit in his friends' mistreatment of Dirk's own wife.

The hum of conversation rose, while Oak introduced Vera to more titled and wealthy people until, by some silent signal, Sycamore and Ash appeared at Vera's side.

"Time to catch a rat?" Cam inquired pleasantly.

"Indeed it is," Oak replied. "I will fetch Longacre. You gentlemen please escort Mrs. Channing to the appointed gathering place." He kissed Vera's cheek, which raised a few eyebrows. "For courage."

"Oak was never this dashing in Dorset," Cam muttered, taking Vera by the wrist. "Come along, for I don't want to miss a minute of the drama. I will pay you an enormous sum for the Stoltzfus odalisque. Ash and I agree that it would look splendid behind the bar at The Coventry."

"Oak says it's one of a pair," Ash added, "and the matching

portrait could hang in the game room. Our clientele would likely try to buy both of them off of us the first night they're displayed. We could hold a little auction."

"Stop it," Vera said. "You are trying to distract me, because you believe I am nervous about confronting Longacre. My only concern is that I will do him a grievous injury."

Ash, a notably reserved man, treated her to a dazzling smile. "Violence can be art too. Cam, we are in the presence of a lady who understands pugilism. I am smitten."

"Not fair," Cam said, holding open the door to Lady Montclair's library. "I was smitten first, and Mrs. Channing likes me better."

She preceded them into the library, surprised to find that her nerves had indeed dissipated, replaced by anticipation.

"I like you both quite well," she said, "though I like Oak best of all, and the pair of you are ridiculous. My heavens, Mr. de Beauharnais has done a splendid job, has he not?"

One of the Stoltzfus nudes was propped on an easel, and beside it was an unsigned work that presented the same subject in the same setting—a forgery, in other words. A very good forgery.

And how ironic was it that a forgery would be the means of exposing the truth?

～

VERA HAD NEVER LOOKED MORE luscious to Oak, so much so that the business with Longacre had become simply a task to expedite. Oak pasted a hesitant smile on his face and approached Longacre, waiting patiently until Longacre deigned to take notice of him.

"Mr. Dorning. Pay attention to Lady Montclair's display. You might learn a few things. If you'll excuse me, I see Mrs. Finchley—"

"If I could have a word in private," Oak said, doing his best to look self-conscious and humble. "I need only a moment of your time."

Longacre wrinkled his nose, sighed gustily, and passed his drink to a waiter. "You might have simply called at the house, Dorning. You brash young fellows always come around eventually."

"I promise to be very brief," Oak said, "and what I have to say is best kept private. Please, Longacre?"

The begging note did the trick. "Very well, Dorning, but only a moment. Lady Montclair expects me to circulate, and there are patrons here to be fawned over."

"I really do appreciate it," Oak said. "The library is right down the corridor. This way." Longacre stopped twice during their progress across the room, once to bow over the hand of their hostess, who had been told exactly what was afoot, and once to try to ingratiate himself with Jonathan Tresham's wife.

A mistake, that.

"In here," Oak said, holding open the library door. "I've asked a few others to join us."

The few others included Vera, Ash, Cam, and de Beauharnais, of course. Also Worth Kettering—a legal perspective could prove helpful—Jonathan Tresham; Nicholas Haddonfield, Earl of Belle-fonte; Trenton, Earl of Wilton; and a few of the other more influen-tial patrons of The Coventry. Stebbins Holmes lurked beneath the overhang of the library's mezzanine, though Oak had not apprised him of the gathering's particulars.

Cam and Ash, by design, stood before Vera so her presence was also obscured.

"I have considered your proposal," Oak said, drawing Longacre into the center of the group, "and found it wanting. You either forgot or did not care that Endymion de Beauharnais and I are sharing quar-ters, and that he and I are friends."

Longacre had by now noticed the two canvases. He withdrew a quizzing glass and bent to examine them.

"These are the work of Dirk Channing," he said. "We can discuss my little commissions later, Dorning. Wherever did you find these?"

De Beauharnais sauntered forward through the crowd. "Don't be coy, Longacre. The one on the left is the one you showed me, claiming Dirk gave it to you. The one on the right is the *study* you painted. When I returned to your town house to retrieve a forgotten walking stick, I happened to take a wrong turning and came upon the work in progress. It's a very good attempt at a reproduction, but you have not appended your signature to it, suggesting it's a forgery in the making."

Longacre straightened. "It's a fine study, de Beauharnais, but I've never seen either of these. Perhaps you've had a bit too much punch again?"

The spectators had gone silent and then remained quiet in the face of Longacre's protestations.

De Beauharnais was not given to overimbibing.

"You claim this one,"—Oak gestured to the unsigned forgery—"is not by your hand?"

"Of course it isn't," Longacre scoffed. "I recognize the model, but I considered Dirk a friend. I would never... Dorning, tell them. I cannot paint. Rheumatism plagues me terribly, especially in my hands. I haven't painted for years. Ask anybody."

Vera began to make her way quietly through the crowd.

"You say you cannot paint," Oak mused, "but you can play a Scarlatti sonata at nothing less than a *vivace* tempo, complete with cadenza. You manage the buttons on your waistcoat easily, your penmanship remains elegant. When, exactly, does this rheumatism come upon you?"

"Do tell," de Beauharnais murmured. "I can't seem to recall you having any difficulty with cutlery or a tea service either."

"But I cannot *paint*," Longacre insisted. "The entire Academy knows I cannot paint."

"Perhaps they know you cannot paint *well*," Oak said, "but copying another's work is a different and more pedestrian talent than creating an original work. A Mrs. Ermentrude Danforth has provided a signed affidavit claiming you sent her a Shackleton portrait of her great-uncle. Shackleton was a court painter, his catalog is well documented, and he created no such portrait."

Jonathan Tresham, who excelled at imperiousness, crossed his arms. "What have you to say, Longacre?"

"De Beauharnais painted the general. Ask him."

"Now that is curious," Oak said. "We never mentioned that Mrs. Danforth's uncle was a general, did we? And Mrs. Danforth never mentioned dealing with de Beauharnais—she bought the painting from you, and paid dearly for it."

A murmur went through the crowd, and Longacre's bravado faltered.

"If I were to bring Mrs. Finchley in here," Oak went on, "she would attest to having eight different portraits of her daughters hanging on her walls. Mr. Tolliver would corroborate that fact. Six of the artists were inveigled into the lady's boudoir, then subsequently told their portraits were inferior and their advances forced on Mrs. Finchley. De Beauharnais and I had the good fortune to be spared her schemes, though in point of fact, those were *your* schemes, weren't they, Longacre?"

"Why would I bother involving myself in—?"

"The artists were all very talented young men," Oak said, "and they all became beholden to you as a result of your trap. Oddly enough, their careers have not prospered. One—Tolliver's cousin—is no longer with us."

"And you think I—?"

"I had an interesting conversation with Mrs. Finchley," Oak said, "to which Worth Kettering was a witness. She paid you for the portraits. She also reports that you assured her your protégés would enjoy a bit of frolic with a friendly lady. Part of the *artistic temperament*, according to you, is an inability to exercise even a schoolboy's self-restraint. Tell me, Longacre, do you approach anybody without a thought for how you can abuse their trust?"

Vera had taken the place at Oak's side. "I don't believe he does, and I can tell you exactly how he got his hands on the painting of the blonde."

Longacre's neck was turning the same shade of pink as a blooming carnation. "I never once, not ever—"

Vera cut him off with a wave of her hand. "Dirk concealed a number of nude studies behind other works hanging in Merlin Hall's gallery. They are all spectacular and quite daring. Last year, I sent you three of those lesser works without knowing what one of them concealed. I, in fact, sent you four paintings, but you returned only three, claiming none of the works had value. Mr. Dorning revealed the treasures hidden in my home. You stole from me, Longacre, and from Dirk's children."

She advanced on Longacre, and he took a step back.

"You stole," she said with lethal calm, "then you copied what you'd stolen to add to your collection of forgeries. I can only guess that you intended to sell the forgery on the Continent and then repeat your crime by selling another version to some unsuspecting American. You stole a Dirk Channing masterpiece. What have you to say for yourself?"

Ash stood to one side of Longacre, Bellefonte—surely the largest peer ever to sit in the Lords—stood on the other.

But Longacre wasn't smart enough to attempt to bolt. He instead struck a *contrapposto* pose, chin up, chest out. He lacked only a helm, shield, and winged sandals to make the heroic farce complete.

"Dirk Channing stole Anna Beaumont and ruined her good name." His chin rose half an inch. "I was owed recompense."

Vera cracked him a good one across the cheek. "*You* ruined Anna Beaumont, with your lies and gossip, with the threat of a lawsuit for breach of promise. You and you alone are responsible for any damage done to her reputation. And yet, she and Dirk were happy, and that is something you will never understand."

And now his cheek also bore that carnation-pink hue. "Anna would have come back to me."

Vera retreated a step and gave Longacre the sort of perusal usually reserved for horse droppings.

"Anna bore Dirk a child and remained by his side despite all your machinations. She would never have come back to you, for which she has my undying admiration."

Tresham, exuding disgust, sent Longacre a glare. "What's to be done with him? The Academy's reputation could be sorely damaged by yonder pustule."

Ash was flexing his fist. Cam had that particularly determined look in his eye.

"Vera?" Oak said. "What say you?" He hadn't discussed this aspect of the situation with her, but apparently he hadn't needed to.

"Richard Longacre," Vera said, "you will sell your worldly goods, including the pathetic assemblage of tripe hanging on your walls, as well as your house, your coach, and your trumpery. You will remove yourself to the Continent, and the proceeds of your estate will be set aside to support aspiring artists new to London. You will return to me the painting you stole, and you will be gone within a fortnight."

"Say yes," Worth Kettering suggested, "and we won't have to involve the gentlemen from Bow Street."

"Write out an apology to Mrs. Channing," Oak added, "and *then* we don't involve the gentlemen from Bow Street—until your remove to the Continent."

"I like that better," Kettering allowed. "Has a bit more menace to it—more justice."

Ash took a firm hold of Longacre's arm. "Pen and paper await you on the desk blotter. You're a creative type, Longacre—or you dreamed of being one. Perhaps your skills are more literary. Beg, grovel, and pray well enough on paper, and nobody will call you out."

Cam sighed. "Nobody? But I do so enjoy a spot of target practice."

"As do I," Oak added. "Start writing, Longacre."

Longacre jerked his arm free of Ash's hold. "As if you could manage a pistol, Dorning. You're barely fit for wielding a paintbrush."

Oak slipped an arm around Vera's waist. "Don't underestimate the peasantry, Longacre. Any younger son raised in the shires will be a dead shot with whatever firearm you care to name. Best start penning your farewell work."

"Make it good," Vera said. "Or I will find time in my busy schedule to drop around Bow Street. Mr. Dorning, I hear the quartet tuning up. I believe the dancing will soon begin."

Oak gestured toward the door. "May I have the honor?"

She kissed him, with a good portion of polite society looking on. "You most assuredly may."

~

THE MORNING after the Montclair reception, Vera rose to find not one but eight bouquets of flowers arranged in the foyer of Sycamore's town house. Jonathan Tresham had sent his regards, as had two earls, a marquess, several anonymous admirers, and a surprisingly tasteful little arrangement of roses from "Your dearest darling Cam."

"You have conquered London," Sissy observed, accepting a ninth bouquet from a footman. "Where shall I put this one?"

Vera took the card. Ash Dorning sent felicitations—and congratulations on her excellent pugilism. "In the parlor. The roses and honeysuckle can go in there as well, lest I foster sibling rivalry."

"Miss Catherine will be impressed," Sissy observed, collecting a bouquet in each hand.

"Miss Catherine will be impatient to take her sketchbook to Hyde Park. Cook should have some stale bread for Alexander to feed to the waterfowl."

The children had taken to London with an enthusiasm Vera hadn't anticipated, and they were soon bustling out the door, both Sissy and a footman with them. The house was quiet in the wake of their departure, and oddly peaceful.

A tap sounded on the door, and Vera opened it herself. "Mr. Dorning, good day."

Oak stood on the front steps, looking as scrumptious as ever. "Mrs. Channing, greetings. How are you?"

She stepped back. "I am well. You?" She gave herself a moment to simply enjoy the sight of him, though sadness pulled at her. She had earned a few bouquets, but the true conquest of London had been Oak's. Before they'd left the Montclair reception, half a dozen members of the Academy had found a way to be introduced to Oak, and another half dozen had been angling for the same courtesy.

Oak came into the house and stopped a few paces from the door. "Are the children on the premises?"

Vera closed the door behind him. "They are not. Cook and the housekeeper have gone to market, the footman went with Sissy and the children to the park. The day is so fine, I do not expect them back soon."

"Then I am not well at all," Oak said, advancing on her. "I am sorely in need of your intimate company. *Now*, Vera. Against the wall would suit me fine. On all fours on the parlor rug, across my lap on the sofa. I am dying for want of you."

So Oak was lusty in victory. She should have anticipated that.

Vera went into his arms. "I miss you too." They had bid each other a decorous farewell the night before, with Oak bowing over her hand as Cam and Ash had waited in the town coach.

"This isn't mere missing," Oak said, wrapping her in a tight embrace. "This is madness." He commenced kissing her in the foyer. Vera whisked off his hat even as she kissed him back. The passion erupted with the suddenness of a summer storm, and before she'd caught her breath, she was upstairs with Oak, behind the locked bedroom door.

"I can't go slowly," Oak said, hopping about as he yanked off his boots. "Not this time, Vera. You were magnificent, and Cam wants the Stoltzfus nudes. Make him pay a fortune for them." He tossed his boots in the general direction of the bed. "Let me undo your hooks."

Oak tried to be gentlemanly with her clothing, but Vera felt a slight tearing before a half-dozen hooks had been undone.

"I could take a knife to your corset strings," Oak said. "Ruck up your skirts and... God, I want you."

Unbridled desire with Oak Dorning had much—*much*—to recommend it. The first coupling was exactly like a summer storm, fierce and fast, an inundation of pleasure. The next was more of an autumn rain, slow, thorough, and quiet.

Vera told herself to fret about the children returning, or fret about something, but she simply could not, so completely had Oak exhausted her.

"That will hold me," he said, gathering Vera against his side, "for at least an hour. I spent a very restless night, Verity Channing, and that is entirely your fault."

"As did I." She put his hand over her breast and closed his fingers in a snug grasp. Never would she have been so bold while married, but with Oak, no shyness plagued her. "Did you engage in self-gratification?"

"I tried to, but it wasn't any good. I wanted you, only you, and all of you. The hands of the clock refused to move. After another two or three bouts in this bed, I intend to take you for an ice at Gunter's. I want all of London to gawk at us and whisper about what might have happened at the Montclair reception last night."

"What will London be whispering?"

"That Richard Longacre will be leaving Town under a cloud of scandal, though the details aren't circulating. That some changes will be made at the Academy, a lot of the old guard retiring from their committees, some new faces taking on the work. De Beauharnais will get the recognition he deserves." He looked at his cock in consternation. "Good God, you are inspiring me once again, Verity. This has to be some sort of record."

"You are inspiring me too. Will one of those new faces at the Academy be yours?"

"Crouch up," Oak said, patting her bum. "I have become insatiable where you're concerned."

Vera obliged and was treated to a loving by turns lazy and passionate. Her pleasure crested higher with each joining, which ought not to have been possible. She was half asleep, Oak spooned around and half draped over her, when he spoke again.

"I have realized something."

"That three times isn't enough?"

"I will never get enough of you, though I might die a premature and happy death making the attempt. What I realized is that I don't love London."

Vera rolled over so she could face Oak, all thoughts of sleep banished. "What does that mean?"

"The London I was besotted with doesn't exist. It's a place where artists are respected and well paid, where jealousy never intrudes, and patrons are uniformly supportive. That London admits of no stupid schemes, backstabbing, or petty politics. It's a pretty picture, but only that."

Vera cradled his cheek against her palm. "I'm sorry. I know what it feels like when a lovely dream is fractured by a less lovely reality. You and London will come to terms, I'm sure."

"We have come to terms," Oak said. "My terms."

A little sadness reappeared through the glow of thorough and repeated loving. "I'm glad, then. London is your dream come true. You deserve to enjoy it, especially now that you've sorted out the Academy's resident troll."

"I do not love London," Oak said, shifting over her. "I came to Town thinking to finally, finally find like-minded company, people passionate about art, people who could appreciate me for my talents. I found evil, grasping, arrogant corruption and others willing to enable it for their own gain."

"You are disillusioned?" A painful process, for a man who sought always to see the truth.

He planted a slow, thoughtful kiss between her brows. "I am less naïve."

Vera scooted a little, the better to wrap her legs around his waist. Her desire had been slacked—for now—but her appetite for closeness was not yet sated.

"I like that," she said. "*Less naïve*. Dirk married a maid of the shires, but I am no longer she, and I like that too. I have made my peace with London, and I wouldn't mind visiting again, but will you come home to Merlin Hall with me?"

She had grown bold indeed, to ask him so plainly.

Oak left off nuzzling her temple to regard her solemnly. "I don't love London, but I do love you. You are my dream come true, Verity Channing. Will you marry a younger son with little means but large ambitions?"

"I have never been anybody's dream come true," she said, trying to grasp that he had used the word *marry*. Not a liaison, not a passing fancy when he was on his way back to Dorset. "Do you know what my dream come true would be?"

"Give me fifteen minutes," Oak said. "Twenty at the most. The wall beside the vanity looks sturdy enough."

She smacked his bum. "My dream come true is to waken every morning in your arms."

"I love this dream," Oak said. "I love you, did I mention that?"

"Only the once."

He shifted up, covering her and cradling her face against his shoulder. "I love you like I love sunlight on water and rain clouds and shadows. I love you like I love the feel of a brush in my hand and a clean canvas awaiting my paint. I love you like all the colors God ever created. Please say you'll marry me."

The moment became sweet and serious as Vera stroked Oak's back and savored a dream coming true.

"You will teach Alexander to ride," she said.

"He's a natural in the saddle. There won't be much teaching required."

"And you will encourage Catherine's art."

"Until she's tired of my critiques."

She smoothed her hand over his muscular backside. "You will sketch nude drawings of me for our mutual diversion."

He raised himself up and hitched closer. "Will I, Vera? Nude sketches of you?"

"Maybe a tasteful oil, in time. Let's start slowly and see if we enjoy it."

"Yes," he said, kissing her. "Yes, and yes."

"You'll help Catherine decide what to do with the paintings of Anna when the time comes?"

"Of course. And I will paint every hillside and cow byre on Merlin Hall land and do a portrait of the Davies sisters if you like."

In other words, Oak was willing to rusticate at Merlin Hall, to set aside anything but an amateur's dabbling for Vera's sake.

"You will have commissions, Oak. I insist on it. Everybody making a sojourn to the seaside spas will come past our door, and we can certainly offer them hospitality if they hire you for their portraits."

She felt him catch hold of her suggestion, the same way he noticed echoing patterns in wall paper, clouds, and garden flowers.

"That might work."

"That *will* work, and we will return to London in spring so you can complete more commissions during the Season, and I can meet the rest of your family. You had mentioned a niece—Tabitha?—I'm sure she and Catherine would enjoy each other's company, and I am looking very much forward to—"

Oak seized her in a bear hug. "Yes. Yes to all of it, of course, yes, but you have to marry me, Vera. You must, or I will never paint anything worthwhile again."

She hugged him back. "I will happily, joyously have you for my husband, Oak, but you will also have your art."

"I will have family and friends to love, which is how the heart makes its art. That creation is more beautiful than any painting ever commissioned. I know that now."

"I want Sycamore and Ash to stand up with us."

"So do I, though Kettering will try to manage the whole ceremony."

They talked quietly of other particulars—where to hold the ceremony; when and how to tell the children and the rest of the Dorning
family, until Oak dozed off in Vera's arms and she in his. When they
woke, Vera declared herself famished for want of a vanilla ice, and
Oak, ever her servant, made that dream come true—that dream come
true, *too*—after proving to their mutual satisfaction that the wall
beside the vanity was, in fact, sturdy enough to meet all amatory
challenges.

TO MY DEAR READERS

To my dear readers,

I did wonder how Oak was going to find his happily ever after between Dorset and London. The quiet ones always bear watching. (Vera says they sometimes bear kissing too). I hope you enjoyed this little tale of true love and determination, because there's more of that in store for Ash Dorning and Della Haddonfield, our next **True Gentlemen** protagonists. *My Heart's True Delight* comes out September 22, 2020 (September 12, 2020, in the **webstore**). I expect Sycamore's story will be published in early 2021, but don't tell him I said that.

A little excerpt from Ash and Della's opening pages appears below.

If you haven't caught the most recent **Rogues to Riches** title, *A Duke by Any Other Name* is hot off the presses. Althea Wentworth approaches Nathaniel, Duke of Rothhaven, to put in a good word for her with the rural neighbors. He's adamantly opposed to embroiling himself in neighborhood politics, but that apparently doesn't preclude enjoying a few of Althea's kisses... my, my, my.

In November, Constance Wentworth gets her happily ever after, which also requires the cooperation of a grumbly duke (by the end of the book, he's not so grumbly). I've included an excerpt from ***The Truth About Dukes*** below.

I will also be this year busy updating, re-covering, and down-pricing the **Lonely Lords** series, book by book, and republishing duets and trios of delisted novellas. Stephen Wentworth's story is in the works for next spring (***How to Catch a Duke***), and I've written three Regency mystery stories for a widowed sleuth named Lady Violet. Maybe I should publish those too...?

If you'd like to stay up to date regarding all this activity, I put out a **newsletter** about once a month. I will never sell, swap, or spam your addie, I promise. Following me on **Bookbub** means you'll get the pre-order and on-sale alerts, and notices of any retail discounts. You might also take an occasional peek at my **Deals** page, where I note all the discounts and sales in my webstore as well as on the major platforms.

Happy reading!
Grace Burrowes

Read on for an excerpt ***My Heart's True Delight***!

EXCERPT—MY HEART'S TRUE DELIGHT

Lady Della Haddonfield has landed in a world of trouble. Ash Dorning doesn't feel he has the right to ride to the rescue, but neither can he stand idly by while the woman he loves faces scandal...

"IF YOU ARE SO UNFORGIVABLY CLODPATED as to challenge Chastain to a duel," Ash Dorning said, "I will not only refuse to serve as your second, Tresham, I will shoot you in the arse myself. Lest you forget, I was raised in the country. My aim is faultless."

"You wouldn't," Jonathan Tresham replied. "Della would never forgive you for wounding her devoted brother."

Ash poured two fingers of brandy from the better stock kept behind the bar in The Coventry Club's game room. At this mid-morning hour, the cleaning crew had already come through. The space was was tidy and deserted, and a perfect place to talk sense into Tresham.

Or try to. "If you add fuel to the flames of gossip," Ash said, "by involving Lady Della's name in a matter of honor, you will be the one she never forgives. As far as polite society is concerned, the Haddonfield menfolk are her brothers. Your involvement in the situation would only cause the wrong kind of speculation."

Lady Della's mother and Tresham's father had had an affair while married to other people. The tall, blond Haddonfields affectionately referred to the petite dark-haired Lady Della as their changeling, but anybody who took a close look at Della and Tresham side by side would begin to speculate.

If they had any sense, they'd speculate silently. Della's oldest Haddonfield brother, Nicholas, was the Earl of Bellefonte, while Tresham was heir to the Quimbey dukedom. Della was fiercely beloved by all of her siblings, and by any number of in-laws and relatives.

And Della was loved by Ash too, not that his sentiments had any bearing on anything.

"Why did she do it, Dorning?" Tresham took his drink to the roulette table and gave the wheel a spin. "Why run off with Chastain? He's a bounder and a rake and the worst kind of inept card player."

Because Ash managed The Coventry Club with his brother Sycamore, he knew exactly what Tresham meant. The more heavily William "Chastity" Chastain lost, the more heavily he drank, and the more heavily he bet.

"To those just down from university," Ash said, "Chastain offers a certain shallow-minded bonhomie. He's good-looking. He pays his debts or we'd not let him back in the door." Though how he paid his debts was something of a mystery.

"His damned father must be cleaning up after him," Tresham snapped. "Last I heard, Chastain was engaged to some French comte's daughter, so Papa is doubtless keeping Chastain out of trouble as best he can. I really do want to kill him."

So do I. "That won't help. Chastain got no farther with Della than some inn at Alconbury. If he wants to live, or ever sire children, he'll keep his mouth shut. The whole business will remain a private regret for both parties."

By daylight, the game room looked a little tired, even boring. The art on the walls depicted good quality classical scenes—scantily clad nymphs, heroic gods, but nothing too risqué and nothing too impressive either. Without the click and tumble of the dice, the chatter of conversation, or the sparkle of the patrons' jewels by candlelight, the room was simply a collection of tables and chairs on thick carpet between silk-hung walls.

Any Mayfair town house would have been at least as elegant and had far more personality. But that was the point: The Coventry was comfortably bland, not showy, not distracting. The focus of the patrons was to be on the play and on each other.

Ash's focus was on Della Haddonfield, whom he had given up trying to forget months ago.

"Chastain drinks when he loses and he loses nearly every time he plays," Tresham said, wandering between the tables. "Sooner or later, he'll drink too much and start wittering on about that time he eloped with Lady Della Haddonfield. He spent half the god-damned night with her in that inn, Ash. I should kill him for that alone."

"I know, Tresham,"—*God, do I know*—"but Della apparently went with him willingly. Bellefonte would tell you if that weren't the case, I trust?"

"I have no bloody idea." Tresham perched on a dealer's stool and took up a deck of cards. "I am not one of them. Your brother Will married into the Haddonfield clan. What does he say?"

"Will and Susannah are ruralizing. I gather several litters of puppies are due any day, and thus Willow remains in the country."

"I hate this," Tresham said, shuffling the deck with casual expertise. "Bellefonte ought to challenge Chastain. Bellefonte's a peer. Nobody would say a word if Chastain got the worse of the encounter."

A peer could not honorably challenge a commoner. "Deal me in." Ash took up a stool at the same table. "Has it occurred to you that

Della might be smitten with Chastain? She might be heartbroken that Chastain's father interrupted their elopement."

"Theo's theory is that Della chose Chastain because he's nothing more than a handsome lackwit. Della could manage him without looking up from her embroidery hoop. She's an earl's daughter, so Papa Chastain would eventually reconcile himself to the match." Tresham gathered up the cards and set the deck in the middle of the table. "I shall beat you at cribbage."

Lady Theodosia, Tresham's lovely wife, had apparently already had a turn trying to speak sense to him. Ash produced a cribbage board from the shelf under the table.

"You don't think Della smitten, then?"

"I know she isn't." Tresham's tone was gloomy. "She once mentioned Chastain to me when I drove out with her. Her tone was less than respectful."

Ash cut for the crib and pulled the low card. "Feelings can change."

"Not those feelings. Della expressed pity for his sire, and the opinion that Chastain will bankrupt the family within two years of gaining control of the Chastain fortune. She's right."

Play moved along, with the cards favoring Ash. His leading peg was halfway around the board when Sycamore sauntered in looking dashing and windblown in his riding attire.

"That is the good brandy at Tresham's elbow, if I'm not mistaken," Sycamore said, pausing to remove his spurs. "Since when do we give away the good stuff, brother mine?"

Ash picked up his cards to find another double run, his third of the game so far. "We are generous with poor Tresham because he needed a medicinal tot for his nerves." As had Ash. "I'm beating him soundly."

Sycamore peered over Tresham's shoulder. "William Chastain needs a sound beating. Who's with me?"

Tresham put down his cards. "What have you heard?"

Sycamore could be tactful—about once every five years—and

then only out of a perverse impulse to keep his older siblings off balance.

"Chastain was apparently in his club last night, lamenting that his French bride refuses to cry off, despite the failed elopement with a certain Lady Delightful."

Tresham was on his feet, so quickly he knocked his stool over. "I will kill him, slowly, after protracted torture. I will *maim* him, and cut the idiot tongue from his empty head. All of polite society knows that Della's given name is Delilah, and Chastain apparently knows it too. By Jehovah's thunder, I ought to ruin his father for siring such a walking pile of offal."

"If you do ruin him," Sycamore said, taking a sip of Tresham's brandy, "please do it here, so the club gets a bit of the notoriety and ten percent of the kitty."

"You *cannot*." Ash said, getting to his feet. "You cannot in any way intimate that Chastain's wild maunderings have any connection to reality or to Della, and you most assuredly cannot strut about all but proclaiming that her ladyship has an illegitimate connection to you."

"But—"

Ash stepped closer. "No. Not if you care for you her, which you loudly claim to do. The Haddonfields have substantial consequence, they have weathered other scandals. You can be a friend of the family, a cordial acquaintance, but you cannot involve yourself in this in any manner that makes it worse than it already is."

And neither could Ash.

Tresham finished his drink and set the glass down on the table with a *thunk*. "I'm supposed to be the sensible one. But then, I'm selling most of this club to you two. How sensible was that?"

"Very sensible," Sycamore said. "We're making you pots of money to go with the barrels and trout ponds worth you already have."

"Della will be a spinster now," Tresham said, and Ash sensed they'd reached the heart of the dilemma. "She's the only Haddonfield yet unmarried. They've all been trying to fire her off—even Theo has tried to help—but to no avail. Now Chastain has botched an elopement, and Della will suffer the consequences. Nobody will marry her."

"Perhaps she doesn't want to be married," Sycamore said.

"Then why elope with Witless Chastity?" Tresham snapped. "That was a desperate measure, indeed, and now she's to be an old maid."

Ash picked up the discarded brandy glass and set it on the sideboard. "She will not be an old maid. Della is lovely, charming, smart, kind, funny, and quite well connected. You are making too much of bad moment."

Sycamore sent him a curious look. "This is more than a bad moment. She spent most of the night in the same room with Chastain at the inn in Alconbury. That news was quietly galloping up and down the bridle paths this morning in the park. I discredited the rumor with vigorous disbelief, but it's as Tresh says: Lady Della has had no offers, and Chastain is not much of a prize. The appearances are dire."

If Ash could have beaten himself soundly at that moment, he would have. Lady Della had quite possibly discouraged many offers while waiting for a proposal from Ash himself.

"This is not dire," he said. "The necessary steps are simple. The Little Season is underway. We will treat Lady Della to a show of support, mustering a phalanx of eligibles to stand up with her. She will carry on as if the gossip is just that. Chastain will learn discretion in a violent school if need be, and come spring, some other scandal will have everyone's attention."

"It's a plan," Sycamore said, in tones that suggested it was a laughably stupid plan.

"And if this plan doesn't work?" Tresham asked, "then may I part Chastain from his pizzle?"

"If the plan doesn't work, then I will marry Della myself."

Sycamore for once had nothing to say, while Tresham looked

mightily relieved. Ash could make this offer because he was sure to a confirmed certainty that he was the last man Della Haddonfield would ever agree to marry.

ORDER YOUR COPY of ***My Heart's True Delight*** and read on for an excerpt from ***The Truth About Dukes***!

EXCERPT — THE TRUTH ABOUT DUKES

Robert, Duke of Rothhaven, is renewing an old acquaintance with Lady Constance Wentworth. His brother is marrying her sister, though Robert first met Constance years ago under trying circumstances. He's delighted that she's called upon him, though his circumstances are still, in a way, quite trying...

"Walk with me to the orchard." Lady Constance did not offer Robert an invitation, she issued him an order—and in his own garden, no less.

"I have not been to the orchard in years." Robert inventoried his reaction to the prospect of leaving the walled garden, and found dread, anxiety, and resentment. Next to those predictable nuisances was a growing impatience with his own limitations. "I might well fail to complete journey."

"This time you might not, but eventually, you will." Lady Constance marched to the end of the garden where the door in the wall had once upon a time loomed in Robert's mind like a portal to the edge of the world.

She kept right on going, and once again, he followed her. Months ago, on a foggy autumn morning, he'd begun experimenting with what lay beyond the garden door, navigating as far as the river. He left the garden only when the mist was so heavy as to obscure anything like a horizon. The thicker the fog, the better he liked it.

A world where he could see only a dozen feet ahead—and could not be seen himself beyond those dozen feet—had suited him splendidly. This sunny spring day, with damned birds chirping and an arrogant hare loping off toward the river, had no appeal at all.

"Come," Lady Constance said, extending her hand. "We will speak of the project you invited me here to discuss."

Robert winged his elbow at her—that was the conventional gesture offering escort, if memory served—but she instead took his hand in hers, her grip warm and firm.

"We have missed the cherry blossoms," she said. "But the plums should be in their glory. Tell me of your project."

Constance was humoring him, jollying him into taking the first few steps on the path to the walled orchard. Robert knew it, she knew it. He went with her anyway, because he had at least as much right to be on that path as the wretched hare did.

Make small talk. Distract yourself. "I would rather return to the garden. We can discuss the project there."

"I would rather wear breeches. I often do, when I paint. Skirts get in the way."

Picturing Constance Wentworth in breeches was, indeed, a distraction. "I have decided that if I'm to be the Duke of Rothhaven, I must behave as a duke. I must look like a duke, speak like a duke."

"Quack like a duke?"

"Don't be impertinent." He failed utterly to suppress a smile. "I can no longer indulge my eccentricities, confident in the knowledge that my brother will carry on as head of the family in my stead. A duke sits for the occasional portrait."

The path angled up slightly, which slowed Constance not one bit. "You'd like me to recommend a portraitist for you? Somebody who will mind his own business and not turn your nose purple?"

"No, thank you. I do not need a recommendation."

"Then you'd like me to confirm the choice of portraitist you've already made. Offer reassurances that he—for only the male gender is suited to rendering portraits, of course—is passably competent."

Constance picked up the pace as they climbed, and Robert had the sense she was annoyed. He did not turn loose of her hand, but rather, lengthened his stride to keep pace with her. She was by no means a tall woman.

"Passably competent will not do. This portrait must convey to the world that I am in every way appropriate to execute the duties of my station." The traveling coach had been sent into York for a complete refurbishment for the same reason.

Appearances mattered.

"You are competent to execute the duties of your station," her ladyship retorted. "Let us not belabor the obvious. That you have handsome features, a compelling gaze, and a fine masculine figure means any half-skilled apprentice could fashion a decent likeness of you."

"Do you mean that?"

"Perhaps not an apprentice, but anybody half skilled. You'll probably let him talk you into painting you wearing coronation robes, the usual castles and churning seas in the background. He'll try to suggest you have blue eyes instead of green, but you must stand firm. Eye color is not a detail and your eyes are *lovely*."

They had reached the orchard gate, which her ladyship yanked open and charged through.

Robert stood for a moment outside the walls.

"Well?" Constance said, holding the gate open. Her question, a single syllable, demanded something—an explanation or justification of some sort, for the human condition, for the evils of the day, for the imponderable mysteries of life itself.

Robert knew he ought to dash through the gate, slam it closed behind him, and refuse to budge until the comfort of darkness descended. Instead he marveled at the view of the Hall amid the fields below. The dread and resentment and whatnot were still lurking in his mind, but they slept like winded hounds, and let him look on his home—his *home*—from a distance for the first time since he'd been sent away.

"Rothhaven is not so dreadful when seen from this perspective." The Hall looked peaceful, in fact, mellow old stone settled on a quilt of green. "Not so bleak."

Constance re-joined him just outside the gate. "It's a fine old place. Perhaps whoever does your portrait would be willing to paint a few landscapes. The portraitists are a snobby lot, generally, but we all pass through a landscape phase, once we leave the still lifes behind."

He took her hand this time, a very bold overture on his part. *She* was not terrified of the out-of-doors, after all.

Though at the moment, neither was he. Uneasy, a bit anxious, possibly even agitated, but not terrified.

"I would like to leave my still-life phase behind," he said. "What could I offer you that would induce you to paint my portrait?"

Constance studied him in that serious way of hers. "Do you mean that? You want *me* to paint your portrait?"

"I'm told as subjects go, I'm not hideous. I want no strangers under my roof strutting about and acting artistic. You are beyond half skilled, and I know you won't turn my nose purple. I am offering you a commission to paint the portrait of the present Duke of Rothhaven."

In Robert's mind, until that moment, the Duke of Rothhaven had been his father, or a role inhabited by Nathaniel. He, himself, had been Robbie, or to old familiars, Master Robbie. Soames had called him Robert, for last names were discouraged at such an establishment.

Watching Constance inventory his features, her gaze roaming from his brow to his nose, to his mouth, to his hair, he felt himself becoming the Duke of Rothhaven. Standing a little taller, adopting a slight air of hauteur the better to withstand her perusal.

"Sitting for a portrait is boring," she said, brushing his hair back from his temple. "You will grow testy." She eased a finger under his cravat and ran it around his neck. "I will grow testy." She gently steered his chin a half inch to the left, then a half inch to the right. "We will disagree."

"I trust your judgment." He would somehow trust himself to withstand her touch too.

She smoothed his lapels, fluffed his cravat, and made another adjustment to his hair. Her smile said she knew his compliment extended beyond her ability with paints and brushes.

"Let's have a look at the trees," she said, leading him through the gate. "I adore the scent of plum blossoms."

She prattled on, about light and seasons, how many different types of green could shine forth from a single tree branch, and why coronation robes were too trite to be endured. Then she shook a branch and showered herself with petals, and Robert knew himself for a doomed duke.

She adored the scent of plum blossoms, and he adored her.

He simply, completely adored her.

Order your copy of *The Truth About Dukes*!

Made in the USA
Columbia, SC
21 June 2020